PRESENT TENSE
Round Two of the Great Game

Other Avon Books in
THE GREAT GAME *Trilogy by*
Dave Duncan

PAST IMPERATIVE:
ROUND ONE OF THE GREAT GAME

DAVE DUNCAN

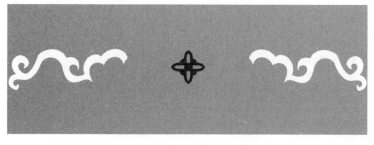

PRESENT TENSE

Round Two of the Great Game

AVON BOOKS NEW YORK

PRESENT TENSE: ROUND TWO OF THE GREAT GAME is an original publication of Avon Books. This work is a novel. Any similarity to actual persons or events is purely coincidental.

AVON BOOKS
A division of
The Hearst Corporation
1350 Avenue of the Americas
New York, New York 10019

Copyright © 1996 by Dave Duncan
Published by arrangement with the author
Library of Congress Catalog Card Number: 96-24540
ISBN: 0-380-97325-1

Library of Congress Cataloging in Publication Data:

Duncan, Dave, 1933–
    Present tense : round two of the great game / by Dave Duncan.
        p.   cm.
I. Title.
PR9199.3.D847P74   1996   96-24540
813'.54—dc20   CIP

First Avon Books Hardcover Printing: November 1996

AVON TRADEMARK REG. U.S. PAT. OFF. AND IN OTHER COUNTRIES, MARCA REGISTRADA, HECHO EN U.S.A.

Printed in the U.S.A.

FIRST EDITION

QM   10   9   8   7   6   5   4   3   2   1

For
Jacinta, Richard & Michael

✤

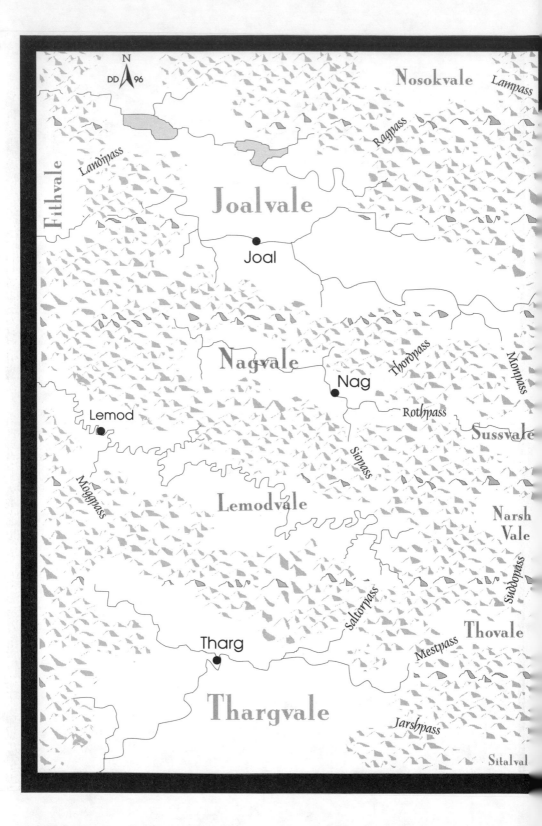

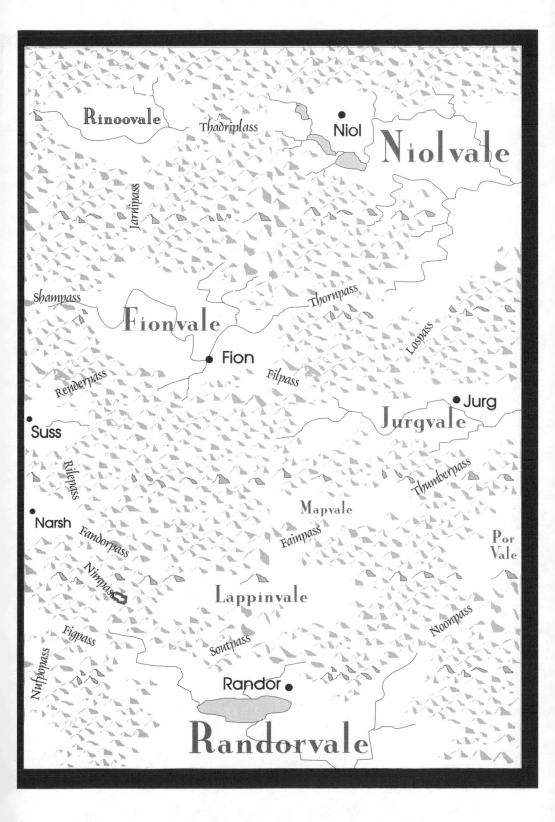

But war's a game, which, were their subjects wise, Kings would not play at.

COWPER, *The Task*

✦

Men plot evil upon the holy mountain. The servants of the one do the work of the many. They send unto D'ward, mouthing oaths like nectar. Their voices are sweet as roses, yea sweeter than the syrup that snares the diamond-Øy. He is lured to destruction by the word of a friend, by the song of a friend he is hurled down among the legions of death.

Filoby Testament, 114

Contents

CONTENTS

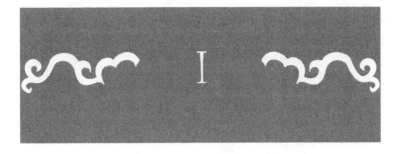

I

Pawn en Passant

꙳ꙮ 1 ꙮ꙳

THE INCIDENT OCCURRED ON AUGUST 16, 1917, DURING THE BATTLE of Third Ypres. The following day, Brig.-Gen. Stringer instituted an informal board of inquiry, consisting of Capt. K. J. Purvis, the medical officer of 26th (Midland Scottish) Battalion, and Capt. J. J. O'Brien, the brigade padre. This procedure was highly improper. The choice of Father O'Brien implies that rumors of a miracle were circulating already.

Apprehension of a suspected spy should certainly have been reported at once to division headquarters, and from there it should have been relayed to Corps and Army, and eventually GHQ. In this case there is considerable doubt that the news ever reached higher than brigade level. Published dispatches and official histories contain no mention of the bizarre affair. Apart from a few cryptic comments in some of the diaries and letters of the period, the only documentary evidence resides in the Stringer family archives.

The four witnesses were examined separately. All four were privates in C Company of the Royal Birmingham Fusiliers, which officially had been held out of the battle on the sixteenth. All four were either eighteen or nineteen years old, and all from the Midlands. Stretcher-bearing duty, to which the four had been assigned, was little less hazardous than combat. They had been on their fourth mission of the day and had been under fire almost continuously. Without question, they were all physically exhausted. Their mental and emotional condition should be borne in mind when evaluating their evidence.

Of the four accounts, that of Chisholm is the most detailed and seems the most convincing. He was the eldest by a few months; he had been a printer's apprentice and had benefitted from two more years' education than the others, Pvts. W. J. Clark, P. T. White, and J. Goss, who had all left school at fourteen.

Considering the danger, the inhuman conditions, and the extreme fatigue under which they had been laboring, the witnesses' evidence is remarkably uniform. They disagree on a few minor details, but—as the board observed in its report—completely identical accounts would be cause for suspicion.

They had paused for a rest in the lee of a fragment of masonry wall, probably the remains of a church which the maps showed in approximately that location. Over the roar of the heavy guns they could hear the repeated *ping* of bullets and shrapnel striking the stones; from time to time a shell would come close enough to spray mud at them. They lay in pairs, two men on either side of a flooded shell hole.

Chisholm later claimed that he had risen to his knees and called on the party to start moving again. None of the other three mentioned this, but in the racket and their own fatigue, they might not have heard or noticed. The important point is that Chisholm was apparently looking toward the rear at the crucial moment, and he insisted that the newcomer did not come from that direction.

The men were unanimous in stating that the fifth man fell into the shell hole between them with considerable force, as if he had dropped "out of the sky." No amount of questioning could shake their testimony on this point. They all claimed to have been splashed by the water thrown up. Three of them insisted that he could not have jumped or fallen down from the top of the wall. The fourth, Pvt. Clark, considered that he might have done, but did not think it likely.

The newcomer floundered and struggled, apparently unable to stand. Clark and Goss waded into the water and hauled him out, choking and still struggling, and completely coated in mud. It was only then that they realized just how remarkable the mysterious newcomer was.

"I saw the man had no tin hat," Pvt. Clark related in the sort of bloodless prose that has obviously been clerically improved. "But the rest of him was just mud. I reached for his arm and at first it slipped through my fingers. I realized he had no coat on. When we got him out, we saw that he had no clothes on at all."

The witnesses agreed that the stranger was having some sort of fit. His limbs thrashed and he seemed to be in considerable pain. He was incapable of answering questions, and they were unable to make sense of what he was saying.

Each of them was asked to report whatever he could remember of the man's words. There the testimonies diverge. Chisholm thought he heard mention of July, railways, and bed socks. White opted for cabbage and ladders and Armentières. The other two had similar unlikely lists, and we can only assume that they were equally mistaken. They all agreed that some of the talk was in English, some of it was not.

They did all agree on a few words: *spy, traitor, betrayed, treason.*

They had come to rescue wounded soldiers. This man had no visible wounds except some minor bleeding scratches caused by his convulsions. He was apparently incapable of standing, let alone walking, even had he been suitably clothed.

That he was a British soldier must have seemed extremely improbable to them, even then. That he was a German soldier was even less likely. Under questioning, they admitted discussing the possibility that he was a spy. Any man apprehending a spy automatically received leave in England, and they did not deny that they were aware of that regulation, although they all claimed that it had not influenced their decision.

Whatever their motives, they loaded the stranger on their stretcher, tying him down securely. They covered him with muddy greatcoats taken from corpses, and waded off through the bog to deliver him to the regimental aid post. It is difficult to see what else they could have done.

The report wastes little time discussing the conditions on the battlefield, which were only too familiar to the examining officers.

Those conditions can be reconstructed from other sources, although at this distance in time the reader's reaction is mostly incredulity. Superlatives pile up in a mental logjam, and the reader is left wondering if any words could ever be adequate. Even the photographs fail to convince. The mind recoils, refusing to believe that men actually fought over such terrain or that any of them could have come out alive to tell of it.

By the summer of 1917, the Belgian plain had been contested for almost three years, and yet the front line had scarcely changed position. The trenches, like insatiable bloody mouths, had subducted the youth of Europe. For three years men had marched in from east and west with intent to kill each other. On both sides they had succeeded. On both sides they had died in hundreds of thousands, yet still they came. Since 1914 the introduction of aircraft and poison gas had improved the technology of death tremendously, but repeated campaigns had barely changed the maps. At the opening of the battle of the Somme, in the previous year, the British Army alone lost over 57,000 men—killed, wounded, or missing—*in one day.* (This is numerically equal to the death toll suffered by the United States in the whole of the Vietnam War, half a century later.)

The battle of Third Ypres lasted for months and much of it was fought in torrential rain. The monotonously flat ground was completely waterlogged, repeatedly churned up by shells. Nothing of the original countryside remained. Nothing at all remained except mud, often thigh deep and in some places capable of sucking men and mules down to their death. It was laced throughout with broken timbers and old barbed wire, with rotting bodies of men, mules, and horses. There was no cover, for every hollow was filled with slime and water, commonly scummed with blood and fragments of flesh. Old corpses thrown up by the explosions lay amid the dying.

Over all this watery desolation hung the reek of death and decay, the garlic odor of mustard gas, the stench of the mud itself. Even a minor wound could cause a man to drown, and in those days there were no antibiotics to combat the frightful infections. The soil was poisoned by gas and virulent microbes. The roar of artillery never ceased. The ground shook as if Earth itself were suffering. Mule trains struggled forward with ammunition; the walking wounded staggered toward the rear. The British Army was attempting to advance across the desolation, while the Germans tried to mow it down with howitzers, machine guns, shrapnel, and poison gas. The field was swept by unrelenting fire and unrelenting rain.

Through this maelstrom of death went stretcher parties looking for wounded. Four men to a stretcher was a bare minimum. Often eight or ten were required, and even then it was not uncommon for the whole party to stumble and tip the wounded man to the ground. After a journey back to the field dressing station—which might take hours—the stretcher-bearers would go back for another. The work had to be done in daylight, for at night there were no landmarks.

Peculiar as the incident itself was, the subsequent behavior of the Army command structure was even stranger.

Suspicion must be directed at the brigade commander, Brig.-Gen. J. G. Stringer, although in all other respects his reputation is unclouded. The son of an Army of India officer, Brig.-Gen. (later Major-Gen.) Stringer had a distinguished career as a professional soldier. Born in India in 1882, he was educated in England at Fallow and Sandhurst. He was a noted athlete, playing cricket for Hampshire and serving as master of the Dilby Hunt. When war broke out in August 1914, he held the rank of major in the Royal Fusiliers, which formed part of the British Expeditionary Force dispatched to France. His subsequent rise was dramatic. He was well-thought-of by both his superiors and his subordinates. He was to die tragically in a motor accident in 1918, shortly before the end of the war.

One man did not testify at the inquiry—the mysterious stranger himself.

Even when the stretcher party had set off with their mysterious patient, their troubles were not over. The British began bringing up reinforcements. The Germans laid down a barrage to stop them. The stretcher-bearers had to run the gauntlet of high-explosives, shrapnel and, at one point, poison gas shells. They took a gas helmet from a corpse for their patient, but some of his exposed skin was blistered.

Their estimates of the time this journey took varied from two and a half to three and a half hours. By the time they arrived at the dressing station, the unknown man was unconscious and incapable of explaining anything.

2

TWO MEN SAT IN A GARDEN AND TALKED ABOUT HELL. ONE OF THEM had been there.

The time was a Saturday afternoon in early September 1917. The site was a sunny corner in the grounds of Staffles, which had been an English country house since the seventeenth century and was now a hospital for wounded returning from the Great War.

The two sat side by side at the top of a short flight of steps leading up to a set of glass doors. Inside those doors, a row of beds prevented anyone from coming out or going in, so the speakers would not be disturbed. It was a sheltered spot. The younger man had found it, and it was probably the best place in the entire hospital for a private chat. He had always had a knack for coming out on top like that. He was not greedy or selfish, yet even as a child he had always been the one to land the best bed in the dorm. Draw a name from a hat, and it would almost always be his.

The steps led down to crazy paving and a lichen-stained stone balustrade. Beyond that, a park sloped to a copse of beeches. The grass badly needed cutting, the rosebushes were straggly, and the flower beds nurtured more weeds than blossoms. Hills in the distance were upholstered with hop fields, their regular texture like the weave of a giant green carpet. Autumn lurked in the air, although the leaves had not yet begun to turn.

Once in a while a train would rush along behind the wood, puffing trails of smoke. When it had gone, the silence that returned was marred by a persistent faint rumbling, the sound of the guns across the Channel. There was another big push on in Flanders. Every man in Staffles knew it. Everyone in southern England knew it.

Men in hospital blues crowded the grounds, sitting on benches or strolling aimlessly. Some were in wheelchairs, some on crutches. Many had weekend visitors to entertain them. Somewhere someone was playing croquet.

In front of the two men stood a small mahogany parlor table, bearing a tea tray. One plate still bore a few crumbs of the scones which had come with the tea. The sparrows hopping hopefully on the flagstones were well aware of those crumbs.

The younger man was doing most of the talking. He spoke of mud and cold, of shrapnel and gas attacks, of days without rest or relief from terror, of weeks in the same clothing, of lice and rheumatism, of trench foot and gas gangrene. He told of young subalterns like himself marching at the head of their men across the wastes of no-man's-land until they reached Fritz's barbed wire and machine guns scythed them down in their ranks. He told of mutilation and death in numbers never imagined possible in the golden days before the war.

Several times during the tea drinking and scone eating, he had reached out absentmindedly with his right sleeve, which was pinned shut just where his wrist should have been. He had muttered curses and tucked that arm out of sight again. He chain-smoked, frequently reaching to his mouth with his empty cuff. At times he would try to stop talking, but his left eye would immediately start to twitch. When that happened, the spasms would quickly spread to involve his entire face, until it grimaced and writhed as if it had taken on an idiot life of its own. And then he would weep.

At such times the older man would tactfully pretend to be engrossed in watching other men in the distance or studying the swallows gathering on the telephone wires. He would speak of the old days—of the cricket and rugby, and of boys his companion had known who were now men. He did not mention the awful shadow that lay on them as they waited for the call that would take them away and run them through the mincer as it ran their older brethren. A war that had seemed glorious in 1914 was a monster now. He did not mention the ever-growing list of the dead.

He was middle-aged, approaching elderly. His portly frame and full beard gave him a marked resemblance to the late King Edward VII, but he wore a pair of pince-nez. His beard was heavily streaked with gray, and his hat concealed a spreading baldness. His name was David Jones and he was a schoolmaster. For more than thirty years he had been known behind his back as Ginger, not for his temperament or his coloring, but because in his youth Ginger had gone with Jones as Dusty went with Miller.

The gasping, breathless sobs beside him had quietened again.

"The swallows will be heading south soon now," he remarked.

"Lucky buggers!" said the young man. His name was Julian Smedley.

He was a captain in the Royal Artillery. He was twenty years old. After a moment he added, "You know that was my first thought? There was no pain at all. I looked down and saw nothing where my hand should be and that was my first thought: *Thank God! I am going Home!*"

"And you're not going back!"

"No. Even better." There was another gasp. "Oh, God! I wish I could stop piping my eye like this." He fumbled awkwardly for a cigarette.

The older man turned his head. "You're not the worst, you know. Not by a long shot. I've seen many much worse."

Smedley pulled a face. "Wish you'd tell the guv'nor that."

"It's the truth," Jones said softly. "Much worse. And I will tell your father if you want me to."

"Hell, no! Let him brood about his yellow-livered, sniveling son. It was damned white of you to come, Ginger. Do you spend all your weekends trailing around England, combing the wreckage like this?"

"Paying my respects. And, no, not every weekend."

"Lots, I'll bet." Smedley blew out a long cloud of smoke, then dabbed at his cheeks with his empty sleeve. He seemed to be talked out on the war, which was a good sign.

"Ginger . . . ?"

"Mm?"

"Er, nothing."

It wasn't nothing. They'd had that same futile exchange several times in the last two hours. Smedley had something to say, some subject he couldn't broach.

Jones glanced at his watch. He must not miss his bus. He was running out of things to talk about. One topic he had learned never to mention was patriotism. Another was Field-Marshal Sir Douglas Haig.

"Apart from school, how are things?" Smedley muttered.

"Not so bad. Price of food's frightful. Can't find a workman or a servant anywhere."

"What about the air raids?"

"People grumble, but they'll pull through."

Smedley eyed the older man with the ferocity of a hawk. "How do you think the war's going?"

"Hard to say. The papers are censored, of course. They tell us that Jerry's done for. Morale's all gone."

"Balls."

"Oh. Well, we don't hear rumors at Fallow. The Americans are in, thank God."

"They're in America!" Smedley snapped. "How long until they can build an army and move it to France—if the U-boats don't sink it on the way? And the Russians are out! Good as. Did you know that?''

Jones made noncommittal noises. If the Hun could finish the Russians before the Yanks arrived, then the war was lost. Everyone knew it. No one said it.

"Do you recall a boy called Stringer? Before my time."

The schoolmaster chuckled. "Long Stringer or Short Stringer?"

"Don't know. A doctor."

"That's Short Stringer. His brother's a brigadier or something."

"He drops in here once in a while. I recognized the school tie."

"A surgeon, actually. Yes, I know him. He's on the board of governors. Comes to Speech Days."

Smedley nodded, staring out over the lengthening shadows in the garden. He sucked hard on his cigarette. Jones wondered if the unspeakable, whatever it was, was about to be spoken at last. It came in a rush.

"Tell me something, Ginger. When war broke out I was in Paris, remember? Edward Exeter and I were on our way to Crete. Came home from Paris just before the dam broke."

"I remember," Jones said, suddenly wary. "Dr. Gibbs and the others never made it back, if that's what you're wondering. Never did hear what happened to them."

"Interned?"

"Hope so, but there's never been word."

Smedley dismissed the topic with a quick shake of his head, still staring straight ahead. "Tough egg! No, I was wondering about Exeter. We parted at Victoria. I was heading home to Chichester. He was going on to Greyfriars, to stay with the Bodgleys, but he wanted to send a telegram or something. I had to run for my train. Next thing I knew, there was a copper at the house asking questions."

He turned to look at Jones with the same owlish stare he had had as a boy. He'd always been a shy, quiet one, Smedley, not the sort you'd have ever expected to be a hero and sport those ribbons. But the war had turned thousands of them into heroes. Millions of them.

"Young Bodgley was murdered," Jones said.

"I know. And they seemed to think Exeter had done it."

"I didn't believe that then and I don't now!"

"What innocents we were . . . fresh out of school, thinking we were debonair young men of the world . . ." The voice wavered, then recovered. "Wasn't old Bagpipe stabbed in the back?"

Jones nodded.

Smedley actually smiled, for the second time that afternoon. "Well, then! That answers the question, doesn't it? Whatever Exeter may have done, he would never stab anyone in the back. He *couldn't* stab anyone in the back!

Not capable of it." He lit a new cigarette from the previous butt.

"I agree," Jones said. "He wasn't capable of any of it—a stabbing or killing a friend or any of that. A quick uppercut to the jaw, yes. Sudden insanity even. Can happen to . . . But I agree that the back part is conclusive proof of his innocence."

"Bloody nonsense," the young man muttered.

"Even Mrs. Bodgley refused to believe he killed her son."

The owlish stare hardened into a threatening frown. "Then what? He escaped?"

"He totally vanished. Hasn't been seen since."

"Go on, man!" Suddenly the pitiful neurotic invalid was a young officer blazing with authority.

Jones flinched like some lowly recruit, even while feeling a surge of joy at the transformation. "It's a total mystery. He just disappeared. There was a warrant issued, but no one ever heard from him again. Of course things were in a pretty mess, with war breaking out and all that."

Apparently none of this was news to Smedley. He scowled with impatience, as if the recruit were being more than usually stupid. "The copper told us he had a broken leg."

"His right leg was smashed."

"So someone helped him? Must have."

Jones shrugged. "An archangel from the sound of it. Or the Invisible Man. The full story never came out."

"And you genuinely believe it was a put-up job? Still? You still think that, Ginger?"

Jones nodded, wondering what lay behind the sudden vehemence. After being through what this boy had been through, why should he brood over the guilt or innocence of a schoolboy chum? After seeing so much death, why become so agitated over one long-ago death? It had been three years. It had happened in another world, a world that was gone forever, butchered in the mud of Flanders.

The mood passed like a lightning flash. Smedley slumped loosely. He leaned his arms on his knees and reached for his cigarette with the wrong arm. He cursed under his breath.

Jones waited, but he would have to run for the bus soon or he would not see his bed tonight. Nor any bed, if he got trapped in the city. Not the way London was these days.

"Why?"

"I don't know," Smedley muttered. He seemed to be counting the litter of butts around his feet.

Nonsense! The man needed to get something off his chest. Well, that was why Jones had come. He crossed his legs and leaned back to wait. He'd slept on station waiting room benches before now. He could again.

"Shell shock, they call it," his companion told the dishes on the table—slowly, as if dragging the words out of himself. "Battle fatigue. Tricks of the mind. Weeping, you know? Facial tics, you know? Imagining things?"

"Maybe. Maybe not. Man has to trust something."

"There's lots here worse off than me, you know?" Smedley jerked his thumb over his left shoulder. "They call it the morgue. West wing. Don't know who they are, some of them. Or think they're the bleeding Duke of Wellington. All lead-swingers and scrimshankers, I expect."

"I doubt that very much."

Smedley looked up with a tortured, frightened grimace.

Jones's heart began to thunder like all the guns on the Western Front. "So?"

"There's one they call John Three. They have a John Two, and there was a John One once, I expect. No name or rank. Doesn't speak. Can't or won't say who he is or what unit he was in."

Jones sucked in a long breath of the chilling air.

"I'd forgotten how blue his eyes are," Smedley whispered.

"Oh, my God!"

"Bluest eyes I ever did see."

"Is he . . . Is he injured? Physically, I mean?"

"Nothing major. Touch of gas burn or something." Smedley shook his head. With another of his abrupt mood changes he sat up and laughed. "I expect I was imagining it."

"Let's just pretend you weren't, shall we? Did you speak to him?"

"No. He was with his keeper. Being exercised. Walked around the lawn like a dog. I wandered over. He looked right through me. I asked his keeper for a light. Said thanks. Trotted off."

Of course Exeter would have enlisted as soon as his leg had mended. It was impossible to imagine him not doing so. False name . . . Tricky, not impossible . . .

"One thing you should know," Smedley said shrilly. "He doesn't look a day older than he did in Victoria Station, three years ago. So a chap really has to assume that he's just a little bit more shell-shocked than he hoped he was, wouldn't you say? Imagining things like that?"

"You're all right, man!" Jones said sharply. "But Exeter? Amnesia? He's lost his memory?"

Smedley's eye had begun to twitch again. He threw down his cigarette and stamped on it. "Oh, no! No, no, old man, that's not the problem at all. He knew me right away. Turned white as a sheet, then just stared at the horizon. That's why I didn't speak to him. Chatted up the keeper to keep him busy till Exeter got his color back, then left without a glance at him."

"He's faking it?"

"No question. Unless I imagined it."

"You didn't imagine this!"

"Oh, I wouldn't say that!"

"Don't be a fool, man!" Jones snapped. "Have you had other delusions? Seen any other ghosts?"

"No."

"Then you didn't this time. He can't reveal his name without going on trial for a murder he didn't commit!"

The eye twitched faster. "He'd better find himself a name pretty soon, Mr. Jones! Very soon! I've been asking a few discreet questions." The twitch had spread to his cheek. "He turned up at the front line under very mysterious circumstances. No uniform, no papers, nothing. They think he's a German sp-p-py!"

"What!"

"That's one th-th-theory." Smedley was having trouble controlling his mouth now. "So he's got the choice of being hanged or sh-sh-shot, do you see?"

"My god!"

"What'n hell're we going to do, Ginger? How can we help him?" Smedley buried his face in one hand and a sleeve. He began to weep again.

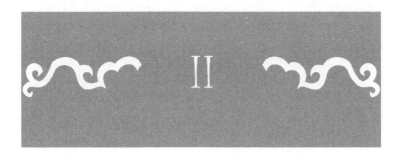

II

White Knight

3

As soon as the nurse turned her back, Smedley spat out the sleeping pill. When the light was turned off, he placed it carefully under his pillow. He would need it later. He rolled onto his back and prepared to wait.

His right hand throbbed. The fingers were tightly clenched, the nails digging into his palm. They were all somewhere back in Belgium, but he could feel exactly what they were doing . . . hurt like hell sometimes. Just part of the trouble of going bonkers.

Staffles had not been designed as a hospital. He shared a room with two other men, and there was barely room to walk between the beds. Rattray tossed and scuffled on the right; Wilkinson wheezed and bubbled on the left, his lungs ruined by gas. Very shortly both men were snoring—those pills packed a punch like twelve-inch howitzers.

Light filtered in from the corridor. The sounds of the hospital dwindled into silence. Once in a while it trembled as a train clattered by, London to Dover or Dover to London . . . no question which was the better way to be heading these days. The guns were still throbbing.

He needed a fag, but the nurses gathered up every cigarette in the building at lights-out. Staffles was one giant firetrap.

He lay and brooded, trying to fit what he had learned about the anonymous John Three in the west wing to the Exeter story he had heard from Jones—how that man had aged! An impossible disappearance and an impossible reappearance? Somehow that was appropriate. At least it made sense to a loony with a bad case of shell shock who couldn't sit still for ten minutes without having an attack of the willies.

I would kill for a cigarette.

He should have done something about Exeter days ago, but he hadn't really been able to believe himself. It had taken Ginger's reassurance to convince him of his own story, to persuade him he wasn't that far gone in the head. Not quite. Close, but not on target.

Exeter had vanished from Albert Memorial Hospital in Greyfriars. Somehow he had passed by the nurses on duty and the doorman, all of whom had sworn he had not. The night nurse had discovered his room wrecked, blood on the floor, and yet no one had heard a thing. Impossible, but Ginger believed, although he admitted it was hearsay. Hearsay from Mrs. Bodgley was good as Holy Writ.

John Three had been brought in from the battlefield with no uniform on. With *nothing* on, so the rumors said—shows how far gone the poor sod must be. No sane skulker would go so far as to strip to the buff in that rain-swept, bullet-swept, shell-swept hell. Mad as a March hare.

There were only two ways into no-man's-land. Either he had come from the British lines or the German lines. Or perhaps he'd cracked up an aeroplane. But why bare arsed? The mud had been known to suck off a man's boots and trousers but not his tunic. Shell blast could collapse his lungs or his brain and kill him without leaving a visible mark on him, but stripping him naked without otherwise harming him seemed rather too freakish even for shell blast.

I would give my right arm for a fag. It's no damn use anyway.

Why John Three? Could he speak at all? Why not invent a name?

Name, rank, and serial number.

The alternative was a bullet.

Why had Exeter not been shot out of hand? Why was he not in a provost cell, at least, instead of a low-security mental ward? There were weird rumors. Or at least there were rumors of rumors, tales of people who knew more than they were able to tell but rolled their eyes expressively.

He might not have been faking when he was brought in. Men picked up in battlefields were usually in bloody rotten shape. The journey back on a stretcher would be enough of an ordeal to drive a chap bonkers all by itself. So perhaps Exeter had genuinely been unable to talk when he was brought in, although Smedley himself had walked on his own feet into the casualty clearing station and tried to shake hands with—never mind.

Exeter had been putting up a stall on Wednesday. He had known Smedley. And if there was one thing Smedley had learned to recognize in Belgium, it was terror.

Exeter hadn't even given him a don't-give-me-away look. It had been an attempt at an I-don't-know-you look. That rankled a little, but if he couldn't trust an old pal not to give him away, then he was in something very deep and ever so smelly.

How long could he swing it? The medicals weren't dumb; they knew a skulker when they saw one. They'd use all kinds of tricks—sneak up behind him and bark orders, ask unexpected questions, leave newspapers lying around. . . .

Thinking about that, Smedley began to sweat. How long could a man go without speaking? It would be like solitary, but solitary in the middle of a crowd. Voluntary Coventry? Never speaking, never admitting that you could understand? Hour after hour. Day after day. It would crack a man. If Exeter wasn't already off his rocker, the strain of pretending to be would make it so. Playing crazy, he'd go crazy!

Smedley realized with a shock that he hadn't been weeping or even twitching. Just lying there, thinking and wishing for a Player's. The Exeter puzzle had given his mind something to chew on.

He had a strange jumpy feeling, not altogether unpleasant. He wasn't going to be in any personal danger. Hell, he could paint his face green or dance hornpipes on the piano and no one would do anything more than sigh and write a note on his file.

The danger would be to Exeter. If Smedley got caught showing interest in the mystery man, then someone might put two and two together. If anyone ever made the Fallow connection, then the jig would be up. Which might be why Exeter was keeping his mouth shut instead of spinning a yarn. An Englishman's voice would place him within a county. Or his school. Put Professor Higgins on the case and he'd say, "Fallow!" in two shakes.

Smedley awoke with a blast of terror, sweating torrents and choking back a scream. He had been asleep! Without a pill! Jolly good! First time since . . . since never mind. Snores to the right of him, snores to the left of him, volleyed and thundered. So he hadn't actually shrieked aloud. He had slept! Perhaps he was getting a little better, just a little? Please, Lord?

He tried to see his watch and couldn't. Still, it felt like time to go. He swallowed the ashtray taste in his mouth and eased back the blankets.

Dressing one-handed was bad enough in daylight. From now on he'd have his suits made with flies that buttoned on the left. He had thought to pull his shoes off without untying them, but getting them on again was harder. Neckties were an invention of the devil. . . . Hairbrush . . .

One wan bulb lit the corridor, invoking vast shadows. He set off on tiptoe, thinking of the poor sods in the trenches in Belgium, going over the top. At least in the artillery he'd never had to do that. Primary target: the linen closet down the hall. Pray it wasn't locked.

It was. Hellfire!

In two weeks he had snooped everywhere in Staffles—upstairs, downstairs, in any chamber he was allowed into—hoping he was doing it from boredom and because it was better than sitting still, frightened he was doing it because his loose brains were looking for bogeys.

Secondary target: one of the doctors' rooms.

He found a doctors' cubbyhole that was not locked, that did have a white coat hanging behind the door. Some kind saint had even left a stethoscope in the pocket. Now that was really shockingly careless! Take that man's name, Sergeant.

His fingers were shaking so much he could barely fasten the buttons. Nelly! He hung the stethoscope around his neck like a gas mask. He tucked a pencil behind his ear and his stump in his pocket and a clipboard under his arm. Then he stiffened his upper lip and marched off boldly in the direction of the west wing.

The house was dim and silent. It stank of disinfectant and the eternal stench of stale cigarette smoke.

A real doctor was the worst danger, and there would be one on duty somewhere. A nurse might be overawed by the stethoscope. Guards . . .

One guard, reading a newspaper.

"Don't get up!" the doctor said, and walked right by him.

It would not have worked in a proper hospital, but Staffles was not a proper hospital. The night nurses were not sitting out at a duty desk where they could view the corridor. Light pouring from an open door was the best they could manage, and apparently no one noticed the white shape flit past. The west wing had been servants' quarters—low ceilings, painted plaster walls. Feeling the guard's eyes boring into his backbone, Smedley chose a room at random.

There were two beds crammed in there. One was empty. The man in the other was bandaged beyond recognition, but he sounded asleep.

Would the guard register that the doctor had not turned on the light?

Smedley waited a couple of minutes, about two thousand heartbeats.

Then he peeked cautiously. The guard was back in his newspaper. The light from the duty room shone unobstructed.

The next room was not the right one either.

Nor the next.

The next was.

A fair-haired head. Asleep. Just a kid, but lying on his back and breathing noisily. Exeter's black hair on the other pillow.

Suddenly Smedley was back in Paris, three years ago, staying at Uncle Frank's on his way to Crete, sharing a room with Exeter. His heart twisted in his chest. Ye gods and little fishes, man! How can you still look so *young*?

He left the door open. To close it would attract attention if a nurse had to pass by. He squeezed in between the bed and the wall, on the right side. He knelt down, dropping the clipboard. He laid his hand over Exeter's mouth.

A wild reaction almost blew the gaff. Bedsprings creaked. Arms and legs flailed; a hand grabbed his wrist so hard he thought it would crack.

"Shush, you idiot! It's me. Smedley. Julian!"

A grunt. A groan. Exeter subsided. The kid in the other bed paused in his breathing—and then resumed. Smedley's heart crawled back where it belonged.

He leaned close. "I know who you are," he whispered. "This is on the level. No one put me up to this. I swear that! I want to help."

The blue eyes were silver gray in the dark, even with his, staring at him from the pillow.

"Ginger Jones came calling today."

Exeter sucked in a long breath and sighed it out again. He was drugged and still mostly asleep. Dopey, trying not to show any reaction.

"I don't believe you killed—I don't think Bagpipe's death was your doing. Ginger doesn't, either. I know you disappeared mysteriously from a hospital. Can you disappear from this one?"

Pause. Very slightly, Exeter shook his head.

That was a very deniable shake. Why wouldn't he trust an old friend?

"Can you talk?"

An almost imperceptible nod.

"You won't fool them for long, Edward! Do you want help getting out of here?"

A stronger nod. More blinks, as if Julian Smedley might not be the only man in the world with eye troubles.

"Can you tell me what's going on?" Smedley begged.

Another faint shake.

"For God's sake, man! Trust me!" He felt his cheek beginning to twitch. Any minute now the tears would start. Then where would trust go?

He waited stubbornly, sweating, gritting his teeth, fighting against twitching and weeping. He thought he wasn't going to get an answer. Then it came, a tenuous sound, like a whisper from beyond the grave and yet so close that he could smell the breath that brought it.

"You couldn't believe me."

"From the rumors I've heard, I can believe anything."

A shake: no.

"Look, I'm not going to be here much longer. I don't know how to get you out of here, and I don't know where I could take you that would be safe. Have you any ideas? Any suggestions? Anyone who needs to be told?"

Exeter's fingers reached out and took the pencil from behind Smedley's ear.

Smedley fumbled awkwardly to retrieve the clipboard. It had slipped under the bed. He passed it up. Exeter turned over the top sheet and wrote on the back of it. He handed them both back.

Smedley took the pencil in his left hand and tried to take the clipboard with his stump.

"Oh, my *god!*"

Exeter had spoken aloud, almost shouted. The kid on the next bed fell silent. Smedley crouched down low, out of sight. He was shaking. He must get out of here before he had an attack of the willies! In a moment the slow breathing resumed.

When he straightened up again, Exeter's hand gripped his shoulder and squeezed like a vise. They stared at each other.

Well! So there were other men who had trouble with watery eyes these days? Lot of it going around.

"Edward—"

Somebody screamed farther along the hall. Then screamed again.

Smedley wanted to dive under the bed. He forced himself to stand up and go to the door. Confused voices rising in protest, more screams . . . Some poor bugger having nightmares. A nurse hurried by. Then another.

Then the heavy tread of the guard. They all went by. Splendid!

He glanced around. Exeter was sitting up straight, face pale, eyes wide.

"Enfilading fire, old man!" Smedley said cheerily. He waved his stump and departed.

If one of the nurses came out to fetch something and saw a doctor in the corridor—but that didn't happen.

Smedley went back to bed and wept until his sleeping pill took effect.

On Sunday it rained most of the day. He practiced left-handed writing all morning. In the evening he walked down to the village and posted two letters, to the addresses Exeter had given him.

4

FALLOW IN HOLIDAY TIME WAS A MORGUE THESE DAYS. IN ANOTHER week the inmates would start to trickle back, and the school year would start up again. Meanwhile, only a half dozen or so masters and three or four wives remained on the premises. Before the war there had always been a few boys in permanent residence, sons of parents abroad. The problems of finding staff, both academic and domestic, had forced the board of governors to abandon the practice of providing year-round board *in the meantime*. A revolution was sweeping England "in the meantime," and only the far future would show how many of those expedients were temporary.

Early on Tuesday, David Jones cycled into Wassal and caught the local train to Greyfriars. The service was extremely poor on that line now, but rural buses were worse, almost as rare as dodoes in the England of 1917. After a twenty-minute wait, he entrusted his mortal coil to the Great Western Railway Company once more and was borne eastward toward London. The express was packed with people, many of them servicemen. At first he thought he would have to stand in the corridor the whole way, but a young gunner rose and donated his seat to the elderly gent, for which the same was suitably grateful. Considering that Jones was bound on paying his respects to the military, the tribute was ironic.

A couple of hours brought him to Paddington. From there he took the tube to Cannon Street and emerged into a dreary, drizzly gray morning, rank with the stench of coal and petrol. Letting the scurrying crowds rush by him, he strolled across London Bridge at a leisurely pace to his destination, Guy's Hospital.

He spent the remainder of the morning in conversation with William Derby, another Fallow old boy—not so old, really. He could not be more than twenty-five. He had been broken and blinded on the Somme, but his morale was heartrending. The ones that needed cheering up were almost easier. Like Julian Smedley, most of them were so happy to be out of the fighting that they regarded their disabilities as blessings. In time the reality would sink in.

By lunchtime, Jones's task was done. He did not like London. Before the war he had rarely come up to town except to pass through on his way to somewhere else. It was too big, too busy, too grimy. The war had brought to it a frantic, hothouse exuberance that did nothing to change his feelings. His new, self-imposed assignment of visiting the wounded had taken him there a dozen times in the last two months. One precaution he had learned from bitter experience was to bring his lunch with him, so today he sat on a damp bench on the Victoria Embankment and ate his sandwiches. Ten years ago all the taxicabs in London had been pulled by horses. Now there was hardly a horse to be seen anywhere. The smell of the city had changed, but petrol fumes were hardly an improvement.

He had the rest of the day before him. There were many other maimed young men he could call on, although none he knew of whom he had not visited at least once. He was haunted by the problem of one he could not visit, Edward Exeter.

In more than thirty years of teaching, he could recall no boy so cursed. His parents had been foully slaughtered in a native uprising in Kenya. He himself had been implicated in another murder, and seriously injured. Now he was in danger of being shot as a spy. It was madness! What had he ever done to provoke the Furies so? Out of all the hundreds of boys Jones had taught in his career, he would have ranked none ahead of Edward Exeter.

The only help he could think to provide was to track down Alice Prescott. He had last met her in 1914, when she had rushed down to Greyfriars to visit her young cousin in hospital. She had been a very self-possessed miss even then. Exeter had been suffering from a severe case of puppy love, but her heart—so Jones had suspected—had been mortgaged elsewhere. She had been fond of Edward, without question, because they had grown up together in Africa, but she had not spoken of him as a prospective lover.

Jones had written to her a couple of times afterward, relaying what skimpy information he had been able to gather about Exeter's disappearance. The correspondence had withered for lack of purpose. When her famous uncle, the Reverend Roland Exeter, died a couple of years later, Jones had sent a sympathy card to her last known address. It had been returned, recipient unknown. The war had raged ever more wildly since then. She might well be married or driving an ambulance in Palestine by now.

But he had promised Julian Smedley that he would try to devise some way of assisting Exeter, assuming that the mysterious John Three confined in Staffles was truly the missing man. In the days since, Jones had experienced no brain waves, had achieved nothing practical. He had written a careful note to the widowed Mrs. Bodgley, but she could hardly be expected to assist a boy she had barely known, one suspected of murdering her only son. The only possible helper in this affair was Alice Prescott. To the best of his knowledge, she was the only family Exeter possessed.

He fed his crusts to the restless pigeons and headed for the underground again. Miss Prescott's last known address had been in Chelsea, a modest location that would have been handy for her clients. She had been a teacher of piano, and the nearby area of South Kensington would have provided many wealthy families with children in need of such social improvement.

He found the flat. There was nobody home, which was hardly surprising in the middle of the afternoon. He rang a few doorbells in the vicinity, spoke with a few harried, suspicious women, and eventually found one who remembered Miss Prescott. It had only been three years, after all. He spun a yarn about news of a long-lost relative; either that or his accent convinced the lady that he was not a bill collector. After a long wait in a dim corridor, he was rewarded with an address in Hackney. Doffing his hat in salute, David Jones departed in search of the nearest tube station.

Hackney, of course, lay on the other side of the City. He could not afford taxis, so he had a choice of bus, tram, or tube. The advantage of the tube was that it displayed maps in all the stations. Even a country yokel could not get lost on the underground.

How often could a young lady change her address in three years?

Twice.

Three times, and apparently never for the better. There had been money in the family once.

The rain had started again. By the time darkness fell, he was in Lambeth, south of the river, and not very far from his starting point at Guy's Hospital. Whatever Miss Prescott was doing in that grim, working-class area, she was not likely to be teaching piano to the pampered offspring of rich matrons.

It had been an exhausting day, and his feet throbbed. Darkness was true darkness, too, for the threat of German air raids had imposed blackout. He knew in a purely cerebral way that the bombs did very little damage and caused few casualties—relative to the millions of people exposed, that is—but emotionally he had no desire to become a statistic.

He found the entrance beside a tobacconist's shop and was happily surprised to see that Miss Prescott did not inhabit one of the horrible egg-crate tenements of the back streets. This was a three-story corner building, proudly bearing the date, 1896. Its yellow brick was stained by the ever-present soot of London, but it was a reasonably appealing edifice. He plodded wearily up two flights of hard, steep stairs, inhaling aromas of boiled cabbage and cooking fat. At the top he was faced with a door, four bell pushes, and four labels he could not read in the gloom. He flipped a mental coin in the dark and pressed.

With surprisingly good reflexes, the door cracked open almost at once. Light knifed out at him. He blinked.

He raised his hat. "I am looking for a Miss Alice Prescott."

"I am she," said an educated, non-Lambeth voice.

Praise the Lord! "David Jones, Miss Prescott."

The cultured voice said, "Christ!" and the door shut.

Jones could not recall ever having heard a woman use that particular blasphemy, and few men either. Before he could catch his breath, the chain rattled and the door swung open.

"Come in, Mr. Jones! This is a welcome, if rather alarming surprise. Let me take your coat. I have just brewed a pot of tea. . . ."

She was a very practical young lady, and self-possessed to boot. He was ushered out of the cramped entrance hall into a small sitting room and urged to take a chair. He glanced around, at first with surprise and then with something closer to astonishment.

The address might be questionable and the wallpaper regrettable, but the furnishings were not. The tiny space was almost filled by an upright rosewood piano, two armchairs, and a sofa; they were old, yet neither worn nor faded. The rug underfoot was thick and bright. The curtains were velvet, the little tables oak. The mantel above the gas fire bore several Royal Doulton figurines and a silver-framed photograph of a man in uniform. A marble-topped cupboard with a two-ring gas cooker and a gently steaming kettle served as kitchen. The cup and saucer were Spode.

The crusts of the family fortune had taken refuge in Lambeth.

His wondering gaze turned to the walls and the watercolors.

"Yes, they are genuine Constables," Miss Prescott said drily. "You will have a cup of tea with me since you are here?"

One of the more embarrassing problems of advancing years . . . "If I may just freshen up first?"

"Of course! First door on the right. Let me find you a towel."

The WC was the size of a chicken coop. The bathroom opposite was little larger, but any indoor plumbing at all ranked the flat well above average for the neighborhood. She would share the facilities with the other tenants on the floor, of course. Considering the housing situation in London at the moment, she was doing very well. Her plain, serviceable suit had suggested that she was in some sort of clerical work, certainly not munitions, like so many thousands of British women now. Idiot!—there were no munitions factories in the heart of London. As he dried his hands, Jones decided that Alice Prescott was almost certainly a secretary of some sort, and she could walk to Whitehall from here.

He returned to the sitting room. She smiled up at him and said, "One lump or two?" Thus might a Roman matron have invoked the household gods.

She was not classically beautiful—her nose and teeth were too prominent. Had she possessed her cousin's jet-black hair and startlingly blue eyes, she might have been striking. Even with nondescript coloring, she was a handsome young woman.

Jones accepted the tea with gratitude, took a sip, and found himself impaled by a very direct gaze.

She wasted no words. "Where is he, Mr. Jones?"

"I am not certain of this, I have not seen him, but . . . Do you remember Julian Smedley?"

"Yes."

"He says Exeter is in Staffles, a temporary hospital in Kent."

"Under what name?"

"A pseudonym, of course. 'John Three.' He is pretending to be suffering from amnesia, but Smedley is certain it's your cousin."

Alice bit her lip. All she said was, "Go on."

With tea soaking through his fibers like ambrosia, Jones recounted the tale. His feet were throbbing and burning inside his shoes; his knees ached. He did not want to think of the journey home that awaited him, but hotel rooms in London were an impossibility now.

She murmured an apology and held out a plate of biscuits. They had not been in evidence when he came in. He limited himself to one. As he talked, he became vaguely aware of other changes in the room. The fire had been lit . . . a table moved . . . Ah! The photograph had disappeared from the mantel. Interesting!

When his tale was done, she did not at first comment, which was a surprise. Instead she said, "And how are things at Fallow?"

"Much the same. We feel the pinch less than most, I expect."

She raised her eyebrows in frank disbelief. "Then how does it feel to be raising the next crop of cannon fodder?"

"Not good."

She smiled bitterly. "How bright and glorious it seemed at the beginning! When I last saw Edward, he was far more upset at his broken leg keeping him out of the war than he was about being a suspected murderer. Another cup? And now we all know better, don't we?"

Uneasy at hearing such defeatist sentiment, Jones accepted another cup.

As she poured, she said, "Edward turning up in Flanders I can understand. He would have enlisted as soon as his leg healed. No question. But to enlist he would have needed an identity. Turning up without any clothes on sounds . . ."

Again she turned her intimidating stare on her visitor. It would not have disgraced Queen Mary. "I do not attend séances, Mr. Jones. I do not read fortunes in tea leaves, nor consult Gypsy witches at fairgrounds. And yet I am convinced that whatever my cousin was mixed up in three years ago was more than natural."

Jones sighed. "I have been trying to avoid that conclusion ever since it all happened, but I think I agree with you. There were too many locked doors, too much of the inexplicable. A rational explanation . . . There wasn't one!"

"Edward thought he was in love with me."

What was the difference between thinking one was in love and actually being in love? "He made no secret of it."

"I mention that only because I really believed he had died. He would never have departed voluntarily without at the very least dropping me a note. Now you say he has returned under equally mysterious circumstances. . . . May I suppose that he was taken against his will and has now escaped?"

"Out of the frying pan?"

She smiled and turned to study the hissing gas.

"I must see him."

"I told Smedley I would visit him again on Friday."

"No, we have departmental minutes on Fridays." A wicked gleam shone in her eyes. "One advantage of being female, Mr. Jones, is that a male employer is always too embarrassed to ask for details if you request a day off."

Shocked again, he coughed awkwardly. "Yes."

"So will you stay over tonight?"

Oh, yes please! "Oh, I couldn't possibly—"

"The settee is quite comfortable, my friends tell me. I doubt if the neighbors will notice, and we must hope the zeppelins don't. Not many zeppelins now, anyway—they have these big bombers instead. I have a largish haddock we can share, and potatoes are back in the shops, thank goodness. If you can manage on half a haddock, two potatoes, and a sofa, then you are more than welcome."

"That is exceedingly generous of you!"

"I am most grateful to you for coming here, Mr. Jones," Alice said somberly. "You must tell me how you tracked me down. What is your normal procedure for organizing jailbreaks?"

5

WEDNESDAY BROUGHT SMEDLEY DISASTER. THREE DISASTERS.

Whatever the war had done, it had not seriously damaged the Royal Mail, which delivered the first two disasters by the morning post. Miss Alice Prescott was "not known" at the Chelsea address. Whether or not Jonathan Oldcastle, Esq. still resided at The Oaks, Druids Close, Kent, the Post Office was not about to admit being aware of the address.

With one hand and a foot, Smedley tore both letters into fragments. Then he had a quiet weep.

The third disaster was even worse. He was told to pack his bags.

He begged. He pleaded. He groveled. Damned tears wouldn't come when they might be useful. The thought of being buried alive in Chichester was the living end. Since his mother had died the house was a tomb. With no servants available now, he would be completely alone with his father. Worse, next Sunday was his twenty-first birthday, so every aunt and cousin and uncle from Land's End to John o' Groats would descend on the returning hero. He would gibber and weep buckets and shock the whole brood of them out of their wits.

"Those are orders, Captain," the medic said coldly. "Besides, we need the beds, old man."

His discharge would take effect as soon as he had been up to the palace to get his medal. Meanwhile he was on sick leave. There was a bus at 12:10. Ta-ta!

Then he remembered Exeter, who would wait and wait and never know why his savior did not return. Ginger Jones was coming back on Friday with whatever plans he had been able to concoct, but Smedley could do nothing by himself. The willies came then. His face did its octopus dance. Tears streamed in torrents. He shook so hard he expected the dressing to fall off his wrist. He gabbled.

"Well . . ." the doctor said unwillingly. "We've got a new lot coming in on Friday. Can put you up till then, I suppose."

Smedley could not even get his thanks out. Two more days! He wanted to kiss the man's hand like a dago.

★   ★   ★

It felt like midnight, and it was still not lunchtime. He wandered out into the entrance hall, which was almost the only public space in the building. On a rainy day, like this one, it was crammed with uniformed men, those mobile enough to leave their beds. Amid all the bandages and crutches and wheelchairs there were dominoes and draughts, bridge and newspapers, and much desultory, bored conversation.

Dr. Stringer came marching in the main door.

Smedley made an about-turn. He headed back to his room and changed into civvies. He would get away with that for about twenty minutes, if he was lucky. He asked a red-haired nurse to tie his Old Fallovian tie for him, so it would look nice.

"Mr. Stringer is extremely busy!" the secretary snapped.

Surgeons were never called "doctor," but fortunately Smedley had remembered that. He should have guessed that surgeons, like golden fleeces, would be guarded by monsters. This particular monster had fortified a stronghold of her own; her rolltop desk was probably armor plated, the wall of filing cabinets behind her cut off half the hallway. Her outer defenses of chairs and tables could not have been bettered by the German high command. It would need at least a full division to advance to that decidedly closed door.

If she could not actually breathe fire, she could certainly look it. "You are not one of his patients, Captain—er . . ."

"Oh, I shan't keep him more than a jiffy! It's a family matter."

The old hussy pouted disbelievingly. "Family?" A surgeon as eminent as Mr. Stringer could not possibly be related to anything lower than a colonel.

"Sort of." Wilting under the glare, Smedley fingered his tie. "Just wanted to pay my respects, don't you know."

Perhaps she had been a schoolmistress in her youth. She wore her hair in a bun and must be at least thirty. Her features had been chipped from granite, but the basilisk eyes narrowed as she appraised the tie. "I'll see if he can spare you a moment, Captain Smedley. Pray take a seat."

He sat on a hard wooden chair and sweated it out. Stringer was another Old Fallovian, but he could not have known Exeter, who had been long after his time. Even by talking to the man, Smedley was breaking trust. But what choice did he have? In less than two days he would be evicted from Staffles and lose all hope of helping Exeter. This was the only lead he had. He need not give John Three's real name. Just make a few inquiries. Find out what the score was. Face seems familiar, maybe? Dare he go that far?

And if the surgeon called his bluff, the provost sergeant would break Smedley into pieces in seconds.

He studied the *Illustrated London News* and saw not a line of it. Oddly enough, though, his hand was so steady that the paper wasn't even shaking. Funny, that. No accounting for the willies.

"Mr. Stringer will see you now, Captain."

The office was a cramped oblong with a small, high window and green-painted walls. It had probably been a butler's pantry originally, because scars on the wall showed where built-in cupboards had been ripped out when the Army took over. There was barely room for a desk, two filing cabinets, and a couple of chairs. The chair behind the desk looked comfortable. The one in front was not.

Stringer rose and extended his left hand. Smedley had not yet decided whether he appreciated that courtesy or regarded it as patronizing. In this case it had been offered to show that the surgeon had fast reactions.

He was short, fortyish, starting to grow plump, and his fair hair was parted in the middle. His suit had cost fifty guineas on Savile Row. His manner was brusque and arrogant, which was to be expected of surgeons. He had an unhealthy hospital pallor, as if he rarely went outdoors. His eyes were fishily prominent, and they had registered the tie.

"Do take a seat, Captain. Smoke?" He offered a carved mahogany box, English and Egyptian.

Smedley accepted a chair and a Dunhill. Stringer took the same and lit both fags with a vesta. He leaned back to put his visitor at ease. He smiled politely.

"I was not aware that we were related."

"Adopted family, sir."

"Esse non sapere?"

"That certainly applied in Flanders!" *To be, not to know.*

Stringer nodded approvingly. "Fallow has more than done its share in this war, Captain. Forty-four old boys have made the Supreme Sacrifice, last I heard. I feel sorry for the youngsters there now. Grim lookout, what?"

"Bloody awful."

The lookout for a sixth former now was a great deal worse than the lookout for a successful surgeon with a prosperous Harley Street practice, who probably regarded his weekly consultation at Staffles as all the Empire could legitimately expect from him in the way of war effort. Field hospitals would be beneath a man of his eminence.

He was smiling the sort of smile that medical professors taught their best students. "You are assured of an honored place in the school annals yourself,

Captain. Sorry I hadn't registered you were here. Jolly good show. We can all be proud of you."

Willies gibbered in the rafters. Smedley shuddered and fought them back. Stringer's eyebrows rose fractionally. "And what can I do for you today?" What Smedley wanted to say was, *Don't let them send me away from here!* What he did say was, "Er . . ."

"Yes?"

"Er . . ." He was choking, he could not breathe. "Er . . . er . . ."

Stringer patiently trimmed the ash on his cigarette in the ashtray, looking at that and nothing else.

"Er . . ."

Still the doctor kept his eyes down. "Take your time, old man. It just takes a little while to get it out of your system. You're still fresh out of Hades."

"Er . . ."

"We've got lots worse than you. Not my specialty, of course. Not my patients, most of them. Can't amputate memories, unfortunately."

They all *said* this sort of guff at Staffles, but it wasn't what they *thought.* What they thought was *coward* and *weakling,* just like the guv'nor did. When Smedley was thrown out of here, he was going to have to face a world that thought like that.

Still Stringer studied his cigarette, while Smedley's face burned like a sunset and twitched and twitched. His lips and tongue would do nothing but slaver. Why had he come here? Any minute he would blurt out something about Exeter. . . .

"Some poor devils can't even remember their own names," Stringer said offhandedly, putting his cigarette back in his mouth. He took a letter from a wire basket and scanned it. "Got one chappie upstairs hasn't spoken a word since the day he was brought in. Understands English, though. He reacts—tries not to, but he does. Understands German, too."

Good God! He knew!

"But I don't really think the German's too significant," Stringer remarked, frowning at the page.

"Probably not," Smedley agreed. Exeter had always been a sponge for languages. Stringer knew who he was!

"Interesting chappie. Picked up in the middle of a battle without a stitch on him, just outside Ypres. No account of how he got there. And he can't tell us. Or won't, perhaps. There was some talk of just standing him up against a wall and shooting him."

"Why didn't they?" said a voice astonishingly like Smedley's own.

Stringer looked up cautiously and seemed to approve of what he saw.

He dropped the letter back in the tray. "Well, it's a rum do. His hair, for one thing."

"Hair, sir?"

"He had a full beard and his hair was down over his ears, like a woman's. I needn't quote King's Regulations to you, Captain, and I dare say the Kaiser feels the same way about lice." Stringer drew on his cigarette, eyebrows cocked quirkily to indicate that this was all frightfully jolly and nobody need get overwrought. The fishy eyes gleamed. He spun his chair around and opened a drawer in one of the filing cabinets. "At any rate," he said over his shoulder, "our mystery man was no soldier. That's certain. And then there was his tan. I suppose the south of France is a possibility."

"Tan, sir?" Hospital pallor?

"He had a tan. A corker of a tan." Stringer spun around to face his visitor again, thumbing through a file. "Yes, here it is. 'When stripped, the patient appeared to be wearing white shorts. This pigmentation is only compatible with recent, extended exposure to a tropical climate.' Then he turns up outside Ypres in the wettest summer in fifty years. Odd, isn't it?"

Now the surgeon put his arrogant stare to work, but Smedley was past noticing. Now he knew why Exeter had not been shot as a spy. But he wasn't much further forward. There was still a murder in the background, and now there was also the problem of how Stringer had known. . . .

The surgeon was smiling.

"How?" Smedley asked weakly.

Smirking. "Best fast bowler the school's had this century. Saw him get that hat trick against Eton."

Lord, who would ever forget that day! The willies grabbed Smedley's eyeballs and squeezed.

"Astonishing thing is that no one else's recognized him yet!" Stringer sighed. "What the hell are we going to do?"

"You? You, sir? You'll help, sir?"

"Don't you want me to?"

"Yes, oh, yes! Would you? I mean he was just about my best friend and I'll do anything I can to get him out and clear his—"

"Ah, yes. There is that, isn't there?"

Smedley considered the awful prospect that he had walked into a trap. He had never spoken to this man before, and now he had betrayed his pal. The chance that Stringer would jeopardize a notable career and even risk a prison sentence for abetting the escape of a suspected spy was not the sort of hypothesis even a shell-shocked . . .

But the doctor had already known.

"Nothing too serious physically," Stringer muttered, perusing the file. "He picked up some scratches in the mud, of course, and that stuff swarms with microbes. Gas gangrene, tetanus—we have antitoxins now, thank the Lord. Not like 1915. And he got some mustard gas blisters." He looked up warily. "But he's basically sound, physically that is. You said you were chums? I'd have thought he was a year or two behind you."

"He seems to have worn well." Smedley had not. "Sir, I will never believe Exeter stabbed a man in the back!"

Stringer pulled a face. "Not what they taught at Fallow in my day! The investigation was thoroughly botched, you know. Some country bobby who'd never dealt with anything worse than poaching. The Home Office sacked the general over it. That wasn't the story, but it's true. He should have called in Scotland Yard or shouted for aid from the next county."

But what did they do now?

"Just as well," Stringer said, glancing at his watch. "No fingerprints on file. So Mrs. Bodgley tells me. I have to make my rounds right away. We'll have the man in here after and talk it over. You can manage for a half hour or so?"

He smiled quietly and eased the file across to the other side of his desk. Then he stubbed out his cigarette, rose to his feet, and pranced out the door in his fifty-guinea suit. Smedley's mouth was still hanging open.

ᔕᕈ 6 ᔓᕽ

HAD SMEDLEY REALLY THOUGHT ABOUT IT, HE WOULD HAVE SAID that he could no more sit still for half an hour in that cramped little office than his battery could have shelled Berlin from Flanders. Yet he did not go off his rocker. The walls did not fall on him. The willies stayed away, although it was probably nearly a whole hour before he was interrupted.

He had serious planning to do. He must devise a way to smuggle Exeter out of Staffles. After a while he decided that could be arranged. But where could the fugitive run to once he was outside the walls?

He considered Chichester and his gorge rose. In theory an empty house with no tattling servants around would be an ideal hideout, but there would be recurring plagues of aunts. Worse, the guv'nor had no use for Exeter. He blamed Exeter's father for the Nyagatha massacre, claiming the man had gone native. He'd acccpted the son's guilt in the Bodgley case right away. Scratch Chichester!

There was Fallow. Term did not start for another ten days. Ginger could arrange something.

So that was settled. Now he had to think of a way to pass the information to Exeter when he was brought in, and right under Stringer's nose, too—another midnight expedition to the west wing would be tempting the gods. He found paper in the desk drawer. Writing left-handed was a bugger. Do *not* begin, "Dear Exeter!"

Tomorrow night will set off fire alarm. Try to slip away in the confusion. Left at bottom of stair. The yard wall is climbable. Go right. Look for Boadicea's chariot at crossroads, half a mile. Good luck.

He added: *God bless!* and felt a little shamefaced about that.

Even folding a paper one-handed was tricky, but he wadded the note small and slipped it in his trouser pocket. Then he sat back to examine the file Stringer had so generously left for him.

Boadicea's chariot was Ginger's Austin roadster. Smedley could write a quick letter and catch the evening post with it. It would reach Fallow in the morning—perhaps. If it did not arrive until the afternoon, that would cut things very fine. He had better walk down to the village after dinner and telephone.

He realized that he was staring blankly at some appalling handwriting and medical jargon. He pulled his wits together—what was left of them—and began to read. He was not much wiser when he got to the end than he had been at the beginning, except on one point. The doctors knew that John Three was a shirker. He would certainly be thrown in the clink very shortly.

Two points. The stretcher-bearers who had witnessed his arrival all swore he had dropped out of the sky.

Smedley jumped as the door swung open. It swung a long way, hiding him from whoever was outside.

"Hand me that chair, would you, Miss Pimm?" Stringer's voice said with breezy authority. In a hospital, a surgeon ranked just above God. "I am not to be disturbed. You needn't wait, Sergeant. We'll send word when we need to ship him back. Come in here, Three."

There was barely room for another chair and two more men and a closing door. Exeter had not expected Smedley. His blue eyes flickered anger for a moment and then went stony blank. He was wearing flannels, a tweed jacket, and a shirt with no tie. He stood like a tailor's dummy as the surgeon squeezed past him to reach his desk.

Stringer sat down and gazed up fishily at the patient.

Smedley shrank back on his seat.

Exeter just stood and looked at the wall. He was tall and lean, as he'd always been. In daylight his cheekbones still bore the inexplicable tan. But his chin and ears . . . long hair like a woman's? *Exeter?*

"Sit down, Exeter," the surgeon said. Nothing happened, and he sighed. "I know you, man! I shook your hand in June 1914. I have discussed your strange disappearance extensively with Mrs. Bodgley. I have read the reports on your equally mysterious reappearance. I know more about your odd goings-on than anyone in the world, I expect."

Still no reaction. How could the man *stand* it? According to the file, he had not spoken a word in three weeks.

"You'll be more comfortable sitting down, Exeter," Stringer said sharply. He would not meet defiance very often. "Cigarette?"

Nothing. Smedley's skin crawled. As the box came his way he shook his head. He needed another Dunhill, but he also needed his hand free.

"Captain?" said the surgeon. "You try."

"I didn't tell him, Edward. He already knew."

No reaction at all.

Smedley felt the willies brush over his skin. Exeter thought he was a traitor. Stringer was scowling at him, as if this were all his fault. Didn't they realize he was just a broken coward, a shell-shocked wreck of a man? Didn't they know he was liable to crack up and start weeping at the first sign of trouble? Please, lord, don't let me get the jitters now!

"I'm leaving here the day after tomorrow, Edward. Dr.—Mr. Stringer showed me your file. They're on to you! I wrote to those two people you named and both letters came back this morning, addressees unknown." He stared up at that unchanging witless expression and suddenly exploded. *"For god's sake, old man! We're trying to help you!"*

He might as well have spoken to the desk. Exeter did not move a muscle.

Stringer chuckled drily. "The most remarkable case of *esse non sapere* I ever saw."

Smedley discovered he was on his feet, eye to eye with Exeter, which must mean he was on tiptoe, because he was three inches shorter. He grabbed at lapels with one hand and a stump, and Exeter staggered back under the assault.

"You bastard!" Smedley shrilled. "We're trying to help! You don't trust me! Well, screw you, you bastard!" Shriller yet. He had not planned this, but he might as well use it. He had his back to Stringer. He stuffed the note down inside Exeter's shirt collar. "I didn't go through all that the other night to help an ungrateful *bastard* who—who—" He was weeping, damn it! His face was going again. Full-fledged willies!

"Sorry, old man," Exeter said quietly, easing him aside. "Mr. Stringer?"

The surgeon rose and reached across the desk. "I'm honored once again to shake the hand that humbled the fearsome ranks of Eton."

"Those were the days," Edward said in a sad voice. He sat down. "You have a good memory for faces, sir."

"Good memory for cricket. Did you kill Timothy Bodgley?"

"No, sir."

"Are you a traitor to your King?"

"No, sir."

Happy to be ignored, Smedley sat down also, and shook like a jelly. He had done it! He had passed the note. "Perhaps I do need that fag, sir," he muttered. He helped himself and leaned forward to the match, sucking a blessed lungful of smoke.

Stringer, too, drew on his cigarette, eying his prisoner.

Exeter gazed back with an unnerving steely calm.

The surgeon blew a smoke ring. "You say you're not a traitor, and I accept your word on it. But when you made your dramatic appearance amidst the battle's thunder, you were talking."

"Just shock, sir. It hits those who— Just shock."

"Daresay. But you were babbling about treason and spies. If you have any important information, I want it. It's your duty to—"

Exeter was shaking his head. "Nothing to do with the war, sir."

"Tell me anyway."

"Friends of mine in another war altogether. I was not expecting to arrive where I arrived. I was tricked, betrayed."

"You'll have to do better than that."

"I can't, sir. You would dismiss it as lunatic babbling. It has nothing to do with the Germans, the Empire, the French . . . no concern of yours at all, sir. You have my oath on it."

The two stared bleakly across the desk at each other.

"You're saying that someone wants you dead, is that it?"

"That is very much it, sir. But I can't even try to explain."

Exeter's foot pressed down on Smedley's instep.

He choked on a mouthful of smoke, remembering Ginger Jones sitting on that bench on Saturday.

"Someone tried to kill him at Fallow," the schoolmaster had said. "They ran that spear right through his mattress. Someone tried to kill him at the Grange and got young Bodgley instead. When he disappeared from Albert Memorial I was afraid that they had scuppered him at last. Now you say he's turned up in the middle of a battlefield? It sounds as if he's a hard man to kill."

Stringer?

Exeter was trying to say that the surgeon wanted to kill him?

Perhaps Captain Smedley was not the worst case of shell shock in Staffles after all.

Suddenly Stringer defused the confrontation with a patronizing chuckle. "Not just the public hangman?"

"Him too, sir. But private enemies also."

"All right! I shall accept your word on this also." He beamed and sat back in his comfortable chair. "All the more reason why we've got to get you out of here, what?"

Smedley gulped.

Exeter showed no change of expression at all. "Why? Why risk your career to help a fugitive escape from justice?"

The surgeon smiled with smug, professional calm. "Not justice, just the law. We can't have the school name dragged in the mud, what? And if some private thugs are after you as well, then that's even more reason. If we can get you out, is there anyone who would take you in?"

Exeter turned a sad look on Smedley. "I thought there might be. Apparently not."

"I think I can arrange a place for him," Smedley said.

"Ah! Somewhere secure?" the surgeon inquired blandly.

Why ask? And Exeter's foot was warning him again.

"No names, no pack drill, sir."

Stringer's chuckle did not quite reach his eyes—or was that just another illusion? "If he is apprehended, Captain, then my part in the affair may become known. I must be sure you have a safe haven ready for him."

Shot while trying to escape?

This was totally crazy! A distinguished surgeon was offering to let a suspected murderer and spy escape from his care, and the aforesaid spy was hinting that the aforesaid surgeon was actually trying to kill him, and Julian Smedley was believing both of them. He had definitely cracked.

"A school friend, sir, Allan Gentile. He and I were in the Somme cock-up together. He got a Blighty."

"A what?" Exeter said.

Smedley and the surgeon exchanged shocked glances.

"A wound. Brought him Home to Blighty—England."

"Ah."

Where had the man been for the last three years not to have heard that expression? Still, Allan Gentile had died of scarlet fever in 1913, and Exeter must remember that, so he would know this was all drip.

Stringer seemed satisfied. "Good. Now, how do you propose to get him off the premises?"

"He can go as me, sir." Smedley fished out his pay book and flourished it. "I've got a chit for the bus to Canterbury, a chit for a railway ticket to Chichester." He turned to Exeter and leaned a foot on his instep. "The window in your WC is directly above the washing shed roof. Sneak out just before dawn on Friday."

Exeter waited inscrutably. He still looked like the peach-faced boy of 1914, but something inside him must be a hundred years old.

Smedley ad-libbed some more. "There's a derelict summer house about halfway down the drive, on the left. Meet me there. My pay book will get you through the gate."

"It will be a very close run thing," Exeter said impassively. "They'll miss me when they do the morning rounds."

"They'll search the house first," Smedley snapped. It was a wet rag of a plan. It would not convince the present audience if Exeter himself started picking holes in it.

Stringer frowned, tapping ash from his cigarette with a surgeon's thick finger. "I'll try and get down here again tomorrow evening and stay over. If I'm around in the morning I may be able to muddy the waters a little."

Now that was definitely going too far! The surgeon had just strayed right out of bounds. Smedley felt a shiver of joy as if the spotters had reported he had found the range. He nudged Exeter's foot.

"I'll look like a scarecrow in your togs," Exeter complained.

"You look like a scarecrow already. I'll try and filch something better from the laundry. If you've got a better idea, spit it out."

"I haven't. But what happens to you?"

"I shall be discovered eventually, bound and gagged in my underwear. How could you do such a thing to a cripple, you rotter?"

"You'll freeze!" Stringer protested. He eyed Smedley suspiciously. "You may be there for hours. Can you really take that in your condition, Captain?"

It would drive him utterly gaga in ten minutes. But it wasn't going to happen. "I'll manage."

"Good show!" Stringer said approvingly. "Now we know how you collected all those medals. It's audacious! And ingenious! You agree, Exeter?"

"I'm very grateful to both of you."

"Just a small recompense for some of the finest cricket I ever saw. Now, where does he find Gentile?"

Smedley almost said, "Who?"

Again the man was showing too much curiosity. Chichester itself would sound a little too convenient. Somewhere handy? "Bognor Regis. Seventeen Kitchener Street, behind the station."

Stringer glanced at his watch and reached for the cigarette box. "Excellent! Now, Exeter, I have a small favor to ask."

"Sir?"

"I want to hear where you've been these last three years—how you escaped from Greyfriars, how you turned up in Flanders. Just to satisfy my own curiosity."

For the first time, Exeter's stony calm seemed to crack a little. "Sir, if I even hint at my story, you will lock me up in a straitjacket and a padded cell!"

"No. I accept that there are things going on around you that have no obvious rational explanation. You can't spout any tale taller than the things I have already tried to imagine to account for your appearances and disappearances." The surgeon was brandishing his full authority now. "I don't expect I shall ever see you again after you walk out of this room. So I want the story. The truth, however mad it may be." The smile did not hide the threat: no story, no escape.

Exeter bit his lip and glanced at Smedley.

"Don't mind me, old chap!" Smedley said. "I'm already round the bend, as the sailors say."

Exeter sighed. "There are other worlds."

Stringer nodded. "Sort of astral planes, you mean?"

"Sort of, but not this world at all. Another planet. Sir, won't you let me leave it at that?"

"No. I can see that there must be some paranormal explanation for the way you come and go, and I won't go to my grave wondering. Talk on."

Exeter sighed again and crossed his legs. "I was on another world, which we call *Nextdoor*. It's a sort of reflection of Earth—very like in some ways, very different in others. The animal life's different, the geography's different, but the sun's the same, the stars are the same. The people are indistinguishable from Europeans, everything from Italians to Swedes."

He paused to study Stringer's reaction. "See? You can't possibly believe I'm not raving or spinning a cuffer."

"It sounds like Jules Verne," the surgeon admitted. "How did you get to Elfinland?"

"I went to Stonehenge, took all my clothes off, and performed a sacred dance." Exeter pulled a shamefaced smile. "You sure you want to hear any more?"

"Oh, absolutely! Why Stonehenge?"

"It's what we—what they call a node. They're sort of naturally holy places. There are lots of them, and they often have churches or old ruins on them or standing stones. You know that creepy feeling you get in old buildings? That's what they call *virtuality*, and it means you're sensing a node. If you know a suitable key—that's the dance and chant—then a node can act as a portal. Somehow the nodes on this world connect with nodes on Nextdoor or one of the other worlds. People have been going and coming for hundreds . . . probably thousands, of years. You have to know the ritual, though."

Smedley wondered how Exeter had managed to dance with a broken leg, but Stringer did not seem to have thought of that. He was nodding as if he could almost believe—or was he just humoring the maniac?

"How do they work, though?"

"I don't know, sir, I really haven't the foggiest. The best explanation I ever got was from a man named Rawlinson, but it was mostly just wordplay. Let's see if I can remember how he put it. It was about a year ago. . . . I'd been on Nextdoor for two years by then, and I'd finally met up with . . . call them *strangers*—other visitors, like me—people who understand all this. Some of them have been back and forth lots of times. They call themselves the Service.

"The Service have a station—much like a Government station in the colonies somewhere. In fact, it's not unlike Nyagatha, where I was born, in Kenya. Prof Rawlinson's made a study of the crossing-over business and come up with some theories. . . ."

Exeter had always carried conviction. As he continued to talk, Smedley found himself caught up in what had to be the strangest story he had ever heard, and somehow he found himself slipping into unwilling belief.

৩ে৫ 7 ৩ে৫৩

"WHAT RAWLINSON SAID WAS, 'IT'S A MATTER OF DIMENSIONS. WE live in a three-dimensional world. Can you imagine a two-dimensional world?'

"Of course I had to tell him that maths had never been my long suit. Then he produced a pack of cards. . . ."

That wasn't quite true, Edward recalled. The cards had been lying on the other table at the far end of the veranda, at least twenty feet away, so Rawlinson had not fetched them himself. He had shouted for a Carrot, and

the Carrot had come and brought over the cards to him. That was how the
tyikank did things in Olympus. But how could anyone ever explain Olympus to these two—the surgeon, as smug in his chair as a Persian cat, almost
purring with self-satisfaction . . . or Smedley, poor sod, with the skin of his
face stretched so tight over the bone that it looked ready to split open, with
glimmers of hellfire inside his eyeballs and little nervous ticks of smiles
jerking the corner of his mouth every few seconds as he listened to poor
crazy old Exeter talking himself into a lifetime padded cell.

"He pulled out a king and a jack. Two two-dimensional people, he called
them—length and width, but no thickness. He put them face-to-face and
then asked me, could they see each other? I said I supposed not.

"He said, 'Right. They can't, because they're not in quite the same plane.
They're separated by a very small thickness, and their world contains no
thickness.' "

Edward remembered how triumphantly Rawlinson had beamed, then.
Prof was a spare, sandy-haired man with the fussy, pedantic manner of an
Oxford don, but he looked no more than twenty, most of the time. His
English had an odd burr, which might be more historical than geographical.
He knew a lot and his mind was quick, but there was something essentially
impractical about Prof, a hint of that most damning of all indictments: *not
quite sound*. If you needed a detailed report with graphs and illustrations and
references, fine—very good chap. Else put him in charge of the sports
program.

Materially, he was doing very well. His bungalow was large, one of the
inner circle of residences surrounding the node, and he must own one of
the finest collections of books in the Vales, where printing was a very recent
innovation. He had at least a dozen servants, all rigged out in snowy white
livery.

But Stringer and Smedley would not be interested in all that.

"I said, 'You're telling me that Nextdoor and Earth are separated in some
other dimension?' and he said, 'It's more complicated. If it were only one
dimension, then Home would have only two neighbors, but there are at
least six worlds that can be reached directly from Home. We know of only
two others from Nextdoor, but then we don't know very much about this
world outside the Vales. So we must be dealing with more than one extra
dimension. I know it's hard enough to think in four dimensions without
throwing five or six at you.' "

Edward was alarmed to hear himself chuckle. "I remember taking a long
drink at that point. I couldn't cope with this while sober."

All the time he'd been on Nextdoor, he'd been homesick for Earth. And
now he was Home, he felt his heart twisting as he talked of Olympus. He
recalled the dry fragrance of the air, tantalizing scents of spice or dried

flowers; hot by day, cooling off rapidly in the evening when the *tyikank* gathered on their verandas to drink gin and blue . . .

He looked again at his audience—Stringer's eyes half closed as he dribbled smoke, Julian's wide, too wide.

"I warned you this was going to take a lot of swallowing! It even stuck in my throat, and I'd *done* it—I mean, I'd actually crossed over to another world. No offense, Mr. Stringer, but this is a too practical, down-to-earth setting for fairy tales. I told you you wouldn't be able to believe me. I had trouble believing Prof, although I knew I wasn't on Earth, and hadn't been for two years. Look here: desk, papers, telephone, filing cabinet! Whereas I was sitting in a wicker chair drinking what they call gin, but isn't, on a veranda with screens around it. The trees had an African look to them, you know?—airy traceries with foliage hovering around the branches more like clouds of smoke or insects than leaves. There were mountains like white teeth behind them, going straight up into a pale, bloodless blue sky. My drink had been brought by a liveried servant who addressed me as *Tyika* Kisster. Prof and I were dolled up in white tie and tails—he'd asked me to come a little early so we could have a private chat, but a dozen or more other guests would be arriving shortly and his wife was indoors overseeing the final touches."

Chattering like this was madness! The sparkle in Smedley's eyes was welcome. The poor devil seemed to be enjoying the guff, and anything that took his mind off his own personal internal hell for even a few minutes was worth doing. But Stringer wasn't going to believe a word of it. Edward Exeter, alias John Three, was cutting his own throat with all this babbling. Trouble was, he'd been silent for so long that now he'd started to speak, he couldn't stop himself. . . .

The veranda fronted on a garden of flowering shrubs and carefully scythed lawn, a surprise of green fertility in the khaki dryness of Olympus. Teams of servants must water it frequently to keep it so lush.

Scattered amid the woods were more of the *tyikank*'s sprawling bungalows, clustered around the node. An irregular line of denser, dark-foliaged trees marked the course of the Cam. The natives' village lay a mile or so downstream.

To the west, the jagged sword of the Matterhorn towered over everything, a stark silhouette. Opposite stood Mount Cook and Nanga Parbat and Kilimanjaro's perfect cone, a poem in itself. All three were flushing pink and salmon and peach in the sunset. The valley lay like a palm between them, the Matterhorn being the thumb and the other three raised fingers. Several minor summits might qualify as the pinkie. He had not learned all their names yet.

"They're two slightly different aspects of the same world," Prof said, "two cards in the same pack, no two identical. Make two slices through, oh, say a Stilton cheese, and you won't get exactly the same pattern of maggot holes each time, what?"

Edward thought longingly of Stilton cheese. "The stars are the same."

"Ah! You noticed that? Small things are different, big things are the same. The beetles have eight legs. The sun looks exactly the same. The planets are very much the same, so far's I've been able to find out. The year's a little shorter, this world's axial tilt's a little less, days are about three minutes longer."

"How can you know that? You can't bring a watch over with you."

Rawlinson smiled knowingly. "But you can go back and forth. Sometimes you arrive at the same time of day, sometimes later or earlier. It works out to about three minutes' lag per day."

Edward had walked into that one. Even so . . . "Nextdoor has four moons. Moons are not exactly small."

"You're wrong!" Prof beamed excitedly. "Oh, they're big, but they may be caused by very small effects. A trumpet can't knock down a forest, can it?"

"No." Edward could not see what a trumpet had to do with moons, but he knew he was about to find out.

"But suppose there's an avalanche poised to fall? Then the trumpet call might set off the avalanche! There goes your forest. Now, it's generally agreed that the Moon was knocked off the Earth by a giant meteor, you know. The Pacific Ocean is the scar remaining. A meteor hit is a very chancy business. If the meteor comes by even a second or two earlier or later, it will miss the Earth altogether. Both bodies are moving at tremendous speed, remember! So it struck Nextdoor slightly differently. The debris coalesced into four small moons instead of one large one. Even Trumb is quite small. It just looks big because it's very close." Prof reached for his glass triumphantly. "Or perhaps there were several hits."

"How about the other worlds?"

"Other slices, remember? More variations. Gehenna has two moons, or so I've been told. Never been there." Rawlinson took a long drink. He was just hitting his stride, glad of an audience. "Back to our flat friends. We agree that they can't see each other, because they're not in the same plane. These cards can't be perfect planes, can they? No such thing as a perfectly flat surface. But if they're face-to-face, then they must touch here and there, what?"

"The nodes!"

"Right you are! The flat cards touch at a few points. And where worlds touch, you have a node—a portal, a hole in reality."

"And the keys pull you through that hole!"

"Across. Or through, I suppose. Apparently."

"But how do they work?"

The enthusiasm faded slightly. "Good question. It's all mental, of course."

"It is?"

"Absolutely. Only people can cross over. You can't bring anything with you—no clothes, no money, nothing."

"Not even the fillings in my teeth."

Rawlinson raised his sandy eyebrows. "Do the cavities bother you?" He grinned, seemingly suddenly very juvenile.

"I picked up some mana, and they healed themselves." Edward could also recall a scar on his forehead that had vanished and certain other scars on his chest that had persisted in trying to disappear when he had wanted them not to.

"That's what usually happens," Prof said smugly. "But whatever makes crossing over possible is something only the human brain can achieve. The keys themselves don't do it, I'm sure. They're not magical incantations; they only work internally. You could teach a parrot the song, but it wouldn't work. Rhythm, words, dance—somehow they induce a particular vibration or something in the mind, a resonance. The music of the spheres, what? The mind soars in splendor, it roams, it drifts across the gap. Then it hauls the rest of you after it. I think that's why we feel so bloody awful afterward. The brain's in shock."

Edward squirmed. "Does it always work? I mean, from what you say, then sometimes the mind might go and the body not follow? Can that happen?"

"Yes, it can. Sometimes. You ready for a refill?"

"Not yet, thank you. Now explain mana to me."

"Wish I could. How much have you learned already?"

How much should he admit to knowing? His report was going to be completely truthful, of course, but there were certain episodes in his recent past that he . . . did not intend to stress.

"I know that Colonel Creighton talked about charisma. I know it's something that only happens to strangers. He had no occult power on Earth, but as soon as he arrived back on Nextdoor he could throw thunderbolts."

"Because he hadn't been born here," Rawlinson agreed. "Where you're born is what matters. If you ever father a son here, my lad, then he'll be a native. Take him back to Earth and he'd be a stranger there. I can't give you an explanation, but I'll give you another picture. Suppose we're all born with a sort of shield, a kind of mental armor. Suppose that it doesn't cross over with us—that fits the case, doesn't it? Without the shield, you can absorb mana. With a shield there, very little can get through."

"And what is mana?"

Rawlinson sighed like an old, old man. "I wish I knew!" he said wearily. "It comes from admiration. It comes from obedience. It comes from just plain old faith. We breathe it in and blow it out again as power. It works most easily on the mind, of course. You must have discovered the authority you have here! Give orders and the natives will jump to obey 'em.

"At higher levels, mana can work on the body, as in faith healing or those yogi chappies who can sit around on an ice field in the altogether. In really high concentrations, it can influence the physical world. Then you're into miracles, Indian rope trick, teleportation, and all that." He discovered his glass was empty. "Carrot!"

A servant hurried out from the house door. He was probably sixty or older, although still trim and alert. His close-cropped hair had once been a fiery red; now the embers were streaked with ash. He wore white trousers with knife-edge creases down the front, a white tunic buttoned to a high collar. Very smart. His shoes were a shiny black.

"Ah, there you are," Prof said. "Sure you're not ready for another, old man?"

"Not just yet, thank you, sir."

The servant bowed slightly and withdrew.

The natives were always referred to as Carrots. Edward wondered if they had any idea what the word implied. He rather hoped they did not. They must have a name for themselves in their own language. Nextdoor's vegetation was completely unlike Earth's; it included some carrotlike vegetables, but they were not carrot colored.

Prof was off on his hobbyhorse again. "Strangers have the ability to absorb mana and redirect it as magic, but even natives can have it in some measure. 'Charisma' is as good a term as you'll find. Napoleon obviously had it. His soldiers worshipped him. He led them into the jaws of hell— they followed him and loved him for it. Caesar the same. Mohammed." He eyed Edward with wry amusement. "You can think of others, I'm sure."

"But Napoleon could not work miracles!"

"Couldn't he? Some of his opponents thought he did. And he was only a native, not even a stranger. Where do you draw the line? If a general or a statesman inspires his followers with a rousing speech, is that magic?"

Edward conceded the point. "No."

"Even if they are moved to superhuman efforts?"

"Probably not."

"Then how about faith healing? Mental telepathy? Foretelling the future?

Where do you draw the line? When does the uncanny become the impossible?"

"When scientists can't measure it?"

"They can't measure love either. Don't you believe in love?"

Edward chuckled. Obviously this speech had been made many times before.

"You came through an untried portal, I hear." Rawlinson rubbed his chin. "That's very interesting! Creighton took a hell of a risk there. Could have landed you anywhere on Nextdoor or on some other world altogether."

"He was relying on the prophecy. It said I would appear in Sussvale."

"I wouldn't have risked it. Still, all's well that ends well. And you arrived in the Sacrarium? That's useful to know. What key did you use?"

Edward tapped out a beat on the table with his fingers. *"Affalino kaspik . . ."*

"Oh, yes, that one," Prof said, watching the Carrot replace his empty glass with a full one. "Don't try that rascal here at Olympus, my boy! It'll flip you to Gehenna. Nasty spot! *Affalino* was a sound choice, though. It does seem to connect Europe to the Vales pretty often. It works the other way sometimes. There's a portal in Mapvale it opens to somewhere in the Balkans. Near Trieste, I think. And others."

The servant stepped backward a couple of paces and bowed before turning away.

Almost like being back in Africa . . . not quite. The natives of the Vales were whites, and in this valley they were all redheads. It happened that way quite often. Blue eyes here, brown eyes there. In one valley the women would all be flat-chested, in the next breasts would be heavy as melons and lush as ripe peaches. The larger vales had varied populations of several "European" types; the little side glens, when they were habitable at all, each cut their sons and daughters from a single cloth. Olympians had hair as red as any Gael. They also had green eyes and skin like sand beaches, freckles on freckles on freckles.

Edward had a houseboy of his own now. Dommi was about the same age as he, but shorter and wider. And freckles! Every time he blinked, Edward expected to see freckles flake off his eyelids. He was a tough little mule. He wore nothing but a loincloth, even first thing in the morning when the valley was decidedly nippy. The soles of his feet were as thick as steaks and hard as iron; he could run along a gravel path like a gazelle. He was as much a white man as Edward—even whiter, really—but he was a native and Edward was a stranger. So he was the servant and Edward the *tyika.*

After roughing it for so long, formal evening wear felt very odd. Three days had not begun to blunt the strangeness of Olympus. Nor had they taught the newcomer all the intricacies of accepted social behavior. Even speaking English again was alien to him now.

The natives spoke a version of Randorian, which was pretty much a dialect of Thargian. They would have their own names for the Cam River and Kilimanjaro and the Matterhorn. They probably did not call the *tyika* settlement Olympus. Edward wondered what they did call it.

The strangers spoke English among themselves. They sprinkled it with Thargian words—or even Joalian—but by and large their English would have been understood on Regent Street. Yet they always referred to themselves as *tyikank*. Odd, that. Why not use the English equivalent, "masters"?

They had a childish fondness for nicknames. Rawlinson was known as Prof, and he seemed to cultivate a dry, academic style. Edward was still "Exeter" to the men, "Mr. Exeter" to the women. Once his status and duties became established, he would probably pick up some informal title of his own. He already suspected it would be "Tinker." His identity as the Liberator was officially a secret, for if the Chamber ever learned where he was, then even Olympus itself might not be safe for him.

"You know mana exists, Exeter!" Prof lowered his voice and leaned closer. "They say you've actually met two of the Pentatheon?"

Edward nodded and emptied his glass. He had not yet learned the levers and switches in Olympus; he did not know who was supposed to know what. The *Filoby Testament* strongly hinted that there were traitors here, in the very heart of the Service. For all he knew, Rawlinson could be one of them.

"Well, you must know that they can work miracles! They draw their power from their worshippers' adoration and sacrifices."

Edward had been expecting questions about his own experience with mana, so Rawlinson evidently knew less than he thought he did. As for his "explanations," they were slick enough, but they left an aftertaste of bamboozlement. The words did not really mean anything.

"Mostly on nodes? How does that fit your picture, Prof? I can see the nodes being portals, but why do they increase the flow of mana?"

"Temperature."

"Temperature?"

"Not real temperature, but something like temperature. After all, if another world is especially close just there, then there could be a leakage of something across the gap. You must have sensed that feeling of awe we call 'virtuality'? Imagine the nodes as being in some way hot and the rest of the world as cooler. Now suppose the shield effect is dependent on this 'temperature.' Sensitive to heat, or whatever the force is. That would explain why the stranger absorbs the mana best on a node and why his worshippers' sacrifices are more potent there.''

More mumbo jumbo, and yet it did have a sort of logic to it.

"What's the limit?" Edward asked. "Telepathy and prophecy—how far does it go?" He knew it could kill.

"A long way. Healing, certainly. And prophecy, as you well know. Legends tell of earthquakes and thunderbolts. Earthly myths do the same. It goes all the way to magic. Miracle, if you prefer." Rawlinson flashed his boyish smile and laughed. He was starting to display the results of the gin. "I have no science to give you, old chap! All I can do is draw pictures."

"They fit the facts," Edward agreed politely. He was becoming a little fizzy, too, and a long evening loomed ahead. He did believe in miracles. He had worked one himself.

Rawlinson peered around angrily at the door. "Where in the world has my wife got to, do you suppose? *Carrot!*"

Edward had a few more questions about keys—who had invented them and who ever dared test a new one—but his host suddenly changed the subject.

"Oh, by the way?"

"Yes?"

"The others'll be here shortly. . . . You hired a houseboy, I understand."

"Jumbo's cook recommended him. A grandson or nephew or something, I expect."

Rawlinson coughed. "Yes. Well, my wife was going by your place this afternoon and saw him. She suggested I drop you a quiet hint."

"I'd appreciate any help you can give me," Edward said, having trouble not adding, "sir," to every sentence. He felt as if he were back at Fallow and had been called into the Head's office. Consciously or unconsciously, Rawlinson was radiating mana at him now.

The manservant glided in, to wait expectantly near the *tyika*'s chair.

Rawlinson did not seem to notice him. "Well, it's just this, old man. We don't encourage the Carrots to run around like savages, you know. That's all very well down in their own wallow, but up here we try to teach them more civilized ways."

Back in the baking heat of the afternoon, young Dommi had scrubbed every floor in the bungalow and most of the walls as well. He'd been working like a horse and sweating like a pig. Shiny shoes and white uniform?

"I'll have a word with him."

"And do see he cuts his hair, old man. Shipshape and Bristol fashion, what?"

Dommi's hair hung down his back like a flag of burnished copper. He was very proud of it.

"It seems clean enough," Edward protested.

Rawlinson pulled a disapproving face. "They look much better with it short. More civilized. You mustn't let them get away with a thing, or you'll never get any work out of them at all. Bone lazy, the lot of them."

Edward had suggested Dommi take the evening off and go courting his beloved Ayetha. The youngster had been shocked. The *tyika*'s house was not yet completely cleaned up. There were still many dishes to unpack and wash. There were the *tyika*'s clothes to iron, and food to be fetched and prepared, and the garden must be dug over. His father would be horrified if he took time off while there was work waiting to be done.

Dommi was pathetically anxious to please.

"So far he had shown no signs of laziness at all! He works like a . . . He works very hard."

"Just you wait!" Rawlinson said. "As soon as he's saved up a few shillings he'll buy himself a wife and that'll be the last you'll see of any work out of him." He frowned up at the waiting Carrot. "What's the *Entyika* doing, d'you know?"

"She is supervising the cooks, *Tyika*."

Rawlinson grunted angrily. "Remind her we have a guest here, will you?" He waved the man away. "Bone lazy," he repeated, "the whole lot of 'em."

࿐ၟ   8   ࿐ၟ

"INCREDIBLE!" STRINGER MUTTERED. HE COUGHED, STUBBING OUT a cigarette. His bulging eyes were red from the bite of the smoke that filled the little office.

Smedley's mind was spinning. *Incredible* did not do justice! And yet no one who knew Exeter would ever doubt his word. He spoke always with a quiet deliberation that compelled belief. Lying would be beneath him, even if his life depended on it. He had always been like that.

"These magical places?" the surgeon demanded. "There was one in Flanders?"

"Must have been," Exeter agreed hoarsely. "There may have been a church there before the war or a cemetery."

"And another in the hospital in Greyfriars?"

"Er, no, sir."

"So someone rescued you and took you elsewhere?"

Exeter set his jaw. After a moment he said, "No names, no pack drill, sir."

Stringer let his annoyance show. Then he glanced at his watch. "By Jove! I must be gone. Dining with some bigwigs tonight! Well, it's a fascinating tale! Wish I had time to hear more of it." His arrogant gaze settled a frown on Smedley, as if he did not belong there. "This meeting has gone on too long anyway. I think you should wriggle out unobtrusively now, Captain. Don't want anyone prefiguring your association with the escaped prisoner, do we?"

He was making sure the two of them had no chance for a private word. But that did not matter. The plan he had been told was not the one Exeter would learn from the note inside his shirt. And already Smedley was drawing up Plan Three in his mind. Other worlds!

He mumbled something and rose, holding out his hand. Exeter stood up also, to clasp it in an awkward grip.

"See you on Friday, old man!" Smedley said, nudging foot on foot.

"Good of you. Damned grateful."

By good luck, the formidable Miss Pimm was absent from her desk, probably having lunch, and Smedley walked away along the hall. He would have to change back into uniform if he expected to eat at the King's expense.

The big hall was almost deserted. Everyone must be in the mess.

Yes, the plan would have to be changed. Stringer was a nark, no question about it. Even if he was not quite low enough for the shot-while-trying-to-escape villainy, he was at least a nark. Exeter caught walking out the gate in a stolen uniform would be exposed as a scrimshanker and the jig would be up. Stringer thought the escape was going to happen on Friday morning, so it must happen sooner. Tonight!

Which was cutting things very fine indeed. Smedley must hare down to the village and phone Ginger to get the chariot fired up right away. How many hours would it take to drive from the West Country to Kent, even supposing the car did not break down completely or have too many bursts?

"Ah, there you are, sir! Been looking for you."

Smedley's eyes came back into focus, seeing the wan face of his roommate Rattray.

"Lieutenant?"

"Couple of visitors for you, sir."

Smedley turned to look, and caught a wave.

Alice Prescott! And Ginger Jones!

Oh, hell! *That's torn it!*

He put his good arm around Alice and kissed her cheek. Despite her astonishment she did not bite him. He could tell she was tempted, though. Quite
a gal, Miss Prescott. He laid his stump across Ginger's shoulders and propelled both visitors toward the door.

"I say, darned good of you to come! You haven't eaten yet, have you?
Let's trot down to the Black Dragon and grab a bite." Then he had them
outside.

It was raining and his greatcoat was upstairs. Oh, well.

"What was all that about, Captain Smedley?" Miss Prescott demanded
as they walked down the driveway, footsteps crunching on the gravel.

"All what?"

"I have never been thrown out of a pub, but I imagine the sensation
would be somewhat similar."

"Edward. He'll be brought through there in a couple of shakes, and
seeing you two might rattle him."

"You've talked to him?" Ginger demanded.

"Yes. He's well."

"No amnesia?"

"No, he's in tip-top shape, actually."

What else could Smedley say? *He's been to visit another world, where he has
magical powers. The magic took him there because it was prophesied it would, and
he was tricked into coming back by people who want to kill him, who happen to
include the doctors here.* And after that, of course, Smedley could explain that
he was inclined to believe most of this. *You'd look neat upon the seat of a
straitjacket built for two. . . .*

"He's slinging it, then?" Ginger demanded.

"Ah, yes. Odd thing, though. Stringer, the surgeon, knew who he was!
Met him at the Eton match, apparently. He's been covering for him. Old
School Tie and all that."

The rain was merely a drizzle. The fresh air smelled wonderful, all leafy
and earthy. They walked hurriedly, and Smedley told the Fallow part of
the story. He left out the Olympus bit altogether. He was asked, of course.
He hedged: "He just dropped a few hints."

By the time he had finished, they had reached the Black Dragon. It was
a favorite outing for the walking wounded from Staffles, serving good English ale and quite respectable lunches. The lounge was packed with patients

and visitors, of course, with more men waiting hopefully on the sidelines, but luckily a group vacated a small table right under Smedley's nose and he grabbed it. Before his claim could be disputed, Miss Prescott sat down and the challengers angrily withdrew.

"My favorite table!" Smedley said with satisfaction.

"I wish I knew how you do that," Ginger muttered.

"Do what?"

"Never mind. A drink, Miss Prescott?"

She requested a sherry. Smedley ordered mild and bitter. Ginger went to fetch them.

Alice had changed very little. Her face had always been a little on the horsey side and still was, but not hard to smile at. Edward had been head over heels back in '14. She was not wearing a ring. How did she feel about Edward? How had she ever felt about him, for that matter? She was two or three years older. She was even older now, and Edward . . .

Recalling how oddly youthful Exeter still looked, Smedley suddenly recalled the remark about curing cavities in teeth. Was that why he still seemed young? He *was* still young? He had not aged at all on his other world. Hell's bells!

"Something wrong, Captain?" Miss Prescott inquired coldly.

He had been staring right through her. "No, nothing . . ."

Ginger laid a foaming tankard on the table; Smedley grabbed for it, cursed, switched arms, and drank. Son of a bachelor!

The fact was, he *believed* in Nextdoor and Olympus! That a man of twenty-one still had rosy cheeks was a very flimsy piece of evidence. Lots did, although lately they had been aging much faster than usual. But it was another piece in the puzzle. There had to be some explanation for that tropical tan turning up in Flanders.

"All they have left is the Melton Mowbray pie." Ginger had brought a beer for himself, but was still standing.

"It's usually pretty fair," Smedley said.

Alice nodded acceptance. Ginger went off to order lunches. Service was something else that had gone to hell since the war started. Now Smedley had his chance to hobnob with a girl and see how often he could make her smile.

"Having a good war, Miss Prescott?"

"You used to call me Alice."

"Horrid little bounder, wasn't I? You called me Spots, as I recall."

"And now I ought to call you Gongs! Well done! I hear you're going up to the palace for . . ."

Oh, God! His eye had begun to twitch. He leaned his face on his head to hide it. No good—he was starting a full-fledged attack of the willies. He wanted a drink, but he couldn't lift the beer with his stump, and . . . *Hell and damnation!* He scrambled to his feet and blundered toward the door.

The cool rain helped. When the tears stopped and he could breathe again, he went back inside. The other two were quietly eating pork pie, discussing the terrible price of food in the shops. They did not say a word as he sat down again, ignoring him as if all grown men had hysterical fits all the time, perfectly normal. He did not try to apologize, for that would just set him off again.

What was the use, now? How could they trust anything he said after that performance? He struggled to cut the hard crust with a fork, keeping quiet in his misery. His companions made small talk across him. As they finished eating, the adjoining tables suddenly emptied and stayed that way. So it was time to talk about the business of the meeting, and he wondered if he could do even that much without foaming at the mouth.

"First," Alice said, as matter-of-factly as if jailbreaks were all in her day's work, "we must get him out of Staffles. Second, we must get him up to London before they bring out the bloodhounds." She had finished her food, but she was still nursing her drink. "And third we must find him a safe refuge so he can stay at liberty. Have I omitted anything?"

She glanced at Smedley. He nodded, not trusting himself to speak.

"I think that's enough to be going on with." Ginger was scratching at his beard. His expression suggested that he was wondering how he had ever managed to get himself involved in such lunacy.

"Good!" she said. "Item one: Can we get him out of the building?"

Smedley nodded again.

"That's your part, Julian," she said. "But how?"

"Two plans," he said hoarsely, clenching his fist under the table, struggling not to let his voice quaver.

"Why two?"

"Because we can't trust Stringer! He was altogether too inquisitive. I think he wants Edward to give himself away by trying to escape."

"I see."

He knew what she was thinking.

"I know it sounds crazy. . . ." Oh, what was the use? He *was* crazy! They both knew that as well as he did.

Ginger grunted. "You say Stringer said he knew Exeter?"

"Shook his hand the day he got the hat trick."

"No, he didn't."

"What?"

Ginger removed his pince-nez and wiped it on his sleeve. It was a trick of his when he was upset. "Short Stringer never had any use for games. It was his brother who was the cricketer. Long Stringer was the one who was there that day at Eton. I know. I was there too. I sat right behind him. I remember Exeter being mobbed. I know there were dozens of admirers around him, but I'd swear Short Stringer wasn't there."

An unfamiliar sensation around his mouth told Smedley that he must be smiling. Another piece of evidence sliding into place! If distrusting doctors was proof of insanity, then Ginger Jones belonged to the club too.

"Long Stringer's the soldier?" Alice said. "Could he be involved in this? Could he have recognized Edward in Belgium and tipped off his brother?"

"I don't think we can trust anyone," Smedley said. "Just the three of us." That was funny, asking them to trust a babbling lunatic.

"I agree! Tell us your two plans."

Keeping Plan Three to himself for the time being, Smedley outlined Plan One, the blind for Stringer's benefit, and then Plan Two, the fire alarm.

His audience did not leap to its feet and applaud.

"Hardly cricket," Ginger said dourly, "to shout 'fire!' in a hospital full of disabled men."

"It's damned near a public service! They haven't had a fire drill since I got there, and the place is a death trap. I just hope the alarm works, that's all." Truth to tell, Smedley was uneasy about the ethics of Plan Two, perhaps trying to convince himself as much as his listeners.

"You're sure it will work?" Alice demanded.

"Certain. There will be chaos unlimited! The yard wall's only head high. Exeter could vault it one-han—easily."

She shrugged and did not argue. "Good. You've taken care of the first problem. How about the second, the manhunt? Spiriting him up to London?"

"That's Ginger's part. He'll have to be waiting with the getaway car. There's a concealed gateway . . ."

He was facing two stares of dismay.

"What car?" Ginger growled.

"Boadicea's chariot."

"The Chariot's out of commission. Up on blocks. There's no private motoring now."

"I—I didn't know!" Smedley felt a surge of panic and struggled against it.

"It's not quite illegal," Alice said quickly. "Not yet. I'm sure it soon will be. There's all kinds of restrictions."

"And the price of petrol!" Ginger added. "It just went up to four and sixpence a gallon! Nobody can afford that!"

Smedley cursed under his breath. He should have thought of this. Bicycles? Horses? No, Plan Two had just sunk with all hands. Oh, God, did that mean he would have to go through with Plan One?

"How much time will he have?" Alice asked.

"He'll be missed pretty soon. I can't cut the telephone wires, or I would. If he can just get up to London, he'll be in great shape, but he's got to go through Canterbury or Maidstone." The coppers could set up roadblocks and picket the railway stations. Kent was a dead end in wartime, with the ports closed. Stringer must have seen that.

"An hour?"

"At the most."

"The same problem would arise with Plan One, wouldn't it?"

Smedley shivered. Cold torrents ran over his skin as he thought of himself lying bound and gagged in the little summerhouse—that tiny, walls-falling-in, *trench*-sort-of suffocating summerhouse. "If Stringer snitches, Plan Two's a dead duck. If not, then my paybook and chits will get Exeter clean away. Just depends how long until they find me." Find a screaming, eye-rolling, mouth-foaming lunatic . . .

Alice eyed him thoughtfully for a moment. She laid down her glass. "I think Plan Two is better. You'll do it tomorrow?"

"Tonight would be even better, but—"

"I know a car I can borrow."

"You do?" Smedley wanted to hug and kiss her. The expression on her face sobered him.

"But I can't drive."

He opened his mouth and then closed it. He felt a twinge of the willies and suppressed them. He would never drive a car again.

"Edward can't," Alice said, "unless he's learned how in the last three years."

"I don't think that's too likely. And it doesn't get the car here, anyway."

"I've only ever driven a little bit," she said, "and I'm certainly not up to driving in London."

They looked at Ginger.

He pawed at his beard, alarmed. "Neither am I! Strictly a back roads driver, I am! And I've never driven anything except the chariot. My license is back at Fallow anyway."

"Come on, old man!" Smedley said. "It's only fifty miles to London from here, and the A2's the straightest damned highway in the country, Watling Street. The bloody Romans built it."

Ginger glowered at Alice. "Where is this vehicle?"

"Notting Hill."

"Don't know London. That's north?"

"West."

"So it's on the wrong side!" The old chap was scowling ferociously, but he had not quite said no—not quite.

Alice drummed fingers on the table. An old, familiar glint shone in her eyes. "Captain Smedley, can you suggest anyone else who might be qualified and willing to assist us in rescuing my cousin?"

"Dozens of chaps, Miss Prescott. All the fellows in his class at school would jump at the chance."

"And where can I find them?"

"Ask around in Flanders. Most of them are there, still fighting the lousy Boche or filling up the cemeteries. The ones back here in Blighty have all had their legs blown off. So they can't help you. Frightfully sorry."

Ginger snarled. "Damn you both! What sort of car?"

"A Vauxhall, I think," Alice said. "Bloody great big black box on four wheels. You won't get wet."

"Does it have electric lights?"

Alice pursed her lips, a gesture which definitely did not improve her appearance. It suggested hay. "I'm not sure. I've never been out in it in the dark."

"Time, gentlemen!" called the landlord.

"We must go," Smedley said.

Jones did not budge. "You're sure the owner will be willing to lend us this vehicle?"

"He would not mind!" she said firmly. "I have the key to the lockup."

"And what will he say if I ram a taxi in the Strand?"

"I am sure it is insured." Her face was bleak. Best to ask no more, obviously.

Ginger polished his glasses vigorously. "Tomorrow night?"

The old chap was not short of courage and definitely long on loyalty. How would Fallow react if one of its senior masters was caught driving the getaway car in a jailbreak?

"Good man!" Smedley said. "But not tomorrow. Tonight! We must get the jump on Stringer and his gang."

Ginger flinched. "Tonight?"

"This is Plan Three! I tried to hint to Exeter that it would not wait until Friday. Even if he didn't understand my hint, though, he'll know as soon as the alarm goes off. I'll bring some spare togs along, in case he has to run in his pajamas." Smedley sighed happily. "I'm coming too, you see."

Other worlds!

9

SUDDENLY THERE WAS URGENCY. SMEDLEY RECALLED THAT THE NEXT bus was almost due, so the three of them ran. Jumpy and chattery, he waited at the bus stop with them until the bus arrived, a creaky old double-decker. Alice and Jones both found seats, but not together, so they had no chance to talk.

Alice was beside a verbose middle-aged lady with pronounced—loudly pronounced—opinions on the Germans, the war, prices, food shortages, the need for rationing, and many, many other topics. Letting this blizzard of complaint drift around her, Alice sat back and marveled at the sudden emergency that had disrupted her life.

She had met Julian Smedley four times previously, with a lapse of years between each encounter. He had always been one of Edward's closest friends at Fallow, and always more of a follower than a friend. It might be more accurate to say that Edward had always been Smedley's friend, for Edward was one of those people who had friendships thrust upon them. Her memories of Smedley were like photographs in an album. Weedy little boy on page one, then pimply adolescent, and now wounded hero on page five. Each memory was strangely different. He had been shy and owlish, yet mischievous and quietly witty. Moreover, as Ginger had pointed out on the train down, Julian Smedley had always possessed a gift for falling on his feet. When the cake was passed out, the largest piece would usually land on his plate, yet nobody ever disliked him.

Perhaps even a missing hand counted as a largish piece of cake in 1917. He had been buried alive by a shell burst and dug out in time. Now he was out of the war, which was what mattered. Ginger said he had medals galore, although she would never have marked Julian as a potential hero. Why had she made that *stupid, stupid* remark about them? Buried alive!

Shell-shocked or not, Julian Smedley had talked Jones and herself into this madness very slickly. She might lose her job over it, although jobs were no problem now. She might even go to jail, although that prospect was sufficiently improbable not to trouble her unduly. She was not the one in danger. If things went wrong, the police would want to know by what right she had taken a motorcar belonging to Sir D'Arcy Devers. The danger was scandal.

The bus groaned into Canterbury at five minutes to three, and there was a branch of the Midland Bank directly across the street. With a wave to Jones, she ran over to it and managed to cash a check just before it closed. Ready money might be useful.

After that she had a chance to talk with her fellow conspirator. They walked side by side to the station. He looked haggard and worried. Jones she had met only once before, and now suddenly they were plotting an illegal undertaking together. He seemed so much a typical, dull schoolmaster, a stolid rock, pitted and barnacled by wave after wave of untiring youth. He was obviously close to retirement, possibly due to having been put out to pasture before now had the war not intervened, a tweedy badger of a man. By no means cuddly, but unthinkable as a criminal.

"Have we both gone insane," she asked him, "or are we merely bewitched?"

"You've been wondering that too, have you? I decided that it's something to do with the war. It's stripping away all our pretences, layer after layer."

"Pretences?"

"Our veneer of culture. Illusions. Everything we hid behind for so long. We see those young men who have gone out into hell to fight for a cause, and we realize that they now know something we don't. Life and youth seem infinitely more precious than they did three years ago. Many other things have become trivial and meaningless."

She considered that thought and decided it was more profound than it had sounded at first. He had an aching conscience, this Mr. Jones.

"I am extremely grateful to you, and—I confess—more than a little surprised that you would let yourself become involved in this for the sake of my cousin."

The schoolmaster cleared his throat. "Ahem! Your cousin is an admirable young man. I feel very sorry for his many misfortunes. But I should be less than honest were I not to admit that my primary interest is Julian Smedley."

"He has severe emotional problems," she said warily.

"He has been horribly damaged, both physically and mentally. We old men who have stayed home and sent the young to fight for us—we do have certain obligations. At least I feel that way. And you cannot conceive the difference between the Smedley you met today and the one I saw last Sunday."

She remembered the tears. "Better?"

"Infinitely better. His efforts to aid his old friend are working a miracle cure on our young hero."

So that was why he had let Smedley talk him into this! What would Smedley think if he knew that? That reasoning would not sound convincing in the witness box at the Old Bailey. How would Smedley react if they failed?

"I wish he were not coming!" she said. "If he would just set off the alarm and then stay with the other inmates, then no harm could come to him." But they had both argued that case, and Smedley had insisted.

"I am sure he has his reasons. We must show him that we trust him. It is the best treatment he could get."

"Your sentiments do you honor," she murmured. "Have you ever had children of your own, Mr. Jones?"

He laughed feebly. "A highly improper question to put to a lifelong bachelor! I suppose I could be platitudinous and say I have had hundreds of sons, but that would not be true. Perhaps twenty-five, a little less than one a year. I always hoped that a year would bring forth at least one. Sometimes it did, sometimes it didn't. Rarely two. Two of them are involved in this."

She squeezed his arm. "I hope they appreciate you."

"Perhaps they will one day. Not now."

They turned into the station. It was ominously crowded.

"They are sending all the engines to France, you know," Jones complained. "And some of the rails, too! Let us go look at the board."

According to the board, there was a train in fifteen minutes. The waiting room was packed to the doors. By mutual consent, they wandered along the platform together, taking the chance to talk.

"May I inquire about this automobile, Miss Prescott?"

It was a very fair question.

"I told you I have the key. Its owner would certainly not object to my using it. He has let me drive it before."

"And why do you think it has petrol available? Why do you believe it to be in operating condition?"

Alice sighed and decided that there had better be honor among thieves. "His wife is a woman with a great deal of influence."

She glanced sideways at her companion, expecting to see a bristling of shock. But Jones had a trick of using his pince-nez to mask his eyes, and his face gave away nothing.

"Does she know you have the key?"

"She does not know I exist. I am certain of that. You know it's illegal now to employ men between the ages of eighteen and sixty-one in non-essential industries, and yet she still has a chauffeur. What strings she pulls I cannot imagine, but she does. Admittedly she is not in good health, but

I feel that morally Captain Smedley has a greater claim on the vehicle tonight than she does."

Jones uttered his quiet chuckle again. "Learned counsel would hesitate to present such an argument in court. And what happens if we are caught and the lady finds out?"

Alice winced. "She will not lay charges, I am sure. It would cause tongues to wag."

That was not true at all. Lady Devers would trumpet it to the four corners of the earth. She was a vindictive, malicious *bitch*. Alice would not tell Mr. Jones that. He was more shocked by bad language than he was by confessions of adultery.

A porter began shouting, "London train!" and they had no further chance for private conversation.

They reached London. They struggled through the traffic, which was already mounting toward the evening rush. They stopped to do some shopping for supper and came at last to her flat.

As always, her hand was trembling when she unlocked the door. The day's post lay on the mat, where it had fallen through the slot. She snatched it up and peered at the envelopes. What she dreaded was not there, and she was another day closer to the end of the war.

The official notice would not come to her, of course—it would go to the bitch in Notting Hill—but D'Arcy had taken his sister into his confidence before he was posted overseas, and Anabel had promised faithfully that she would notify Alice if the dread announcement ever came. Alice could not bring herself to trust that arrangement. Every day she read the obituaries and casualty lists in the *Times,* although no one knew how out-of-date those might be. On Sundays she would sometimes go up to Notting Hill and walk past the house, looking for the drawn blinds that would be evidence of mourning. That was how she knew about the chauffeur.

She made tea and prepared a drab meal. She suggested that Jones take a nap, in preparation for a sleepless night, but he was too anxious about the coming ordeal to relax. They must be out of town before dark, he insisted. He dare not try to drive in traffic in the dark.

Alice prepared some sandwiches from the ugly wartime bread. She dressed in the warmest tweeds she possessed. She took the precious key from her bottom drawer, and pressed a kiss on D'Arcy's photograph. Then she went back into the sitting room and found Jones nodding before the gas fire. He looked up with a guilty start.

"Come, my lord!" she said. "We must embark upon our pilgrimage to Canterbury, as in days of yore. You shall be my verray, parfit gentil knyght!"

He hauled himself out of the chair, blinking behind his pince-nez. "And you, my lady? The prioresse?"

"The wif of Bathe, I think, is more my role. Shall I tell you a tale upon the way to lighten the journey?"

Mr. Jones looked deeply shocked that she should even know that story.

They sallied out into the streets again. They took the tube, and then a bus, and so they came to Notting Hill. It seemed a very mundane way to embark on a mission of romance and high adventure. And all those long miles must be retraced.

The lockup was one of six, in what had been a stable until five or six years ago. There was no one else about in the gloomy little yard. The rain had ended, but the skies remained gray and gravid.

The key still worked. Jones groaned loudly when he saw the size of the motorcar. The great black dragon almost filled its kennel, so that there was hardly room to move around it. Alice had only been here two or three times, and she could not recall why D'Arcy had ever given her the key. She could remember every drive she had ever had in the car, though— wonderful, intoxicating journeys out of town with her lover, stolen hours of happiness together.

Jones inspected every inch of the monster. Alice fidgeted, fearing that some neighbor would come driving in and think to investigate the strangers, although it was more than probable that the cars in the other lockups had been abandoned for the duration of the war. Adjacent houses overlooked the yard. Would some kind friend think to telephone Lady Devers and inform her that her car was being stolen?

Jones checked the fuel tank with the dipstick and examined the jerry can chained on the running board. Both seemed to be full, he said glumly. He had been hoping for a last-minute stay of execution, perhaps. The oil in the lamps was low, he said, and he could find no spare oil. They must stop somewhere and buy some before the garages closed.

That was not enough excuse to give up the expedition. Alice found a motoring rug in the back. She adjusted it over her knees as she settled herself in the seat next the driver's. Jones turned the crank. The motor caught at once. He backed the car out of the lockup and went to shut the doors. The adventure had begun.

Sometime in the small hours, Julian Smedley would set off the fire alarm in Staffles. Edward, who would not be expecting the signal this night, would be jerked out of his sleep by bells ringing to signal his escape. . . .

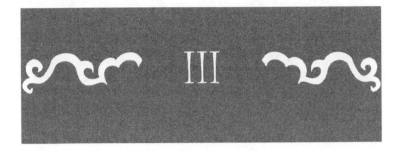

III

Illegal Move

౭ 10 ౨

Escape! Escape!

Edward Exeter had escaped from Sussvale.

He stalked along happily, encrusted in red dust. His boots were rubbing his toes, but the ache in his legs was almost pleasurable. Rothpass was one of the easier passes in the Vales, and now the road led downward. He matched strides with Goathoth Peddler, who was also on his way to Nagvale and enjoyed company on the road. Ahead of them trudged the peddler's packbeast, to whom Edward had not been introduced, but which generally resembled a jackass designed by a committee of iguana. Goathoth was expounding on his daughter-in-law's childbearing problems in a Sussian accent like a knife on a tin plate, quite unaware how little his young friend understood. Neither of them was particularly worried by trivia on such a fine morning.

"————," said the peddler, "another miscarriage. That made three. A few fortnights later they went to ———— and sacrificed a ———— to ————."

"A very wise decision," Edward remarked.

Jagged peaks towered on either hand. Once in a while the trail would emerge from forest and offer a glimpse of scenery ahead. From that height the world stretched out forever. Nagvale was another intermontane basin, of course. It seemed narrower than Sussvale, but he could not discern the end of it; the bordering ranges trailed away into hazy distance.

He was enjoying himself, although his conscience said he should not be. He had betrayed little Eleal, who had befriended him and saved his life. He had left a trail of dead friends and would-be helpers—Bagpipe, Creighton, Gover, Onica—not to mention an unknown number of slain foes, one of whom he had dispatched personally.

By all rights, he should have died in Sussland. Zath had been waiting for him to arrive there, as the *Filoby Testament* prophesied he would. The god of death had set his deadly reapers to trap the expected Liberator. Julius Creighton and Gover Envoy had died, but Edward had escaped. Zath's killers had set another ambush for him, and Onica Mason had died; but again Edward had beaten the odds and escaped. Tion, Suss's patron god, had let him go, which he had never expected either.

He could claim very little credit for himself, but he had escaped from Sussvale. He was going Home. In a few more weeks, he would be back in England, ready to fight for King and Country—under an assumed name, of course, but in time to help humble the Prussian Bully. Nextdoor would be nothing but an incredible memory, a month missing from his life.

A party of pilgrims came riding up the western slope, taking it easy to spare their moas. They waved cheerily at the two men heading down but did not break off their conversation. Clearly they had seen nothing odd in either of the two. They had probably not noticed the younger one taking an unusually hard look at their mounts.

Edward, for his part, was amused at how easily he now accepted the idea of creatures that had hooves and fur and yet looked like birds. In less than two weeks, he had already adjusted to the lesser oddities of Nextdoor. It was a fascinating place. Perhaps one day, after the war was over, he might try to come back, to explore it in detail—or even fulfill a prophecy or two.

"———" Goathoth announced triumphantly, "bouncing baby boy! Named him ——— after his ———!"

"May the gods be praised!"

Tangles of purple and bronze creepers in the woods sent out waves of pungent scents, while shrieking birds fluttered and stalked around—feathery birds and furry birds also, for Nextdoor had a wide variety of bipeds.

Just once, near the summit, Edward had sensed the eeriness of virtuality, but very weak and localized. An ancient mossy shrine stood there, a curved wall around a weathered statue of a woman, which would be some aspect of Eltiana, the Lady. His companion had lingered to say a prayer; Edward stayed well back from it, although he doubted that there would be any resident numen at such a minor node. They had continued on their way unmolested.

The previous day he had stopped at a lonely farmhouse in the mountains and offered to work a few hours in return for a meal and a place to sleep. He had chopped wood and milked goats. He had raised some blisters and been butted a couple of times and enjoyed himself thoroughly. The food had been tasty and filling, the soft hay fragrant. The farmer's eldest daughter had offered more than customary hospitality and been mildly peeved when her advances were declined, but apart from that all parties had been satisfied by the arrangement. A stranger's charisma would take care of most problems; youth and honest labor guaranteed untroubled rest.

He had certainly had an interesting couple of weeks since leaving Paris.

"———— Thargians," the peddler grumbled. "All over Narshland like ———— around a mating ————!"

"Murderous scum," Edward agreed.

Joalia versus Thargia was another war, but one he must stay clear of. He was just the right age to be handed a spear and told to form up. He wondered which side Goathoth spied for. It soon became evident that Goathoth was wondering the same about him, for he began spinning a string of leading questions.

Oh, the temptation to tell the truth!—*I'm D'ward, the Liberator whom the Filoby Testament predicts will kill death. I'm a stranger in this world. When I get down to Sonalby, I'm going to seek out an agent of the Service, which is another group of strangers. They will send me Home. In another couple of fortnights, I'll be in England. That's on Earth. Yes, Earth. Well, I'd never heard of Nextdoor until a couple of weeks ago. Any other questions?*

It was not on. Instead, Edward explained that he was a wandering scholar from Rinooland, a vale far enough away to explain his accent and his ignorance of the geography.

Joal versus Tharg was one war. There was another, older war that he must also stay out of. Odious as Tion had turned out to be, the Youth was not as despicable as some of the others, the ones known as the Chamber— Zath and his allies. Obviously Tion conspired against other members of the Pentatheon—the Parent, the Man, the Lady, the Maiden. That was the Great Game, which the strangers played to relieve the tedium of immortality. His personal recreations might be vicious, but the Lord of Art did not use murder to earn his mana. He seemed to keep his subordinates under reasonable control. He was certainly not a member of the Chamber, or he would never have released the Liberator to find his foretold destiny. Did he disapprove of Zath on ethical grounds, or was he merely resentful of his ill-gotten influence in the Great Game?

The struggle between the Service and the Chamber was yet a third war. Somewhere in a place nicknamed Olympus, the organization Edward sought was trying to do something about the appalling injustice of a deceitful religion, to bring enlightenment to an oppressed and benighted population. It was a new version of the White Man's Burden. His father had favored the cause, and anything the guv'nor had supported would be worthy of Edward's loyalty also.

But that was not his war either, no matter what the *Testament* predicted. He had duties elsewhere, a fourth war.

He must not—could not—stay and play missionary in this alien world while his friends were dying for England. He heard Alice's voice whispering *starry-eyed romantic idealist!* in his mind's ear, and he chuckled. Long might he remain one!

A bend brought another breathtaking glimpse of the great valley ahead, framed between rocky spurs. Sunlight gleamed on a winding river.

"Susswater again?" he asked.

The peddler frowned. "Nagwater."

Well, that was absurd! Susswater flowed west. The road had followed it for a while, detouring into the hills when the gorge became too narrow. Now both trail and river had emerged from the mountains. Obviously that was the same river!

But apparently it was not the same river to Goathoth Peddler, so each vale must have its own river. That was a strange concept of geography, another stumbling block to understanding the language—the many languages.

"Those mountains? What are they named?"

This time the peddler's sun-reddened eyes were frankly incredulous. "Nagwall, of course!"

Edward thought about that for a few paces. He used gestures to aid his next question. "Nagwall this side. What name on the other side?"

"Joalwall there." The peddler waved his stick northward. Then southward. "Lemodwall there."

"And in the middle what are they called?"

The old man seemed completely at a loss. "What pass are you looking from?"

What a range was called depended on where it was seen from? If mountains were all about you, always, then perhaps you had no concept of classifying mountains, like fish in an ever-present sea?

Why did Nextdoor have to be confoundingly interesting?

It was late afternoon when he limped into Sonalby. His feet hurt and his legs ached, and Nextdoor no longer seemed quite so fascinating as it had done in the morning. The peddler had stopped off to trade at an isolated ranch house, leaving him to walk alone for the last couple of hours.

Nagvale was different. Where Sussvale had been lushly tropical, with farms and orchards packed in from wall to mountain wall, here the flat land was semidesert. The grass was scrubby and well grazed; trees were rare and spiny. There were no hedges or fences; houses were grouped into small, widely scattered settlements, which he assumed were ranches. The only industry he had detected so far was herding. The livestock were gangling, hairless beasts as angular as camels would be without humps. The males sported elaborate branched antlers and looked potentially dangerous. He was relieved that none came near the road.

The herders were grown men, and they carried spears and big circular shields. Many of them were astride moas or had moas tethered nearby. He wondered if the weapons were for defense against the male cattle or against predators, and if those predators had four legs or two.

Sonalby was a larger village than any he had seen in Sussvale, although smaller than Suss itself. It had no wall or palisade around it, which meant either that Nagland was peaceful or that the inhabitants relied on their weapons for defense. It sprawled for more than a mile along the bank of a wide, reedy river, which clearly provided building material as well as drinking water. The houses were wicker walled and thatched, none higher than one story. There seemed to be no pattern to them, no streets.

He was parched, footsore, hungry. His first need was to locate Kalmak Carpenter and enlist the aid of the Service. Onica had not lived to carry word to Olympus, so he would have to improvise. Kalmak himself was only a native, not a stranger, but he would recognize the password and put Edward on the road Home.

Nagvale looked more like Kenya than England. From the road he had seen Nagians only at a distance, but he began to catch closer glimpses of them as he approached the town. They were about the color of well-tanned Spaniards or Italians. Most were lanky and leathery, their dark hair and beards long and untrimmed. Seeing both sexes dressed in leather kilts or loincloths, he found himself thinking of them as savages and that discovery annoyed him. Their way of life was well adapted to the climate. They might have a sophisticated literature and culture for all he knew to the contrary, although Eleal had never mentioned the troupe performing in Nagland.

Women going around bare-breasted had seemed quite unremarkable during his childhood in Africa. He found them more interesting now.

The village had no wall or stockade, or even any well-defined borders. He passed the first houses without being challenged. To his left a group of women pounded meal, to his right young men were practicing spear-throwing. Neither group seemed especially promising—or especially interested—although he was an obvious outsider in his Sussian smock. His hair was as black as theirs, but he doubted that anyone else had blue eyes. He had decided to go on a little farther when faint sounds of shouting came drifting out from the town.

The warriors stopped their spear-throwing. The women looked up.

Then the men took up their spears and began to run. The women rose to their feet, hastily gathered small children, and set off to follow.

So did Edward. Pushing his blistered feet faster, he hurried after them. Soon the shouting grew louder; he saw more people running. Something of importance was happening. It could have nothing to do with him, but if everyone was there, then he had better attend also. A stranger caught skulking around deserted houses would be suspected of ill intentions.

He saw smoke. One of the houses was burning, which could hardly be a rare event in a village built like this one. The houses were spaced well apart, undoubtedly for just that reason. With no set street pattern, the people were heading more or less straight to the emergency. He followed until he reached the assembled crowd. He peered over heads. Half the building had gone already, red flames shooting skyward. Through a window he could see the interior glowing like a furnace and could feel the heat on his face, even at that distance.

He sensed something amiss. However strange the language, he could read the tone of the shouting. There ought to be wailing and lamentation. There wasn't. He heard jeering and anger. This was a mob. Someone was in trouble, and ten to one that house had been deliberately torched.

He located the center of the agitation, the men in charge of this riot. Their green robes, their shaven heads and faces, all confirmed that they were priests. They were haranguing the crowd, rousing it to ever-greater fury.

His skin prickled. An outsider had no place in a nasty business like this. Mobs were fickle. Furthermore, green was the color of Karzon, the Man, one of the Five. In the popular mind, Zath was an avatar of the Man, but in Zath's case the vassal was the stronger of the two. Zath was certainly one of the Chamber, and Karzon must be assumed to be so also. This affair might very well concern Edward, therefore, and the sooner he made himself scarce the better.

He stepped back one pace, then stopped as the crowd howled, a hungry, bestial sound. Four men came forward, carrying another prone between them. The priests yelled something. The crowd howled again.

Then the lynch party ran forward to the flaming house, two holding their victim's ankles, two his wrists. They swung in unison, and hurled him bodily through the doorway. They beat a hasty retreat from the heat. The man screamed from inside the furnace. Edward watched, appalled and help-less. He thought he saw the wretch rise to his feet, already wreathed in flame, only to stumble and collapse. There was one more scream and then nothing but the roar of the fire and the wild hollering of the mob.

"Karzon!" they screamed. "Krobidirkin Karzon! Karzon Krobidirkin!"

The priests waved a signal, and the execution squad came forward again. This time they were carrying a woman.

Edward began to push his way through the crowd. He was a stranger; he had charisma; he might be able to do something. He was too late.

Sickened, he turned away, hearing the lustful howl of the mob and the woman's horribly prolonged dying shriek.

An elderly man stood beside him. His graying beard hung to his waist, but it did not hide old ritual scars on his scraggly chest. The wrinkled face above the beard was painted with a complex design, mostly in white, but with minor elements in the other sacred colors. He was grinning and rubbing his hands on his leather skirt.

"What have they done?" Edward demanded in Joalian. "What is their crime?"

Filmy eyes inspected the stranger suspiciously. Then the old man bared his teeth and barked out a string of words.

Edward caught very little of the explanation, except for one name: Kalmak. Another howl from the crowd made him look around. He caught a glimpse of an adolescent boy cartwheeling through the air, following his parents into the pyre.

So the priests of Karzon had just taken care of Kalmak. They had also destroyed Edward's only lead to the Service. Without the help of the Service, he could not return to Earth.

No escape! No escape!

He was trapped on Nextdoor, with no way to escape.

He watched in dismay as all his hopes went up in flames.

What was that confounded noise? He was in a bed. A bell ringing? A fire alarm. Not on Nextdoor any longer. Eyes gritty with sleep, head like a swamp. Back on Earth, in England. Dreaming of three years ago. Smedley had set off the alarm to help him escape from Staffles. . . .

ᡒᡅᡅ **11** ᡅᡅᡒ

Aᴳᴬᴵᴺ Jᵁᴸᴵᴬᴺ Sᴹᴱᴰᴸᴱʸ ʜᴬᴰ ᴰᴵsᴘᴏsᴇᴅ ᴏꜰ ʜɪs sʟᴇᴇᴘɪɴɢ ᴛᴀʙʟᴇᴛ. Aɢᴀɪɴ he struggled to push his feet into laced shoes. This time he had pulled his greatcoat on over his civvies—no old campaigner ever forgot his greatcoat. He had noted where Rattray had put his blues. Rattray was roughly Exeter's height, although much broader. With a stolen bundle under his maimed arm, Smedley stole out into the dim, hushed corridor.

The fire alarm was right beside the bathroom door—a real spot of luck, because he was going to provoke a very fast reaction, and he did not want to be caught in the act. He paused for a moment, heart pounding, wondering for the thousandth time if there was any horrible miscalculation in his plan. Suppose nothing at all happened?

Over the top! he thought, and pulled the lever. Noise roared through the silent mansion, louder than the guns opening up at the start of a major battle. He turned the door handle the wrong way and began to panic; he almost fell into the bathroom—should have opened the door first, of course—he counted to ten and then emerged again. Other men were coming out of other doors, nurses flitting like moths already, lights dazzling bright.

He had expected to be first down the stairs, but several men were ahead of him, staggering in the way of the newly awakened. They might be cursing, but the clamor of the bells drowned out all sound. More were already streaming out into the chilly night, some on crutches, some helping the disabled. Like him, many had thought to pull on their greatcoats. Then he was outside on the lawn.

His first error! He had expected darkness, but light was streaming from every window—so much for regulations! The sky was almost cloudless and a gibbous moon had etched the grounds into a silver lithograph. His companions had stopped to take stock, muttering angrily. He pushed past and kept on going, around the west wing and the big greenhouse, past the sheds, across the rose garden, and through a narrow arch into the yard.

Second error! The yard was already full of men, and more were pouring out the kitchen door. He should have foreseen that! And the light would make it impossible to climb the wall unobserved. Oh . . . heck. Keep calm! It could be done yet. All it needed was a cool head.

Some meddling officer began shouting, ordering everyone out to the garden. The yard was too close to the house.

Splendid! Smedley backed away and then stood against the wall near the arch, watching the faces coming by him—pale blurs, but he could imagine the angry, unshaven faces, the tousled hair. Cold, shivering men in pajamas. If they knew who had ruined their sleep, they would lynch him. And indoors, the bedridden, the crippled, the crazy . . .

Where was Exeter? Could he have vaulted that wall and gone on ahead? Not without raising a hue and cry, surely? Had he been rounded up by a guard? If Stringer had reported that the malingerer was preparing to break out, then anything was possible.

Then one of the taller ones . . .

"Exe—er, *Edward!*"

Exeter parted from the mob and grabbed Smedley's shoulder.

"Where to?"

"This way."

They moved along the side of the wall, and Smedley plunged into bushes. He heard crackling behind him. A voice shouted, "I say!" in the background. He kept on going. Twigs scratched and clawed at his face, tugged his clothing. There were no more shouts.

The shrubbery offered no foothold, only obstruction. Then it ended. Ahead was a lawn, and there were men on it, although none near the wall. They would all be looking toward the house, wouldn't they? Not staring out into the night?

"This'll have to do!" He panted. "There's glass on top here. Can you manage?" He thrust Rattray's uniform at his companion.

Exeter eyed the height. "I think so. Thanks, old son! You've been a real brick. Never forget this." He chose a spot clear of branches and swung the garments up to cover the glass.

"Wait! I'm coming too."

Exeter turned to stare at him. "Why?"

"I just am. Don't waste time arguing. I'll need a hand."

Funny ha-ha.

"Don't be an idiot! There's nothing to connect you with this. Don't stuff your neck in a noose!"

"I want to come!"

Exeter put his fists on his hips. "What are you planning?"

"Nextdoor. You're going back, aren't you? Take me!"

"No, I'm not going back! I don't know that I could, even if I wanted to. I don't know how to get in touch with Head Office. I'm not sure that you can cross over with only one hand. No. You stay here."

They were wasting precious seconds! This was madness.

"Exeter!" Smedley heard his voice crack. He felt his face starting to twitch. "Please!"

"Look here, there's no need to implicate yourself! I'll get in touch with you later. Your people still in Chichester? That's where you're going?"

"The coppers!" Smedley said, choking. "They'll watch me!" He was sobbing already. Must he beg, too? Must he explain that if they locked him up he would go out of his mind? "Please, Exeter! They'll question me. I'll give the others away! Ginger Jones! For God's sake—"

"Oh, right-oh!" Exeter stooped and cupped his hands.

Smedley placed a foot and jumped. He got his arms over the wall and heard glass crack, felt pain. He swung a leg up, banged his stump, scrabbled, and tipped over. Fire tore at his leg as it dragged over the coping. He fell bodily onto the grass verge. Impact knocked all the breath out of him. God almighty!

He hurt. He felt sick.

Exeter came down with a curse and hauled Smedley to his feet. Then he tried to pull the uniform loose from the wall. There was a loud ripping noise.

"That's torn it! Leave it. Come on!"

They began to run along the lane, through blackness under tree branches. Smedley could feel hot blood on his ankle. He lurched and stumbled; Exeter steadied him as they ran. The road was muddy and uneven.

"We're going to look like a pair of real ninnies if the car isn't there," Exeter said.

Smedley tried to explain about the concealed driveway, but he lacked breath. He should have remembered the glass on the wall sooner and brought his own blues as well as Rattray's. Or another greatcoat. Exeter in pajamas would have a deuce of a lot of explaining to do if they ran into anyone.

Twin orange moons dawned ahead of them, reflecting on puddles, shedding uncertain light on the hedges.

"Someone's coming!" Exeter said. "Into the ditch!"

"No! Be . . . Ginger . . ." He'd have seen the lights going on in Staffles. "Too big for the chariot!"

Smedley made a gasping sound of disagreement. The car went spraying by them and stopped. A door flew open, and Alice's voice yelled, "Edward!"

He should have had the wit to go in the front, beside Ginger. The back was roomy enough, but the other two fell into the car and each other's arms and on top of him, all at the same time. Even before the door slammed, he was in a scrum.

By the time he had escaped to the fringes, the big car had swept past Staffles and was hurtling recklessly along the dark lane. He sank back with a shivery feeling of release. Done it! They had done it! Exeter was bubbling his thanks to Alice and Ginger. The old man was managing the driving very well. All they needed now was a burst tire.

Miss Prescott took Smedley's face in both hands and kissed him as if she really meant it.

"Well done!" she said, sounding quite emotional.

"My pleasure, ma'am. I should warn you . . ."

"What?"

"Nothing."

He was bleeding like a pig all over her fancy automobile. But there was no light, so it would have to wait. It would stop soon.

"Yes, well done," Exeter said from the far side. "Anyone mind if I wrap up in this rug?" His teeth rattled.

Alice squeaked in a motherly fashion and helped him. Smedley thought about offering his greatcoat, but that seemed like a lot of effort.

Ginger roared, "Crossroads! Which way?"

"Left," Smedley said, and they rushed through the village.

"Lights?" Exeter asked, peering back. "What's wrong with the street-lights?"

"Blackout," Alice said. "The lamps're painted so they just throw light downward . . . German planes."

There was a moment's silence, then he said incredulously, "They drop bombs?"

"On London, yes. They used to use zepps—zeppelins. *Airships*. We started shooting those down, so now they use aeroplanes. Big jobbies, with four or five engines."

"But bombs? On *civilians?* Women and children?"

"Indeed they do. Now you tell me exactly where you've been these last three years, baby Cousin, because I'm—"

"No! First you tell me all about this war!"

"You don't— You really have been away? You don't know?"

"I don't know a thing except what I've overheard when I wasn't sup-posed to be listening. I saw a bit of a battlefield. I thought I'd died and gone to hell. It's still going on, after three years? I'd never imagined it would be like that!"

"Nobody did! It turned out much worse than anyone ever thought it would be."

Smedley was trying to remember the way in case Ginger needed guid-ance. He stopped listening as Alice talked about the war—planes and U-boats and trenches, the Tsar deposed and the Yanks coming someday. He fingered his leg and discovered his pants leg and sock were soaked. He had gashed his calf in two places. It was sticky, but he thought the bleeding had more or less stopped. It throbbed nastily. It was his right one, unfortunately, hard for him to reach.

A lorry rumbled by in the opposite direction, and he realized that they were on a main road now. If it didn't go to Canterbury, it would go somewhere. Every mile made their escape more likely, as long as they didn't end up at Dover. He was shivering with reaction.

"Speak up!" Ginger shouted over his shoulder.

"Sorry," Exeter said. He had started to tell his story. "I've been in an-other world. Can you believe that?"

"We'll try," Alice said. "How did you get out of the hospital in Grey-friars?"

"I had supernatural aid. Call him Mr. Goodfellow. I don't know his real name. Perhaps he doesn't, any more."

"He made you invisible? No one saw you."

"I didn't see them. I just walked out, on crutches. Then we were met by a man named Creighton. Colonel Julius Creighton. Said he dropped in at Nyagatha once. Remember him?"

"Can't say I do."

"Average height . . . Doesn't matter. He was Service. And so was the guv'nor."

It was strange to hear that old familiar voice, would know it anywhere. Those dry, quiet tones in the dark, bringing back memories, bushels of memories.

"No, not the Colonial Office. This is another Service altogether. There's two Services, really. The one on this world we call Head Office, but it's not really in charge of the Service on Nextdoor. They're more just allies, sort of in cahoots. Service and Head Office are the goodies. There are also baddies, which on Nextdoor are the Chamber and here are the Blighters. I don't know very much about them here, except that they had a lot to do with starting this awful war. Mr. Goodfellow took us to his, er, residence, and he cured my broken leg."

"Snap of the fingers cured?"

"Pretty much. Yes. Then Creighton and I traveled down to Wiltshire. I didn't want to, of course, but he insisted I owed him that much. There's a portal there, a magic door. It let us cross over to Nextdoor. Trouble was, there were baddies waiting on the other side, and Creighton got killed. So there I was—stranded. Stuck. All washed up. Robinson Crusoe."

Ginger was following a lorry. Its stronger headlights were lighting the road for him, and they were doing a steady thirty at least.

"I really wanted to come back and do my bit in the war," Exeter said. "But the only way I could come back here was to find the Service, and I didn't know how to do that. I had what I thought was a lead, but it didn't pan out. When I did get in touch, they were pretty reluctant to help me. Three years, it's taken. You see, there's a prophecy about me."

Houses now. Perhaps this was Canterbury already. Smedley was feeling dizzy. Perhaps he had banged his head falling off the wall. Perhaps he was suffering from lack of sleep. He wouldn't have nurses popping pills at him every night now, so he might not sleep much in future. But he did have a strange tingling in his head.

The car jerked, coughed, and then purred again.

Alice: "What was that?"

Jones: "Dunno."

Dirt in the petrol, likely. That would put the hen among the foxes, wouldn't it? If the car broke down with Exeter in nightclothes and him with blood all over his bags . . . Even a modestly intelligent bus conductor might be suspicious enough to blow the whistle.

"You cross over," Exeter was explaining, "by doing a dance, a particular mixture of chanting and rhythm and words, done at a particular place. It used to be quite a common accident, I think, because the nodes are very often holy places. You know that sort of *awe* you feel in old churches? You're sensing what the Service calls 'virtuality,' although no one knows what it really is. So in primitive times, when the shaman called the tribe together to do their sacred leap-about, they would do it at a node. And if the routine was good, they'd feel that virtuality more strongly. Why do you think people sing in church? The shamans would experiment with the ritual, I expect. Try different words, different movements, to increase that sense of the holy presence or whatever they thought it was. And one day— one night, more likely—someone would hit the right mixture and *pouf!* Clarence and Euphemia had disappeared. Big feather in shaman's cap! Do it again next Thursday."

The car coughed again, twice, and then resumed its low rumble. Everyone was silent, but nothing more happened.

Smedley jerked his head up. He seemed to be drifting off to sleep. His leg had stopped throbbing. Come to think of it, his leg was numb. Were legs usually numb?

". . . set themselves up as gods," Exeter said from a long way away. "I expect many of the old myths relate to strangers from Nextdoor or one of the others: Hercules, Apollo, Prometheus. And on Nextdoor, they may be from either this world or one of the others. The more worship they get, the stronger they become. The stronger they become, the more worship they can demand."

"Absolute power corrupts absolutely," Alice muttered.

"It certainly does. On Nextdoor . . . Well, actually, the area I know is called the Vales. It's not much bigger than England and I haven't seen all of the Vales even. So there's an awful lot of the world I know nothing at all about. But in the Vales, there are five or six dominant gods. Well, they call themselves gods, but they're really just magicians."

Oh, that made things a lot more believable, Smedley thought drowsily.

"Each one has a retinue of lesser gods. Some of them are jolly nasty types. The Service refers to those as the Chamber of Horrors, and they're the ones trying to kill me, because of the prophecy. The worst is Zath, who calls himself god of death." Exeter paused for a moment. "I know this must sound dodgy, but they caused the Nyagatha business."

"That sounds dodgy," Alice agreed, "but keep talking."

"You know when the guv'nor was born?"

"Yes. Roly told me. He certainly didn't look his age."

"Because he'd spent thirty years or so on Nextdoor. You pick up mana even without trying. . . . He helped found the Service there. Then Zath tried to kill him, and failed. That brought the prophecy to light. The prophecy foretold that Cameron Exeter would father a son who would be a sort of messiah, who would kill death. It's very muddled, most of it, but that bit was clear enough."

The car coughed again.

When nothing more happened, Exeter continued. "So Zath was gunning for the guv'nor. He went to earth. That's a joke, actually."

"I expect you're out of practice. Carry on."

"Well, it was very ironic. Zath tried to stop me being born, but the attempt drove the guv'nor into coming Home—meaning home to Earth—and about the first thing he did was meet the mater and fall in love and, whoops, there was me. These things happen.

"If Zath had only known it, the guv'nor wasn't in favor of the prophecy either. It leads to all sorts of evil complications. So both sides in this business wanted to break the chain! The guv'nor thought that all he had to do was stay out of the Chamber's reach until after the prophesied date, which would have been August 1914 by our reckoning, and then keep Baby Exeter, that's me, from crossing over. Then the chain would be broken and nothing else would apply. Head Office wangled him into the Colonial Office and got him posted to Nyagatha . . ."

His voice kept fading away and coming back. Smedley was having a deuce of a job keeping his eyes open. Funny, that. Heavenly choirs.

". . . like everyone to take Home leave every few years. A little refresher course as a mortal is very humbling, and it keeps people in touch with the language and customs, and so on . . . Jumbo Watson and Soapy Maclean dropped in on Head Office in 1912. Jumbo inquired about the guv'nor . . . when he heard about me the penny dropped. Edward is a common enough name in England, but it begins with a vowel, which would make it feminine in the Vales; the masculine would be D'ward.

"There's actually more about D'ward in the *Filoby Testament* than there is about the Liberator, but nowhere did the seeress say that they were one and the same chappie. Soapy headed for Nyagatha to explain this and find out if the guv'nor was still opposed to the prophecy. Somebody tipped off the Chamber's agents—or perhaps they followed him. Anyway, Soapy arrived the day before the massacre. . . ."

Bad business, that massacre, but perhaps Exeter Senior had not been as much as fault as everyone had thought. . . . Smedley started awake. He had dozed off but not for very long. Exeter seemed to be talking about the gods again.

"Some of them aren't so bad. I've met a couple of the Pentatheon, the five Great Ones. When I first crossed over, Zath's assassins were waiting for me and almost nobbled me. They're rather like Kali's thugs, in India

. . . wander around killing people at random. Fortunately that was in Sussland. That's Tion's manor, and he was miffed. . . . Tion's one of the five,
the Youth. He's a sort of Apollo figure, if you believe his advertisements,
god of art, and beauty, and sport. He holds a big festival every year, like a
miniature Olympic Games."

"Sounds all right," Alice said.

"Well, he's not very *likable*, but he let me go so I could settle Zath's
hash. He did warn me about the prophecy that said the Liberator would
be betrayed by his friends and thrown among the legions of death. That's
exactly what happened. There's a traitor in the Service, and I know who
it is, and I absolutely must get the word back to Olympus."

Alice spoke from a long way away. "But you did find the Service in the
end?"

"I found the Service right away, the next day. But I was too late. Zath
got to their agent before I did. I saw him being burned alive by—"

"Excuse me," Smedley said. "Frightfully sorry and all that, but I think
I'm going to faint."

12

THE PRIESTS WERE STILL HARANGUING THE CROWD.

As subtly as drifting snow, the young men of Sonalby closed in around
the stranger in their midst. Just as unobtrusively, women, children, and older
men left his vicinity, leaving Edward surrounded by youths. They all
seemed intent on the funeral pyre, but he knew better than to try to escape.

Most of them leaned on spears, and some had shields also. Every one had
a wooden club dangling at his side; none wore more than a leather loincloth.
Their hair and beards were trimmed short, so they could not be caught
hold of in battle, and they all had painted faces. They all had scars on their
ribs, too regular to be accidental—some old and healed, others still raw and
oozing.

The Carpenter house collapsed into ashes, and there were no more
heretics to burn. The priests departed, and the mob began to disperse.

The young men turned to the next item of business, the stranger in town.

They opened up into a circle around him and proceeded to discuss him as if he were a piece of furniture. He was footsore and thirsty and melting in the heat. The debate seemed likely to go on for the rest of the day. It might eventually conclude with a decision to put him to death or perform something less fatal but more unpleasant.

There were two factions involved, one slightly younger than the other. The younger group were clean shaven or just beardless, and their faces were painted in a complex design, mainly yellow, with very minor amounts of blue, white, red, and green. The older group had beards and another pattern, in which blue predominated, with lesser amounts of the other colors and an ominous addition of black.

Had Edward been a native-born Englishman, he would probably have demanded at that point to be taken before the village headman, and that would have been a very serious error. Fortunately, he had been raised among the Embu of Kenya, so he had some idea of what he was dealing with, although he could not make out a word of the jabbering talk.

Finally heads began to nod; some sort of agreement had been reached. One of the blue-painted older ones said in heavily accented Joalian, "Do you wear merit marks?" He tapped the scars on his ribs.

Sussian smocks left arms bare, but concealed chests. "It is not the custom of my people."

The debate resumed, as incomprehensibly as before.

Then the same man asked a second question. "How old are you?"

"Eighteen."

"How long since you shaved your face?"

Edward rubbed his stubble. "Two days ago."

There were grunts, then. And more jabber. At last the younger, yellow-faced youths just melted away. They had conceded that the beardless stranger belonged to the other group.

He belonged to them outright. He was fairly certain that he was theirs to do with as they pleased. There would be no headman, no council of elders to whom he could appeal. A young male stranger in town was a matter for the young warriors.

There must have been fifty of them around him now. By and large they were too swarthy to be a typical crowd in England, but they would not have been out of place in Southern Europe. They varied from lithe to beefy, from short to tall, although few were six-footers like himself. They were all about his own age. Now they were debating who should interrogate the prisoner, with much pointing. Eventually one of the tall ones was selected; he stepped forward and the rest fell silent.

"Foreigner, what is your name?"

Edward had already given that matter considerable thought. He had decided to stick with D'ward, having learned that it was not uncommon, the name of some minor god or other—who might be an interesting stranger to meet sometime, possibly a fellow countryman. To use an alias would be to concede to himself that he was frightened of the Chamber. D'ward he would remain, but in the Vales a man's name included his trade. He could think of only one skill he possessed that might be of any value at all in Sonalby.

"I am D'ward Spearthrower," he said.

It was an insane gamble. He would have to prove himself in the eyes of men who had been practicing all their lives, and he had no idea of the technique required for their weapons. But he had always had a knack for throwing things. He had set a school record with the javelin.

Now he had won the interest of his age group. They marched him back out of town in very short order, to the practice field he had seen on the way in. An audience of women and the younger youths watched curiously from the sidelines.

He would need to work a miracle. He had done so once, after picking up mana by playing holy man on a node. Later he had absorbed some from the audience in the theater, but that had been trivial and he must have used it up in the exertions of the last two days. Now he was so tired he doubted he could summon up any charisma at all.

A couple of warriors offered him a choice of spears. They were heavier than he had expected, with leaf-shaped metal blades. He selected one of medium length and weight and hefted it a few times. At that point someone thrust one of the round shields at him, a massively heavy circle of wood and thick leather. He was supposed to hold *that* while throwing *this!* His confidence plummeted.

"This weight is not familiar to me," he announced brashly. "I shall try for distance first." After that he might attempt to hit a moderate size barn at close quarters. He nudged the tall man with the edge of his shield. "Give me a mark." He could watch how it was done.

He expected the tall man to run, but he barely moved. He just leaned back, took one long pace with his left foot, and hurled. The spear flashed in the sky and dropped into the scrubby grass about a hundred miles down range.

Merciful *heavens!* Wasn't that out of bounds?

"Good throw!" Edward said. He could sense that it was a good throw from the reactions around them. He steadied himself for the roll of the dice, braced his left arm to support that pestilential shield. . . . He threw.

His spear fell well short of the other, but he heard no sniggers. He thought he sensed some grudging approval. He snarled angrily.

"Let me try again, with a longer pole!"

He was given a longer spear. This time he did better, and the audience was moderately pleased.

"Good throw!" said the tall man. "I am Prat'han Potter." He gripped Edward's left shoulder and squeezed. Edward did the same for him.

Then the fifty or so others went through the same procedure, each announcing his name in perfectly understandable Joalian, although the accent was harsh. Their trades were not what he had expected—tanner, shoemaker, tentmaker, yes, but also wheelwright, silversmith, printer, musician, and many others.

Now Edward must show that he could hit a target, and he discovered just how seriously young Nagians took their spear-throwing. One of them stalked forward about thirty paces, then turned and waited. His shield covered him from his shoulders to halfway down his thighs, but that still left far too much of him exposed. The blades were not honed to battle sharpness, but they could still maim.

"I will not throw against that target!"

Suddenly the blue-painted faces were dangerous again. The circle seemed to close in with menace.

"Your spears are not what I am accustomed to!" he protested.

"You are so good that Gopaenum cannot block your cast?"

"I don't mean that. It is unfair to the man to throw against him until I have practiced more."

"It is perfectly fair," Prat'han said. "That is a very easy shot. You throw to Gopaenum Butcher's shield. Then he throws to yours. Throw, D'ward!"

Hmm! Like that, was it?

"It is still not fair. He is at much greater risk than I shall be."

He provoked another debate. Did they *never* sit down in Nagvale? The human target was called back for the discussion, but in the end nothing was changed. Edward asked that Gopaenum stand closer, which was folly because now he had complicated the matter with questions of courage. Of course Gopaenum went out even farther than before, making the range greater. They really did seem to think the shot was an easy one.

Fortunately there was no wind. Wiping a sweaty palm on his smock, Edward summed up the problem. His bluff had been called. Only the most incredible luck would let him hit that shield, and even then he might be expected to repeat the throw. Gopaenum probably could block a single spear, and obviously this exercise was shield practice as well as spear practice, but Edward would not risk wounding a man just to carry off a fraud. It is better to have leaped and lost than never to have stuck your neck out. . . .

He missed the shield. His spear passed three feet over Gopaenum's head, and that was still a yard closer than he had planned. The audience burst into howls of ironic laughter. Their accent suddenly became incomprehensible again.

Out in the field, Gopaenum Butcher retrieved the spear and turned to throw.

The spectators moved back a pace or two, but probably only so the marksman could see his target more easily. None of them expected Gopaenum to miss.

Edward looked around for a safe place to hide, and of course there was none. The sprawling village was the only settlement in sight. Beyond the river, bare plain stretched out to the misty peaks, shimmering in the awful heat, and behind him the rocky face of Nagwall. At best he would be driven out to die of thirst and hunger. At worst the warriors would all use him for spear practice.

He should have claimed to be a traveling scholar. Then they would have assumed he was a spy, but they might have allowed him a night's sleep before they ran him out of town. He had gambled and lost.

He put down the shield, lower edge resting on the ground just in front of his toes, upper edge leaning against his thighs, leaving valuable parts unprotected. He straightened and folded his arms.

"What are you doing, foreigner?" Prat'han demanded.

"Waiting for Gopaenum."

The target was the same, but now the human part of it could not dodge or move to block the throw. Edward felt a strange tingle as his words registered; he knew it for the touch of mana. In the end these warriors would be more impressed by courage than by anything else. He had never thought of himself as being particularly brave—in fact, he was sure he was not—but he was not going to have them laughing at him, even if this mess he was in was all his own fault. Now he had captured their imagination.

Someone shouted an explanation to the waiting Gopaenum Butcher.

Gopaenum hesitated, then raised his spear. He hefted it a few times, judging the throw. Edward wished he would get on with it.

He felt a spasm of terror as the pole arced through the air. It struck the shield on the extreme end, jerking it away from him. Even so, he felt as if someone had kicked his knee. He almost fell over. He winced, staggering to regain his balance and wondering if a direct hit would have broken his legs. Gopaenum had either almost missed altogether or had deliberately aimed off to the side. The blade had gone right through the wood and leather—a possibility that Edward had not even considered.

The audience broke into cheers and rushed forward to thump him on the back. Their admiration sent intoxicating waves of mana surging through him. Willing hands thrust a spear at him and retrieved his shield. Gopaenum was waiting for the next throw. Again?

Oh, hell! How could he fail now? Too elated to stop and consider the risk, Edward drew back his arm, stepped forward, and hurled with all his strength. He could not tell how much he used mana on his arm and how much on the missile. Probably most of it went on himself, because to influence material objects must require far more power. He felt the sudden loss, the drain of mana, exactly like the time he cured Dolm Actor's despair. Again the results surprised him. The spear flashed over the field in an arrow's flat trajectory. Gopaenum did not have to move his shield an inch and perhaps did not even have time to react. The spear struck it dead center. The impact threw him flat on his back, the pole quivering upright. The spectators yelled out an incredulous whoop, and Edward felt his confidence return with a rush, greater than ever. Bizarre!

Honor was satisfied. Gopaenum came running up to give D'ward a hug of congratulation. There was much laughter and shoulder squeezing. Then the entire age group trotted off to their barracks to discuss the situation over warm beer. At last their visitor had a chance to sit down.

The barracks was a long building of wicker and thatch, as barren inside as an empty bottle. What need for closets when you owned only one garment? Where else would warriors sleep but on the bare ground with their shields as pillows?

The culture was not organized in quite the same way as the Kenyans', but there were strong similarities. These were the young men of the village. They had no designated leaders, for everything was resolved by consensus, but some were more respected and listened to than others. They had been together since they were children. Forty years from now the survivors would still be together, but by then they would be elders, with other responsibilities. There was a class of senior warriors three or four years ahead of them, and another of adolescents close behind, the yellow-faced Boy Scouts who had contested jurisdiction over the visitor.

The newcomer was questioned closely, because any traveler in the Vales was automatically assumed to be spying for someone, probably several someones. He did not mention the Service, which was obviously out of favor just then. Again he said he hailed from Rinoovale, because that was a long way away. Ah, they said—Rinoo was a vassal state of Nioldom, so he was a Niolian spy, was he? No, he was traveling because he was curious to see the world. They all thought that a very weak excuse. How would he ever earn enough money to buy a wife?

After more beer and prolonged debate, though, the junior warriors of Sonalby decided that D'ward Spearthrower was acceptable. Niol was too far away to worry about. He was given a leather loincloth, which was manly wear; his boots were removed, probably going in trade for it. Two of his new brethren brought paints and proceeded to decorate his face, instructing him carefully in the meaning of each of the symbols they had chosen for their mark. Blue spears and shields were for Olfaan Astina—blue was sacred to the Maiden. The black skulls showed that they served Zath and did not fear him. Two yellow triangles and a frog because they still owed allegiance to the Youth. Blue crescent, hand, and scroll for other aspects of Astina. A small white sunburst as a token to Visek. No red yet, because they were virgins. The green hammer of the Man for strength, and so on and so on.

There was a brief debate about whether he had earned one merit mark or two, and they agreed on two—one for being accepted and another for his dare with the shield. Raucous, tipsy, but probably not very dangerous, the age group set out to escort D'ward Spearthrower to the shrine of Olfaan Astina. In this aspect the Maiden was goddess of warriors and also patron deity of all Nagland, her main temple being located in Nag itself.

When they reached their destination, Edward could feel virtuality from the node, but the shrine seemed to be on the edges of it. He was now fairly confident that a shrine, unlike a temple, would contain no resident numen. This one was only a shabby—and smelly—leather tent enclosing an altar and a carved image of a young woman in armor. The figure was about half life size and surprisingly well made; he wondered if it had been looted from somewhere, sometime. If there was no numen present he was probably in no danger from Astina or any of her vassals.

But directly adjacent stood the temple of Krobidirkin the Herder, an aspect of Karzon. He was a definite threat. Kalmak Carpenter's auto-da-fé had been organized by priests of the Man, and the timing was too slick to be a coincidence. Either Karzon or Zath had guessed that the Liberator would seek out the Service, and might suspect he was in Nagvale. Edward had a strong hunch that a stranger would be able to detect the presence of another on his own node.

Yet he could think of no way to avoid the ordeal his classmates had planned for him. Merit marks were awards, a source of pride, recognition from his peers. His newfound brethren cheerfully inked lines on his ribs for him to cut along. They provided the stone knife; they offered the salt he had to rub in to stop the bleeding and create a lasting scar. Then they watched critically to see how he would perform. It was a sacrifice to the goddess, of course. It was a demonstration of his manhood. It was a damnable risk, because he was a stranger. The mana that should flow to Olfaan might stick to him and be detected by Krobidirkin Karzon, or he might be drained of the little he had collected that afternoon, or . . . or all sorts of things.

But he had no choice, so he cut and rubbed and shook away the tears before they could smudge the paint on his face. He felt nothing except anger and extreme pain. The first touch of the salt was the worst shock he could remember. The second time his hand shook so much that he cut too deep and the salt hurt even more. But nothing miraculous occurred. He was probably too exhausted and too intoxicated by the rotten beer to notice mana now.

His brothers carried him back shoulder-high to the barracks and cheerfully informed him that it was his turn to be cook.

Still, he had found a home and without it he might well have been facing starvation or execution. A few weeks to polish his skill with the language and he could hope to set off in search of the Service somewhere else.

If the Service was still worth finding, that was.

The only Service personnel he ever met always died very quickly.

13

"THERE'S A HORSE TROUGH!" GINGER WAS BRAKING. "HE CAN GET a drink there."

Smedley had admitted to feeling thirsty. Mostly he was feeling very foolish, and everyone kept pestering him, asking if he was all right. The gash on his calf was not serious. He did not think he had lost very much blood, he had just lost it rather quickly. They had bandaged his leg with strips of blanket, but he was respectable again, keeping it stretched out along the seat. He was all right now, just thirsty.

The car came to a halt alongside the trough. Where else could one find anything to drink at two o'clock in the morning? Windows overlooked it; Jones turned off the engine, which shuddered into silence broken by irritated tickings.

"Damn!" Alice said. "We don't have anything to drink out of."

"I can walk!" Smedley protested. "Really, you're all making a frightful fuss about nothing."

Exeter opened the door and climbed out. Smedley moved to follow. *Humiliation!* "Where did my shoes go?"

Alice tied the laces for him.

He shook off Exeter's helping hand and limped over to the water pipe, feeling nothing worse than a little shakiness. He bent his head to the stream, he drank and drank. That definitely helped. The sky was streaked with silvery clouds, the moon playing peekaboo. Moonlight showed the black blood all over his clothes. Exeter joined him, bundled up in the greatcoat. Even the greatcoat had blood on it. By the time they returned to the car, Jones had brought one of the oil lamps and was inspecting the interior.

It looked like a slaughterhouse.

"I hate to ask this," Exeter said, "but whose car is it?"

"It's stolen!" Alice said quickly.

He yowled like a hyena.

"Quiet, ninny!" she snapped, looking at the cottages flanking the road.

"Seriously, whose is it?"

"Don't worry about it. How much farther, Mr. Jones?"

"Oh, we're about halfway, almost at Chatham. Once we cross the Medway, we could get off the A2."

"What do you think, General Smedley?" Alice asked.

"Backroads'll be slower. I'd say keep on making a run for it."

"I won't argue," Jones said. He sounded very weary. "On irregular French verbs, yes. On strategy, no. Where do we go in London? Your flat, Miss Prescott, I assume?"

"Why don't we drop our jailbirds off there, then you and I go and return the car?"

He grunted agreement and took the lamp away. In a few moments he turned the crank and the engine caught at once. It had not done its worrisome coughing for some time. The car pulled smoothly away from the curb and resumed its journey.

Smedley had arranged himself along the back seat again, with the other two fitted in around him. He was starting to feel quite hopeful. True, they might yet blunder into a police blockade at any minute. The coppers could react very quickly at times, but would they in this case? Officially Exeter was just a shell-shocked soldier with amnesia. To reclassify him as an escaped German spy would require some explanations. The news of his disappearance must be in Whitehall by now, but at this time of night who was going to waken whom to do what or find which file where?

Whose car was it anyway? Alice had been reticent yesterday. Today she seemed even more determined that they not know.

"So I needn't have worried at all!" she said brightly. "Here I thought the Devil himself had carried you off bodily to hell, and all the time you were running around with a spear, stealing cattle?"

"It wasn't hell," Edward admitted, sounding as if he was smothering a yawn. "Actually it was almost fun. They were a likable bunch in their way. A different sort of college."

"But what did you do all day? Throw spears and rustle cattle?"

"No rustling at all. As for what we did . . . Well we all began by jumping in the river, except the day's cook, who made breakfast. Then we divided up in pairs and painted each other's faces. After that we went to work, usually."

Incredible! Smedley shuddered to think what his father would say about the Exeter family if he ever heard this confession. The fellow had gone completely native, it seemed—scars and war paint and all. This Nagland story was quite unlike the hints he'd dropped earlier about Olympus, where people had houseboys and dressed for dinner.

"What sort of work?" Alice asked. "Silversmithing, you said?"

"All sorts of work." Exeter chuckled, not sounding at all ashamed of himself. "Nobody worked very hard or very long, but we all had some sort of morning job. In the afternoon, we usually knocked off to go fishing or spear-throwing. Sports, exercise. We taught the juniors, the seniors taught us. In the evening we sat around and made weapons, gambled, or just talked about girls. None of us knew anything about them, of course."

"How long did you stay there?" Smedley asked, trying not to sound disapproving.

"Much longer than I intended. I soon learned that Kalmak Carpenter had been martyred because he was involved with a new sect, the Church of the Undivided. I could guess that the Service was behind it—the only way to break the tyranny of the Pentatheon would be to start a completely new religion, so that made sense. But the persecution had not been restricted to Sonalby; it had happened all over Nagland. The order had come from Karzon, but no doubt Zath was behind it, so I was probably the immediate cause. I was not very happy when I thought of all the innocent people who had died because of me.

"The new church might put me in touch with the Service, but it had been wiped out in Nagvale and nobody seemed to know anything about it—or even want to discuss it. If my interest in it got back to the wrong ears, then I might wake up dead one morning. I had no other leads, so I just stayed where I was and waited to be rescued. That wasn't very likely, of course. I knew the Service believed the reapers had killed me in the

Sacrarium, the night I crossed over. It had sent Onica Mason to confirm this, and she had disappeared also. So the chances that it was still searching for me were about two thirds of zero.

"All I could do, I concluded, was try to find out as much as I could about the Vales. And learn the local jabber, of course. Perhaps one day I might pick up some mention of the Church of the Undivided that would tell me where to look for it. My group brethren were as informative as anyone, which wasn't informative at all. At least I could trust whatever they told me, which was more than you could say for anyone else. Most of them had never been outside Nagvale in their lives, and never expected to be, but there were a dozen or so who had jobs that required them to travel—peddlers and drovers, mostly. A couple had gone off to work in the capital, Nag. As they drifted back home, to stay a while before their next excursion, I got to know them and questioned them. I didn't learn much. I was lazy, I suppose, or just windy. Having nowhere to go, I kept putting off my departure.

"Obviously I needed a job. The group talked it over and decided I was tall and would be good on roofs, so about a dozen of them took me along to see Gopaenum's uncle's brother, Pondarz Thatcher. They suggested he hire me. He didn't argue, because a village has to support its militia. Also, he had a daughter."

"Aha!" Alice said. "Describe this daughter."

"Absolutely gorgeous. About ten, I think . . . I don't know, I never set eyes on her. I never saw much of my supposed wages, either. They went toward her bride price. It didn't matter to me, as long as I ate twice a day. All I had to do was toss bundles of reeds up to the workmen on the roof. The job was well within my capabilities.

"But I agree that the original purpose must have been cattle stealing, just as in Africa. In the olden days—whenever those may have been—a young man's occupation in that herding society would be stealing the neighbors' livestock. He would give his loot to some older man of the village as payment on a wife. When he had paid enough cows and proved his mettle in more or less serious battles, he would marry the girl he had bought and retire. Thereafter he would just watch his own herds grow and his wife do all the work. War he would then leave to the young men, because that was their business."

"If that were true here," Ginger Jones said, "then we might not be in the mess we're in."

Nobody commented for a while. The car roared on through the night. Smedley decided that the remark had been very close to defeatist. The war existed, so it must be won. He had done his bit.

When Exeter spoke again, his tone was more somber than before.

"You can't imagine how strange it feels to be back in England, spinning through the night in a motorcar like this! It feels odder than all these things I've been telling you. I'm sorry to chatter so much. It's such a relief to be able to talk again."

"We're all enjoying it," Alice said. "It is better than having Baron Munchausen along. You're leading up to something. You're going into all this sociology for some reason?"

"Absolutely! You remember Nyagatha and the Embu. A lot of Bantu peoples had that sort of age-group arrangement, or something similar. When the English arrived they usually said, 'Take me to your headman,' and the natives would look blank, not knowing what they meant. Who you talked to depended on what your business was! So the English would appoint a headman and tell him to stop the cattle raiding. Then they wondered why the whole culture collapsed. What astonished me about the Nagians was that they had managed to make a transformation to a money economy without losing their social structure. A lot of the Vales are very close to an industrial revolution, you see, although they don't have guns yet, thank goodness. The Joalians play the part of the English, but without firearms Joalia can't ever make a real colony out of Nagia. They had imported a mercantile culture, though, and yet the traditional ways had very largely persisted. The Nagians had managed to blend the old and the new. I was very intrigued to know how they'd done it. The answer was obvious, but I didn't think of it."

"But who do the warriors fight?" Smedley asked.

Exeter chuckled. "Nobody. Oh, they have periodic brawls with neighboring villages, but they're prearranged, show affairs. A few bones get broken and teeth knocked out and a deuce of a lot of betting goes on, and that's about it. I never saw one.

"The most exciting thing that happened in my first few fortnights there was that Toggan Silversmith got married. His father had money, of course. He was the first of our age group to tie the knot, and it was a big milestone for all of us. I swear it took half a fortnight to decide how our face design should be changed. We could add some more green emblems, you see, because that is the color of manhood. We could introduce some red, which represents the Lady, Eltiana, who's goddess of motherhood and, um, related matters. But if we overdid it, the senior warriors would get in a snit and the juniors might start crowding us on the blue. So we had to appoint delegates to negotiate with other age groups. Everyone found it fascinating.

"As soon as Toggan got married, he wasn't a warrior anymore, but he was still one of the group. He slept with his wife and came around in the morning to get his makeup on. After the first fortnight, we saw a lot more of him than she ever did. Being a warrior just seemed like being in a boarding school. So I assumed. Until the war came."

"Followed you, did it?" Alice said. "Oh, sorry! I didn't mean—"

"No, this was a different war. The first I knew of it was when a priest turned up one evening, an elderly chap in a green robe. I smelled trouble right away. He sat down and negotiated with us. I suppose there were about sixty of us there, sitting around sharpening spears. We didn't stop because of him, either! He said that the temple had learned that the junior warrior age group had adopted a foreigner. Well, the whole village had known that for fortnights. He said that Krobidirkin was Sonalby's patron god, and the foreigner really ought to make a sacrifice to the god and ask for sanctuary— matter of protocol, you see.

That debate lasted all night. A lot of the fellows said the priests just wanted a free meal, but eventually the group decided that it was a good idea. I considered making a break for it, but Krobidirkin must have known about me all along anyway. Moreover, I could see that if I did a bunk, I would get my pals in trouble with the numen and probably with the elder groups. And I was curious.

I couldn't be expected to take part in an important ceremony without the backing of my peers, so the next afternoon the whole age group assembled. We bought a bullock from Gopaenum's uncle and drove it along to the temple.

There we were right on the node. The virtuality made my scalp prickle, as usual. There were shrines to Olfaan, and Wyseth—he's the sun god, and in that climate you don't ever forget the sun. And there was one to Paa Tion, the god of healing, and one to Emthaz, goddess of childbirth. The usual Pentatheon representation. But the temple was the center of the village, and it was Krobidirkin the Herder's.

It was one story high, made of leather and poles. If you can imagine a leather labyrinth, that's what it was. Smelly and hot. The others knew what to expect because they'd been there before, but all the way in I was shivering from the sanctity and thinking I would never find my way out again. The middle was open, a big courtyard: sand underfoot and the sky overhead. There was a paved place for making sacrifices. The priests were waiting eagerly, because they would have red meat for supper afterward. And there was a small, round tent in one corner. A yurt, I think they're called. That was the house of the god. If there was an image of him, it was in there. All we could see was the tent.

I was introduced as D'ward Roofer and put in the front. We all knelt down on the sand and bowed our heads and the ceremony began, chanting and praying and so on. In a few minutes I looked up. The flap of the tent had been pulled aside, and there was a little man standing there, holding it. He smiled at me and beckoned, and I knew that he was the numen himself, Krobidirkin. I could see no alternative, so I just stood up and walked over, and the priests did not notice. I was surprised they couldn't hear my knees knocking.

He took me inside, and the inside was much larger than the outside. There were several rooms to it, and flaps of the roof had been opened to let in the air and light. There were rugs and cushions. It smelled of spices. Someone was playing a zither or something softly in another room, and I could not hear the temple priests doing their awful wailing. It was exotic, but quite pleasant.

"Do sit down, Liberator," he said. "I regret that I cannot offer you tea, but I have a reasonable substitute."

We settled on the cushions, and he poured from a silver pot that stood on a brazier. The cups were beautiful porcelain.

You can't tell how old a stranger is from his appearance. They have a sort of agelessness. Krobidirkin was small, as I said, but tough and wiry looking. He had the serenity of a landscape and could have been eighty, but he had the skin of a youth. He wore only the local leather loincloth, and his face was quite the ugliest I had ever seen, all slanty eyes and squashed nose. His ears stuck out, and his mustache turned down at the ends. He had a whimsical grin that I found reassuring.

It took me a minute or two to find my voice. This numen was a vassal of Karzon's, remember, and therefore an ally of Zath, the god of death, whom I was prophesied to kill and who had been doing his level best to kill me. I had met Tion and escaped unharmed, but he was not allied with the Chamber. This Krobidirkin must be. He had immolated Kalmak Carpenter and his family, and here he was offering me tea!

"I am honored to meet you, sir," I said, or some such nonsense.

He chuckled. "No, the honor is mine. May I say that your father would be proud of you?"

I spilled half a cup of scalding tea down my chest.

"You knew my father, sir?"

The little man was much amused by my reaction. "Yes, indeed. I met him several times. A good man. He made a special journey all the way from his home world to consult with me. He even gave me a picture of you."

I think that was probably the biggest surprise I have ever had in my life. There I was, an infinite distance from home, a stranger in a very strange land indeed, and this all-powerful local god handed me a photograph of the station at Nyagatha! It showed the mater, and you, Alice, and me. We were sitting on the veranda. The gramophone was there, and the parrot's cage, and all sorts of details I had forgotten. I was about three, I suppose. I had never seen that picture before. I made rather an ass of myself over it.

Of course Krobidirkin was pleased, because that was the effect he had wanted to produce. He refilled my cup.

And then I said, "But surely this is impossible! I thought nothing could cross over except people?"

He chuckled, as if he had been waiting for me to work that out in my dim-witted way. "Memories can cross over," he said. "And there is mana." He took the photograph from me—it did seem to be a real, honest-to-god photograph, black-and-white, not colored—and he turned it over. I expected to see the photographer's name there, but it was blank. Then he waved his hand and the back showed another picture. It was the guv'nor, sitting in that very tent, where I was sitting, wearing a Nagian loincloth and smiling.

Well, that floored me.

"May I guess?" I said when I recovered. "He had been put in charge of some people who had once had a society very similar to the Nagians', and he knew that you had managed to preserve their institutions in the face of progress, so he came to ask your advice?"

Krobidirkin's ugly face split in a wide grin. "Of course! Unfortunately, it takes mana to guide such a development, and in the post he then held, Kameron was only another native. A culturally advanced native, and a well-intentioned one, but not a stranger in his own world."

"You have been a good father to your people, sir," I said. "You also are from our world?"

He smiled and nodded. "A very long time ago, yes. I can recall very little of my youth, I am afraid. One forgets. A new world brings a new life, and the old days become unimportant when one decides one will never return. I do remember that my people were very warlike. We had a notable leader, named . . . I forget. He led us against a civilization of great cities, and we were badly defeated. The next year he tried again, and this time he was turned aside by an army led by a priest. The mana was very strong, and he retreated before it, knowing that he could not win against the god power. He died not long after."

That may have been the second worst shock, I suppose. It is one thing to know intellectually that strangers live a long time. To run into a man who remembers battles fought fifteen hundred years ago—that brings it home with a vengeance. "Was his name Attila?" I asked.

The little Hun clapped his hands and said, "That's it! A wonderful leader of men! Great native charisma."

So we sat and talked about the battle of Châlons—which was fought sometime in the middle of the fifth century, in case you forget—and Pope Leo, who somehow persuaded the Huns to withdraw from Italy the following year. How he did it has always been a great historical mystery. My host was delighted to learn that his comrades in arms were still remembered after so long, but I was careful not to go into details about their reputation. He probably wouldn't have minded. Krobidirkin had been a sort of medicine man with the horde, and in his old age he had accidentally crossed over to Nextdoor and become a god.

He soon eased the conversation around to the *Filoby Testament* and the Liberator.

"I greatly regret what happened to the carpenter and his family," he said. "I had direct orders, and I dared not disobey them. One hates to treat one's people so, however misguided their heresies."

"And what of me?" I asked. "Have you direct orders about me?"

"Oh, yes. But you are the son of my old friend Kameron! Zath does not know where you are. He does not know that I know, and he is furious that you have escaped him. He is a very frightened god!"

"He need not be," I said. "I have no plans to kill him."

The little man chortled. "The prophecy says you will! Zath has tried everything he can think of to break the chain of events and failed every time. So he fears you, and rightly so."

"What of Karzon?"

He screwed up his ugly little face, making it even uglier. "He fears Zath! And that brings me to the reason I invited you here, D'ward. Zath has decreed that there must be war, and more war. War brings him mana, and he is hungry for all the mana he can get, because the Liberator is a threat to him. Now it has begun—in Narshia, which was part of Joaldom, but lies between Thargvale and Lappinvale. Lappinvale has been a Thargian colony for half a century, you know? But recently the Randorians have been stirring up trouble there, urging rebellion and independence."

He looked expectantly at me and I nodded as if it all made sense. I was actually thinking that it didn't, but it still sounded less insane than all Europe exploding over the death of one Austrian nobleman.

Krobidirkin chuckled. "Thargians dislike being inconvenienced or worried by uncertainty. They had been trying to subvert the Narshian government for years, and this summer they ran out of patience. They invaded Narshland. The Joalians plot reprisal." He sighed. "It will be bloody, I fear, and Zath will benefit greatly."

As you may guess, I was not very happy to hear this. "What has it got to do with me?"

He smiled cryptically. "The Joalians plan a lightning raid on Tharg itself, while the Thargian army is absent—that is exceedingly brave of them! To reach Thargvale, they must cross both Nagvale and Lemodvale. Lemodia is part of Thargdom, but we belong to Joal. Our queen is a Joalian puppet. Their vanguard is already here, in Nag, demanding her help. She will muster her warriors as they demand."

I felt ill, and the more I thought about it, the more ill I got.

"I must give myself up!" I said. I probably didn't mean that, of course. It was just the first thing that came into my head.

Krobidirkin looked shocked. "Oh, no! That will not help at all! The war is inevitable now. No, I wish to ask a favor."

"Sir . . . ask!" I owed him my life, remember. He had given me sanctuary, even if I had not realized it until then.

He nodded, well pleased. Numens usually get their own way.

"The summons will arrive soon. I knew you would be tempted to leave. This is not your cause, after all—or at least, you would not have thought it so, had I not invited you here and told you. The Joalians will require each village contingent to have a leader. Nagians prefer to debate and argue, but they do appoint leaders in time of war. In this case they will have to. There is no question whom the Sonalby contingent will choose."

I could not argue with that, because I knew they reacted to my stranger's charisma no matter how much I tried to hide it. "I know little of war, especially this sort of war."

"It is not necessary that you do. The Joalian generals will provide all the skill needed to spill all the blood possible. And I think you would have been my boys' choice even had you not been a stranger." That was just flattery, of course.

"What do you want of me?" I asked gloomily.

"Stay and lead them, D'ward! With you at their head, they will not suffer quite so much. More of them will return to their homeland. Believe me, this is so. You will ease the suffering and reduce the deaths. I fear for my people if their young men are dragged into this without your guidance.''

What could I say to that?

I hedged at first. "I was hoping to find the Service and enlist their help in going Home.''

He scowled and tugged at his droopy mustache. "Beware the Service, D'ward! They will betray you—it is foretold.''

Everyone seemed to have read that damnable *Filoby Testament* but me! In the end I agreed to accept the leadership of the warriors. One cannot easily refuse a numen, and he had obviously kept my presence in Nagland a secret from Zath. He had probably taken quite a risk doing that. Although he did not labor the point, I knew I was in his debt.

"Your presence honors my humble tent," he said then. "I would be happy to keep you here and talk. I should have invited you before, but it is not safe for either of us. Zath suspects me, and he is far stronger than any of us.''

It was dismissal. We rose. He offered to give me the picture. I was sorely tempted, but I had no pockets. Reluctantly I declined it, and promised that one day I would come back, after the war. He showed me to the door. The priests were still at their work, and they did not see me return to my place.

That was the third time I had met a god. He was a true father to his people, the most impressive of the three by far. And he had been one of Attila's Huns! In my innocence, I thought that very wonderful.

Much of what he had told me was true, actually. I later confirmed that the guv'nor did make a flying visit to Nextdoor in August of ninety-nine, and he did go to Nagland. The picture may well have been what Krobidirkin said it was, although he could just have pulled all the images out of my memories as easily as out of the guv'nor's. What the Herder was really doing was playing the Great Game. By enlisting the Liberator in the war, he had made a very cunning move—from his point of view, at least.

14

SMEDLEY AWOKE WITH A START. THAT TIME HE HAD REALLY BEEN asleep. The car was doing its coughing and stuttering again. He peered out the window and saw buildings, darkened shops. The blackened streetlights threw tiny puddles of brightness; here and there another vehicle showed or a chink of window high up.

"Where are we?"

"Greenwich," Alice said.

London! They must be safe now!

The car choked, slowed, and then picked up again.

"Does anyone know anything about the workings of these infernal contraptions?" Ginger demanded.

Alice and Exeter said, "No," simultaneously.

"A little," Smedley said. "Have we any tools on board?"

"No," said Ginger.

"Is it short of petrol?"

"No."

That settled that, then. Nothing to be done.

London never slept, but it was pretty drowsy out in the suburbs at this time in the morning. There were no traffic policemen at the intersections, but usually Ginger had the right-of-way. He was driving quite slowly. The old boy must be completely exhausted.

Smedley's leg throbbed. So did his missing hand. Perhaps in time he would discover that this was a sign of rain or thunder or something.

Exeter had refused to talk any more, claiming he was hoarse. He had demanded to know more about the war, about what this Lawrence character was up to in Palestine, about zeppelins and poison gas, and what sort of allies the Italians and Japanese were. Alice had talked for a while. Smedley had stayed out of it, and started nodding off.

"Somebody talk!" Ginger said. "I'm getting sleepy."

Smedley roused himself. "So that's what you've been doing these last three years? Fighting with spears?"

Exeter sighed. "Not all of it, no. But some. I knew there had been an out-of-valley campaign about twenty years ago. As soon as we left Krobidirkin's temple, I went off to talk to the fathers at their clubhouse. The whites, we called them, because Visek's—doesn't matter. That evening I brought a couple of them to the barracks and got them to tell us about it. I said I'd had an inspiration in the temple. Everyone assumed it was a message from the god, which was perfectly true.

"They told us how the Joalians had made them march in rows, and I suggested we practice that. There was a lot of grumbling, but I could always get my way when I wanted, being a stranger. A couple of days later the queen's envoy arrived in Sonalby. He went to the senior warriors and eventually they summoned us. We marched up in a phalanx and their eyes just about popped out of their heads."

Alice chuckled, although it sounded forced. "So you were elected general?"

"Of course. My group all voted for me, and we outnumbered the seniors. Half of them were married and didn't count—married men stay home as defensive reserves. We roped in a few of the big ones from the cadet class. In a day or two we set off for Nag, about a hundred of us."

The car coughed, coughed, coughed. It faded to a stop, then suddenly lurched forward. Everyone breathed again.

"Keep talking!" Alice said.

"Lordie! I'm sure you don't want to hear all that. Nag is a fair-sized city by Vales standards. Not like Joal or Tharg, of course, about the size of Suss. We'd call it a modest market town. That was where I met the heir apparent, Prince Goldfish."

"You are making that up!"

"No. Cross my heart! Well, it was pronounced more like 'Golbfish,' but I always thought of him as Goldfish. He was the queen's oldest son and his name was Golbfish Hordeleader. He was in his late twenties, I suppose, and one of the tallest, biggest men in Nagland. He was rich, had three gorgeous concubines, and he was heir to the throne. What more can a man want?"

"To play the mouth organ?" Smedley said grumpily.

"I told you you wouldn't want to hear all this."

"Yes, we do!" Alice said. "What about Goldfish?"

"And he was absolutely miserable! To start with, he was big, but he was shaped like a pear. Also—"

The car coughed and slowed, the motor silent.

Ginger guided it into the curb, and it came to a halt right by a streetlight. It hissed and clinked.

Alice said, "Hell's bells!"

Ginger had slumped over the wheel. After a moment he turned around. "Anyone got any ideas?"

"It may just have overheated," Smedley said. "Let's give it a few minutes and then try cranking it." If he had some tools he might be able to do something, or at least show Exeter how to do something . . . but he hadn't.

A lorry went rumbling by.

"We're not supposed to park here," Alice said, her voice brittle. "And I don't imagine the buses are running yet. Care to explain all that blood on your coat, Edward? Or your trousers, Julian?"

"Or why I am wearing pajamas," Edward said. "The old crate's done very well."

"But not well enough!" Now there was no hiding the overtones of panic in her voice.

"How about a taxicab?"

"At this time of night? Away out here? Explain the bloodstains?"

"Just a thought."

"Telephone the Royal Automobile Club," Smedley suggested.

"Don't be stupid! We have no papers!"

They sat in brooding silence for a while.

Failure was a bitter taste in Smedley's throat. So near and yet so far! The sun would be up soon, and they must look a hopeless bunch of guys. You could get away with a lot in London, but marching around covered in blood was not one. Without his folly, the others would have had a good chance, even yet. All his fault.

Lorries rumbled by in both directions. There were no pedestrians in sight, but the capital awoke early. Covent Garden would be stirring by now, and Billingsgate.

Smedley stiffened. He must be imagining things. That wasn't just traffic he was hearing. It must be! Or was he starting to have delusions in addition to all his other madness?

"What's that noise?" Exeter said.

"Oh no!" Alice said. "Look!"

A policeman had just passed under the next streetlight. He was heading their way with the solid, unhurried tread of the bobby on his beat.

"I don't have my license!" Ginger wailed.

"I don't have anything at all," Exeter growled. "Will he take me for a deserter?"

"Julian," Alice said wildly, "you're on convalescent leave, and we're taking you to my home in—"

"I don't have my hospital discharge yet and why at four in the morning and Exeter has no papers at all and the blood—"

There was no innocent explanation! No one answered. They all just stared helplessly as their nemesis approached relentlessly along the pavement. With his helmet on, he looked about eight feet tall. He would have to stoop to see in the window.

He did.

"Morning, Officer!" Ginger said in his best Cambridge drawl.

Pause. "Good morning, sir."

"The jolly old engine's overheated, you see. Just giving it a moment to calm down, and then we'll be on our way."

Pause. "Will you tell me the purpose of your journey this morning, sir?" The copper glanced at the three passengers in the back. He did not shine his light on them, not yet.

Ginger said, "Er . . ."

๛ 15 ๛

GINGER SAID, "ER . . ." AGAIN.

Smedley could feel Alice shaking. Or maybe it was him.

Somebody think of something!

"Yes, sir?" said the voice of the law. A regulation notebook appeared in the bobby's hand.

"Well, it's like this," Ginger said and fell silent.

"Convalescent leave!" Smedley said loudly, and leaned forward to wave his paybook at the policeman.

The law was becoming suspicious. "In a moment, sir. First may I see your driving license, sir?"

Ginger drawled, "Well, actually, officer—"

Behind the car, the night exploded in fire. Not a furlong away, a building sank to its knees and toppled forward into the street. The car jumped bodily. Gravel rattled on roof and windows. The policeman vanished. Before the roar had died away, another . . . and another . . . and another . . . all around. Glass tinkled in deadly rain.

"Out!" Exeter shouted, struggling with the door.

"Get down!" Smedley barked. The others jumped at his tone of authority. "This is as safe as anywhere. It's raining glass out there."

He pushed Alice down on the floor. Exeter went on top of her. As Smedley followed, he caught a glimpse of the policeman, on his feet again, staggering toward the nearest burning ruin. *Boom! Boom!* The car rocked. *Boomboom!* Hail spattered on the roof. Guns crumped regularly in the background between the bomb blasts. *Boom!* The car leaped, windows shattering. People were screaming right outside, they must be pouring out of the houses, idiots.

From underneath, Alice said, "My God!"

"This is nothing!" Smedley said scornfully. "Throwing darts. It'll take a direct hit to hurt us." Or the adjacent building falling on them, of course. He felt quite unworried. Odd, that. After the creeping barrages of the Western Front, this was a very pathetic fireworks display. The last few bombs had been farther away. The noise was mostly people yelling and the roar of fires.

Boomboomboom! Closer again.

"Nothing, you say?" Exeter's voice sounded strained. This was not spear-throwing and shield banging.

"Kids' stuff. You all right, Ginger?"

A distant voice said, "I just died of fright, that's all."

"Good show."

Heartbeat—beat—beat—beat—beat—

"Is it over?" Alice said. "Someone is kneeling on my kidneys."

"Wait and see. Later planes aim for the fires."

BOOM! The car rose a foot and fell back with protesting squeaks. Something sizable struck the roof, but now the clamor of hail was briefer.

"No, it's not over."

Minutes crawled by. Distant clanging of a fire engine bell. A lot of shouting and cursing now, some very close. More explosions very far away. The futile hammering of guns.

"I think we can risk it," Smedley said. "Watch out for glass in here." He sat up. The car had lost all its windows. A fiery dawn lit the street and the frightened crowds, many people still in their night attire. "Exeter, old man, I do believe you're wearing the proper kibosh now."

They emerged cautiously from the battered vehicle. Ginger had lost his hat and his pince-nez, he was blinking and mumbling. Apparently all four of them had escaped uninjured. The same could not be said for the inhabitants of Greenwich, or possibly this was Deptford. There were bodies on the road, wailing children, and hundreds of people in night attire. Policemen were trying to move the crowds back and let the ambulances and fire engines through. No one was interested in the fugitives now.

"That was very tricky timing," Smedley said. "How far is it from here?"

He looked at the other three, who were staring aghast at the burning build-ings. *"Alice!* How far is it from here?"

"What? Oh, miles!"

"Let's get started, then! Don't wait to say good-bye to everybody."

Alice stared at him. "How can you make jokes?" she shouted. "There are people dying, bodies—"

"If you don't laugh you cry. Come on!"

"But you can't walk in your condition!"

"Then you can carry me. Come on! No one's going to question how we're dressed! Or where the blood came from." Smedley took Ginger's arm and urged him into motion. He assumed Exeter and Alice were fol-lowing, but he did not look back. He felt the same wild exuberance he had known when he lost his hand—saved! No matter the cost, deliverance was what mattered. They could explain their bizarre appearance now, if they were asked. It could not be more than five miles or so to Lambeth, and he was sure he could manage that. He had walked almost that far with a tour-niquet on his bleeding stump. Alice would find it harder in her fashionable shoes.

That was a very strange journey along the winding darkened streets of the great city. Half the population had emerged to look at the fires and the searchlight beams playing on the clouds. They cursed the Hun and called out condolences in incomprehensible accents.

About half an hour later, as the fugitives emerged from the affected area, they began to attract more attention. People started asking questions. It could not be long before another policeman appeared. Then a lorry pulled up and asked in very thick Cockney if they needed help. Alice rode in the cab with the driver, denouncing the bombs and explaining about going to stay with a mythical aunt. The men rode in the back, and a few minutes later they all arrived safely at her flat.

16

ALICE HAD NEVER HAD FOUR PEOPLE IN HER SITTING ROOM BEFORE. She had far too much furniture, and it was all designed for greater, grander rooms. The three men standing there, blinking in the harsh light, seemed to fill every inch. This was the first time she had been able to see Edward properly. He had not changed in the slightest from the gangling, fresh-faced boy he had been three years ago. Except that now his expression was murderous.

"Do sit down, please!" she said. "And I'll make some tea."

They were all beat, as if they had mud smeared under their eyes. The two youngsters were blue chinned, old Mr. Jones's beard was frazzled. His thin hair lay all awry over his bald crown, while his fingers kept touching the bridge of his nose, feeling for lost specs. She probably looked a hag herself. She ought to be exhausted, yet she seemed to be floating in unreality, a bubble on a sea of illusion.

"So the old bastard did steal it all?" Edward said.

"Don't speak ill . . . You do know he died?"

"Glad to hear it. And for all eternity, he will wonder why he's in hell!"

"Edward! Go and wash out your mouth."

Still glowering, he removed the greatcoat and spread it on the sofa, bloodstains out. He gestured for Julian to sit there, while he flopped into a chair, apparently unaware that his pajamas were blood spattered also. Mr. Jones sank into the other with a long sigh, like a collapsing balloon. Alice took the kettle from the counter and headed for the bathroom to fill it, stepping over feet.

She heard Julian say, "Your late lamented uncle Roland, I presume?"

Edward growled something she did not catch; probably just as well. She returned to put the kettle on the gas ring, then stepped over all the feet again and went into the bedroom. D'Arcy's photograph was safely hidden in the drawer. She had only one other thing to remember him by, the bottle-green velvet dressing gown he had kept at her flat in Chelsea. Many of her favorite memories of him involved that gown—sitting on his lap, watching him take it off, or taking it off for him, or stepping inside it with him and feeling its soft touch on her back as he closed it around them both, body against body. . . . *Every day I do not hear is one day closer to the end of the war.*

D'Arcy would not mind her lending his dressing gown to Cousin Edward. Young Cousin Edward had been a little too friendly in the car. He should have grown out of his romantic illusions by now.

She went back into the sitting room and dropped the gown on him. "Here. You can make yourself a little more respectable."

Then she went to the cupboard and began taking out cups and saucers, not watching what was happening behind her back. Edward must have risen and donned the gown and sat down again, because she heard the chair squeak. Presumably three grown men knew a man's garment when they saw one. The silence was pregnant. *Extremely* pregnant.

She turned enough to see Julian. If that was an owlish look in his eye, then it was an owl trying very hard not to hoot.

"We must take a gander at your leg," she said. "It may need a doctor."

He blinked solemnly. "Then it won't get one. It's only a gash. A scar there won't ruin my looks."

Scar! She spun around to look at Edward. His eyes had never been bluer, but she did not read in them what she had expected—reproach, self-reproach, humiliation, anger, all of them? No, Edward was amused, and suddenly it was her face that was burning. He had seen through her little ploy. However he looked on the outside, there was an older, more experienced Edward inside there.

Ignoring the embarrassment she had brought on herself, she touched his forehead. He jerked his head away.

"You had stitches!" she said.

He smiled sardonically. "Now you believe me?"

"I believed you before." But that physical evidence made her feel creepy. He had no scar at all, which was impossible.

"The sawbones have some new techniques," Julian said. "They're using them on the—" He yawned. "'Scuse me! On the wounded. They say they can put a chap back together so the scars don't show."

"They couldn't three years ago. Get those bags off, old man," Edward said without taking his mocking gaze away from Alice. *We're all men of the world here.* "Want to take a look at your leg."

Julian yawned again. "In a minute. Alice, how safe are we here? How about the neighbors?"

She turned back to the kettle, feeling it. "The old lady across the hall is as nosey as they come but deaf as a pole. The two couples at the end are away all day. You may be noticed when you go to the loo, though."

"Do it in squads and march in step?" He grinned wanly. "Or do you have a bucket we can use?"

"Good idea," she said. Julian had a foxy streak, an echo of his boyhood mischief.

She sat down on the end of the sofa, and all her bones seemed to creak. The bubble had burst. She felt old. She wished the watched pot would boil. She did not want tea, she wanted a mattress. "Two of you can share the bed. If we—"

"Tommyrot!" Julian said. "I can sleep in two feet of mud with shells falling all around. Nagian warriors lie on the ground, so I'm told."

"'Sright." Edward yawned also. "That's why they sleepwalk so much."

Well, well! Big boy now.

"I'll remember to lock my door."

Jones, too, was having trouble keeping his eyes open. "And I made out very well on the settee last night, or whenever it was. Feels like a week ago."

"We'd better draw up some plans, though," Edward said sadly. "A couple of hours' shut-eye until the shops open won't hurt, but we can't stay here longer."

"Why not?" Alice had been wondering about that, and had decided that they had left no trail. "There's nothing to connect the car to us." She had dropped the lockup key down a drain in Bermondsey.

"No. It's Stringer. If he was telling the truth, we're all right, of course. If he was just protecting the Old School Tie, you see. But if he was trying to trap me and calls in the law . . . He knows who I am."

Now it was Jones who hid a yawn. "I tracked you down in one afternoon, Miss Prescott. The police should be faster."

Edward nodded and rubbed his eyes. "And if Stringer is on the side of the Blighters, then I've put you all in mortal danger."

The kettle began singing a warning.

"The who?" Alice said.

"The Blighters." He glanced around bleakly, as if expecting to see doubt in the weary faces. "They're the Chamber's allies in this world. They contrived the massacre at Nyagatha. They're a damned sight more dangerous than the law, although they can warp the law to their own ends if they want to. They have powers you can't imagine. They killed Bagpipe."

Alice caught Ginger's eye, and his expression frightened her. He believed. Timothy Blodgley, she recalled, had been nailed to a draining board with a butcher knife. In a locked room.

"How could they know you were in Staffles in the first place?" she demanded. "And if they're so clever, why not kill you on the spot? Why ever let you reach England alive?"

He shrugged.

"Well?" she demanded. "You can't just issue cataclysmic warnings and then not explain them!"

"The man who tricked me into landing in Flanders expected me to die," Edward said. "But he knows I'm extremely hard to kill, because of the prophecy. So it would make sense for him to have put a mark on me, like a ring on a pigeon. Then the Chamber passes word:

"Dear Messrs. Blighters,

"The indicated subject has just returned to your manor. If he is alive, would you please stop him breathing at your earliest convenience. If you will do same, you will oblige,

"Your humble servants, etc.

"The car broke down exactly where the bombs were going to fall! Or vice versa. I really oughtn't involve you lot anymore, but I'm frightened that the Blighters may decide to take you off as witnesses or even just for spite. In that case, my luck may help shield you also."

Ginger said, "Good Lord!"

"They're not infallible," Julian said sleepily. "The bombs missed. You are heading back to Nextdoor, aren't you? To pass a message, you said."

"No."

Alice rose and stepped over Edward's feet to reach the kettle. She poured some water into the pot to warm it. She wondered why Smedley was so eager to cross over to this other world of Edward's. Running around with spears did not sound like his cup of tea, especially since he would have to throw with his left hand and carry the shield on his stump. Did he seriously believe that magic could give him back his hand?

After a moment, Julian said, "Why not? Why aren't you going back?"

"Lordie!" Edward said. "You should know! Because I came back here to fight in the war I'm supposed to fight in, that's why! How much identification will I need to enlist?"

"If you can breathe you're in," Jones growled.

It would not be that easy, Alice thought. And how long could he stay in? Her indestructible cousin was trailing a remarkable history behind him now. Too many people knew of him and knew him by sight. The thought of another loved one at the Front was a horror, and yet that confession made her feel guilty and unpatriotic. He would have to enlist under a false name, so she could no more be listed as his next of kin than she could be D'Arcy's. She would have two names to look for in the casualty lists.

"What about this prophecy?" she asked. "Did you kill the Zath char-acter?"

"No. And I never will."

She made the tea and covered the pot with the cozy. "So that's all? You walk out of here at daylight and enlist?" The night's efforts seemed strangely futile if all they had achieved was to deliver another living body to the abattoir.

"There's one thing I must do first," Edward said through a yawn. "And that's get word to Head Office about the traitor back in Olympus. I hope they can tell me if the Blighters are still after me."

"I thought only people could cross over?" Julian said. "Letters won't? So how do you get word back to the Service?"

"I've got three leads. Yes, one of them might require a trip back, but if I do have to go, it won't be for long. They all require heading down to the West Country. You going back to Fallow, Ginger?"

"I must. First thing."

"Then I'll come with you. Soon as I have something to wear. Can you think of anywhere I can lay low for a couple of days?"

Jones fingered the bridge of his nose and jerked his hand away angrily. "I do have one idea. If we can't trust Stringer, then the school itself's too obvious."

Edward nodded, yawning again. "Smedley?"

They all looked at Julian.

"I'll tag along," he said quietly.

"Tea, anyone?" Alice said, but it turned out nobody wanted tea. Prob-ably, like her, they wanted only to close their eyes and disappear. "Well, if you men are sure you'll be all right in here . . ."

Today was Thursday. She would likely be sacked if she missed a second day's work, but she knew she could not just walk out of this affair now.

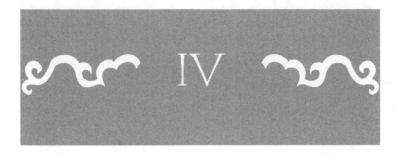

IV

Queen's Gambit

17

DAYLIGHT AROUND THE CURTAINS WAKENED HER. SHE FUMBLED FOR her watch. *Ten o'clock!* Now she could hear the rumble of traffic to tell her that business swirled as usual through the city. She reeled out of bed, buttoned up her housecoat, disciplined her hair viciously, and then hurried through to the sitting room.

A man in a bottle-green dressing gown was reading yesterday's *Times*. The sight was a stake through her heart, but of course it was only Edward. He lurched to his feet as she entered. He smiled, all blue eyes and white teeth.

No one else around—damn! She was not awake enough yet for the bleeding-hearts scene. "They can't both be in the bathroom. Is there a cup left in that pot?"

"Yes. It's fresh. Ginger went out shopping."

She moved to the counter, turning her back on him. She laid out cup and saucer, bracing for the inevitable questions. She heard a floorboard squeak as he moved to the fireplace, a rustle of paper.

"Tell me about him," Edward said.

"No." Perhaps when she was properly awake.

Or perhaps not.

She poured the tea. It looked well stewed.

Edward said, "He's rich, but his wife controls the money. He smokes cigars. He's a barrister and probably in the army."

The teapot clattered on the counter. She spun around, heart pounding madly.

Edward's smirk changed to alarm. "I say! Didn't mean to startle you!"

"Is this some of your witchcraft?"

He blushed like a child caught in wickedness. "Of course not! Not in this world!"

"Then how do you know all that?"

He shrugged, smiling thinly. "The cigars I can smell on this dressing gown. You don't wear a ring, so he's probably married. He buys his clothes at Harrods and drives a cathedral-size car, so he's rich. But you live in a slum, so he can't afford to give you money. Reasonable guess that he's in the Army, living on the King's shilling."

"And a barrister?"

Edward hesitated. Looking thoroughly ashamed now, he pulled a paper from his pocket. "Envelope addressed to Sir D'Arcy Devers, QC, at Gray's Inn."

She took up her tea with shaking hands and went to the sofa. "Elementary, my dear Watson!"

"Bloody cheap trick," he muttered. "I'm sorry. Soldier by choice or conscription?"

"By choice."

Edward said, "Oh!" and there was silence.

She finished the tea and laid down the cup and saucer.

"And you used to call me a starry-eyed romantic idealist!" he said.

She did not look at him. "They're all over the place. He was in line for a judgeship. A messy divorce would have finished that. His wife is vindictive and well-connected."

" 'I could not love thee, dear, so much, Loved I not honor more'?"

"You could say that."

"Herrick said that, actually."

"It was Lovelace. And, no, it doesn't feel good to come second to a war."

"Oh, Alice!" he said sadly. "Oh, my poor Alice!"

"Save your pity. I was a kept woman and happy in the work, until the Kaiser spoiled the show." She forced herself to meet his stare. "I should have told you. I nearly did, but you had so many other troubles. I'm sorry."

"That long?"

"Since October 1913."

"Oh." He winced and turned to face the mantelpiece. "I must have seemed a bloody fool!"

"No. Not a fool. Young men in love are foolish, but not fools. I told you, I love you as a brother."

"A kid brother!" he said angrily. "I was eighteen and you were twenty-one. I'm still eighteen!"

"And I'm an old crone of twenty-four!" He looked more like sixteen standing on a box, but she could hardly tell him so. "I still love you as a brother."

He turned back to her and smiled. It was a brave effort, but his eyes were glistening.

"And you're not eighteen on the inside, Edward. In some ways you seem older than Julian, who's been tempered in the flames of hell. What have you been through, to do that?"

"Nothing like what he's seen. Just experience."

Grim, grim experience, she thought.

"You didn't grow out of it?" she asked sadly. "Did you really carry a torch for me all those years on your magic world?"

He bit his lip. "I still had hopes, I suppose. You were another reason for wanting to come Home."

"Oh, come on!" she persisted teasingly. "You have all my secrets. In the car you displayed a certain assertiveness I do not recall noticing before. You've had practice in clinches."

He squirmed. "No love affairs! But—but there could have been." When she let the silence age, he said, "She indicated that she was inclined in that direction."

He sounded so incredibly Victorian she almost laughed aloud. He was still the paradigm of the romantic.

"Go back to her and try a few more of those clinches," she said.

He stared down at the cold gas fire. "I am never going back, so it isn't possible. It wasn't possible then. I had given my word to you."

She rose to go and dress. "But I had refused. You were under no obligation to me." She turned her back on him and suddenly his arms were tight around her.

"I expect I was using you as my excuse," he said in her ear. "How could I let myself fall in love on a world I was trying to leave? Yes, I was tempted, very tempted. It was my memory of you that sustained me."

Her baby foster brother was a man now, and this was the first time she had really appreciated the difference. Not being able to see his face helped. A man was embracing her, a determined, strong-willed man. No boy.

"Let me go, please."

"I'm not going to rape you. I just want to know if you're happy."

"If the war would end and D'Arcy come back safe, then I would be very happy. His wife's an invalid; she won't live much longer."

"You trust him?"

She would not take this inquisition from anyone else, but he was not anyone else. "Absolutely."

"Because if you have doubts . . . If you want to change your mind, Alice darling, then you still can. You can go to Nextdoor."

"What?"

"I'll go fight the Kaiser. You go to Nextdoor. In six years we'll be the same age."

"Edward! That is not the problem! Now let me go and stop talking nonsense!"

He released her. When she turned, she saw that he was furious. His voice had given no hint of that.

"You'd rather stay and fester in this slum? Uncle Roland blew it all on his precious Bibles, didn't he?"

She sighed. She was not at her best first thing in the morning. "Not really. Some man he had trusted embezzled it."

"Someone in his precious Missionary Society, of course?"

She nodded. "He had no idea. He wept when he told me, Edward. I think it killed him."

"So it should have!" He scowled at her frown. "Oh, I don't care about the money. It was his damned sanctimonious holier-than-thou-ness! I hate people who think they know what's best for the whole world."

There were probably many good responses to that, but she could not think of one. "There's a little left, your share. Just a few hundred quid, and it's all tied up in chancery or something."

"Garn! Cheese in a mousetrap?"

"Not worth your neck to claim, no."

With relief she heard the door open. Julian came limping into the room. His hair was wet, but he was unshaven and his clothes were still caked with dried blood. His eyes flickered appraisingly from one to the other.

"Good morning," he said.

"Good morning. How's the leg?"

"Stiff, that's all. I made a mess of your clean towels, I'm afraid. Have you found any breakfast? We cleaned out the larder like a herd of locusts."

"Horde," Edward said. "Horde of locusts."

"Plague," said Alice. They were playing silly games to cover the tension, and it annoyed her. "I'll go and get dressed before Ginger comes back."

The bell rang then. Julian went. Ginger entered with bulky brown-paper parcels under each arm. He blinked short-sightedly in her direction.

"Morning, Miss Prescott."

"Morning, Mr. Jones. My, you have been busy! I apologize for being such a terrible hostess."

"Nonsense. The old need very little sleep." He dropped the parcels. "This one's five-nine, eleven stone. This is five-foot eleven and three-quarters, ten stone seven pounds." He reached in pockets. "Razor, shaving soap, brushes of diverse types, all as per your favor of today's date."

"Savile Row?"

"Off a barrow." He sat down heavily. His hard night still showed. "I made a phone call and I have a refuge for you."

Edward sighed. "Ginger Jones, you are a prince among men! I am so grateful I could weep."

"So could we all," Julian agreed.

Jones coughed disapprovingly. "Steady, there!" He was genuinely embarrassed.

"Where is this haven, then?" Edward asked.

"The Dower House at Greyfriars."

Edward's eyes widened in shock, making his bony face seem skull-like. "The *Grange?*"

"Mrs. Bodgley lives in the Dower House now. The general died, you know."

"No, I didn't. I'm truly sorry to hear that. The lady hasn't had much luck, has she!"

"But she knows you were not the cause, and she is anxious to meet you. And a friend. I didn't give your name, Smedley, in case of accidents. There's a train in a little over an hour. Think we could make that?"

Julian and Edward dived for their respective parcels.

"Wait!" Alice said. "I hate to be rushed. Why don't we travel separately? Wouldn't that be safer?"

"All four of us?" Jones asked, frowning, touching his nose.

"Two and two. You and Julian. Me and Edward on the next train."

Everyone looked to Edward.

He nodded. "It can't be any riskier, can it? If I write a letter, Ginger, would you post it in the Fallow box for me?"

The schoolmaster raised his eyebrows and again reached to adjust his absent pince-nez. "Why should it matter what box I put it in?"

"I think it does," Edward said. "And the handwriting will. It may even matter whether you pop it in the box or I do, but we can try this first."

Julian made a snorting noise of disbelief. "May I borrow your bedroom, Alice? I'm slow, I'm afraid."

"Go ahead." Alice wondered how she could ever dispose of such horribly bloodstained clothes.

He limped out, carrying his parcel. When the bedroom door clicked shut, Ginger turned to her and smiled triumphantly—the invalid was shedding no tears today.

"What's so funny?" Edward demanded, seeing her answering smile.

"Nothing," she said.

"Next train's not till four-something," Ginger said.

Alice relaxed. "Then you and Julian go first. Edward and I can follow."

They would have time to hammer out his emotional problems, and she could hear more of his adventures in that magical world of his. She had a suspicion that he had been harping on the Nagian savages to discourage Smedley's interest. There must be a brighter side to Nextdoor—perhaps that mysterious Prince Goldfish he had mentioned.

18

GOLBFISH SLAMMED THE BEDROOM DOOR ON YMMA'S MOCKING laughter and stamped off to face his ordeal. He stopped stamping quite soon, because he was barefoot.

His honor guards were waiting in the antechamber. He had expected them to be in dressed much as he was, but they all wore Joalian-style armor of shiny bronze. The colored symbols of their devotion to Olfaan and the other gods were marked on the armor, not slobbered in paint all over their faces. The leader saluted. Puish Lordservant bowed and waved forward two flunkies. One presented Golbfish with a spear, and the other a circular shield. It was so massively ornamented with gold that he almost dropped it. Anything less useful for battle had never been invented.

He glowered around the guards, searching for any hint of a smirk hiding inside a helmet, but their expressions were all studiously noncommittal. Growling angrily, he strode off without a word, leaving them to follow in any order they liked.

For the first—and, he fervently hoped, the last—time in his life, he was clad in the traditional garb of a Nagian warrior. Not that there was much garb to it—a skimpy leather loincloth. He felt naked. His face was ludicrously painted up with colored hieroglyphics. His hair and beard had been trimmed short, because that was warrior style, but he knew how it emphasized the smallness of his head. He felt a freak. He knew he looked a freak, too. Perhaps there was a funny side to it, and someday, at some elegant dinner party, he would laugh with his friends, relating how he had been forced to dress up as a barbarian. Perhaps. But if his friends back in Joal could see him now they would . . . they would laugh just as hard as that slut on the bed was laughing.

He was not the right shape. His torso tapered upward instead of downward, although that did not stop him worrying that his absurd garment might slide right off him in the sweltering heat. With both hands occupied, he would be able to do little to stop it if it tried. He had no hair on his chest—and no ritual scars, either. If Mother thought he would rouse the warrior caste of her primitive kingdom to blood lust and patriotic fervor, then she was going to be sadly disappointed.

Even stupid Ymma knew that. Her mocking words still rang in his ears: "What will they think of you? What will your precious friends think of you when they see you like that? What verses will your poets compose, what songs will your singers sing? And that sculptor man—will he carve your likeness?" She had started to laugh again—hard, cruel laughter like the strokes of a lash.

Golbfish shuddered. Fortunately his best friends were all far away in Joal, and the few he had in Nag would not be close enough to see any of the details. They were civilians all, talented artists whom he had brought back from Joal to aid him in his efforts at improving the cultural life of the kingdom. Civilians would be kept to the back of the temple.

The Joalians will understand! he told himself. *They know I must conform to local custom in raising the horde. They trust me, as they will never trust Tarion. It was the Joalians who insisted Mother appoint me hordeleader.*

But Tarion had been made cavalryleader, and Golbfish did not understand why the Joalians had agreed to that. They were relying on the Nagian cavalry far more than on the Nagian infantry, which would be of little help to them. Nagland had plenty of moas, but no tradition of using them in warfare. Joalian lancers were as good as any in the Vales—except the Thargians, of course—but they had not been able to bring their mounts over Thordpass. A moa was a one-man steed that needed many fortnights to be imprinted by a new rider. Little brother Tarion would be technically under the hordeleader's command, but he was far more likely to win glory in the coming war than Golbfish himself was.

He was not looking forward to the war at all. He was a patron of the arts, not a fighter. He was looking forward to this afternoon's mustering ceremony least of all. He would rather face a horde of armed Thargians than go before his own people dressed like this, but there was no way he could escape the ordeal. Joalia had demanded the support of its ally, and the horde must be mustered in the ancient ways.

What Joal wanted, Joal got. That was the law in Nagia.

The palace was a dingy affair of endless stone corridors, badly designed and poorly built, an insipid imitation of Joalian architecture. There was no decent building stone near Nag, not like the lustrous variegated marbles of Joal. Everything was made of the same drab, purplish sandstone. It was so

soft it crumbled, and the floors were permanently gritty. Nagland had no
tradition of building in stone.

Nagia had no tradition of hereditary monarchs, either. The Joalians had
imposed the monarchy by force of arms when they put his grandfather on
the throne. His mother, it must be admitted, had astonished everyone by
managing to hang on to it, crushing the predictable revolts with Joalian
help and ruthless cruelty. It was true she favored Tarion as her successor,
for she made no secret of the fact. She maintained that Golbfish was not
sufficiently ruthless. She was right about that, but was ruthlessness necessary
anymore? After three generations, he thought, the Nagians had adjusted to
the situation. They would tolerate a king to keep the Joalians quiet, just as
long as he was benevolent and well intentioned.

Mother did not agree.

Golbfish's left foot was already sore by the time he reached the Garden of
Blessings, which was a feeble copy of the Garden of Blessings in Joal. Anyone who had seen the original found this one pitiful. Imported Joalian seeds
never thrived, and Nagian vegetation just did not have the same luster. The
wickertrees gave a feeble shade, the sunblooms and starflowers were almost
invisible amid their rioting leathery leaves. Now, in late summer, the fountains had run dry and the ornamental pools looked scummy and dead, as if
they should have fish floating belly-up in them. The statuary had been
carved from the inevitable purplish sandstone, so that most of the figures
were weathered to faceless mummies already.

The honor guard had halted somewhere. Golbfish advanced alone, following the winding path through the shrubbery. He heard voices ahead,
many voices, and felt a twinge of uneasiness. He had expected only Mother
and Kammaeman, the Joalian commander. Possibly Tarion. He could hear
a large party in progress.

Rounding a tangle of bamboo, ruby bushes, and salmon vines, he
came in sight of the throne. The queen was holding court, elevated
above the crowd. She seemed to be the only woman present. As he approached, he searched in vain for signs of anyone at all gaudied up as he
was. Some were clad in bronze, gleaming and warlike, the rest were
dressed in the loose breeches and tunics of Joalian civilians. He recognized the usual ministers, envoys, and secretaries. He could understand
their being here, but there were others he would never have expected.
Mother seemed to have invited every officer in the visiting Joalian army,
plus all the court officials and most of the important local notables—and
all Golbfish's personal friends, too! There were dozens of faces he had
never seen within the palace before: Toalmin Sculptor, Gramwil Poet,

Gilbothin Historian, and innumerable others. These were the people he had happily assumed would be relegated to the back of the temple. Why had they been invited to this reception?

And why was the reception being held at all? He had not been told of it. He wondered if Ymma had known about this.

He reached the back of the crowd and said, "Excuse me." The closer men looked around and gaped in astonishment. Then they backed out of his path, but their eyebrows soared high as flags.

I shall run my spear into any man who smiles! he thought, and then realized he would have to commit a massacre. Faces were averted, but he dared not look behind him to see what effect he was leaving in his wake. He could hear much coughing.

"Excuse me, please!" he said again. And again . . .

The one advantage of his grotesque war paint was that his blushes would not show. He could feel his ears glowing hot, though.

He was tall enough that he made out Kammaeman Battlemaster even before he reached the throne. The Joalian leader was standing at the foot of the steps, joking with the queen. Despite the gray in his beard, he was still one of the best warriors Joalia had produced in a generation. Kammaeman could be relied on to lead the combined armies with imagination and the necessary ruthlessness. The Thargians would not find him an easy opponent. He was also a shrewd politician, shrewdness in politics being an important survival trait in Joal. Golbfish had met him there often enough, but their friendship had been purely ceremonial.

Needless to say, Golbfish intended to leave all the military decisions to Kammaeman. He also intended to stay very close to him during the battles. An heir to a throne could not take risks like other men.

There was Tarion Cavalryleader, also close to the queen, smirking ominously.

Admittedly Tarion was only his half brother, but the two of them could not have been less alike. He was a pure Nagian type—lean as a whip, tireless, brown skinned, and dark haired—and touchy and dangerous. No one ever outrode Tarion; he seemed to merge with his moa and make it part of himself. If anyone else in this assembly ought to be exhibited in a loincloth and emblazoned with war paint like Golbfish, it should be Tarion, leader of the cavalry. But no. There he was, undeniably handsome in a shiny bronze helmet and Joalian riding wear of blue cotton, bearing himself with all the menace of a naked sword. He was good, and he knew it.

At last Golbfish came to the steps of the throne, stopped, and nodded his head in an excuse for a bow. He dare not ask why his mother was not also wearing national dress for the solemn occasion. If her subjects expected to see the scrawny royal bosom bared, they were going to be disappointed. Her blue gown was as Joalian as could be. She was tiny and frail, her thin white hair hidden by a jeweled tiara. Her face was painted even more heavily than his, but in her case the covering was wax and rouge, to hide the lines of pain and the yellowing skin.

Emchainne was dying. Everyone knew it, even she, and nobody dared say so. A few months at best were all she had left, but the illness that racked her had not yet blunted her will. She was still queen; she ruled Nagia yet, as implacably as she had ruled it for thirty years.

How had anyone so puny ever produced him? He was half again as tall as she was. At the moment, though, her eyes were higher than his, and they glared.

"You're late!" she snapped. "Have you already forgotten the correct form of military salute?" Her voice was croaky.

Grumpily, Golbfish slammed his shield with his spear and almost let it slip from his sweaty fingers. A couple of the onlookers leaped back out of harm's way.

The queen of Nagia looked over her older son with undisguised contempt. "And do you not also salute your commander in chief?"

Now there Golbfish felt he was on firmer ground, if there could be any firm ground in this quagmire of intrigue. He favored Kammaeman with a nod. "Battlemaster?" Then he turned back to the queen. "You are our commander in chief, Mother. I am your appointed deputy. The battlemaster is merely commander of our allies. Of course, I defer to his overall leadership, but by treaty we are equals. We march together against the common foe."

The older man raised a grizzled eyebrow.

With sudden apprehension, Golbfish glanced around the onlookers. Most of them were making an effort to conceal amusement. Not Tarion, though. His helmet did not disguise his sneer. He must know something Golbfish did not. Had Ymma also known it? Did everyone know but him?

"Ah, yes!" The queen glanced over the nearer courtiers. "Who has a copy of my son's speech?"

Golbfish could feel himself starting to grow angry, which was an unfamiliar feeling and an unwelcome one. When he lost his temper he usually became very shrill; he tended to stamp his feet. "I know my part, Mother!"

"We have decided to make a small addition to the ceremony."

"The form is traditional!"

Emchainne sighed, but the glint in her eyes showed that she was enjoying herself. "Monarchy is not. Historically, hordeleaders were elected, not appointed. You are our heir apparent. We have concluded that you are too precious, Golbfish, dear. We have decided we cannot allow you to risk yourself in battle. Nobody doubts your courage, of course. We know how you must regret this, but our Joalian allies agree—do they not, Battlemaster? So you will have to remain here in Nag, with us, my son."

His first reaction was a surge of relief. Tents and coarse food and sleeping on hard ground held very little appeal. Feather beds and silver spoons were more to his taste. Then he remembered Tarion's cryptic joy and knew that there were snakes here somewhere.

"But—" he said.

"No argument! Where is that speech? Ah, yes. Give it to him."

Gragind Chancellor thrust a paper at Golbfish. Having a shield on one arm and a spear in his other hand, he ignored it.

"Tell me!"

Faint cracks showed in the wax coating on his mother's face, as if a smile were struggling to break out. "At the conclusion of the oath-taking, when all the warriors have sworn allegiance to you, Hordeleader, you will announce that you are unable to lead them in person and therefore you transfer their loyalty to Kammaeman Battlemaster."

"What?" Golbfish screamed. "They swear to die for me and then I tell them I am staying home?"

"It is a regrettable necessity, son."

"I cannot do that! No man could!"

Satisfaction glowed in his mother's eyes. "You refuse a direct order from your sovereign, Hordeleader?"

That was a capital offense.

"No," Golbfish moaned. "Of course not! But—"

"No buts!" Emchainne said firmly, glancing askance at Kammaeman to see his reaction.

The barbarians would never stand for it!

Tarion was smirking from one ear guard to the other.

19

TWO TERRIBLE HOURS LATER, GOLBFISH STOOD BESIDE THE ALTAR, A few steps up from the temple floor, his head almost level with the goddess's toes. The heat beating down off the rock behind him was a torment.

Astina, the Maiden, was one of the Five, the Pentatheon. Her temple in Joal was one of the wonders of the Vales.

In her aspect as Olfaan, goddess of warriors and presiding deity of Nagvale, she had to make do with very much less. The Joalian influence that had transformed the secular capital had been balked when it tried to replace the ancient sanctuary with something more dignified and artistic. Golbfish's grandfather had laid out foundations for a great religious complex on the far side of the city. The priestesses had refused to sanctify it, whereupon the people had downed tools and offered to die before they would offend Holy Olfaan. So the old temple had remained much as it had always been. Queen Emchainne had added a grandiose pillared entrance, but that was the only change.

Visitors, especially the all-important Joalian visitors, were always astonished by it. They complained that a hole in the ground was not truly a temple, and of course they were right. Not that it was strictly a hole—only half a hole, a semicircular embayment in a cliff. Its floor was a plain of shingle that often flooded in the rainy season. The image of the goddess had been carved into the vertical stone many eons ago. On dull days it was hard to make out, but when the sun shone, as it usually did, her outline was clearly visible. Nagians could boast that their goddess was the largest in the world and the acoustics were splendid. But it was still only a hole in the ground, and on a day like this it was a god-sized pit oven.

Before Golbfish, in massed array, stood the young warriors of Nagland, summoned from all over the vale to pledge their loyalty in the ancient ritual. Interspersed among them was a very large contingent from the Joalian army, presently encamped just north of the capital. Officially they had assembled to honor the goddess and their allies. Unofficially they were there to see that nothing went wrong, and the way they had segregated the Nagians into small groups proved that.

At the back of all this blade and muscle stood the queen's civilian subjects, come to watch their sons and brothers be inducted to fight a war that no Nagian truly cared a spit for. They had cheered Her Majesty when she was borne in. They had sung the praises of Holy Olfaan with a genuine verve that had probably been audible halfway up Nagwall, thanks to those superb acoustics. All in all, they were putting a brave face on this latest evidence of Nagvale's lowly status as a colony of Joalia.

After the initial invocation, the priestesses had slunk back to their caves. This was strictly a military ritual.

It had been going on for hours, and had a long way to go yet. The queen's litter had been located well off to one side, its draperies closed against the raging sun. Her attendants kept peering in at her. Golbfish assumed that she must be having one of her bad turns. There was nothing he could do about it, and he could not help thinking that it served her right. Admittedly she could not have refused the Joalian demands, but she had certainly used the situation to dispose of her elder son. He was doomed to die here today. Tarion had won.

The brawny young warrior on the other side of the altar took up the arms he had dropped earlier. He saluted Golbfish and the goddess overhead, then stalked away down the steps, following the last of his contingent. The steps were spotted with blood.

In the center of the altar a stone knife lay on a drying red stain. Beside it were half a dozen gold dishes. Three were empty now. The others were heaped with sparkling white salt, too brilliant to look upon.

Golbfish sighed and glanced down at the handwritten list that had been placed on the stone table to prompt him, weighted with gold coins in case a wind developed later. No such luck! The air was still, the temple an oven.

"I call on Her Majesty's loyal warriors from Rareby!" His throat was parched as the Western Desert. He seemed to have stopped sweating. Probably he had just run dry, like the palace fountains. Earlier, he had worried that he might have washed all the paint off his face.

A massive young man came striding up the steps, bearing his shield and spear. Now that was how a warrior should look! His shoulders were as broad as a wagon, his hips slender. The muscles of his calves bunched as he walked. Golbfish squirmed with shame to look at him.

The giant laid his shield and spear on the altar and spoke the words of the dedication. "Her Majesty's warriors of Rareby swear obedience to Holy Olfaan and to all your commands, Hordeleader." He had a strong voice, in keeping with his appearance, and the cliff threw it back over the weary multitude who had heard all this so often before. "They offer their blood and their lives and their absolute allegiance. They pray to Olfaan to guide them, protect them, and make them worthy of her service."

"Amen," Golbfish said for the eighth or ninth time that afternoon.

The man was sweating like a burrowpig, of course, but that could charitably be attributed to the heat. The way he set his teeth as he lifted the knife could not. He was dreading his ordeal. He already bore four merit marks on his ribs, but that knife must be thoroughly blunted by now.

He surreptitiously scraped it on the edge of the altar. That was not part of the service, but he was not the first to do so, and the marks there showed that these warriors' forefathers had done the same thing many times in past centuries. One scrape would not add much sharpness.

Then he slashed at his ribs.

Golbfish never watched this part. The sight of blood made him nauseous. He heard a faint gasp as the warrior rubbed the salt on his cut. Gods, how that must hurt! Two youngsters had fainted earlier and been dragged away by their friends. Officially they had to be put to death for that display of frailty, but more likely they would be allowed to escape and flee the country.

The troopleader sighed with relief as the pain eased. Then he stepped to the far side of the altar. The first of his men came hurrying up, eager to undergo his ordeal and get it over with. He had hardly stopped moving before he hurled down his shield and spear and grabbed for the knife. He made his cut so fast that Golbfish barely had time to avert his eyes.

"Not enough!" snapped the troopleader.

The warrior scowled at him and cut again. He let the blood run for a moment, as if waiting to be told it would suffice. Then he reached for the salt.

Barbaric! Unspeakably barbaric! The Joalians present would be appalled. When they sacrificed to Olfaan, or even to Astina herself, they offered a chicken, or a calf at most. They would think this deliberate self-mutilation utterly depraved, as did Golbfish himself. It was a primitive, savage custom.

He bore no merit marks. Because of that alone, he must have seemed a very spurious war leader to the real Nagians when he paraded through the town on his way here. He had been secretly ashamed, but he had certainly never considered mutilating himself just to please the rabble.

The warrior retrieved his weapons and departed. Another Rarebian followed, and another. At least they were moving quickly. Some villages tried to drag it out.

Golbfish ought to want it to last. Almost certainly he would die at the end of it. When the last warrior had sworn, he would have to make that dread speech that had been laid out for him. If he didn't, then the Joalians would know that he had disobeyed a direct command from his queen, and they would not tolerate an untrustworthy officer. So they would not help him.

The Nagians would not, either. They had laughed aloud as he marched through the city. Everyone else had been in armor, or mounted on moas like handsome brother Tarion. Only the hordeleader had been stripped down to a loincloth, to show his flabby hips, his narrow shoulders, and his hairless, unscarred chest. The queen had very cruelly demonstrated to her Joalian visitors that her elder son had no following among the people.

Tarion and his cavalry had been cheered! That rankled worse than anything. Tarion cared nothing for the people. Tarion did not know a sonnet from a drinking song. He had no interest in advancing Nagian culture and raising the people from barbarism, as Golbfish had. The Joalians did not trust Tarion, which was wise of them, but now they would have to. Tarion would go off and earn military glory in the war. Golbfish, even if he managed to escape assassination this afternoon, must needs skulk at home in the palace, and everyone would assume he was a coward. He wasn't a very brave man, but he would have gone to the war if he'd been given the chance. It was not fair!

His final act of the ceremony, rejecting all these oaths, was very likely going to be his last. The bloodied warriors would not stand for such an insult. A hundred spears would flash in the sunlight, and Golbfish's blood would mingle with theirs on the steps. A hundred? There were close to a thousand of them out there, and it would only take one.

The heat might kill him first. He lacked the lifelong tan of the peasant. His skin was being fried by the sun. What penalty did the ancient rituals prescribe if the hordeleader himself were to faint during the ceremony?

Oh, goddess! The troopleader was scooping up his shield. Next village, then. Had that one been Rareby or Thoid'lby? For a moment Golbfish almost panicked. Then he decided it had been Rareby, and called for Thoid'lby. No one corrected him.

The Thoid'lby leader was older than most, an ugly, weathered man. A widower, likely. His look at Golbfish was openly contemptuous as he spat out the oath.

The bloodshed continued.

The temple shimmered in the hellish glare.

Only one more village to go! Death was moving in very close to Golbfish Hordeleader now. He could think of no way out. If he did not resign his command as ordered, he would be arrested and executed for mutiny. If he did, the warriors would riot and use him for target practice. And even if by some miracle they didn't, then Tarion would see that he did not remain around long as a rival claimant to the throne. Not one Nagian or Joalian would lift a finger to save him.

He was doomed.

Warrior followed warrior. Cut followed cut.

He wanted to shout out that they were going too fast. Life had become a blur.

Thoid'lby completed its ordeal, and its surly troopleader departed.

The last village! He worked his mouth until he could find enough spit to speak.

"I call on Her Majesty's loyal warriors from Sonalby!"

A murmur of surprise rustled through the temple. Golbfish's eyes snapped back into focus. The Sonalby contingent was not milling forward in a mob, as all the others had done. It was marching four abreast, with its spears on its shoulders in parallel rows like the teeth of combs. Every foot moved in perfect unison as if an invisible band were playing somewhere. The Joalian infantry drilled no better.

"Troop—halt!"

A hundred feet came down together. Their hundred partners joined them, and the warriors stood motionless at the base of the steps. Not a spear wavered. Another bark, the poles sprang to the vertical, then the butts struck the ground. Somebody cheered at the back of the temple and was hushed.

Kammaeman Battlemaster had laughed out loud at the idea of teaching proper drill to Nagians. Past experience showed that it would be a waste of time, he insisted. But Sonalby must have found a veteran leader, one who had at some time served in the Joalian army and learned the advantages of discipline. Somehow he had trained this band.

Who had worked that miracle?

This man?

The troopleader alone had continued. He came marching up the steps toward Golbfish.

Yet he was only a boy, although a very tall one. He bore only three merit marks. One was very recent, probably acquired when he was elected troopleader, but even the others were still red and therefore not more than a dozen or so fortnights old. As he came to a halt, Golbfish saw with astonishment that the youngster's eyes were brilliant blue, bluer than the blue of his face paint, a shade Golbfish could not recall ever seeing combined with hair so black.

For a moment the two stared at each other, and there was a significance in that steady gaze that startled Golbfish utterly. He could not place it. It was something he had never met before. He thought it mattered greatly.

Then, very slightly, the boy smiled.

Bewildered, Golbfish smiled back, and felt an inexplicable sense of relief.

With a couple of smart military movements, the young troopleader discarded his shield and spear. He spoke the words of the oath loudly and clearly, and if as he meant them. He had a faint, unfamiliar accent.

Never taking his eyes off Golbfish, he took up the knife and cut his chest.

He salted the wound without a flinch, as if he were barely aware of what he was doing, and all the time that steady blue gaze was asking some impossible question.

He marched to his place at the far end of the altar, and swung around. Again he looked meaningfully at Golbfish. Who was this cryptic youngster? What message was he trying to pass? He seemed almost to be offering sympathy, as if he were aware of the terrible problem. That was impossible!

Then the first of his followers arrived to perform the ritual, and the young leader turned his attention on him.

One by one, a hundred men and boys came to shed their own blood before the goddess and their so-temporary hordeleader. But this time there was a curious difference. They did not look up at the goddess. They did not even seem to notice Golbfish. They watched their leader, and he watched them, and each time Golbfish detected a curious little smile of encouragement pass. The youngster's lips did not move, but his eyes brightened, and every man of the hundred seemed to appreciate that tiny signal, as if they drew inspiration from this juvenile soldier. *I did it. It's not so terrible.*

Then it was done. The last man marched smartly away.

The leader came over, picked up his arms, shouldered his spear. For a moment his eyes wandered past Golbfish and he frowned slightly, then smiled.

Golbfish looked around uneasily. There was no one there, only the bare rock of the cliff, radiating heat like a forge. He turned back to confront that same blue, quizzical stare. The barbaric face paint made the expression difficult to read. Now the boy would go and leave Golbfish alone, to meet his fate.

But he didn't. Instead he raised his eyebrows in a question. What? A suggestion? An invitation? He almost seemed to be offering to stay and help as if . . .

Merciful Goddess! Perhaps there *was* a way out!

Golbfish's knees began to tremble. Mindful of the phenomenal acoustics, he spoke in a tiny whisper. "Could you make me a warrior too?"

The boy smiled, pleased. He spoke as softly. "Only you can do that, sir. But I can show you how."

Golbfish nodded in bewilderment.

The boy marched back to the far end of the table, grounded his spear, and stood at attention—watching Golbfish! Again a mutter of surprise rustled through the crowd.

The prince glanced over to the queen's litter. A curtain had been raised so she could witness his coming resignation—and death. The monarchy had always mattered more to her than her disappointing son did. Golbfish was the product of a loveless, dynastic marriage. Tarion had been born of passion.

Tarion was a bastard in every sense of the word.

The shadows made Mother invisible. Kammaeman Battlemaster stood alongside her litter, tense and expectant. A glance to the cavalry at the other side of the temple showed Tarion—too far off for his gleeful smirk to be seen, although it could be imagined.

I shall cheat you all yet!

Golbfish took one last look at the boy from Sonalby, and received that same little smile of reassurance and encouragement that the others had.

At least one man was on his side!

He ignored the written speech. His voice burst out clear and strong, so suddenly that he hardly knew it was himself speaking. "Warriors of Nagland! I have accepted your oaths in the ways of our ancestors!" That was how the prepared text began, and it was a lie because he had not one drop of Nagian blood in his veins. Tarion did. Tarion was the son of a palace guard.

Golbfish sucked in another deep breath. "I shall be honored to fight at your side—but I am not a general. I am not worthy of your allegiance! I now command you all, in the first and last order I shall give you, to obey the noble Joalian battlemaster, who can lead us to victory in our righteous struggle against Thargian aggression."

He paused, sweating and shaking. Could he really go through with this? Rip his own flesh? He glanced again at the Sonalby troopleader, and again the boy smiled approvingly, urging him to continue. A low but rising growl from the audience warned him he must decide quickly.

"As for me, warriors, I shall fight as one of you, in the ranks."

He turned and took up that odious knife with a shaking hand. He poked the edge with his thumb and knew he would have to strike very hard to make a visible cut—it must be visible. To his horror, he felt a stirring in his groin, a rising thrill of sexual excitement. What foul perversion was that?

In a quick gesture of revulsion, he cut. It felt like molten iron poured on his skin. He had never known real pain before. It was frightful, worse than he had ever imagined. But at least it had banished the deviant surge of lust. He felt panic in its place. Hot blood trickled down his ribs. He was bleeding!

He stared doubtfully at the salt. That would be a hundred times worse. Could he bear even that? Supposing he screamed? Frozen in terror between fear of pain and fear of bleeding, he looked again to his inspiration.

Again that nod, that smile. *I know how you feel,* the steady blue eyes said. *A thousand men and boys have done it already.*

Golbfish grabbed a handful of the gritty stuff and did it. Gods, gods, gods!

Agony coursed through every nerve, every vein. He bit hard on his lip. He would faint! He must faint! Then the torment slowly faded to a fiery burn. He was still bleeding. Not so much, but still bleeding. Unable to suppress a moan, he took another handful and the torture came again. He blinked at the tears.

"Come," said the boy softly.

Golbfish staggered back to his own spear and shield. His head swam when he stooped, but he managed to lift them. He tottered down the steps behind his new leader. A hundred astonished Sonalby faces stared up in amazement at the unexpected recruit. The whole, vast congregation had frozen into statues.

The boy barked an order. The warriors snapped their spears to their shoulders. Another word and they spun around to face the other way. One error and those poles would have tangled in chaos, but there was no error. A third order, and they began to march. Their commander followed, and Golbfish tottered along at his side, struggling to keep in step.

He might die in battle, the rigors of training might kill him, but he had survived the ceremony! He stole a glance sideways at the lanky youth who had inspired his dramatic gesture. He felt a strange conviction that his new-found leader would look after him. He had found a friend. He had found someone he could trust.

20

"So what did she look like, this goddess?" Alice demanded.

"Didn't get much of an eyeful," Edward said. "She was there and then she was gone. You've seen one goddess, you've seen them all."

The two of them were strolling through St. James's Park, Edward casually swinging her overnight bag. It was a beautiful autumn afternoon. They had lots of time, and a straight line from Lambeth to Paddington would take them through the fairest parts of London—over Westminster Bridge, past the Houses of Parliament, across St. James's Park, Green Park, and Hyde Park. Then they would be almost there.

It was wonderful to have Edward back, after three years of wondering and worrying and almost but not quite giving up hope. He was more than just a cousin. He was her foster brother, her only living relative. She had not yet plumbed all the changes in him—strength and firmness of purpose. The schoolboy honor would be more deliberate and perhaps more practical, but no less firm.

This should be a marvelous day, a day to savor and remember, yet she could not shake off a creepy sensation that she was being followed. She glanced behind her once in a while, although reason told her that any follower could hide amid the milling crowds.

Edward noticed, of course. "What's the matter? You're jumpy as a grass-hopper."

"Guilty conscience. I ought to be at work."

"They'll hold the war for you. What sort of work do you do, anyway?"

"Can't talk about it. Official Secrets Act." If he were to guess that pianists made good typists and very few secretaries in London could type Kikuyu, he would not be far off.

Policemen bothered her. She kept thinking they were staring at her.

Half a dozen young men walked past talking loudly. Edward glanced back in surprise. "Americans?"

"Canadians, I expect. On leave."

He shook his head disbelievingly. "The whole world at war! It's mind-boggling."

"They all seem to come to London," she said. "I don't know how they stand it—a few days in civilization, knowing they have to go back to the trenches, to be scarred and tortured—or killed."

Edward said nothing.

"That wasn't exactly tactful of me, was it? Edward, are you sure your duty is here?"

He looked down at her quickly, then away. He pointed. "Never thought I'd see guns in London. Antiaircraft, I suppose?"

"Answer me!"

He frowned. "Of *course* my duty is here! You know! We weren't born in England, you and I, but this is our native land. Nextdoor isn't."

"But you know you can achieve something worthwhile there, in your storybook world, because of that prophecy! Here you may just become another number, one of millions."

"I will not be less than those millions!"

"But you could be one *in* millions."

He scowled. "Alice, can't you understand? You might have talked me out of it before, but now I've seen what it's like! Those men carried me for hours across that hell, and I saw. I had never imagined war could be so horrible. I had never imagined *anything* could be so horrible. But now I've seen it. Now I know. I have to go back there! I can't run away now."

That seemed a very stupid, masculine way to think. "We have to win the war," she said. "It's cost so much that we can't stop now. But I don't know that you belong in it." Or D'Arcy, either. "We aren't all called to serve in the same way. You don't pull carts with racehorses."

"You don't make pets of them, either."

They paced on. The park was surprisingly crowded. She took his hand, though she had promised herself she wouldn't. He squeezed her fingers without looking down at her.

"What amazes me," he said after a while, "is how you all seem to accept my story. I'd have expected you to have me locked up in Colney Hatch as a babbling loony."

"You carry conviction. You always did. Have you ever told a lie in your life?"

"Course I have! Don't be ridiculous! Everyone has."

"About anything important?"

He took some time to answer, staring woodenly at nothing. "Lying isn't important. Betraying friends, now . . . that's worse."

"I won't believe you ever have."

"Well, that's where you're wrong!" he snapped. "Twice! That damned prophecy keeps trying to make me a god. . . . And I keep thinking of Holy Roly. . . . Telling people what they must do—what's right and what's wrong!" He looked down, and she was astonished to see that his eyes were shiny with tears.

She reminded herself that something had changed him and to pry might be needless cruelty. This day was much too precious to spend quarreling. "Tell me what magic feels like?"

He smiled. "That's impossible! Like describing color to a blind man. When you have mana you know it, but I can't say how. It's a little like having a bag of money, so you can feel the weight of the coins. You're a great pianist—"

"I had some talent."

"How did you *know* your talent? Mana's like that. How does an athlete know his strength? It's a fizz in the head. It's an excitement. I thought I knew what it was like, but I didn't really. Not until that day in Olfaan's temple. Oh, I'd picked up scraps now and then, but nothing like that. Having a troop of warriors to lead had been giving me some, but we hadn't been on a node. Nodes make all the difference. That's why strangers find themselves nodes and become numens—gods, if you want to call them that. As soon as we marched in, my chaps realized that my drill had made them superior to all the other contingents. They were thinking, *Good old D'ward!* and I could feel that pride and admiration like a shot of hot brandy."

"You weren't frightened of the numen, Olfaan?"

He laughed. "I was a complete innocent! I still trusted Krobidirkin, you see. I thought he would have foreseen that ceremony and warned Olfaan I was coming and won her approval. Astina's lot were not part of the Chamber—so I thought, and in a very rough sense I was right about that. I was wrong about Krobidirkin. The Herder was just using me. There's the palace!"

"It's usually around here somewhere."

They stopped at the curb, looking across at Buckingham Palace, waiting for the policemen controlling the traffic.

"Ugly heap, isn't it?" Edward said. "You'd think that the King-Emperor of a quarter of the world would have a more impressive residence. Pity he isn't home, or we could drop in for tea." The royal standard was not flying.

"He's doing his bit. He does a lot for the troops."

"So he damned well should! They're certainly doing enough for him."

Alice glanced up, surprised. "What's wrong?"

"Oh . . . nothing."

"Come on! Out with it."

He shrugged, frowning. "I wish I understood how it works here. That was something we didn't talk about much in Olympus. A couple of thousand years ago, yes. Then it worked on Earth very much as it still does on Nextdoor. I think there really was a god at Delphi, then. When the Greeks went to consult the oracle, there was a numen present and the prophecies were genuine. Or some of them at least. When the Romans prayed in the Capitol to Jupiter Optimus Maximus, someone was listening. But things changed a few centuries back."

Alice had been wondering about that. "Nietzsche? 'God is dead'?"

"No. The gods are not dead. They're still here, or else there are new gods. People stopped taking them literally when the Enlightenment came, but they didn't die. They've taken some other form."

"You're not saying King George is a stranger?"

He laughed. "Hardly!" His mood darkened. "No. Creighton said the Blighters started this war, but there's no nominal god of death receiving the sacrifices. That doesn't mean the sacrifices aren't being made. Who is lapping up the mana?"

"Edward! Are you saying that all gods—all gods—throughout history . . . that all gods and all religions have been fakes, frauds?"

He hesitated. "No. No, I'm not saying that. You see, what the Service is trying to introduce in the Vales is a system of ethics that you would recognize. You would approve. I do. It has a lot of Christianity in it, and a lot of Buddhism. . . . The Golden Rule, mostly—the sort of thing that has cropped up in our world and in that world many times. It has to come from somewhere and— Come on!"

The policeman was waving. They crossed the road. She kept trying to release his hand, but he was holding her fingers tightly. Passersby shot them disapproving looks.

"It's incredible to be back here," he said. "To see all the old familiar sights again."

"And yet the differences? What do you notice?"

"Crowds. The whole population of the Vales would not fill London. People overdressed, because of the climate. Walking their dogs! How absurdly, typically English! Mothers pushing babies in prams. Tourists and late holidaymakers, soldiers on leave. Policemen. Do those barrage balloons really do any good?"

They talked of the war for a while. They crossed Piccadilly and entered Hyde Park. His sinister talk of sacrifice bothered her, though, and eventually she asked him how it worked.

He sighed. "Know that, and you would understand all mysteries! The essence of sacrifice is that you do something you don't want to do because you think it will please your god. If you're lucky, you get a pat on the head and feel good. If I hadn't known that before, then I'd have learned it that day in Nag. All those warriors from Sonalby sacrificed to *me!* They didn't mean to. They didn't even know they were doing it, but each of them had to perform a very unpleasant ritual with a blunt knife and a handful of salt. They thought they were doing it for their own manhood, their goddess, and poor old Golbfish, but I was their leader and their friend, and there I was, right on the node. I had charisma! So they did it for me, and pretty soon I was gibbering drunk with mana."

"That was what you used on Golbfish?"

"Not really. I didn't use anything on him except charisma, and I couldn't help that. Oh, I suppose I was being a little more than naïve. Right at the beginning, as soon as he went up to the altar, I knew he was a very worried man. Probably no one else knew. I had no idea what the matter was, but I felt sorry for him. When I finally got my chance to march up the steps, I tried to give him a bit of cheering up. I gave him one of those looks you do when you want to tell someone something without actually speaking, you know? He sort of grabbed at it, and I realized that he was in mortal terror."

"Then the goddess came?"

"At the end she did. If I was tipsy, she must have been completely bung-eyed by that time. She'd all those thousands of people singing hymns to her and then hundreds of men offering blood and pain, all right on her node— mana in torrents! I don't suppose she'd had a feast like that in a generation.

And suddenly it was cut off. It was all coming to me, see? So she came to find out what was going on. I'm sure nobody else saw her. I caught a glimpse and thought, *Whoops!* and she saw me and I'm sure she guessed right away who I was. I was very bad news, because I might queer her with Zath or Karzon or with major intriguing in the Pentatheon. The lady did not want to be involved! So she scarpered."

"But what did she look like?"

"Nothing special, as I recall," he said vaguely. "Big woman. Hardly saw her. It was like two friends passing in a busy street. They tip their hats to each other and are gone. I was more worried about Golbfish."

"Why? Why did you decide to help him?"

Edward shrugged, almost shyly. "I didn't do anything, really. He needed a friend and my charisma made him trust me. He thought up his own way out. I was amused to discover I now had a prince under my command. I wasn't thinking too clearly, as I said. I felt invincible! Good day for sailing boats!"

Alice looked to where the children were playing by the Serpentine.

"Is that what you want to do? Stop and play with toy boats on a lake, just let the world go by? Two worlds?"

"I want to enlist."

"Edward, what exactly is prophesied about you in the other world? What does the Liberator actually *do*?"

He turned on her in sudden anger. "I told you: He kills Death. Not real death, just Zath, of course. And that's disaster! It leads to disaster! There's only one way it could be done, and that's for me to set myself up as a god and collect more mana than Zath—and he's been at it for a hundred years. I can't imagine what horrors I'd have to invent to squeeze worship on that scale out of the masses, and what happens after? What happens to me? What happens to them? All that just to kill one stranger, who'll probably be replaced by another in two shakes? Zath's the first one nasty enough to claim to be god of death, but it's such a great swindle he invented that he certainly won't be the last. The guv'nor saw all that, and when I finally got to read the bloody Filoby thing, I saw too, and I won't have anything to do with it! I came Home to enlist, but I also came Home to break the chain, and I'm never going back! Never! I won't! I mean it! That's final!" He spun on his heel and stalked away, walking faster than before.

She ran after him. "No, I don't see. Are you sure you can't kill Zath without using mana?"

"Absolutely certain."

"Then you could take the god of death office yourself, to make sure it isn't abused."

"Faugh! No. Don't worry about it. It won't happen. I'd rather stop a

German bullet any day. What else do you want to know, apart from that?"

"What happened to Golbfish?"

Edward sighed. "Ah, that's quite a story. If it wasn't for Golbfish I wouldn't be here. First thing, of course, when we'd barely left the temple, was that a couple of heralds appeared, demanding that he return to the palace."

"And?"

Edward grinned, looking suddenly very juvenile. "I told them that Golb-fish Warrior was now under my command and I refused to release him. I had a hundred spearsmen with me, so the argument was brief."

Alice glanced at her watch. They still had an hour before train time.

"Of course," he said, "I realized that I had blundered into a major po-litical crisis. We'd hardly got back to camp before I was summoned to appear before Kammaeman Battlemaster, the Joalian general. I was told to bring my new recruit with me, but I didn't. I went alone and explained that the prince couldn't come—he was too busy digging latrine ditches. After that, they sort of lost interest in us."

"Never mind your confounded modesty! What did you really do?"

"Nothing much," Edward said blandly.

ꙮ 21 ꙮ

"TWO FRIENDS ARE BETTER THAN ONE," SAID DOSH HOUSEBOY, kneading Tarion's calf, "especially if they are enemies."

"Sounds like one of my dear brother's aphorisms. It's enough to send a whole dining room of sycophants into hysterics."

"It's from the Green Scriptures, Canto 1576." Dosh turned his attention to the other leg.

Tarion was stretched out naked on an auroch hide. The tent was dim and hot. It smelled of leather, his own sweat, and the fragrant oil Dosh was using. After hours of standing in the temple, a massage felt very good. Massages from Dosh always did—he had skill and his hands were much more powerful than they looked. All the thousands of other people who had endured that ceremony would perhaps appreciate similar treatment, but none of them would be getting it.

"What two friends do you have in mind?" he asked sleepily.

Dosh chuckled throatily. "You and Golbfish."

"The Joalians can still play us off against each other, of course."

"Of course. And the fat man did not die . . . which may have been the plan, possibly?"

Tarion chuckled. "Do my thighs now." He sighed sensuously as those powerful fingers began to work on the muscle.

"So you will have to behave yourself, or they can bring him back," Dosh said, phrasing the words in time with his thrusts. "They do not trust my beloved master." He was as nosy as an old woman.

After a while Tarion roused himself to answer. "Mother cannot last much longer. Then the Joalians will have to decide which of us to put on the throne. I think we shall have just time to slaughter a few Lemodians before then. Before the terrible news arrives."

It would be better for Tarion himself if the time was insufficient for the Lemodian's Thargian allies to arrive on the scene—Thargians were dangerous—but that was in the lap of the gods. "It seems most unlikely that my dear brother will survive more than an hour or two of infantry training. He has the muscle tone of a milk pudding. His comrades will laugh him to death. There must be a limit to the amount of humiliation even that man can absorb. Besides . . . Do you want to hear a little secret, dear boy?"

"You know I love secrets."

"Then work harder. Harder! I won't break. Ah! Lovely! My whimsical brother took refuge in the Nagian infantry. You know what the Joalians think of the Nagian infantry?"

"They think it a useless rabble," Dosh said, panting with effort as he pummeled.

"Exactly! Our cavalry—*my* cavalry I mean . . . They will allow us to play some minor part. Nothing too critical, I am sure. I hope showy. But the infantry is a mob. A peasant's idea of fighting is to throw his spear at his opponent's shield and then charge him with a club. Even Lemodians can massacre Nagians. They always have in the past. Start on my back now. Kammaeman will hurl the Nagians in first to use up the Lemodians' arrows. That's what they're for. Dear Golbfish's chances of surviving his first battle may charitably be defined as, 'remote.' "

He grunted as Dosh's strong hands pressed down on his torso. He had allowed none of his subordinates to bring personal body servants along to the war, and only the very senior Joalians had them. As leader of the cavalry, though, he needed someone to attend to his mount, his weapons, and equipment. And his more personal needs. Dosh was a real joy, in every way.

"The Joalians do not trust you, master," Dosh repeated.

"I am heartbroken," Tarion said drowsily. "I wonder why not?"

"Because two friends are better than one, especially when they are enemies."

Tarion spun over on his back, grabbed a handful of Dosh's hair, and hauled him down. Dosh squealed in surprise and ended leaning on one elbow, nose to nose with his prince and frantically trying not to spill the oil bottle in his other hand.

"What are you implying?" Tarion said menacingly.

He saw none of the fear he had hoped to provoke, only amusement.

"Oh, beloved!" Dosh said in a fake whine of humility. "Who am I to lecture my master on political affairs?"

"Did I ever tell you you had beautiful eyes?"

"I don't think so. You've praised just about every other part of me excessively, but I don't recall you mentioning eyes."

"I do so now only to stress that I should hate to have them put out with red-hot irons. That would spoil your perfection. What were you saying?"

Dosh still showed no alarm. He smiled, as if this bullying were a form of foreplay—which it probably was, Tarion realized.

The beautiful eyes twinkled. "I mean that Thargia would be very happy to see Nagland recover its independence. Thargia is not close enough to be a threat to you in itself. I think you are a man of Nagvale, beloved master."

"My father was a peasant," Tarion agreed. "And then a palace guard, and then royal gigolo." He twisted the boy's hair. "Is this what is said about me—that I would sell out to Thargia?"

"It is what is thought. Nobody says it. Ouch! That hurts!"

"It is meant to. Do you spy on me for the Thargians or the Joalians?"

With his head bent over at a critical angle, Dosh regarded the prince sideways and then said, "Both. Whoever pays me."

"Good. I appreciate honesty and a proper respect for money. Spy all you want, but remember this—while you are mine, you let no other man touch you! Unless I say so, of course."

"Of course not. I have my standards."

Tarion chuckled and released him. Then he put an arm around Dosh's neck and hauled him closer. "I love you, you little monster! When we have overrun a village or two in Themodvale, we shall enjoy the spoils of war. What would you like me to bring you? Girls or boys?"

Dosh's white teeth shone. "Either, as long as they are young and pretty. Like you, I am not fussy."

"I am extremely fussy."

"I am flattered."

From outside the tent flap came the unmistakable sound of a spear being thumped against a shield.

"Curses!" Tarion said, pushing his body servant off his body. "Just when things were starting to become interesting! See what he wants."

Dosh rose, straightened his hair, adjusted his loincloth, and took the oil bottle with him.

Tarion sat up, hearing the Joalian voice outside summoning him to the battlemaster's tent. He had half expected this, and of course he must go. He would be very surprised if his beloved half brother Golbfish was not the first item on the agenda.

The camp was not large enough to justify riding; the two men walked. With the sun now dipping toward Nagwall, the temperature was becoming bearable, but Kolgan Coadjutant set a very leisurely pace. When the second-in-command of the Joalian army came in person to conduct a mere Nagian to a meeting, one could reasonably assume that he had an ulterior motive. Tarion was now Nagian heir designate and Kolgan was an important Joalian politician. They had never spoken in private before.

The camp bustled all around them. Troopleaders were drilling long-shadowed squads on the dusty plain; moas were mewing for their evening meal. Smoke trickled up reluctantly from cooking fires.

"How soon do you expect the final contingents from Joalvale, sir?" Tarion inquired politely.

"In a few days." Kolgan was very tall, and even his armor failed to make him look broad. He had a hatchet face and a reddish beard.

"I hope we shall move out at once. The enemy must know about us by now."

The tall man chuckled. "And the army is eating the heart out of your capital?" Tents ran off in rows for miles, enough to hold five thousand hungry men.

"Certainly. Mother will have to raise taxes to pay for it." On the other hand, the crown's levy on brothels must be paying royally just now.

"Ah. But the queen's health distresses us all. That unpopular task may fall to her successor."

"Or, if Karzon favors our cause," Tarion prompted, "loot from Lemod-vale may solve the problem?" But would the Joalians let the Nagians have a significant share?

"Possibly," Kolgan said vaguely. "Do you know how I got to be where I am, Tarion Cavalryleader?" He glanced down with a meaningful glint in his eye.

"Not in detail," Tarion said diplomatically, "but I have heard how the people's assembly in Joal rejected the Clique's nominee for the position of coadjutant and demanded you instead. Riot was threatened. A great tribute to your reputation, of course."

"A great tribute to graft. I have no military experience to speak of. I had been sponsoring public games on a scale not seen for many years."

The People's Assembly was the ultimate authority in Joal, but it was very expensive to buy. Tarion distrusted candor. Candor was dangerous to both candorer and candoree. "How wonderfully public-spirited of you!"

"I staked everything I possessed and everything I could borrow. Unless I return gloriously victorious and loaded with loot, then I am a ruined man."

"We must trust in the gods and the justice of our cause," Tarion said, wondering what this frankness could possibly be leading up to.

Kolgan's angular face twisted in a grin—or possibly a sneer. It was hard to tell under his helmet. "And you, Prince? How did you come to be where you are?"

Candor was for others. "Mother has long believed that I would make a better king than my poor brother."

"Quite!" Kolgan Coadjutant snapped. "But her Joalian allies have never agreed with that viewpoint. Our distinguished ambassador recently switched his support to you—in direct breach of the Clique's instructions."

"He did," Tarion agreed blandly. The Joalian ambassador was effectively the resident Joalian governor of Nagland, although one did not say so openly. Bondvaan was another devious politician, a human snake.

The commander's tent was in sight now. Kammaeman had appropriated the best campsite, under the only decent shade trees. He was sitting on a stool, still wearing armor and watching his subordinates approach. Beside him sat that very same Bondvaan.

"Three years ago," Kolgan said, "the old man spent five million stars, bribing the Clique to appoint him. I am sure he has made it all back by now."

"In his first ten fortnights here, or so he boasts."

"Well, then!" Kolgan said triumphantly. "Bribery on his scale would be well beyond your means. How did you work it?"

"Mother persuaded him."

This time the sneer was unmistakable. "That is not what I heard. I had hoped we might exchange confidences, Tarion Cavalryleader."

Tarion sighed. "What did you hear?"

"He is a notorious lecher. He hosts orgies of the foulest perversions. What his age makes impossible for him personally now, he stages to watch.

I heard you participated in certain memorable performances at his residence."

Tarion had never found a smile harder. "I am no prude, but I prefer not to be reminded of those nights." Candor!

"Understandably!" The tall man chuckled coarsely. "Great causes require great sacrifices?"

"Yes."

"Do we appreciate each other now? Do you know why I dismissed the messenger and came for you myself?"

Tarion gritted his teeth. "Of course. Kammaeman Battlemaster must be aware of your need for personal glory. A wise Joalian commander never turns his back on his deputy. By arriving with me, you are undermining my reliability in his eyes, and thus hope to enlist me to your side."

Kolgan laughed. "We do understand each other! Let us make an agreement, then. Help me come out on top in this and I shall give you Bondvaan Ambassador's privates on a plate. Interested?"

"Fervently," Tarion said. "Fried."

The guards let the visitors pass. They came to a halt and saluted the man who was at the moment autocrat of Nagland. Kammaeman's word could stop any heart in the vale.

He was close to sixty, a seasoned warrior. He must also be one of the most successful and ruthless politicians in Joal, as he had hung on to his membership in the Clique for more than ten years. The fact that he had dared take command of the army in person and thus absent himself from the city showed how firm his grip must be. He was physically powerful, too. His armor covered his torso and shins, but his bearlike, matted arms and thighs were exposed. Dust and sweat had muddied in the wrinkles in his weathered face and in his beard. His eyes were inflamed by the sun. He nodded at the newcomers without rising or even offering them a seat, although there were stools standing unused at his back.

Beside him—silver-haired, short, and blubbery—Bondvaan Ambassador favored Tarion with a buttery smile that awakened memories to make his skin crawl.

Kammaeman was peering up at him from under grizzled brows thicker than many men's mustaches. Black hairs sprouted from his ears and nostrils.

"Did you enjoy the ceremony today, Cavalryleader?"

Kolgan alone had been bad enough. Tarion braced himself to deal with three of them. "I hope someday to wean my people from ritual scarring, sir. It is a holdover from our barbaric past and contrary to the enlightened civilization that Joal has brought us, for which we are all so grateful. However, the sight of blood excites me, and you certainly cannot doubt the young men's courage."

"I can doubt their sanity. Did you find the conclusion at all surprising?"

"Astonishing!" It would be more truthful to call the conclusion deeply disappointing. Some blood would be more exciting than others. "I never suspected my brother of such patriotism."

Without even looking, Tarion could sense the smirk on Bondvaan's suety face. Oh, he must be pleased! The Joalians still had a second string to their bow in Nag.

"That was not quite what I . . . Ah!" Kammaeman gestured for Tarion and Kolgan to step aside. "Here comes the man I want to see."

Tarion watched with interest as the guards confiscated the new arrival's spear. He was a fairly typical Nagian—black haired, slender, and tall; taller than most. Still bearing his shield, he marched up to the commander and slapped a palm on it in salute. Then he stood stiffly at attention, staring over the commander's helmet. His grotesque face paint made his expression almost unreadable.

Having seen him earlier only at a distance, Tarion had not realized how young he was. He felt a stir of interest. A straight diet of Dosh Houseboy would soon pall. If rank did not suffice, a few coppers would seem like a fortune to such a peasant.

"Your name?" Kammaeman demanded, looking the youth up and down, mostly up.

"D'ward Troopleader, sir."

"And before that?"

"D'ward Roofer."

"From Sonalby?"

"Yes, sir." He had a faint accent that Tarion could not place. He was showing no signs of nervousness, which was exceedingly curious.

"I ordered you to bring your new recruit with you."

The young man did not look down. "With respect, sir, my oath was made to another, who then transferred it to you. I take orders only from you directly."

Kammaeman's face reddened under the dust. His hairy fists clenched.

"If you order me to go and fetch him now, sir," the youth told the tent in the background, "then of course I shall obey."

"That is exceedingly kind of you!"

Tarion detected a suitable moment to win the boy's gratitude. "If I may speak, Battlemaster? Technically he is correct. That is the way things stand at the moment. He cannot be expected to understand proper military procedures."

The youth glanced briefly at the speaker and Tarion saw with astonishment that he had brilliantly blue eyes. How bizarre! How very intriguing!

And why was he not quaking in his shoes—apart from the fact that he was barefoot, of course? This lad must definitely be investigated more closely. Nasty, fat old Bondvaan had obviously had the same idea. He was almost slobbering on his stool.

"I see!" Kammaeman growled, mollified. "Well, I can't have a dozen troopleaders pestering me all day. I have to appoint an overall commander for the Nagian infantry, do I? Someone responsible to me?"

Tarion opened his mouth and then hastily closed it. The question had been directed to the peasant.

"As I understand, sir, there are no precedents. No hordeleader has ever resigned before."

He was not speaking like an ignorant rustic. He was quite right, though, and Kammaeman's proposal was the only possible solution. Tarion had carefully not mentioned the problem earlier, but he was prepared to undertake the additional responsibilities if they were offered. Then he would command the entire Nagian army. He did not say so yet, for Kammaeman was still intent on the youngster.

"What military experience do you have?"

"None, sir."

"Who taught your squad to drill?"

"I did, sir. I asked some of the elders in the village how Joalians made war." He was showing no pride or satisfaction or . . . or anything! He was as impassive as a veteran of innumerable campaigns. His confidence was positively eerie. Tarion wondered if Kammaeman might order him flogged, just on principle. But there was nothing in the boy's manner to indicate insubordination or hidden mockery. He was being completely factual, and his manner carried conviction.

"How long did it take you?"

"Two days, sir, was all I had—I do have a request, sir."

"Yes?"

"I have nothing more to teach them. If you could send us a Joalian instructor, he could further their training."

Kammaeman snorted disbelievingly. "It has been tried before! Nagian warriors insist on fighting in their traditional fashion. They will not listen to a Joalian."

"They will listen if I tell them to, sir."

At Tarion's side, Kolgan Coadjutant chuckled. Kammaeman shot him a glance that silenced him, and then looked back to D'ward. Up to D'ward.

"Give me your oath on that, subject to a flogging if you are wrong."

"I so swear," the boy said at once, still staring over his head.

Tarion felt a stab of alarm. What was going on here? Was the old rogue going to take the word of a raw laborer? He glanced at Kolgan and saw a scowl that mirrored his own feelings exactly.

Kammaeman said, "Kneel."

The boy knelt. That put their eyes on the same level.

"So you can make them march in step," the commander said. "I admit that. I admit that I am surprised by that. But how do you make them remember that spears are for thrusting? In the heat of battle, they will throw their spears away! They always have in the past."

"I was planning to tie the poles to their wrists with leather thongs," D'ward said simply, "to remind them."

"Indeed?" Kammaeman raised those jungly eyebrows. He was obviously impressed. "How long would it take you to train the rest of the Nagian contingents to the same standard you have brought Sonalby's?"

Even the youth looked startled, but he barely hesitated. "I can talk to them this evening, sir. If you will assign a Joalian instructor to each troop in the morning, I will guarantee that they will obey him and do their best."

The battlemaster scratched his beard. "On the same penalty? No, I'll raise the stakes. Make that two floggings."

The boy grinned. "Done!"

"By the five gods, lad, you're either crazy or just insane! Your new recruit? What is he doing now?"

"Digging a latrine ditch, sir."

Tarion exploded. Oh, *joy!* Oh, perfection!

Kammaeman shot him a disapproving glare, but he was having trouble hiding his own amusement. "Why that?"

The boy seemed surprised, as if the answer were obvious. "I told him that was the worst job I could give him. Once he has done that, then he has nothing more to fear."

The Joalians exchanged glances. Old Bondvaan ran soft fingers through his skimpy silver hair. Kolgan was chewing his lip thoughtfully. Kammaeman seemed to be at a loss. "Did your group accept him?"

"Yes, sir."

"Oh? What did you tell them?"

"I said we were very honored to have the prince enlist with us. That they need not show him any special favor, but they should try to be patient with him, because he has had a deprived upbringing and has everything to learn about true manhood."

This time even the commander grinned. He turned to Kolgan.

"Well, Coadjutant? Do we have a native military genius here?"

"He appears to have flair, sir."

"Stand up!" Kammaeman said, heaving himself to his feet. Even in his boots and helmet, he was shorter than the boy, but twice as wide. "Take good care of him!"

"Yes, sir."

"We don't want him to have any accidents—do we, Cavalryleader?" He favored Tarion with a threatening glare.

"I hope my brother survives to dig many, many latrine ditches, sir," Tarion said crossly. If the Nagian rabble was to be turned into an effective fighting force, he could no longer count on Golbfish dying in the customary massacre. How annoying!

Kammaeman thrust out a hairy arm and grasped the youth's brown shoulder.

"I shall make you a wager! D'ward Troopleader, I appoint you acting commander of the Nagian infantry. Any instructors you need, just ask this man. His name is Kolgan Coadjutant. Three days from now, you will parade your horde for me. I shall then either confirm your appointment or have you beaten to jelly. Do you accept those terms?"

"Yes, sir," the youth said calmly. "Thank you, sir."

"My pleasure! Dismissed."

With a smart salute, the new troopleader spun around and marched away. The guards gave him back his spear.

Kammaeman watched him go and then turned to his deputy with the sleepy content of a bearcat that has just eaten a band of hunters. "You are dismissed also. Give him the best men you can, all the help you can. You two gentlemen wait a moment."

Kolgan flickered anger, but he saluted and marched away.

Tarion moved forward. Bondvaan rose, looking completely perplexed. Tarion hoped his own face did not show his fury. That young upstart was doomed!

"You two gentlemen," Kammaeman repeated as soon as Kolgan was out of earshot, "were both making slobbering spectacles of yourself. Keep your filthy habits to yourselves, do you understand? Leave D'ward alone!"

"Sir!" Tarion protested. "I don't underst—"

"You understand perfectly! He is not to be molested in any way. *Any* way! I think I may have found a secret weapon in this war."

Tarion decided he had better make some new plans.

His FIRST FEW DAYS IN THE INFANTRY WERE CONTINUOUS TORMENT for Golbfish. Going without shoes, he shredded the soles of his feet; his skin blistered in the sun; his ritual cut suppurated. The sheer physical exertion was worse than all of those. He dug ditches, he marched, he ran. Every muscle in his carcass throbbed and ached. He fainted and was kicked awake and told to stop slacking. Time and again he came to the breaking point, when even death seemed preferable to this unending torture.

But whenever that happened, by some curious coincidence, he would look up to see a pair of steady blue eyes watching him. He would hear a few words of encouragement and recall that this youth had saved him in the temple at no small risk to himself. Somehow, then, Golbfish would find the strength to struggle on a little longer. He owed it to D'ward, who had trusted him.

He fully expected one of Tarion's assassins to come calling on him with a thin dagger, but that never happened. He awoke every morning, never quite sure whether to be surprised or disappointed. And by the fifth or sixth day, he realized that he was going to live through this and be a warrior. Even more astonishing, he came to understand that his rough companions were sympathetic to his sufferings and approved of his efforts. Then a thin sliver of pride began to glow in the darkness.

Just when he had begun to cope with life in camp, the army moved out, almost seven thousand strong. About a quarter were Nagians, a thousand on foot and eight hundred riding moas. Their road took them east, past Sonalby, and then south into the wilds of Siopass. For three days they made a cautious ascent of the winding valley, through dripping forest and along stony watercourses. The march brought Golbfish new impossibilities of fatigue and hardship.

It also brought danger, for every military campaign in the Vales inevitably began with a contested pass. The Lemodians could not but know that the combined might of Joalland and Nagland was coming against them. Already they must have reinforced their defenses and called for help from their fearsome Thargian masters. There were very few places where an army could cross the ranges.

Fortunately, there had not been time for Tharg's assistance to arrive. The battle was fought long before the Nagian contingent reached the summit. Word was sent back down the line that the pass was cleared and Lemodvale lay open before the invaders. Then the warriors cheered and sang songs as they marched. Golbfish saw the bodies as he stumbled past, but he was not involved in the fighting. He had no breath for singing, and he did not know the words of those songs anyway.

Thereafter the road led downward and the pace quickened. Two days later, the army camped by a shallow lake in the foothills of Lemodslope. The talk now was all of conquest and the joys of loot. The warriors assured one another that Lemodian girls were famous for their beauty.

Eventually the Sonalby troop received its turn to bathe in the now very muddy lake. The warriors stashed their arms, but did not bother to strip. They charged into the water with whoops and set about making it even muddier. Golbfish avoided the horseplay, but he enjoyed the soak and the chance to reduce his personal population of vermin. What small things could please him now!

He limped out to dry off in the sun. A gangly young man was sitting on the grass, leaning his head and arms on his bony knees, his bright blue eyes watching Golbfish with amusement. He must have been in the water also, for his hair and beard were wet.

"Congratulations, warrior!" he said. "You've done it, haven't you?"

"I think you deserve most of the credit, sir." One thing Golbfish had certainly learned, and that was humility. He knew he could not have managed without D'ward's help and inspiration.

"Nonsense! Sit down here and relax a minute. I said I could show you how, but you did it." D'ward chuckled, shaking his head at Golbfish's tattered appearance. "You just need to grow a new skin and you'll be done. How do you feel?"

Golbfish considered the question. It seemed like centuries since he had held a real conversation with anyone—meaning anyone with intelligence. "Surprised, mostly."

"But proud?"

"Yes," the new warrior confessed. "I wouldn't have believed that a fortnight ago—but, yes."

"You should be proud. Even the men are proud of you, you know! They were laying bets on how long you'd last. Nobody won—or rather you won! They admire courage. Anything you need?"

Golbfish smiled, and it was a long time since he'd done that, too. "Ymma or Uthinima or Osmialth."

The blue eyes blinked. "Who?"

"My concubines."

D'ward laughed. "You are better, aren't you! Sorry, I can't help there. Well, I just thought I'd congratulate you and tell you how much I admire what you've achieved. It would have broken most men. Well done!"

He moved as if about to rise.

"Sir?"

The hordeleader settled back with a wary look. "Yes?"

"May I ask . . . No. May I make an observation?"

"Observe away."

Golbfish turned his head to watch the splashing mob in the lake. "This is impertinent and rash of me, but I have overheard enough to know that you are not a native of Sonalby."

There was no reaction, just a terrible stillness that was more eloquent than a scream or a string of oaths.

"Sir! . . . I am sorry. . . ."

"I'm not originally from Sonalby, no," D'ward said, very quietly. "The Joalians don't know that, though. At least, I didn't tell them, and I don't think they know. Carry on."

"No. I should not have—"

"Carry on!"

"Sir!" Why had he been such a fool as to bring this up? "You arrived there in early summer. I suspect it was soon after the seven hundredth Festival of Tion, in Suss."

There was a long pause, and then the young man said, "Who says so?"

"Nobody. I worked it out. Very few of the lads can read. If they have ever heard of the *Filoby Testament,* they certainly know none of the details."

D'ward sighed. "But you do, of course. What details do you have in mind?"

"Oh . . . just that it implies the Liberator will be born then, but that isn't what it actually says. It actually says that he will come into the world naked and crying. Not quite the same thing!"

The piercing blue eyes raked the prince's face, then suddenly began to twinkle. "How else does one come into the world?" D'ward demanded with a grin that washed away the guilt and tension.

"Well . . ." Golbfish felt a twinge of nostalgia, remembering table talk in Joal, the long philosophical debates when every word must be combed for subtleties of meaning. He gazed for a moment at the peasants roistering in the water. "Those who enter convents or monasteries are said to leave the world. So I suppose a man who was, say, evicted from a monastery might be said to enter the world again?"

"You believe that is what is meant?"

"Perhaps. Or there may be an arcane meaning. Other references suggest that the Liberator is something other than a normal man."

"Are you trying to blackmail me?"

Golbfish looked around in horror, momentarily speechless. Even worse than the suggestion itself was the realization that a fortnight ago he probably would have been thinking that way. *"You?* When I owe you my life?"

His companion smiled again. "Sorry! I must have been consorting with that blackguard brother of yours too much. You don't really owe me anything, you know—but carry on."

"Nothing! I wish I hadn't mentioned it."

"Have you discussed this with anyone else?"

"No, sir! Sir . . . you can trust me!" Golbfish was suddenly seized with a need to weep. Why had he ever blabbed all this out?

"You are implying that I am something other than a mortal man?"

"I think you have powers that others do not."

D'ward said, "Damn!" and studied his toes.

"Are you a god?" Golbfish asked nervously.

"I'm definitely human. I am probably the man mentioned in the *Testament,* though. Shrewd of you to work that out." He sighed. "I don't know if I shall ever be the Liberator. I have no ambitions to be any sort of liberator. I just want to go home! Will you keep this to yourself, please?"

"Of course. I swear it."

Obviously D'ward did not want to talk about the prophecies, which was a pity, because Golbfish did. The *Filoby Testament* never mentioned Nagland, so he had never paid much heed to it. It did mention a prince. About half the Vales were monarchies, so there must be many princes around, but he and Tarion were certainly the only princes available at the moment.

The blue eyes were smiling again, and D'ward unrolled, stretching his bony form out on the grass. "I trust you! So let me ask you something. The day I arrived in Sonalby, I saw a family murdered by a mob."

Golbfish shuddered. "Led by Karzon's priests? It happened all over the vale."

"Because they were heretics?"

"Yes. We didn't have very many in Nagland, but the Man decreed that they must be stamped out."

D'ward raised his head and frowned at the troops in the water. "I think we'll have company in a moment. The Church of the Undivided? Tell me about that."

"It's a new faith," Golbfish said hastily, racking his brains for the little he knew about it. "Where it started, or when, I don't know. It's fairly widespread in Randorland. It may be cropping up in other vales too—I have no idea. It preaches a new god, a single god. That sounds like Visek, but it isn't. All gods are the Five and the Five are the Parent, you know? But this god is none of them. His followers claim that he is the only true god, and all the others are . . ."

"Yes?"

"Demons," Golbfish said reluctantly. It was a heresy almost too foul to repeat. Why in the world was D'ward interested in that obscure sect of deluded fanatics?

"Has he a name, do you know, this new god?"

"Apparently not." Vague memories of drunken dinner conversation stirred. "If he has, it is too holy to be spoken. And his followers do not pray to him directly."

D'ward grunted. "This is very interesting! What are his teachings, his commands to the faithful?"

"I really don't know, sir! I wish I could be of more help! They wear a gold earring in the left ear."

D'ward turned his head and stared. "Even the men? And only one ear?"

"Apparently."

"Peculiar! That must make them very conspicuous. It will be dangerous, if they are being persecuted. Or is that the whole idea?" he added thought-fully.

"Perhaps not all of them do," Golbfish suggested. He had always taken the gods for granted. Philosophy was interesting, but religion he had left to the priests.

"Perhaps not," D'ward agreed. He sat up as a mob of wet warriors emerged from the lake, eager to greet their former friend, now elevated to giddily high rank. "One last question. Quickly! If I wanted to find this church, where should I look?"

"Randorvale, I suppose," Golbfish said. "But we're going the wrong way."

23

"WHITE TABLECLOTHS!" EDWARD SAID IN A TONE OF WONDER. "SIL-ver cutlery! Civilization!"

Outside the dining car window, the Thames valley rushed by in a blur of hedgerows and hamlets, evening sun on woodlands and church spires. Even in the mere ten years of Alice's experience, rural England had changed, although much less than the cities, where the inrush of motor vehicles and power lines was more visible. Out here the plodding horses still hauled mountainous hay wagons, but lorries and omnibuses were pro-liferating on the country lanes. Tradition was a personal thing, she supposed. The landscapes Constable had painted had long since been blighted by railway lines and then telegraph wires.

The carriage swayed in hurried rhythm. *Clickety-click,* said the wheels, *clickety-click, clickety-click* . . .

"I think I'll try the Scotch broth," she said. "How long since you saw tablecloths?"

"Ages. We had them at Olympus, but I didn't stay there very long."

He had been attempting to turn the conversation away from his adven-tures, inquiring about her life in wartime London. She kept steering him back to Nextdoor. Even then, he would obviously rather talk about Olym-pus than relate his experiences as a warlord. She was curious to know why. Either he had something to be very proud of and was being typically modest about it, or he had done something shameful. Which?

Was he concerned that she would think he had gone native? Julian and Ginger had both been shocked by the little they had heard, although neither had said so. In their view, the code of the English sahib did not include self-mutilation and spear-throwing. Having spent much of her childhood playing in the dust of an Embu compound, Alice had few such prejudices. As far as she could see, Edward had had no choice. Marooned on another world, he could hardly have appealed to the British Consul.

"The lamb may be safest," she said. "Railway food is not what it was before the war. Tarion sounds like an interesting character."

Edward snorted. "He has charm, when he bothers to use it. He's a superb athlete and tough as an anvil. That about sums up his good points, I'd say."

"How about his bad points?"

"Please! That would take all night. I swear the man has not one trace of morals or ethics or scruples. Nothing is beneath him, absolutely nothing!"

"He tried to bribe you, I suppose?"

Edward looked up from the menu again and rolled his eyes. "Dozens of times. You can't imagine some of the offers he made me!"

Alice thought she could, but she knew he would not mention them in the presence of a lady.

She wondered just what it would take to bribe her idealistic cousin into doing something he felt was wrong. The Imperial Crown Jewels, perhaps, as a start? Edward had no family responsibilities; he was young enough to have few needs beyond his daily bread. He had been taught to believe that honesty and willingness to work would suffice to carry him through life. Vast estates would just seem a burden to him, and his education had armored him against depravity. He probably still took a cold bath every morning. He would be true to King and Country, decency and fair play—and seek nothing else. His education had been designed to turn out incorruptible administrators, the men who ran the Empire. Even Edward Exeter might slip in a year or two, when idealism faded in the light of experience, but at the moment he was as close to incorruptible as any mortal could be. The Tarion man must have been very puzzled by the response to his offers.

Where Tarion had failed, how could Alice Prescott succeed?

Whatever had happened to her patriotism all of a sudden? She recalled the recruiting posters of the early months of the war, before conscription: THE WOMEN OF BRITAIN SAY "GO!" She had been horrified when D'Arcy enlisted, and yet proud of him. Like everyone else, she knew the war must be fought and must be won—she just did not think that it was Edward's war. He had been called to other duties. The very laws of nature seemed to bend around him. But if she could not justify this feeling even to herself, how could she ever convince him? What would it take to change his mind?

"You declined, of course?"

"Alice, darling! What do you think I— Don't answer that! Of course I did. Even if he'd come up with anything really tempting, Tarion's promises are mere wind and always will be."

"Did you tell him so?"

"Of course. He would just laugh and agree. In a day or two he would try me again."

Edward smirked. He knew what she was thinking. He knew he was good. Well, she could deflate him. She could still make him blush.

"You're young and winsome," she mused. "I assume he also made indecent advances?"

He blushed an unbelievable scarlet. "How did you guess?"

"From things you didn't say. Golbfish was no pillar of virtue either, I gather."

"Not by our standards," Edward said primly. "But he was merely debauched, whereas Tarion was depraved. There was a real man inside Golbfish's blubber. He'd just never had reason to call that man out before."

> *"Not for the sake of a ribboned coat,*
> *Or the selfish hope of a season's fame,*
> *But his Captain's hand on his shoulder—"*

"Oh, cut it out!" Edward said testily.

"So you turned a frog into a prince? And then—"

The waiter appeared beside them as if condensing out of the air. They ordered dinner. Up ahead, the engine came into view, snaking around a curve, smoke pouring from its funnel. Some poor devil of a fireman was shoveling his heart out there. The dining car rocked unevenly as it reached the bend.

They sat for a while in silence, Alice reviewing a mental list of things she should be asking. Talking was difficult in the crowded train; when they arrived at Greyfriars they would have Julian for company again, possibly Ginger, and also the formidable Mrs. Bodgley. Mrs. Bodgley would probably demand Edward's story from the beginning. She would certainly want an account of what had happened to her son. Alice must put this brief dining-car privacy to good use.

The waiter slid soup plates in front of them and departed.

"This is not bad at all!" Edward announced.

"But look at this awful wartime bread!"

Everything went black.

"Don't eat it!" he said over the racket. "It makes you go blind." The acrid reek of coal began to foul the air. Then the train burst out of the tunnel, gradually shedding its cocoon of smoke.

"You are still the idiot I used to know," Alice said affectionately. "Tell me. You want to get in touch with the Service? You said you had three ways in mind."

Edward nodded glumly. "They're all very flimsy leads, though. One of them is that letter I asked Ginger to post for me. Do you remember Mr. Oldcastle?"

"I remember you talking about him."

"He wrote to me just after—after the news." His bony face seemed to grow even thinner for a moment, remembering the bad times, when Cameron and Rona Exeter had died in the Nyagatha massacre. "Claimed to be with the Colonial Office. He wasn't, of course. He was with Head Office."

Alice had known only that Oldcastle had been an absentee father to Edward. In retrospect, he had been too good to be true. His Majesty's Government would never take so much interest in the orphaned son of a very minor official.

"When you disappeared, I wrote to Mr. Oldcastle."

Edward grinned, popping a crust in his mouth. "What address?"

"I tried Whitehall, and I tried the one Ginger had, at the school."

"Whitehall had never heard of him and the GPO had never heard of Druids Close?"

"Right on."

"There is no Druids Close. There was no Mr. Oldcastle. He was a committee, or so Creighton told me, although he always wrote back in the same hand. Head Office were keeping an eye on me, you see, as a favor for the Service. The Blighters were after me then, too."

Clickety-click, clickety-click, clickety-click . . .

"So if Oldcastle doesn't exist, how do you get in touch with him now?"

"I do what I always did—I write him a letter! I already have, and Ginger will have posted it by now."

"I thought Julian had already tried this for you?"

Obviously she had been expected to ask that.

"Ah! But this one has my handwriting on the envelope, which may be important, and it's going in the right box." Edward smirked like a schoolboy demonstrating his first card trick. "I know a little more about magic now, you see. It would take a great deal of mana to bewitch the entire postal service, but not much to do one pillar-box."

"That is certainly logical."

"And as soon as I worked that out, I remembered several times when Mr. Oldcastle warned me that he would be away—at about the same times I was going to be away from Fallow! So any postcards or letters I sent him, from anywhere else, might reasonably not get answered! Simple, isn't it?"

"And you think the magic is still on that box?"

"Well . . ." He frowned. "I have no idea. It may not be. I warned you all these ideas were dishwaterish."

"Let's hear the next one."

"The next one is even dicier. The, er, man who rescued me from the hospital was a numen. He used to go by the name of Robin Goodfellow, a fairish time ago."

Blue eyes studied Alice solemnly, waiting for her disbelief. The waiter removed the soup plates and served the roast lamb.

"*Puck*?"

"The same. One of them. A local representative of the old firm, was how Creighton put it. Forgotten now, and ignored, but still residing on his node, amid the bracken and brambles and the standing stones—husbanding scraps of the mana he received back in Saxon times or the Middle Ages, when people still believed in the People of the Hills."

Gods on a storybook world were one thing. In modern England they took more believing. "What was he like?"

"Nice enough old boy. At least, he was nice to me. Mad as a rabid bat, really, I think. He can't have had anyone to speak to in centuries."

"He's with this Head Office bunch?"

"He's a neutral, but he must know how to find them."

"And where do you find him?"

Edward shrugged, struggling to cut an extra tough slab of mutton. "Not sure exactly. I was half out of my skull with pain that morning, but not far from Greyfriars, on a little hill. I'll know it when I see it."

This sounded even weaker than the first idea. It would take time and transportation to inspect all the hilltops around Greyfriars. The police must be after Edward Exeter now. The ominous Blighters might be. Looking at him, it was hard to believe that he was twenty-one and a man of two worlds. She felt a motherly obligation to dispatch her hopelessly idealistic young cousin off to Nextdoor as fast as possible, whether he wanted to go or not. Details to be arranged.

"Will Puck help you again?"

"I can only ask. He's a stranger here, of course. Originally from Nextdoor. From Ruatvil, in Sussland. I could sacrifice a bullock, perhaps."

He was being remarkably generous with her money.

"A bullock? You'll get thrown in jail if you waste food like that, these days. There's a war on, my lad!"

"Oh. Well, I shall think of something."

"Tell me the third lead." Alice forked up some well-named string beans.

"I think I still remember the key I used with Creighton, the ritual. Anyone who goes to the same portal and does that dance will arrive at the Sacrarium—that's the ruined temple in Sussvale." He gave up on the mutton and poked angrily at a soggy potato. "But that's a fair way from Olympus, and who could I ask to risk it? Arriving naked, not knowing the language?"

"You'd have to go yourself!" Now they were making progress!

He must have sensed her approval, because he scowled. "No. It would take too long, and I'd have to find my way back here all over again."

"It would only be a flying visit, surely? There and back." Another three years and the war would be long over.

"I don't trust the Service! They wouldn't let me come Home before, and they might try to hold me again. You think Smedley really wants to cross over?" he added hopefully.

"I don't know. I don't know if he knows. He's pretty badly shaken, Edward. Don't think any the worse of him for that! He's got enough medals to start a pawn shop and lots of fellows have been—"

"Shell-shocked. Yes, I know. I saw some of them, remember." Again he hacked angrily at the meat. "Smedley's a brick, I don't doubt it. But I can't send him over alone, not knowing the language. I damned nearly died myself, and I would have done if I hadn't had Eleal to help me."

"Suppose none of these plans work?"

"Then I can't warn the Service about the traitor, that's all."

"So you just stay here and enlist?"

"Enlist or hang. Or both."

"Where is this portal you mentioned?"

"Stonehenge." Edward peered out the window. "What town is this we're coming to? Swindon already?"

Alice laid down her knife and fork. "Edward, Stonehenge is on Salisbury Plain."

"Of course I know. . . . Why? Why does that matter?"

"The Army has taken over all of Salisbury Plain now. There's an aerodrome at Stonehenge itself. There's even talk of knocking down the stones because they're a danger to planes landing and taking off, it's so close."

He stared at her in frank dismay.

Clickety-click, clickety-click, clickety-click . . .

"You were counting on that one, weren't you?" she said. "Stonehenge was your trump card?"

"Final stand, more like."

"You won't get near it," she said.

"After the war?"

"Perhaps after the war, whenever that is."

He pushed the remains of the meal to one side of his plate and laid down his knife and fork. "Damn!"

Damn indeed!

Then he grinned. "So I can't go back! Clear conscience. Good!"

"Do you wish to try the sweet, madam?" the waiter inquired. "Dundee pudding and custard?"

"Cheese and biscuits, please," Alice said, suppressing a shudder, "and coffee."

"The same for me," Edward said, not even looking up.

Waiter and plates disappeared.

Edward poked at some crumbs. "Let's just hope the letter works."

"Yes."

"And let's hope that the Blighters don't get it instead."

"What! Is that possible?"

He smiled bleakly. "Definitely possible. Head Office suffered a major defeat. I don't know what their English equivalent of Olympus is, but it may have fallen to the enemy since I was a kid. If that's the case, then I just wrote to the enemy, saying where I am."

"Oh."

"I should have warned you."

Disbelief swirled around her like a sudden squall. Two days ago Ginger Jones had walked into her life and now she was a character in a John Buchan thriller. *The Black Stone is after you! Flee, for all is lost. . . .*

"In fact," Edward said sternly, "I should never have let you come. You had better catch the first train back to town."

"Not Pygmalion likely!" Alice said. "Tell me more about your experiences as Chief of the Headhunters."

He frowned.

"Sorry," she said. "That was a cheap shot. So what happened when the old queen died? Who got the crown? The reformed Golbfish or the unrepentant Tarion?"

Edward sighed and turned to look out the window.

"The news arrived early one morning, just after we reached Lemodvale, before we got trapped. Old Kammaeman called me in to ask my opinion—which brother should he send back? I couldn't help feeling flattered, although I knew it was nothing to do with me personally, just my charisma at work. I told him any man who trusted Tarion ought to be chained in a padded cell."

She could guess what was coming from his disgusted expression.

"But by then it was too late?"

Edward looked up with rueful surprise, spoon poised. "Right on! Tarion had taken his Nagian cavalry and gone. Deserted in the middle of a war!"

She sipped coffee. "You expected better of him?"

He tried to laugh and swallow at the same time, and shook his head. "No! It was perfectly in character. He got the news even before Kammaeman did, so he must have bribed somebody somewhere. Personally, I was glad to see the back of him, but it left us seriously short of cavalry. Moas are one-man beasts. They fix on one owner when they're only chicks—calves I mean, I suppose. They're closer to mammals than birds. English doesn't have the right words. Anyway, it takes fortn—months, that is, to imprint one to a new rider. The Joalians hadn't been able to bring very many over Thordpass—it's too high—so they'd been depending on Tarion's troop. He upped and left, and that put us in the soup."

24

"WAKE UP, BEAUTIFUL," SAID A WHISPER.

Dosh jumped, feeling a hand over his mouth. "Mmmph?" The hand was removed. He could see nothing except a faint hint of moonlight under the flap of the tent. He was lying on his sleeping rug, and the ground below it was hard and stony. He heard the voice again, very close to his ear.

"Awake?"

"Yes, master."

"Good. Keep your voice down. It is time to play a little game."

"Again?" The man was insatiable! "How long have we slept?"

"I have not slept at all, and this is another sort of game. We begin by tying you up."

Dosh's heart made a mighty leap and began racing all around his chest, looking for a way out. "No, master! Please! I have had some very unpleasant experiences with those sort of—"

Tarion's strong hand pushed a cloth into his mouth, and Dosh's protests subsided into whimpers. It was the rag he used for cleaning the master's saddle. He did not resist as rope was wrapped around his ankles, harsh fibers biting into his skin. Tarion had never bound him before and had never really hurt him—not too much—but he was capable of anything. There were bloodcurdling tales of orgies at Bondvaan Ambassador's house. . . .

"Roll over!"

Dosh rolled over on his belly and put his wrists together. As the rope tightened about them and then was pulled tighter and even tighter, he said, *"Mmmph!"* urgently through the gag. It did no good. Then his elbows were lashed together also, and finally his knees. *Holy Tion, preserve me!*

For a moment nothing more happened. He lay in the dark and sweated, while his imagination rioted with macabre thoughts of what Tarion might be going to do to him. If it took very long his hands would fall off.

It started—Tarion flipped him over, so he lay awkwardly on his bound arms. There was a sharp rock under his shoulders. To make matters worse, the prince lay down also and leaned one arm heavily on Dosh's chest. Something cold caressed his neck.

"That is my dagger you can feel, lover," Tarion said softly, a few inches above Dosh's nose. "I'll take the gag out, but if you make any noise, I shall cut your throat while the second word is still in it. Understand?"

The cloth was removed. Dosh gulped and tried to work the taste away. "Yes, master," he whispered.

"Good. Now listen carefully. I must leave. My dear mother has been called to take her place in the heavens, among the shining blessed."

"I am sorry, master."

"You needn't be—I'm not. It is Thighday already and she died on Ankleday, so our beloved battlemaster should receive the news before nightfall. I prefer to depart before he does, just in case he makes the wrong decision."

"But how—"

Dosh felt Tarion's chuckle more than he heard it.

"Just say I have a premonition. I am quite confident that she died on Ankleday. A monarchy should not be left without a monarch any longer than absolutely necessary. And I cannot take you with me, dear boy, much as I long to, because you have no moa and we shall be going very fast. So what am I to do with you, *mm?*"

Dosh managed a small moan, but his throat seemed to have closed up completely.

A wet tongue touched his nose. "I love you so much," said the dread, mocking whisper close above him, "that I can hardly bear the thought of leaving you to another master. But we have had such good times together that it does seem unkind to put you to sleep. Do you wish to express an opinion on the matter?"

Dosh believed. He knew the prince was quite capable of killing him here, now, on the tent floor, in cold blood, with a single slash of his dagger. "I love you!" His voice quavered.

"And I love you, too, darling. I considered just cutting your beautiful throat while you were asleep, but there is something I am curious to learn, most curious to learn. Men always tell the truth on their deathbeds, did you know that? And wise men tell the truth to avoid deathbeds. So you tell me now, lover: Who are you spying for?"

"I've told you before! Anyone who pays me."

"My, you are sweating, aren't you? I have known you sweat often enough, dear one, but never quite like this. So you do understand that I am going to kill you if you continue lying to me? Last chance, Dosh House-boy. Who are you spying for?"

Dosh tried to speak and discovered he was weeping. Sobbing was not easy with so much of Tarion's weight resting on his chest. "Nobody."

"Oh, now that is absurd! Really silly. Everybody spies for somebody. The day I hired you, you hid two stars and some small change under the

Niolian vase in my bedroom. You now have five stars in the bottom of my brush case. Three stars in seven fortnights? That isn't nearly enough for a clever sneak like you to earn by tattling. You probably made that much selling your pretty body around the palace guard, but you'd have gained far more if you were peddling information about me to anyone local. So you're spying for some outsider. Who?"

"I love you," Dosh whimpered. "I don't tell anyone anything!"

A sudden searing pain at his throat and he thought he had died. . . .

"That's just a flesh wound," Tarion said. "At least, I think it is. It's hard to tell in the dark. I may overdo it next time. You still alive?"

"Yes."

"Good. This is taking too long. Somebody sent you to Nag to worm your way into my service and spy on me. You were not exactly subtle in your approach, I'm afraid. You claimed to be a Narshian, but you're not. Now I shall put the gag back and rip your guts open and you will die very nastily—unless you tell me who it was that sent you."

Trouble was, Dosh knew he could not answer that question. He was not spying on Tarion at all, only on the Liberator, but he could not explain that either.

He was dragged out of the tent in the bitter light of dawn. He should have been ashamed of his nudity, his tears, the dried blood on him, but the pain in his limbs drowned out everything else. His legs would not support him, and when he was brought before Kammaeman Battlemaster, he collapsed in a sniveling heap.

"Oh, sewage!" said the general. "That will be all, Captain. You may go."

The tent flap closed. There were two other men there, and they stayed. Through the blur of his tears, Dosh recognized Kolgan Coadjutant by his great height. The other was wearing face paint and a loincloth and was almost certainly the Liberator.

"All right, scum," Kammaeman said. "Talk! When did he leave?"

Dosh's mouth was a foul desert, still tasting of the oily rag that had spent so many hours in it, but he managed to croak, "Middle of the night, sir. I don't know the hour."

"Who brought him the news?"

Normally Dosh would lie in response to such a question or demand money for an answer—or both, but he was too weak to maintain a good fiction, and his hatred of Tarion maddened him.

"I don't think anyone did. He said the queen died on Ankleday, as if it had been arranged."

The Joalian grunted. "That's entirely possible, I suppose. Coadjutant?"

"I agree."

"Hordeleader?"

"I'd believe anything of that one, sir."

Yes, it was the Liberator. Not that anyone but Dosh knew that D'ward was the prophesied Liberator, of course.

Kammaeman growled angrily. "If we believe this wretch, then they've got too good a start for us ever to catch them. Hordeleader, send for the other one."

The tent flap lifted, and the Liberator said something to someone outside. Then he returned. He came over to Dosh and offered him a water bottle. Seeing that Dosh's hands were not functioning yet, he went down on one knee and held it to his lips so he could drink. Water went everywhere, but some found its way down into the desert. Bliss!

"I'm not sorry to be rid of the royal bastard," Kolgan muttered, "but we can ill afford to lose the mounts. It leaves us too damnably short."

Kammaeman grunted agreement. "But it'll be much worse if I detach a troop to follow him." The Joalians moved away, to sit on the stools at the other end of the tent.

The Liberator was peering at Dosh's face. "Why did he cut you up like that?"

"Just his idea of fun, sir," Dosh mumbled, hoping nobody put a mirror near him. He did not want to know how bad it was. The slashes on his throat wouldn't matter, but Tarion had done things to his cheeks and forehead, and close to his eyes.

"Mm?" the Liberator said quietly. His paint wrinkled. "Did you tell him what he wanted to know?"

Startled, Dosh shook his head. He had tried to! He had tried desperately, but his real master had made that impossible. His real master could not be named. It was hard for Dosh even to think his name.

Of course the Liberator did not know that, and he misunderstood. "Good for you!" he murmured. "Amazing he didn't just kill you, then."

That was certainly true! Dosh shuddered at the memory and could not speak.

"There's a surgeon's apprentice in the Rareby troop. He could stitch those slashes so they don't scar so badly."

Astonished, Dosh said, "I'd be very grateful, sir."

The Liberator chuckled drily. "After all, your looks are your stock in trade, aren't they?" He stood up and walked over to the others.

Who was he to sneer? A warrior sold his body too, and in worse ways. Beauty was a talent like strength or courage. If the gods blessed a man with those, he was expected to use them to benefit himself and other people, was he not? Then why not the same with beauty?

What chance had Dosh ever had, an abandoned Tinkerfolk brat? His own people had thrown him out. His body was all he'd ever had to offer. It had needed to be fed, just like any other. He had served women just as willingly as men—more so, actually, because they were less dangerous—but he had never found a woman with the money and the freedom to offer him long-term employment.

For a few minutes the soldiers talked tactics and battle plans, while Dosh brooded, wondering what was going to happen to him now. He had been wondering that for hours, ever since Tarion had given up and left him. When he had decided that he was not going to bleed to death, he had concluded that he would probably be lucky if the Joalians just ran him out of camp at spearpoint. Then the Lemodians would kill him. He hardly cared anymore. He was desolated by the thought that he had failed his master, his real master. The pain in his hands was a sickening throb. He stayed where he was, keeping very still, hoping to hear something of importance.

Then the other prince was ushered in, gasping and coughing from running. His face paint was patchy, as if he had been interrupted during his morning touch-up. Nevertheless, even Tarion had conceded that the fat man was far more convincing as a warrior now than he had been in Nag. He was still just as fat, though.

Kammaeman informed him that the queen was dead. Golbfish expressed suitable regrets, but he was probably even less upset than his half brother had been. No one had ever described old Emchainne as likable, and she had conspired to have this son murdered in front of her eyes.

"So either you or Tarion must be recognized as her successor," Kammaeman announced, belaboring the obvious. "As he has betrayed our trust, you are our choice. Even if he hadn't, of course! I mean, we had already decided that. Long live the king!"

"Thank you, Battlemaster," the blubber-man said. "Joalia will find that her trust in me is not misplaced."

Kolgan chuckled in the background. "There may be some delay in arranging your coronation, though."

"Yes," Kammaeman said. "First we shall have to hang your brother. However, you have my word. As soon as we return to Nag, he is a dead man, and you shall have the throne."

"I am very grateful, sir."

"I suppose we had better have him proclaimed in the camp?" Kolgan said.

"I suppose so." Kammaeman sounded displeased.

There was a pause, then Golbfish said, "That will present difficulties. I shall automatically become hordeleader." He even sounded like a prince now. How extraordinary!

"You are welcome to it," the Liberator said.

"But I swore before the goddess that I would fight in the ranks."

Dosh looked up in amazement, and saw that the two Joalians were equally at a loss. As for the Liberator . . . Face paint tended to mask expressions, but his jaw was hanging down.

Then everyone spoke at once: "That is not necessary!". . . "Do I understand that you wish to remain a simple warrior?". . . "It does you great honor!"

Golbfish shrugged. "If you will permit it, Battlemaster, that is what I request. I wish to fulfill my oath. When we return to Nagland, then I shall be free to assume my new duties."

"By the five gods!" Kammaeman exploded. "I confess I did not expect this of you . . . Your Majesty."

"It is gravely out of character, I agree," the fat man said, and chuckled. For a brief instant that chuckle made him their equal, or even their superior, and they responded with smiles and laughter. Then he sank back into his humble warrior role. "But my people will approve. Lately I have been studying leadership, under a remarkable teacher. Do I have your permission to withdraw?"

He must have been given a nod of consent, for he went strutting out, stalking past Dosh without even a glance of distaste.

"Miracle!" the battlemaster said. "May the gods be praised! D'ward, what have you done to him?"

"Me? Nothing! Nothing at all!"

"Somebody made a man of him!"

"Well it certainly wasn't me!" Kolgan said, laughing.

They all stood up. Then, of course, they remembered Dosh.

"Yuuch!" Kammaeman said. "What do we do with this dreg? Either of you gentleman need a catamite?"

"Throw him out and let the Lemodians have him," Kolgan suggested, looking down from his enormous height. His red beard twisted in an expression of extreme contempt. "He can only tend to corrupt the camp if he is allowed to stay. I despise such degenerates."

That was hardly honest, Dosh thought, considering that Kolgan had borrowed Tarion's houseboy twice since leaving Nag, for massage and other purposes. He was a stingy tipper, too.

The Liberator sighed. "Can you run, lad?"

"Run, sir?"

"I could use a messenger." He looked to Kammaeman. "If I send warriors, they spend half the day chattering when they get there."

The battlemaster chuckled. "I believe you! Take him by all means. If he causes trouble, though, he'll have to go."

"I think he'll behave, sir. Will you, Dosh?"

Dosh stood up shakily, hardly able to believe his ears. "Oh, yes, sir. Thank you, sir!" Personal messenger for the Liberator? Wonderful! How pleased his real master would be with him!

"Come on, then. Here, you carry my shield until we can get some clothes for you."

They all went outside, blinking at the sunlight. As he set off through the camp with the Liberator, Dosh tried to hold his head up and ignore the laughter and jeering his appearance provoked. It wasn't easy, though. There was a lot of it.

"Clothes first," D'ward said. "Then we'd best get those stitches done as soon as possible." He grinned down at Dosh. He was tall. "Perhaps you'd better try some face paint!"

Dosh laughed as a good servant should when his master makes a joke. He discovered that laughter hurt his face.

"Then food," the Liberator went on. "I wonder if we can find you some decent boots? Hatchet, knife? . . . I assume you're going to make a break for it?"

"No, sir. I want to stay with you, sir. I'm terribly grateful for—"

"Stuff that! I don't need your flattery. Why didn't he kill you at the end, when you wouldn't tell him what he wanted to know?"

"I think he was fond of me in his way."

"Curious fondness. All right, stay. I do need a messenger. But you will not sleep anywhere near me, understand?"

"Yes, sir."

"He offered you to me several times, did you know that?"

"He offered me to many people, sir. Many accepted."

The Liberator pulled a face under his paint and looked away.

Then Dosh felt a sudden blaze of inspiration and joy. He had completed his mission! He had solved the riddle in the prophecy: *Eleal shall be the first temptation and the prince shall be the second.* Prince Tarion had tempted the Liberator by offering him Dosh. That was all there was to it! The prophecy had already been fulfilled, so now he could report back to his master, his real master, his *divine* master.

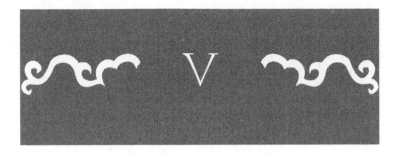

Pawn Takes Castle

25

A SCHOOLBOY OF ABOUT THIRTEEN CAME OUT INTO THE CORRIDOR and offered Alice his seat in the compartment.

She smiled winningly at him. "That's very kind of you, but I'm all right here. Thank you, though."

Blushing, he went back inside and slid the door shut.

Since Swindon, the train was far less crowded. It was possible to talk in the corridor.

"Tell me what happened after you arrived in Lemodvale and Tarion departed."

Stooping to peer out the window, Edward scowled. "I'd just as soon not talk about it, actually. Have you noticed how much luggage everyone seems to have? I think they're running away from the air raids in London."

"Possibly. And you're running away from my question."

He sighed. "I'm not proud of what happened! It was a mess. Kammaeman may have been a crafty politician, but he was no general. He hadn't done his homework."

He drew cucumber shapes on the greasy window and explained the geography. "Thargia had taken Narshvale, which had been Joalian. The Thargians are the bullyboys of the Vales, like the Prussians in Europe or the Spartans in Greece. Nobody calls out the Thargians!

"But Joalia needed to save face to keep its other colonies loyal. The original plan was to cross over Lemodvale and attack Thargvale itself, while it was still digesting Narshvale. It was to be a punishment raid—loot, rape, burn, and scram. Of course, the Thargians would have retaliated, probably the next year. I expect Joalia was counting on Nagvale taking the heat. That's what junior allies are for, isn't it? It was all business as usual, and nasty.

"But Tarion took almost all of our cavalry, so the plan collapsed. Even hitting and running wasn't in the cards without cavalry. Kammaeman had to do something with the forces he had, or face impeachment when he went home. He decided to conquer Lemodvale instead. He probably thought he could trade it back to Tharg in return for Narshvale." Edward smiled quizzically. "Does that sound logical?"

"But not practical? Like offering to give Southwest Africa back to the Boche in return for Belgium?"

He grinned. "Something along those lines. Cavalry would be useless in Lemodvale, anyway, which probably convinced him, but Joalia had never conquered Lemodvale before, and that should have warned him. All the vales are different, and Lemod is more different than most. First of all, it's hilly. There's no—I suppose *Lemodflat* would be the English equivalent."

He paused to think. Alice watched the telegraph wires dip, rise, dip, rise . . . *Clickety-click, clickety-click* . . .

"Valian languages use prefixes where we have suffixes," he said vaguely. "Roughly—very roughly—it would go like this. Say Nagvale is the general term, the whole basin. The mountains all around it would be Nagwall, the foothills Nagslope. Roughly. The arable part would be Nagflat, and in most vales it truly is flat. In Nagland itself it's a plain, almost a desert. Everything that's habitable is called Nagland and everything that's not has another name—Nagwaste? The capital would be Nagtown, or just Nag. The political entity would be Nagia, I suppose. They have other terms. You could say that Nagslope is the usable foothills, and the higher bits are Nagmoor or something like that. It's not a bad system. English doesn't make so many distinctions."

"I imagine words like *ebb tide* would confuse the Nagians just as much as you are confusing me. What has all this to do with the war?"

"Just that Lemodflat isn't. Flat, I mean. It's all cut up by streams. There wouldn't be enough level ground in the whole country for a good nine-hole golf course. And the Lemodians don't have farms, they have trees. They're strange looking trees, but all their crops come from trees. Something rather like a breadfruit gives them their basic starch, but they have others that provide stuff like flax—also cotton and fruits and nuts and wine berries and things just like potatoes . . . everything. The whole country is one enormous orchard."

"Which isn't too good to fight in?"

"It's great to fight in," Edward said bitterly, "if you happen to be a guerrilla."

He sighed and turned around to lean on the brass rail across the window. He folded his arms. "I should have seen what was going to happen. I should have guessed. But, damn it all, Alice, I was only eighteen! I was a stranger in their world. I thought they knew what they were doing in their shiny armor and fancy helmets."

She had never known him to make excuses before. "You couldn't have done anything, surely?"

"Surely I could have! I still had the mana I'd collected in Olfaan's temple. It wasn't much by the gods' standards, of course. I knew it wouldn't build any magic castles, but I thought I might manage a faith healing or something, so I was hoarding it. But even with just my stranger's charisma I could have talked some sense into Kammaeman if I had seen the problem." He pulled a face. "The only man with any brains was Tarion, who got out while the going was good."

He turned back to the glass and added to his map. "Lemodvale's shaped like a snake, very long and thin. We came in here, at the eastern end. That's where the main passes are. Lemod, the capital, is up here, at the western end. Nobody thought to ask what sort of openings there were thereabouts. It was autumn." He frowned at the map he had drawn or perhaps at the scenery sliding by outside. The train was slowing for a station, but she thought he wasn't really looking, just reluctant to tell her more.

"You'd think Kammaeman would have studied the geography, wouldn't you?" he growled. "Or at least the history. He wasn't the first Joalian general to die in Lemodvale."

Houses flowed past the window, slower and slower.

"He wasn't the first Joalian general to be murdered by his deputy, either. And when the Chamber learned I was with the army, then we were fighting gods."

26

FOUR DAYS AFTER THE ARMY REACHED LEMODFLAT, GOLBFISH HAD his first experience of battle. The battle itself was not nearly so bad as the getting ready for it.

He hated Lemodvale. All the Nagians hated Lemodvale. Their own land was flat, dry, and treeless, with rarely a day when a man could not see all the way to Nagwall in every direction. At night the stars and the moons roamed overhead like fireflies in infinite space.

Lemodvale was different. Sky and mountains vanished; the world became nothing but trees, with rarely enough space to pitch a tent and no level ground anyway. Lemodflat wasn't even a decent jungle, because the trees were planted in rows, curving around the slopes. Usually there was no undergrowth, but the lowest branches sprouted at shoulder height and men became hunchbacked from creeping under them all the time. There were no open fields and few trails wide enough to let the sun through. Day after day a man saw no farther than twenty yards, and then only in one direction. He could walk for hours and the view never changed. It was like being shut up indoors, in a maze of pillars, with the roof leaking all the time. Some of the Nagians were almost out of their minds.

Rain fell every day, sometimes only a brief shower, often a dawn-to-dusk downpour. Face paint washed off and stained beards like rainbows.

Droppings showed that wildlife or packbeasts grazed the orchards, but they were never seen. The Lemodians themselves had vanished also. When cottages were located, they were always deserted, often burned. The army advanced unopposed—except by cold and constant wet and the ravages of unfamiliar food.

The scouts had finally located a village, name unknown. At last there could be a fight.

Kammaeman Battlemaster had decided to attack at dawn. He had given the Nagians the honor of leading the assault because he thought they could approach more quietly than the armored Joalians, or so he had said. The rain had stopped. Trumb was almost full, his eerie green light filtering dimly through the foliage. It was just possible for a man to see the man in front of him, as long as he stayed close. It was not possible to move without walking into tree trunks and branches. By day the warriors held their shields up until their left arms were ready to fall off, but shields would make too much noise now. So they wore their shields on their backs and felt their way forward with their hands. Golbfish followed Pomuin, and Dogthark followed Golbfish, each trying to keep the other in sight and not ram him with his spear. It was easy to lose track of where those sharp blades were in the dark.

Feet squelched on dead leaves, but otherwise there was no sound. For all Golbfish knew, they might have walked in a circle and returned to camp. His back and neck ached from stooping.

He was shivering, telling himself that the clammy morning air was at fault and knowing it was not. His feet were icy. He did not think he was afraid of dying so much as of exposing himself as a coward in front of these young peasants. What would they think of their future king if he fainted, froze, or just soiled himself with terror when the fighting started? He was probably the oldest Nagian in the army, because only single men had been conscripted and villagers married young.

They were ignorant, uneducated. They took life as it came, not questioning its meaning or the gods' purposes, or asking about ethics.

Courage was easier for the young. Life felt permanent to them. Probably every one of those rustic warriors was a virgin. Back at the camp, they had been cracking cheerful jokes, speculating about the Lemodian women they would capture and the sport that would follow. Golbfish was no warrior. He was no virgin either. He knew that the transient pleasure was not worth the risk of being maimed or killed.

Pomuin stopped and turned. Golbfish moved closer, watching where he put his spearpoint, then swung around to find out where Dogthark was putting his. They stood side by side, then, listening to the footsteps dying away behind them. A faint rustle of sound came along the line as the men sat down in obedience to some whispered command at the front. The move was not easy in the dark with trees all around and a ten-foot pole spear attached to one's wrist by a leather thong. But Pomuin sat, Golbfish sat, Dogthark sat, the activity moving away into the distance.

They were under strict orders not to talk. Golbfish did not think he had enough saliva to move his tongue anyway. Fear was an awful tightness in his chest, a terrifying insecurity in his bowels. What if he shamed himself right here, with men on either side of him who could not fail to notice? Even in darkness they would hear him and certainly smell him. And could he ever bring himself to thrust this spear into a living man? He had no quarrel with the Lemodians. The Thargians had taken over Narshvale, so the Joalians attacked Lemodvale. Why should a Nagian care, any Nagian? He kept imagining his spear impaling some young peasant, blood and guts spilling out, the victim's scream of agony, the accusing look on his face as he felt himself dying . . . rank, uncouth barbarism!

He thought of his friends in Joal, poets and artists and musicians.

Or the peasant might impale him. Somehow that did not seem so terrible, or at least not so shameful. Then it would be over and there would be no memories.

He sniffed. Smoke? The landscape was waterlogged, so smoke meant hearths. The village must be very close. Downhill, Prat'han Troopleader had said. When the signal came, they were to move downhill, and they would come to the village by the ford. Kill all the men, even if they try to surrender. Don't touch the women until the officers give permission, and then wait your turn. Go easy on the children lest you anger the gods.

Golbfish could hear quiet whisperings to left and right. He thought he could hear something from downhill, but the trees muffled sound so much that he could not be sure. Running water, probably.

What would Ymma say if she could see him now, sitting on wet leaves in a dark forest, damned nearly naked, waiting to kill or die? She would roll around on the bed screaming in hysterics, with her big breasts flopping from side to side. . . .

He jumped as an icy hand took hold of his. He looked around, into Dogthark's eyes, glistening bright in the green moonlight.

Dogthark's hand was shaking. He squeezed Golbfish's fingers.

Golbfish squeezed back. "What's wrong?" he whispered.

"I'm thkared!"

Dogthark was one of the youngest, but big. He had lost all his front teeth, which gave him an idiot look and slurred his speech. He was a troublemaker, a bruiser. Golbfish was afraid of him and avoided him normally, not wanting to get involved in a pointless brawl he would certainly lose. Dogthark was just the sort of moronic kid who might find it amusing to beat up his future king. He was exactly the sort of dolt Golbfish had been envying for his unthinking courage.

"We're all scared!" he said.

"Not you, thir!"

"Yes I am."

"But everyone elth was making thilly jokes and you were jutht quiet, all confidence, quiet courage!"

How wrong could one be?

"I am scared shitless," Golbfish said. "Like you. Worse. I've never been in a battle either. Keep thinking about the girls down there. How many girls can you rape in one morning?"

Dogthark made a strange panting sound that was probably a laugh. "Three?"

"Oh, come on! Husky young fellow like you ought to manage four or five."

"You really think tho? I've never had a girl before, thir."

Golbfish sniffed again. Smoke! How long until dawn? "They're nice. Lot of hard work after the first couple, though. It'll really make you sweat."

"I think you're marvellouth, thir! A king fighting in the rankth! We're all tho proud of you!"

"I feel like a bloody fool," Golbfish confessed. "I . . ."

Only his own stupidity had brought him to this. Why had he refused royal rank and insisted on remaining a warrior? What did he really owe to D'ward that he so much wished to be worthy of that youngster's approval? He was certainly acting out of character these days.

Sounds. Men rising, unslinging shields. Leaves crackling underfoot. It was not dawn yet, but the attack had begun.

"Come on!" he said, clenching every sphincter. "Save a few girls for me."

A hundred yards downhill and they saw the flames.

There were no women. There was no battle. Half the cottages had collapsed into embers already. Howling and yelling in disgust, the Nagian warriors milled around in the single street that had once been a village.

"There'th no girlth!" Dogthark wailed. "No wariorth! They all ran away! Cowardth!"

Golbfish felt drunk with relief. No battle! No need to impale men, no men to impale him! He wanted to dance and sing with joy.

"Tie a knot in it until the next time, son!" he said. "Next time you can try for a dozen!" He laughed aloud. The warmth from the fires was a caress on his permanently damp hide. But, oh, all that warm, dry bedding going up in . . .

Dogthark said, "Huh?" He looked down in surprise at the arrow protruding from his chest. Then he dropped.

Golbfish realized that he was well illuminated. Pomuin toppled forward on his shield with a shaft sticking out of his back. Arrows were everywhere and men were falling.

That was how it began.

Sometime in the next couple of fortnights, Golbfish decided it was all just a matter of numbers. Nagland sent out its unmarried adult males to make war. The Joalians allowed any man to volunteer, but in practice few but young bachelors chose to do so. Those were barely a twentieth of the population. When a Lemodian village was threatened, everybody fought, even the children. Their bows were crude, homemade affairs and their arrows merely fire-sharpened stakes. That did not matter, because the range was rarely more than a few yards and often only feet. The guerrillas hid in the branches or behind the trunks and waited until a warrior came within reach. If the victim's companions gave chase, then as often as not there would be an ambush waiting.

Progress slowed to a crawl. Every morning the army marched; by noon it had to stop and begin chopping trees. It spent far more time building stockades and huddling inside them than it did waging war. It killed a million trees and hardly a single Lemodian.

With every precaution the officers could think of, sentries died at their posts, sleeping men had their throats cut, fire arrows came over the palisade. Moas and packbeasts were slaughtered in the night or driven off. Day after day the wastage continued, while the army blundered its way through the unbounded woods of Lemodflat.

Lemod itself was the answer, Kammaeman insisted. Lemod was a fair city. When the capital fell the country would fall. Lemod was the prize and the sanctuary. The army marched on Lemod.

But there was no road to march on. The trails and lanes wandered all around the countryside, and every mile brought another ambush. On rainy days—and most days were rainy that fall—even the leaders lost their sense of direction. Streams and rivers wound and twisted like tangled wool. In some lands rivers were highways; in Lemodland they flowed in gullies or gorges and were barriers.

Officially the sick and wounded who could not keep up were left to die, but in practice their friends made sure the enemy did not take them alive. Knowing how they themselves interrogated prisoners, Joalians considered such murders a kindness.

"There's a new plan," D'ward Hordeleader said.

He had called the troop in around him to hear the new plan. It was midday break, and raining. The closer ones sat down on the soggy ground, wet and dispirited. The rest just stood or leaned against trees to listen. The supply of face paint had run out, and now they had nothing to hide their despondency. They were cold and deeply frightened, naked before their unseen foe and the anger of the gods.

Golbfish sat in the front row. The closer he could get to the Liberator, the better he felt afterward.

Even D'ward did not look happy. His eyes were raw, as if he did not sleep much; he was leaner than ever. He came around at least once every day, and his daily pep talk always raised the men's spirits. It was the only thing that ever did. He visited every Nagian troop every day.

But today even he did not look happy.

"Casualties, Troopleader?" he asked.

Prat'han had been elected to lead the Sonalby contingent when D'ward had been promoted. He was a good kid, but he was not the Liberator.

"Just one today, sir. Pogwil Tanner. Booby trap."

D'ward bared his teeth in anger. "Just one is too many! Well, there is a change of tactics. We're going to make a forced march. We're going to outrun the monkeys."

He glanced around and won some smiles.

Golbfish did not smile. He sensed desperation. Regular forces could not outrun guerrillas. These peasants would not know that. They would find out soon enough.

"No more wasting half the day building forts!" D'ward said. "We're going to push on now until dark, at the double. Then we'll bivouac. Same thing tomorrow. We'll set triple watches all night. Grab any chance for sleep you can get! Some of you have complained about getting blisters on your hands. From now on you're going to get them on your feet—and you certainly won't get any on your backsides!"

More smiles.

"A few days and we'll be in Lemod itself. I told Kammaeman Battle-master that we Nagians could run rings around his metal-plated Joalians. Was I wrong?"

Loud jeers . . . Golbfish wondered what the Joalian leaders would think if they heard this pep talk. Every one of them would just snap out the new orders to his troop and leave it at that. None would ever bother explaining an order—but D'ward always did.

"By the time the monkeys realize where we are," he was saying now, "we'll be miles away!"

What difference would that make? The whole of Lemodvale was full of people. The enemy was everywhere, endless as the trees.

D'ward began talking details—foraging must be done on the way, no squad ever to be less than six . . . He was proposing a rout and making it sound like storm tactics. Soon he had the men twitching with eagerness to try this new plan.

Eventually he even had them laughing. He did not speak very long after that. He rarely said even as much as he had today. It was the way he said it that left everyone smiling and chuckling.

At the end he caught Golbfish's eye and jerked his head in a beckoning. Then he left, and Prat'han ordered the troop to its feet.

The Liberator was waiting a few trees away, leaning on his spear. His sky-blue smile jerked Golbfish's backbone a few notches straighter and dispelled the cold. He wanted to ask if Kammaeman had gone completely insane, but he knew he wouldn't. D'ward would not criticize the battle-master, even to a prince.

"How are you surviving, Your Majesty?"

"Better than I would have expected, sir. Er, may I ask that you not call me that?"

D'ward held the smile for a few seconds in silence. Then he said, "War-rior, then. It is a more honorable title, because it is one you have earned for yourself. Do you think this experience will make you a better king?"

"It will make me or break me, I suppose. Yes, of course."

"If it were going to break you, you'd have broken long ago. You even look like a warrior now, you know. You stand like one, walk like one. I suspect Joal may eventually find you a tougher nut than Tarion. If all kings were trained this way, there would be fewer wars. . . . But that wasn't what I wanted to talk about. How well do you know the *Filoby Testament?*"

Golbfish sighed. "Not at all well! I tried to read it once, but it's such a muddle I lost interest." He wished he could be of more help to this young-ster who had helped him so much. "I've heard bits of it quoted, of course."

"Does it say anything about Nagvale?"

Golbfish shook his head. "Not a word. That I do know."

D'ward frowned thoughtfully. "How about Lemodvale?"

"I don't recall anything about Lemodvale. That doesn't mean it isn't— You mean you—"

The blue eyes twinkled. "No, I've never read it. None of it. I'm not sure I could, since it's written in Sussian."

"Oh, that's not so far from Joalian. But—" Golbfish choked off the question. Why would the Liberator not have read the prophecies about himself?

"I just wondered if there was anything that might be relevant." D'ward sighed and straightened up. He hitched his shield to a more comfortable position. He hesitated. "You haven't any idea how far it is to Lemod, have you?"

"None at all."

"Mm. Pity. Well, keep up the good work. You're a great inspiration to your countrymen, you know."

With an encouraging smile, the Liberator strode away.

Golbfish wondered afterward if he should have mentioned the *Filoby Testament*'s prophecy about a prince.

ᵜᵜ 27 ᵜᵜ

LESS THAN THREE QUARTERS OF THE ORIGINAL ARMY ARRIVED AT Lemod. There it was thoroughly balked. Lemodwater, the main drainage of the vale, writhed like a mad snake in a deeply incised canyon. The city stood on a Ω-shaped salient, practically an island, its fifty-foot walls poised on the brink of sheer cliffs, a hundred feet above the torrent. The only approach was along a narrow neck of land from the north, which dipped almost to river level, so that attackers must charge uphill to reach the gates. Needless to say, those gates were closed. Lemod had been starved into submission a time or two, but even the Thargians had never taken it by storm.

Lemod was a very easy city to invest, for the white-water river was neither fordable nor navigable. The Joalians settled in. Relieved to be out of the pestilential trees at last, they cleared a campsite and a safety zone around it. They set up barricades against any attempts at sorties; they laid out sanitary trenches and generally established a proper military camp. Then they sat back and waited—to sicken, starve, and rot.

At first it was not too bad. The orchards provided food, but five thousand men ate many tons of fruit a day. As days stretched into fortnights, the foragers must go ever farther in search of fresh trees to strip. The greater the radius, the greater the guerrillas' opportunity for ambush.

Attempts to storm the gates failed before a blizzard of arrows and missiles from the defenders. Casualties were heavy. The attackers began digging trenches, building breastworks and siege engines, and generally going through all the proper motions of investment that Lemod had seen a dozen times before. Periodically the defenders would sally out to burn or smash what had been achieved. The earthworks crept steadily up the hill, but progress was desperately slow.

Disease spread through the camp. The temperature fell steadily, and the snow line slunk downward on the peaks of Lemodwall. Soon it became obvious that the city could endure the siege far longer than the besiegers could.

The mutiny took Edward by surprise. He had little to do with the Joalian officers and too much to do keeping the Nagians in line. He worked day and night at keeping up their morale. Without his steadying hand they would have broken long ago. They would have fled in a mob for home and been cut down in the trees. Old Krobidirkin had foreseen that.

Besides, Edward was not familiar with Joalian customs, and Kolgan Coadjutant had the law on his side. When he convened a meeting of the officer cadre, he invited the Nagian commander along to witness Joalian democracy in action.

The rain had stopped at last, but a bitter wind blew. Ropes creaked and canvas thumped. The meeting was held in the general's own tent. It did not take long. Kolgan denounced Kammaeman as incompetent. Kammaeman blustered. The troopleaders voted. Kammaeman was taken out and beheaded.

Kolgan assumed command.

★   ★   ★

"Thank you, citizens," said Kolgan Battlemaster. "I shall endeavor to be worthy of your trust. Pray inform the army of your verdict. Tomorrow I shall issue new orders."

The officers saluted and trooped out into the thin sunshine.

Edward wandered over to a stool and sat down.

The tall man scowled at him and then pulled another stool up close, very close. He sat down and said, "Well, Hordeleader? You wish to see me?" Their knees were almost touching.

"Very democratic!" Edward said. "How long do you have before someone pulls that trick on you?"

Kolgan glared. Facing challenge, he went on the offensive. "As it happens, I wish to speak with you. I hear reports that you have been releasing prisoners."

Who had been blabbing? "One prisoner."

The admission made the Joalian pause. "Any lesser man guilty of that offense would be executed on the spot. You had better explain, Hordeleader."

"I was out on patrol," Edward said, knowing that Kolgan would not have raised the matter if he were not aware of the details. "A couple of the fellows captured a girl. She was no more than fourteen, I should say. Not a warrior."

"She might have provided valuable information."

"Under torture?" Edward let his disgust show. "The only thing she could provide was sport. They told me I had the right to go first, as I was senior. I said that the gods damned men who made war on children and that a rapist was about the next lowest slime I could imagine. Then I asked who wanted to take my place. When no one offered, I told the child to make herself scarce and she did. What did I do wrong?"

Kolgan stared at him blankly. Finally he said, "Don't you have any balls at all?"

"The same number you have, I'm sure. But I don't let them rule me."

The big man curled his mustache up in contempt. "You prefer Dosh Houseboy?"

"I don't spin in that direction, Battlemaster."

"Ha! That reminds me—all this damp is making my back ache. I am told he is an accomplished masseur. May I borrow his services this evening?"

"No," Edward said. "You may not. That would be rape too."

The tall man flushed almost as red as his beard. For a moment the confrontation teetered on the brink of open quarrel. Then Edward turned on a grin, consciously using his charisma. "I am sorry about old Kammaeman," he said, "but not terribly sorry."

After a brief hesitation, the tall man grinned back. He was in armor but without a helmet. There was gray in his hair, and that was new. He was deeply worried, trying to hide the fact.

"Just an old Joalian custom, Hordeleader!"

There was another old Joalian custom that Edward did know of—betrayal of allies. He had even less confidence in Kolgan than he had lately had in Kammaeman. Too lately. Obviously this expedition was a disaster. His own loyalty was to his Nagians, and they were going to be slaughtered unless he could pull off something dramatic. He should have been smarter sooner; he felt responsible.

"So now it is your turn, sir. How long do you have to find a solution?"

"A fortnight at most, if I stay here." The new commander glanced around the unfamiliar command tent. His angular features were somehow reminiscent of a pointer sniffing the air. "The old fart used to keep some damnably good Niolian brandy hidden away somewhere."

"Not for me. What do you plan to do?"

Kolgan's gray eyes narrowed within their wrinkles. "What plan do you propose, Hordeleader?" He would put no stock in Edward's judgment. Charismatic or not, D'ward was merely another peasant.

"You summarized the situation clearly, sir. Winter is almost here. Food is almost out of reach. We take the city soon or we die."

Coppery eyebrows rose ironically. "I did not put the question quite like that. Have you a solution?"

"I am only a village laborer. Instruct me."

If the Joalian was needled by this sudden assertiveness from his colonial subordinate—his *juvenile* colonial subordinate—he was still sufficiently under the spell of the stranger's charisma to reply civilly.

"I must rescue the army. If I can lead it safely back to Nagland, or get even a substantial fraction of it back safely, then I shall be in the clear, and possibly a hero."

So his motives were purely personal, which Edward should have expected. "And how can you rescue the army?"

Kolgan scratched at his beard for a long moment, as if weighing his words carefully. "The prisoners tell us there is a rarely used pass to the north. Tomorrow we strike camp and head for it. The season is late."

"Your men are far better dressed than mine, Battlemaster. Can you supply us with warm clothing? Is this road passable for men going barefoot?"

"No, to both questions."

Without warning, fury was a tight hand around Edward's throat, making normal speech almost impossible. His voice came out so harsh he did not recognize it. "Are you certain this is not a trap? Can armored men carry enough food to cross the ranges? Do you expect the Lemodians to let you leave unopposed? What happens if a storm strikes while you are in the high country? Can you carry the sick and the wounded? What of *my* men? You just abandon your allies?"

Kolgan had paled until the rough weathering on his face seemed lit from within. He raised a clenched fist like a mace. "Have you a better plan, Nagian? If we stay we starve. If we try to fight our way back the way we came, we shall be butchered in the woods. The Thargians will hold Siopass in force by now. Do you propose to parley? Kammaeman tried it and was refused. The Lemodians think they have us by the testicles."

And so they did, Edward thought, except for one factor. They could not know that the besieging army included a stranger with a store of mana. He did not want to use it for so fell a purpose, but he had been left no choice.

He sprang to his feet, rage pulsing in his ears and a sour taste in his mouth. "I need to borrow a bugle!"

Kolgan rose also, half a head taller. "What for?"

"Trumb will eclipse tonight?"

"I believe so. Why?"

"Tonight we Nagians will force the gates for you. When you hear the bugle, advance and take the city!"

Edward turned around and stormed out of the tent.

Cursing his folly, he stalked off through the camp, heading downhill. He could feel his store of mana like a pocketful of gold, but how much would it buy? Major gods like Tion or Zath would have power to blast a hole through a city wall as easily as Apollo leading the Trojans through the Achaeans' stockade. Or levitate the invaders to the battlements. Or just convince the Lemodian guards that they should throw open their gates, which would be the simplest solution. Edward did not think he could even do that much. If he tried and failed then he would have spent his mana to no purpose.

Nevertheless, he had taken up the ball and he would have only one shot at the wicket, so he had better think of something before dark.

The wind was icy on his bare hide. Fallow had encouraged toughness, but running around naked in winter was a little more stringent than cold baths. Lemodwall shone with fresh snow. The peaks to the north looked higher than any he had yet seen on Nextdoor. Those to the south were lower, but behind them lay Thargvale.

Kolgan's rumored pass to Nagvale might not exist; it might be already blocked; it certainly could not be attempted without warm clothes and stout boots. The Nagians were doomed unless their madcap leader could deliver on his boast. Probably the Joalians were too.

As he neared the edge of the camp, he sensed that he was being followed. It was Dosh Houseboy, of course, now formally Dosh Envoy, although no one but Edward ever used that name. Edward waved for him to come closer, and then walked on. In a moment the youth was pacing at his side, decently dressed in a blue Joalian tunic, yellow breeches, and a stout pair of boots. Where or how he had acquired those was a mystery. He might have stolen them. If he had bought them, Edward preferred not to know what price he had paid.

Except when running errands, Dosh clung to Edward like a shadow. None of the warriors would have anything to do with him, lest their friends suspect them of unmanly desires. He could not even find a meal or a place at a fire unless he was with the hordeleader. The Nagians left him alone because D'ward had commanded them to, but he had been punched up by Joalian troublemakers at least twice. Perhaps Dosh's life had never been easy. At the moment it was certainly not, but he never complained.

He might be years older than he looked. He refused to give his age, or say much about himself at all. He was short and slight, had fairish curls, and his face had been childishly pretty until Tarion took a knife to it. Now it was scrolled with crosshatched red lines that bore a bizarre resemblance to railway tracks on Ordnance Survey maps, although only one man in this army would ever notice the resemblance. He had let his downy beard grow in since his promotion to messenger, but it was invisible at a distance. At close quarters it made him seem like a boy playing at dressing up. He could be mawkish or servile or acidly witty as circumstances required. And underneath the professional softness, he was as hard and bitter as a harlot—at least, Edward assumed a harlot would be like that, having never met one. He felt sure that sweet little Dosh was as tough as any bruiser in the army and much less trustworthy than the average tarantula.

"How long would you need to round up all the troopleaders for a council?" Edward asked.

"An hour. Half that if you'll let me delegate some to fetch others."

"Have the forager leaders returned?"

"No. You want substitutes?"

"Yes. Stay with me awhile, though. I have a problem."

They came to the lowest point of the neck, flanked by the river on either hand and barely above its level. Beyond them the land rose steeply to the gates. Joalian soldiers were working on breastworks and siege engines just out of bowshot of the defenders. Edward stopped and stared at the activity without going any closer.

If he were defending the city, he would be about ready to make another sortie and burn those scaffolds. He wondered if they were dry enough for the attempt to come tonight. Probably not. It would take many fortnights for the earthworks to reach the gate. Winter was at hand. Tomorrow Kolgan was pulling out.

He turned his attention to the city itself, the high wall and the tall build-ings within. The toothed battlements went all the way around, which seemed unnecessary—why build walls on the edge of vertical cliffs? Was there some reason to expect attack from the flanks, or was that merely an artistic conceit?

The cliffs were not perfectly sheer, and the plateau was irregular. In places the ground projected out beyond the walls, although those salients had mostly been beveled away to steep slopes. Between them, where the ground dipped, the walls were necessarily higher. An army could not march around the city, but possibly an active man could work his way along there, if he had time and was sufficiently suicidal. A squad of sappers might find a place to undermine the foundations, but how could they possibly do so unde-tected? The defenders would drop rocks on them. Still, there were spots where a man might stand back a short distance from the wall, so that he would not be looking straight up at it. Or shooting straight up it? Or? . . .

He felt that there was an idea there somewhere, but he could not find an end to tug on. Many generals much wiser than he must have considered all these possibilities in the past. Lemod had never been taken by storm.

"It should be possible to walk right around the base of the walls," he said, shivering.

"If they didn't see you. A couple of the Rareby kids claim to have done it."

Edward glanced down at the guileless blue eyes in their long golden lashes. "How do you know that?"

"Eavesdropping."

Obviously. Nobody spoke to Dosh unless it was absolutely necessary.

"Bring them to the meeting too."

"Want me to ask if any others have done it?"

"No." Edward chuckled. "Did you speak to Tarion this way?"

"What way?"

"All terse and efficient and military."

"No."

"How did you speak to him?"

Dosh looked away for a moment, then turned back to Edward with tears glistening. "I love you," he said with a break in his voice. "I will do any-thing for you, anything to make you happy." He seemed completely sin-cere. "I love you for your smile, for the touch of your—"

"That's enough, thank you! I get the gist."

"You asked."

"And I should not have. I didn't mean to humiliate you."

"How could you humiliate me? You don't know what humiliation is."

"No, I suppose I don't. I am truly sorry."

"Don't be," Dosh said. "*Sorry is a waste of time.* The Green Scriptures, Canto 474."

"Really?"

"Who knows? Who ever reads that junk?" He smiled ruefully at Edward's laughter. "What's your problem?"

"Can I trust you?"

"If you mean will I tell anyone in the camp what you say to me, the answer is no. Who would listen?"

"Can you talk to anyone outside the camp?"

Dosh flinched. "Of course not!" he snapped.

Which confirmed what Edward had suspected for some time. The wind was gnawing through to his bones now and he was probably turning bright blue, but this was important.

"You were spying on Tarion, weren't you? Who for?"

"I won't answer that."

"You *can't* answer that! And you couldn't tell him, either! That's why he cut up your face!"

"You calling me a hero?"

"No, I'm not. You're not spying for a mortal, are you?"

A spasm that might have been pain twisted the red scars beside Dosh's eyes. "Can't answer that," he mumbled.

"Then you needn't try. If I name a name, can you—"

"Don't, sir! Please?"

"All right," Edward said, still uncertain how much of this performance was real. "If you get the chance, will you stick a knife in my back?"

Dosh curled his cherubic lip in contempt. "You would be well rotted by now."

"Yes. I see. Thank you." Not Zath, then. "Did you ever wear a gold rose in your hair?"

Dosh stared at him, then nodded. A boyish blush spread around his scars. What did it take to make a harlot blush?

But the answer to the real question was obviously *Tion.* "Just snooping?"

"Just snooping. Now, what's the problem?"

He was a born spy, curious as a cat about everything. Even little Eleal had been no nosier than Dosh. Edward did not like to think about Eleal.

He hugged himself, hunching against the wind. "I told the new battlemaster that I would take the city for him tonight, and I don't know how. Haven't the foggiest."

"Oh, you'll find a way."

"You display a gratifying confidence in . . ." Edward stared at that cryptic, mutilated face. "What do you mean by that?"

Dosh smiled slyly, twisting the crimson railway lines around his eyes. "Nothing, Hordeleader."

"Out with it!"

"The prophecy?" Dosh said reluctantly.

"What prophecy?"

Surprise . . . disbelief . . . "The long one? The one about the city? The *Filoby Testament*, about verse five hundred, or four-fifty?"

"Tell me!"

"You don't know? Truly?"

"No, I don't know."

For a moment Dosh seemed to think Edward must be joking. He shook his head in astonishment, thought for a moment, then declaimed: *"The first sign unto you shall be when the gods are gathered. For then the Liberator shall come forth in ire and be in sorrow revealed. He shall throw down the gates that the city may fall. Blood in the river shall speak to distant lands, saying; Lo—the city has fallen in slaughter. He shall bring death and exultation in great measure. Joy and lamentation shall be his endowment."*

28

TOO MUCH HAPPENED THAT NIGHT. IN RETROSPECT, DOSH WAS NOT to recall ever panicking or disgracing himself. He was never to doubt that he had remained clearheaded during the events themselves. He did what was needed, with far greater courage than he had ever known he possessed.

It was his memory that betrayed him. Terror piled on terror and horror upon horror until his mind could not retain them all. Reality faded like a nightmare, so that afterward he recalled only glimpses, the highlights mostly, but also a few unimportant incidents like incongruous flickers of dream. It was as if the turning point of his life had been written in a precious book and then he had lost all but a fraction of the pages before he could even look at them. Long stretches were evermore blank.

It was a night of quadruple conjunction, a wonder that few mortals ever see, coming only once in generations. Even then, most people will not be alerted in time; it never lasts long. Neither Niol nor Tharg would admit afterward that the great event ever happened. The Niolians insisted that Ysh passed close by Trumb that night, but not actually behind, while the Thargians claimed it was Kirb'l who narrowly failed to cross over Trumb. In Joal the weather was bad and no one noticed anything at all.

Dosh knew better. He witnessed the gathering of the gods that had been prophesied, and his world was changed forever.

As for all the rest . . . just pictures on a wall.

The first picture: faces around a campfire at sunset. . . . He huddles silent on the outskirts, ignored. A dozen or more near-naked Nagians shiver in the dusk, their unpainted faces listening in awe as the Liberator promises a miracle.

He does not mention the word. He does not tell them he is the Liberator; he seems not to believe that himself. In his own mind he has no great faith that he can deliver a miracle—Dosh knows this from what he heard earlier—but certainly no one else around this fire will guess as much from D'ward's manner. He gives orders calmly, with perfect poise. He needs a miracle, so he will attempt one. To profit from it he must have his troops standing by, so he is promising them that he will open the city. If he fails he will have destroyed himself, but he is the Liberator and they believe him. It shows in their wild, childlike eyes. They would follow him into a furnace, these crude peasants. They are all muscle and faith and no brains.

They will be the Warband, the first of all his followers.

Does Dosh sense that, even then?

What says the Liberator in this image by the campfire? Alas, most of that precious speech is written on pages lost. Dosh will recall no words, except a few, right at the end, when the Liberator turns and points at him and all the warriors scream in fury.

Their hordeleader has told them he will take only one man with him to help carry the ropes. A dozen strong voices have cried out, demanding the honor. No, none of them, D'ward has said. Not the troopleaders, for they must lead their men. Nor the prince, nor even Talba and Gospin, although they know the way. No, he will take Dosh Envoy and no one else. Only he ever calls Dosh by name. Everyone else has other terms for the despicable catamite.

This is the second picture—a dozen furious warriors howling in outrage and the Liberator shouting them down. To Dosh his words are to be the beginning of the other miracle, his personal miracle, but he does not know that yet.

"Because you ask," D'ward is saying in that second picture, "and only because you ask, I will tell you why. I need a man whose courage I cannot doubt. Be *silent!* Look at those marks on his face! They were made in the dark, while he was bound and gagged. See how close they come to his eyes? See how his throat was slashed? That man endured vile torture, yet did not tell his tormenter what he wanted to know. Will any of you now claim to be this man's better in courage? Will any of you exchange your merit marks for his? I will have Dosh Envoy at my side tonight, for I trust him beyond all others."

Another glimpse: Dosh weeping, as the warriors come, each in turn, to embrace him and beg his forgiveness for past slights. . . . Some also whisper in his ear that he will die most terribly if he fails D'ward this night, but he ignores that. He is finding the experience very strange, for many reasons. The body contact arouses him, and he knows that will disgust them if they sense it. Their admiration distresses him—why should he care what these bullocks think?

Not the least strangeness is that he knows the Liberator is lying. The Liberator is fully aware that Dosh could not have given Tarion the information he wanted. Dosh does not understand why the Liberator should tell such a falsehood now, nor why he apparently believes his own lie enough to trust Dosh, or why Dosh himself in his present terror is not refusing the suicidal honor. He has not been asked, and he does not refuse.

Do the wonders begin here?

The waiting in the trenches as the sky darkens . . . gut-wrenching anxiety. Dosh and D'ward crouch amid timbers and stonework while the weary soldiers trek back to camp for the night. Below an empty sky, the temperature drops by the minute. Trumb's green disk peers between the eastern peaks, huge and ominously perfect. Nights are bright when Trumb is full.

Has the Man already eclipsed? Will he wait for true darkness? The Liberator is counting on those few precious moments of distraction to let him approach the city unobserved. An eclipse of Trumb is a time of dread, when reapers claim souls for Zath. The guards will be watching the sky and praying. It is a time of ill omen, the last time anyone should choose to launch a mission such as this.

Trumb did eclipse, of course. Trumb must have eclipsed. At D'ward's side, Dosh must have sprinted through the darkness under the stars, stumbling up the slope under his burden, forcing legs and straining lungs to greater effort before the brief blessing was withdrawn. He must have reached the base of the walls before the light returned and hence escaped the notice of the watchers above. If he hadn't, he would have died. He must have done.

He just lost the memory somewhere.

★   ★   ★

Terror.

Fingers scrabbling in dirt for purchase, feet fumbling and slipping, the coiled rope a crushing weight on his back threatening to pull him out into the abyss, a hundred feet of nothing above the rumble of the torrent. His face pressing into the rimy grass.

Why did he not remember sooner how much he hates heights?

His nose against the gritty surface of the masonry as he edges his way along, spread-eagled against the wall . . . Nothing below him at all, just a hundred feet of vertical rock in the ghastly green moonlight, and below it the raging cataracts of Lemodwater. How many seconds would a man have to scream as he fell? How often would he bounce on the ledges?

Wind.

Cold. Icy, biting cold, and he is swaddled in a double layer. He has wool underwear that nobody knows about, except the three Joalians who sold it to him all through one very hard night. D'ward must be frozen to the marrow of his bones.

Slippery wet grass and steep slopes. Not a bush, not a root.

Greasy rock with nothing to grasp hold of.

Always the smooth face of the wall above, merciless and uncaring.

Always the thought that someone up there may chance to look down and see the two intruders. They will be amusing target practice. Even in moonlight, fifty feet straight down is not a difficult shot.

Dosh will remember quite a lot of that journey. Too much.

The *dike* . . . that is the Liberator's name for it, not a word Dosh has ever heard. It is only a narrow buttress jutting out from the cliff face a few feet below the brink, a crumbly black rock about ten feet across. Here D'ward can stand a small way back from the wall to work his miracle. Of course they are much more visible here than they were earlier, directly underneath. Watchers on the battlements will see them easily if they look down.

That is what watchers on battlements are supposed to do, isn't it?

The wind tugs and pushes viciously, striving to throw them both from their perch. D'ward curses under his breath as he fights with the thin line and the wind tries to carry it all away or tie it in tangles. His teeth chatter. In the lurid green light he looks like a walking corpse.

Picture: Dosh unbuttoning his tunic and pulling it off—he offers it to his near-naked companion and it streams out sideways like a flag.

D'ward's angry snarl: "Stop that! Are you *trying* to get us killed?"

"You need it."

"No. The others do not have it. Put it on again." He goes back to tying knots with numb fingers.

The others are not crouched on this accursed ledge a hundred feet above the rapids.

The throw . . . the beginning of the miracle.

In the wind and the dark at that impossible angle, the Liberator succeeds at his first attempt. It is beautiful: the log rising into the night, trailing the string behind it, the wind arcing it away.

D'ward teetering on one leg, flailing his arms, and somehow recovering his balance. For a moment Dosh is sure he is about to fall. That image will remain always, one of the clearest—the Liberator poised over the abyss, with one leg and both arms outstretched, face rigid with terror, and Dosh leaping forward to catch him just in time. . . .

If the log makes a noise as it falls on the parapet far above, then the wind steals it away.

There must have been a hasty scramble then, back up to the base of the wall, into relative cover. Dosh does not recall it. That is a moment of terrible danger, for if anyone has heard or seen that log arriving then he must inevitably peer down to see where it came from.

The waiting.

How long it lasts, he will never know. The two of them huddling up against the cruel masonry, waiting, waiting . . . D'ward looking as if he will freeze to death. Again—perhaps several times—he has refused to accept a share of Dosh's garments. In the end Dosh wraps him in his arms, and the Liberator does not resist the embrace.

It is hardly romantic, anyway, like hugging a glacier.

The fading of hope. The despair . . .

The moons. Trumb's glare drowns out the stars, but Ysh had risen soon after him, and then Eltiana. Three moons shine together, close together: a huge green disk, a tiny blue disk, and a red star. In the required order. Not quite a straight line, but close enough, yes? Please! Imperceptibly but inevitably, the red and the blue catch up with the green.

The prophecy is being fulfilled. Three of the gods gather, as they do every few years. It is awesome and auspicious, but it is only three. Three are rare; four are epochal.

Where is Kirb'l, the Joker?

The Maiden and the Lady edge closer to the Man. Where is the Youth?

No one can predict Kirb'l. He moves in strange patterns, straying far to north and south. He appears and he disappears at will. Sometimes, at his brightest, he travels from west to east.

Dosh praying.

The Joker!

Dosh will never forget that dramatic entrance. It will be the sharpest of all his recollections of that night—the tiny, brilliant, golden moon flashing into view ahead of Trumb, so that all four gods blaze together in the velvet silver of the sky. Kirb'l, visibly moving, moving *east!* Four lights. Four shadows.

Eltiana and Ysh on one side, Kirb'l on the other, almost in a line, in perfect order and relentlessly closing on the great disk of Trumb.

Quadruple conjunction, a gathering of the gods!

Wait for it . . .

The Liberator's sudden hiss, and the brightness in his eyes . . .

"What?"

"Someone's coming!"

Dosh peers all around, and of course there is no one on this accursed windswept cliff top. Someone up on the battlements, then? How can D'ward possibly know?

(Perhaps that was the beginning of belief.)

"He's found it!" D'ward pushing free, sitting up, tense in the moonlight. "Here it comes!"

The *miracle!*

Some weary sentry, cold and bored, walking his beat on the parapet, has found a chunk of firewood. His superiors will not approve of litter where a fighting man may trip over it.

Perfectly natural for such a man to pick up the log and heave it over the side and then resume his march. He will be watching the skies tonight, like any other man.

Not natural for a sentry to overlook the twine attached to the log . . . that is the real miracle. Not entirely luck, either, that he does not throw it out the same crenel it came in by. But he does *not* notice the twine he is thus looping around a merlon, and he does *not* notice that twine running out as the log slides down the wall, snagged on a stone tooth.

He plays his part in history and walks away to die, and at the base of the wall the Liberator relaxes with a sob, a gasp of breath held far too long.

Miracle.

There are more pages missing here.

One of the two invaders unfastened the twine and attached it to the heavier rope. One of them hauled on the twine, muttering prayers that the string would not wear through on the crenelation or just break under the strain. One of them then grabbed the rope when it came and tied a noose in it and hauled it tight.

It may have been Dosh. It may have been D'ward. It must have been one of them.

The four moons closing.

Faint sounds of chanting coming down on the wind. The priests of the city are rousing the people to come and praise the miracle in the heavens.

They do not notice the miracle on the walls. So small a thing, to bear such fruit—a length of twine looped around the battlements, and then a rope.

The Nagians will be on their way now.

The quadruple conjunction.

Side by side, sapphire Ysh and ruby Eltiana vanish behind Trumb. A moment later Kirb'l slides in front, and the gold speck is lost in the green glare. Only Trumb remains.

A gathering of the gods, omen of great destiny.

No one ever forgets seeing that.

D'ward has gone, gone up the rope. His corpse has not come back on its way to the river; there has been no sound of challenge. He must still be alive up there. Dosh waits to show the way.

He is to remember that waiting as being worst of all, because D'ward is up there alone.

Then the cream of the Sonalby troop emerges out of the darkness in single file, bringing more ropes. Bringing no spears or shields, only their clubs, clambering along that same perilous road.

Dosh insists that he be allowed to go next, first after D'ward. . . . They argue and Prat'han concedes, letting him go.

Stripping off his clothes so that he will not be mistaken for a defender.

Climbing near-naked and unarmed up a vertical wall in the dark.

That image will remain, always.

And after that . . . a great blank.

The Sonalby troop followed the Liberator into the city. They overpowered the watch. They opened the gates for the rest of the Nagians, the spearsmen who had crept forward while the defenders watched the conjunction.

Someone sounded the bugle to summon the Joalians.

The Joalians arrived as the defenders rallied and began to slaughter the club-wielding, unarmored Nagians.

Dosh was to remember none of that. None.

The memories that came after drove them away, perhaps—bitter memories, better forgotten: glimpses of battle in near darkness, blood splattering on walls, bodies in the streets, much screaming, panicking mobs. Dead babies.

A man run through dies cleanly, showing only surprise. Men dispatched with clubs have their heads beaten into shapelessness like broken jam pots.

Women cower in corners or lament over the bodies.

Children, tiny children, running, screaming. With blood on them. Clinging to their fathers' corpses.

Great fires stream up into the night as the failing defenders try to deny their city to the victors.

The chapel of Yaela Tion, the goddess of singing—an avatar of the Youth . . . Dosh has found it somehow, he cannot remember how.

The main temple is full of hysterical refugees, but this little crypt is deserted, dark and silent, lit by one flickering candle before the diminutive image of the goddess. He will not remember entering, kneeling, or performing the secret ritual given him for this purpose.

He remembers the coming of the god, the blaze of his beauty and glory . . . although that particular recollection may have blurred and merged with those of other, similar, occasions when the god has come in response to his call. He never can remember afterward just exactly what he has seen—only the impact and the beautiful voice of the god. Sobbing with happiness, barely able to speak because of the love that fills his throat to choke him, he whispers his report to the stones of the floor.

And is praised!

"You have done well so far, Beloved," says the god. "Quite well. The prophecy of the city is fulfilled, yes. I feel the prophecy of the prince is not. Tarion offered you to the Liberator, certainly. I expect he offered you to just about everyone, but you were no temptation to D'ward. There is more to come, and it would seem that Golbfish is the prince to watch now. Carry on."

Despair! Sorrow! "Take me, master! Take me with you!"

"No, dear boy! Not yet. You must stay and watch, for my sake. And report of course. When the prophecy is played out to the end, when you have completed this task I gave you, then I promise you will be reunited with me and my love. Stop slobbering . . ."

This above all will remain with him: the drab emptiness when the god has gone, the unbearable pain of knowing that his mission is not complete.

Later came an unfamiliar gnawing doubt, a reluctant, treasonous, blas-
phemous sensation that obedience to his real master, which formerly filled
him with unalloyed joy and pride, now bore an odious aftertaste, the cer-
tainty that he is betraying the Liberator.

✌ 29 ✌

Ysian Applepicker did not know the city well. She had arrived
there only a couple of fortnights before the war came. She should have
gone home again while there was time—her parents had written, urging
her to do so—but the marriage had already been arranged and to leave
would have seemed like terrible cowardice. Everyone had insisted that Lemod was impregnable. Soon all the rope bridges over Lemodwater had
been cut down to prevent the invaders crossing, and then it had been too
late. So she had remained at her uncle's house, patiently waiting until the
siege was lifted and a day could be set for her wedding.

She had been all ready for bed when Aunt Ogfooth had come flustering
into her room in great excitement to announce that there was going to be
a holy event, a quadruple conjunction, and Ysian must come and watch.
Such a once-in-a-lifetime opportunity was not to be missed; she had dressed
in her warmest furs and gone out into the night with her uncle and aunt
and with Cousin Drabmere, who wore his sword.

The best view would be from the battlements, Uncle Timbiz had explained, but the wall was off-limits in this time of siege. They had gone
instead to the great square, which wasn't truly great, even to the eyes of a
rustic orchard girl, but was the largest open space in the city. The palace
fronted it, and the temple too. The entire population seemed to have had
the same idea, so the crush was enormous.

To be perfectly honest—although Ysian already knew that honesty was
one virtue that should be exercised with discretion—the quadruple conjunction was not especially impressive. She could recall a couple of triple
conjunctions, and this was not all that much more. The excitement she felt
came from the crowd itself, like an infection. People wept and sang hymns

and called out praises to the gods who were thus promising to protect their loyal and faithful worshippers in Lemod. Ysian wondered if the besiegers viewed the sign that way or if their interpretation might be very different. Time would doubtless tell who was right.

The singing faded, the conjunction ended as Kirb'l parted from Trumb. Ysh reappeared shortly thereafter.

Ysian looked around and realized that she had become separated from her companions. Well, her highly respectable aunt and uncle could always be relied upon to do the right thing, and in this case the right thing was obviously to attend the inevitable service of thanksgiving in the temple. At least half the crowd had come to the same decision, so the squash inside was frightening, the air chokingly stuffy. The high priestess made the service brief, almost indecently brief, shorter than the conjunction itself had been. Soon, but not too soon, Ysian found herself back outside in the welcome cool of the night.

She could still see no signs of her family. Being all alone did not bother her unduly. Indeed it was an adventure. An unmarried maiden should not wander the streets alone, even by day, although that was more a matter of propriety than safety, for Lemod was very law-abiding. She hung around the square as the crowd dispersed, looking for her relations until she was forced to conclude that they must have gone home. Quite likely they had all been separated and each would assume she was safe with one of the others.

She set off to make her own way home. Lemod's streets were narrow and winding, all very dark, and she had no lantern. Anytime she had been out of doors in the past, she had been accompanied by her aunt or Cousin Drabmere or by *someone,* and everything seemed different by night, anyway. Propriety made her reluctant to ask strangers for directions. She wandered around for a while, and all the time the city was growing quieter and quieter around her, the roads emptier and emptier, as the citizens repaired to bed. Very soon her sense of adventure became a feeling of misadventure, of being incredibly stupid. Somehow or other, she had managed to get lost.

Then the shouting began. Alarms rang. People started running. She guessed what was happening, but soon she was caught up in the panic. There were still no lights, only the eerie colored glow of the moons. Even the few lighted windows winked out into darkness. She ran away from the clamor, but invariably it circled around in front of her again. Shouting became screaming, and the clash of steel. She could not tell if the screams came from men or women. Once she almost tripped over a body.

But then—Oh, praise the gods!—she recognized an elaborate marble horse trough. A few gasping minutes later, she stumbled against the great double doors of her uncle's workshop. To her intense astonishment, the little postern door was not merely unlocked, but ajar. She could clearly remember Cousin Drabmere locking it behind him when they left. She hesitated, wondering if this might possibly be some sort of danger signal. Common sense told her that the invaders were charging around the streets killing people, not lurking in dark interiors, but still she hesitated. Then a howling, battling mob surged around a corner into the street. Ysian jumped through the door and shut it behind her.

The big shed was as black as a cellar, but she knew her way, roughly. At the cost of a dozen or so bruises on her shins, she reached the stairs. She crept up them, making no more noise than a growing mushroom, stepping very close to the wall, so that the stair treads would not creak. The house itself was dark and silent. Only the big clock in the living room made any sound at all.

She crept into the kitchen and armed herself with the biggest, sharpest knife she could find. Then she explored every room, all the way to the attics. She found no one, not even the servants, which explained the unlocked door.

She worried about that door. Common sense . . . Her parents had been great believers in common sense and had made an appreciation of its importance a central element of her education—common sense told her to keep it locked. But suppose her aunt or some of the others in the family came home seeking refuge as she had done? That thought brought immediate nightmares of them being cut down on their own threshold. Furthermore, if the Joalians succeeded in seizing the city, they would mount a house-by-house search for defenders, while the Lemodians, if they won, would go around rooting out any stray invaders. The door could certainly be forced easily enough, which would mean damage to her uncle's property. To leave it open might divert suspicion. In the end she went back downstairs and opened it again, leaving it ajar as she had found it. Then she hurried back upstairs to find a hiding place.

The big closet in her aunt and uncle's bedroom seemed a likely choice, but when she went to look at it, she decided that it was all too obvious. She sat down on the edge of the bed in the dark to think. Faint but horrible noises kept drifting in through the open window, sounds of death and violence. As always, the big room was scented with her aunt's favorite perfume. It was warm, this room, never chilly. A soft, friendly room.

She wondered why she did not feel more frightened, even terrified. She decided that there was a blanket of unreality over the events of the night. Quadruple conjunction, big disappointment . . . on her own for the first time since leaving Great-uncle Gooba's orchard . . . unvanquished Lemod about to fall . . . at least it sounded as if it was falling. She really could not believe any of this! Some prayers to the gods would likely be a sensible precaution, especially to Eth'l, patron goddess of Lemodvale. . . . Eltiana had been eclipsed by Trumb tonight. . . . Ysian decided that praying could wait until after she thought of a good hiding place. She would likely have more than enough time for praying then.

A house was burning a few streets away, ruling out any temptation to consider the attics. The workshop downstairs? The big laundry copper where the clothes were boiled?

Cousin Drabmere was probably caught up in the fighting, although he had been an inoffensive, bookish man until the war came. If her aunt and uncle were not already dead, then they had probably fled. Common sense— Ysian could not help wondering now if common sense might be a poor guide to wisdom in such an *uncommon* event as a sack—common sense suggested that she ought to go out and discover who was winning. If the Joalians were, then she should flee also. Trouble was, she knew she could not find her way to the gate. Other refugees would guide her, but she would be just as likely to blunder into a gang of murderous Joalians or Nagian savages, who would be worse. She would be killed or raped or both.

Well, if she was going to be raped, she would rather it happened in a private bedroom than out in a cold public street. She might well be carried off into slavery. A virgin of sixteen was probably very valuable slave material, although she would not count on remaining a virgin much longer. She clutched the big knife tightly to her chest. The first man who tried was going to regret it!

The second one would probably succeed, though.

Probably her marriage had been postponed indefinitely. She might never even know the name of the man she had been about to marry! Aunt Ogfooth had revealed only that he was a widower, wealthy, and a prominent citizen. And a man of mature years . . . The one member of his family Ysian had yet met had been a nasty old harridan with a million wrinkles and few teeth, and even her name had not been disclosed. That was the custom in Lemodia. Ysian had assumed at the time that this antiquated crone was negotiating on behalf of a son or more likely grandson, but then Aunt Ogfooth had let slip the word *brother*. . . .

Why did Ysian not feel dismay at the thought of losing the advantageous marriage she had been promised? It was for that purpose she had been sent to the city. Her parents had very little money. A well-married daughter was their only hope of comfort in their old age. She should be heartbroken at the collapse of all her prospects, so what wickedness was this sense of relief she felt? Had she no shame?

It was at that point in her meditations that she heard men's voices downstairs.

30

" 'THE CITY WAS SACKED,' " EDWARD SAID BITTERLY. "YOU READ about it in history books, but that doesn't prepare you for the real thing. Drogheda, Cawnpore, Boadicea in London, or the Goths in Rome . . . the Saxons, the Vikings. Just words."

The train had slowed to a crawl, waiting for a clear signal to pull into Greyfriars station. Only the grassy sides of a cutting crept by the windows, with a single church spire bright against the evening sky.

"It can't possibly compare with what's been happening in Europe lately," Alice said. She had been wrong to make him speak of it.

"In some ways it's worse, because it's more personal. You pull the trigger on a machine gun and you don't see the blood spurting, I suppose. But battering a man to death with a club—that's real."

"Well, don't talk about it anymore."

"Why not? If I'm ashamed to talk about it . . . I mean, I did it. I opened the city. I knew there would be killing, didn't I? I must have done, mustn't I? It was them or us. The old, old excuse. If I wasn't ashamed to do it then, why should I be ashamed to talk about it now?"

He was ashamed, she knew, deeply ashamed. This was part of the change she had sensed in him. He had brought about the death of thousands.

"Fire and slaughter?"

A clamor of couplings ran down the line and the carriage lurched. Picking up speed, the train began chuffing toward the station.

"There was some fire, yes, but the defenders did that. Men were slaughtered. Children and the old were mostly driven out. The thing had not been properly planned, of course . . . too many deaths. The Lemodians out in the woods reacted very quickly. They broke into the camp and killed all our sick and wounded. In the end it was a reversal of positions—us inside, them outside. But we had the supplies and could wait out the winter. That was what mattered."

People were emerging from the compartments, bringing their bags.

"And rape, I suppose?" she said. "You haven't mentioned the rape."

He shrugged. "That really wasn't so bad. Gosh, I know that sounds awful, but being gutted with a spear is frightfully permanent. There was no violence, no public violence at least. The women knew the rules. When the killing was over and the Joalians held the city, then every man just picked out a woman and said, 'I'm so-and-so. You're mine now.' They submitted and made the best of it."

"Edward! How can you be so . . . callous?"

He looked at her oddly. "That's how it's always been—in their world or in ours. That's more or less how the women were married in the first place. No one ever asked their opinions. Like in Africa, women are property; you know that. This isn't Kensington we're talking about. Even in Kensington it happens. Ask some of the debutantes! Valians live closer to the ground than we do."

She shook her head in disbelief. Was he serious?

"And the men were *dead*!" he added bitterly. "They had it worse, wouldn't you say?"

The station slid into view, and a sign saying GREYFRIARS. Some of the people standing on the platform were waiting to board, standing patiently until the train came to a stop. Others were there to meet friends, and were waving and running. Porters scanned the windows, hunting for hire.

"There was no numen in Lemod," Edward said, peering out the window. "That was probably lucky from my point of view. Most cities in the Vales are sited on nodes, and I think that's true here, too. Lemod had been chosen for its defensible location. It had just a trace of virtuality near the north wall, and there were shrines there and a small temple to Eltiana. But no numen."

Clattering and huffing, the train came to a stop. He slid down the window and reached out to the door handle. He went first with the suitcase and handed Alice down to the platform.

"So there we were, locked up snug in Lemod for the winter, knowing that the Thargians would arrive in the spring. I had fulfilled the prophecy and given the first sign, so I had advertised where I was to Zath. Apart from that— By Jove, there's Mrs. Bodgley!"

31

JULIAN SMEDLEY HAD HAD A BAD DAY. THE CROWDS NIGGLED AT HIS nerves; the close-packed mob in the train suffocated him. He felt as if everyone were watching him, especially men in uniform. He developed an absurd tendency to sweat whenever he saw a policeman. He was frightened he would suddenly start weeping in public.

Women bothered him, especially young women. He found himself staring at them, even while terrified that they would notice his attention. At his age he ought to have learned something about affairs of the heart, but the war had stolen those years out of his life. He was still the innocent virgin he had been when he left Fallow. How could he ever catch up now? No girl would be interested in a cripple—a cripple with no profession, a part man who burst into tears without warning.

His invisible right hand was tightly clenched, aching and cramped. He could feel the nails digging into his palm. Even if he pushed the end of his stump against something to make it hurt, he could not convince himself that those fingers had rotted away in the Flanders mud.

He exchanged little talk with Ginger, except when they changed trains at Chippenham. There they paced the platform together, but they seemed to have nothing left to say each other. In the cold light of day, the previous night had taken on a tinge of nightmare. They did not mention Exeter at all. His story now seemed like the wildest sort of jiggery-pokery, a tale of the horse marines. Perhaps both he and Ginger were ashamed to admit having believed it.

Even now the cops might be informing the guv'nor that his lunatic son was not just a physical and emotional cripple but also a criminal.

The local train was as crowded as the express, puffing along from station to station, full of farmers and West Country burr. Jones disembarked at Wassal, hoping his bike was still where he had left it, chained to the railings. Smedley carried on alone to Greyfriars.

And there he was met by Mrs. Bodgley. Surprisingly, she was just as large and loud as he remembered her, a weathered dreadnought armored in Harris tweed. Her hair was streaked with silver now; there were lines like trenches radiating from her eyes. She beamed at him and boomed at him, saying nothing that might surprise anyone overhearing. Luggage? No luggage? Well, that made things simpler. The cart was this way, for of course motorcars were out of the question these days. He braced himself for questions about medals and the war, for mention of his mother's death or her husband's or Timothy's murder—and none came. He realized as they strode up the station stairs together that Ginger would have warned her about his nerves.

The dogcart might have belonged to Queen Anne, and the shaggy pony between the shafts was almost as ancient. Before Smedley could protest, Mrs. Bodgley scrambled up nimbly on the near side. There she sat, calmly adjusting her skirt, apparently engrossed in watching a gaggle of children playing hopscotch. For a moment he dithered. Of course, when a couple rode together the gentleman must drive, but . . . but she knew about his hand. With a rush of both gratitude and embarrassment, he heaved himself awkwardly into the driver's place. He almost tied himself in a knot reaching the brake. He jiggled the reins. The pony did not know he could not use the whip. It wandered off homeward, dragging the dogcart behind it.

Timothy Bodgley, poor old Bagpipe, had been Exeter's friend, not especially Smedley's. Smedley had never visited the Grange. He whistled under his breath when he saw it in the distance, a crenelated backdrop to a hundred acres of stately park. There were *sheep* grazing in that park! Nothing he had seen that day had so clearly shown him the changes that war had brought.

Now the Army occupied the Grange, and his destination was the Dower House—a gloomy, ugly box buried in monstrous yew trees, ancestral storage for unwanted mothers-in-law. As he drove into the yard, three enormous dogs came roaring to greet him.

"Down, Brutus!" Mrs. Bodgley bellowed. "Be *quiet,* Jenghis! Oh, do stop that, Cuddles! There was a most beautiful house here, you know, designed by Adam. There's an etching of it in the Grange library. But Gilbert's grandmother had it torn down and put up this *dreadful* Victorian barn. I shouldn't complain. I can't imagine what I should have done if the Army hadn't taken over the big house. Oh, these dreadful pigeons! They turned it into a hospital, you know. Can't get servants for love nor money these days, and with just myself, it would be far too . . . Heaven knows what I'll do with it after the war is over. Let me do that. And I'll give Elspeth her rubdown. Please don't argue. She's used to me. Just go on inside, dear boy. Captain, I mean. Make yourself at home. If you want to put the kettle on we can have a cup of tea. Jones said the others would be arriving on the four fifteen, so we've lots of time. . . ."

The Dower House was dark and smelled of damp. Its furniture was old and lumpish, its plaster stained. There was no electricity, not even gas. Smedley filled the black iron kettle from the pump and carried it indoors. He poked up a flame in the range, which would have roasted oxen in herds. Just a little place, this—only seven bedrooms. It was a mausoleum, but at least his nerves would not be troubled by crowds. The kitchen was the size of a ballroom, a vast expanse of shadow and stone. It echoed, full of emptiness. He thought of prisons. He sat on one of the hard wooden chairs and wondered what life should have been.

"There you are!" Mrs. Bodgley boomed, bustling in with the dogs all around her. "I can show you to your room if you like. No, don't thank me. It is I who should be grateful. I have so little company these days. Stop that, Brutus! One tries to keep busy, you know, and do one's bit. Knitting for the troops and war bond committees and visiting our poor dear boys up at the Grange, but I do confess that sometimes the evenings drag, so I was only too happy when Mr. Jones called, and I do so want to hear Exeter's story from his own lips because I never for one moment believed he had anything to do with what happened to Timothy. And where he went to! I have some Madeira cake around somewhere. That inspector man was utterly incompetent, and Gilbert himself was quite distrait at the time. Where did he disappear to so dramatically, do you know?"

Exeter, not the general. "He went to another world, Mrs. Bodgley."

Mrs. Bodgley had been rummaging in a drawer for spoons. She straightened to her full height and transfixed Smedley with a stiletto eye.

"Did you say, 'Another world'?"

"Yes, I did."

"Oh." Mrs. Bodgley pursed her lips and thought for a moment. "How very curious!" she murmured, and returned her attention to the cutlery.

He had never felt so helpless in his life. He was appalled to discover that his hostess had no resident servants, only "old Tattler's daughter who comes in twice a week to do the rough cleaning." Moreover, Mrs. Bodgley did not seem to find that situation remarkable. He had not realized how much the war had changed things.

She began peeling spuds. He could not help with that. He might possibly make beds, but she assured him the beds were already made up. There was no shortage of linen. She had *trunks* and *trunks* of stuff she had brought from the big house, she said. Perhaps he could just look through *that* one and find some more plates?

He had run out of fags. He could not even walk into town to buy some—partly because he was a hunted fugitive, mostly because he had no money. Oh hell! How had he ever blundered into this bog?

Rumbling nonstop as she prepared dinner, Mrs. Bodgley spouted news of his old chums, and he felt the chill of the war's grim shadow. Wounded, wounded, dead, dead, dead . . . She talked of the difficulties the school was having now, for although she was no longer wife of the chairman and hence Honorary Godmother, she had maintained her interest.

She asked what his plans were now. He had to confess that he had none. He had always assumed that he would return to India, where he had been born, following in the guv'nor's footsteps. The Government of India would probably prefer men with two hands, but he had some gongs and he was Sir Thomas's son . . . but the police were after him now. Whatever happened in the next week or two, that blot would never fade from his record. Scratch India.

He kept thinking of Exeter's Olympus—dressing for dinner in the jungle, house servants galore . . . but that mythical world was wilting under the clammy breath of reality. Magical powers and miracle cures, prophecy and vindictive gods . . . how could anyone believe such ravings?

Oh, for a cigarette!

The time came to harness up the pony again. Mrs. Bodgley set off for Greyfriars and the station. Smedley wandered out into the garden. The vegetables were well tended, the flowers needed work. He removed his jacket and tie. Clippers or lawn mower were beyond him, but he found a hand fork in the shed and set to work on the weeds. When that palled, he established that he could use a hoe, after a fashion, and even rake leaves.

The scent of fresh earth reminded him of the trenches. But this was an autumn afternoon in England. He was Home. Thick hedges and ivy-furred walls enclosed him like a womb. There were leaves overhead and white clouds. He could hear a chaffinch and the pigeons. He had done his bit, his war was over. Home! Blighty! A fierce contentment seized him.

After a while he realized that his invisible hand had gone, and he had not wept all day.

The trap came jingling back, with Exeter driving. Smedley went to open the yard gate for them, but of course Alice was there. Alice was a *girl*. Confused by the strange shyness that suddenly possessed him, he hastened back to his gardening. There, at least, he would not have to listen while Exeter discussed old Bagpipe's murder with his mother, if they had not already gone over that.

An hour or so must have drifted by before he heard a mechanical rattling. Exeter came around the corner, grinning cheerfully and pushing a lawn mower. "Escaped!" he said. "Tired of talking! You've got a good show going here."

He hung his jacket and tie on a branch. After a few passes across the straggly lawn, he stopped and glanced at the hedges. The lane outside was a cul de sac, with no traffic. He took off his shirt, to work in his undervest. The ladies were busy in the kitchen, he said. They wouldn't notice. It wasn't quite gentlemanly, but it did make sense. Smedley removed his shirt also, and went back to killing weeds.

His mood of lonely content had faded. Every time he caught sight of Exeter's bronzed shoulders he thought of those ritual scars the man must still have on his ribs. How could he have gone native like that? What little he had said about the Service had made it seem like a very worthy cause. Olympus had sounded like a true outpost of civilization. But spears and mutilation and painted faces . . . those were not pukka!

Dinner was a strange meal. Even with all the windows open, the sepulchral dining room was dim and breathless. Its monumental mahogany furniture would have seated twenty without trouble, so the four of them clustered at one end of the table, Smedley paired with—and tongue-tied by—Alice Prescott. If either of the ladies had ever studied the culinary arts, the food did not bear witness. They both wore dresses, but not evening dresses, and of course the men had nothing except the clothes that Ginger had acquired for them from the mythical barrow. The total absence of servants screamed wrongness.

As compensation, the wines were superb. Everyone became a little louder than usual.

Exeter hardly had a chance to eat. Whenever he paused, either Alice or Mrs. Bodgley would fire more questions at him. He repeated much that Smedley had heard before. He added a lot more. Mrs. Bodgley raised her eyebrows a time or two, but never expressed a doubt as the unlikely tale unfolded.

If Exeter was making it up, or had imagined it all, it was astonishingly detailed and consistent. Reluctantly, Smedley began to sense belief creeping back again, and odd stirrings of something that felt strangely like relief. He was too close to being tipsy to work that out.

After the cheese, the men declined port, and all four moved out to the little crazy-paving terrace to sit on a pair of extremely uncomfortable wrought-iron benches and watch the sky darken and the stars awaken. Alice brought coffee. Mrs. Bodgley disappeared and returned with cobwebs in her hair and a very dusty bottle in hand.

"This is older even than I am," she said. "It's part of a stock of wines and spirits that Gilbert laid down for Timothy when he was born. It seems only fitting that his friends should enjoy them. Edward, will you do the honors, please?"

It was an angel of a brandy.

There was only one thing wrong with the day now.

"Captain?" Mrs. Bodgley boomed. "Mr. Exeter? What am I thinking of? I do believe there are still some of Gilbert's cigars in the humidor. Would either of you care . . ."

It was a goddess of a cigar. Corona Corona, finest Cuban.

"Listen!" Alice said. "That can't be a nightingale? This late in the year?"

"Well?" Mrs. Bodgley demanded, shattering a reflective silence. "What are your plans now, Mr. Exeter?"

Smedley jerked out of a reverie. Good question!

"I do wish you would go back to calling me Edward, Mrs. Bodgley."

He had asked that several times. Smedley was amused to see the redoubtable Mrs. Bodgley not in perfect control of her tongue, but he knew that this evening must be a devilish strain on her. She must feel haunted by ghosts of past, present, and future—son, husband, and better days. She deserved a medal for even trying.

"Tch!" she said. "I keep forgetting. What are your plans now, Edward?"

"I want to enlist, of course; do my bit."

"Naturally. I would not expect anything different of a Fallow boy."

Alice shifted on the bench at Smedley's side. He thought she was about to speak, but she did not.

"Preferably not in the Foreign Legion," Exeter added.

Mrs. Bodgley thundered a brief laugh like a signal cannon. "Indeed not! But from what you say . . ." She was talkative but her wits were not befuddled. "Oh, some of Gilbert's friends will help. I'll think of someone in the morning."

"That would be wonderful! Thank you." Exeter's gaze flickered toward Smedley's empty cuff—and then away again, quickly. "But I also must get word back to the Service, on Nextdoor. About the traitor. That is urgent."

Even the deepening twilight could not conceal the shrewdness in the old lady's stare. "But you say that only people can cross over? You cannot just drop a note?"

Again Exeter glanced briefly at Smedley.

"That is correct. All messages are verbal. Someone will have to make the trip there and back. One possibility would be Stonehenge, the portal I used before, but Alice says the Army has it shut off."

"I am sure that is correct."

Smedley waited for her to invoke some more of her late husband's friends, but she just sipped her brandy in silence.

Exeter scratched his chin. He had cut it while shaving for dinner, and now he was making it bleed again. "Another approach would be to get in touch with the, ah, the numen who cured my leg. The one I called Mr. Goodfellow."

"And where is he?"

"Not far from here, but I'm not sure where. Do you have any local Ordnance Survey maps around?"

"Gilbert had reams of them, but they're packed away in boxes somewhere. And I don't think you can buy any just now—in case of spies, you know. Why do you need them?"

"To find a hill with standing stones on it."

"Nathaniel Glossop."

"Beg pardon?"

"Nathaniel Glossop," Mrs. Bodgley repeated infallibly. "A neighbor. He knows all the local archaeology. I shall call on him in the morning."

"Oh, jolly good!" Exeter said. "Spiffing! That would be very good of you."

"No trouble, Edward. But tell me something. Why did it take you three years to return?"

His hesitation was interesting.

"Well, the Service weren't frightfully helpful, I admit."

"You were a prisoner?"

"Er, hardly! But they'd suspended all Home leave during hostilities, and the Committee didn't want to make a special case for me. They kept saying that the war would be over before I could do any good. Olympus doesn't keep up to date very well, you see. The *Times* doesn't circulate there. We knew the war was still going on, but months would go by without news, and the war always seemed to be on the point of ending. And . . . they had this conviction that I have a destiny to play out as the Liberator."

Mrs. Bodgley made clucking noises of disapproval. The moon was rising, silver behind the sable yews.

"Well, naturally they're more concerned about what's happening on Nextdoor than here," Exeter said defensively. "They're very dedicated to their own cause. And it did take me almost two years to arrive at Olympus in the first place."

"Why?"

He peered at his fingers and found the blood on them. Muttering angrily, he fumbled for a handkerchief. "What? Oh, the Vales are primitive compared to Europe. The distances are not great, but it's like wandering around Afghanistan or ancient Greece. Strangers attract suspicion. Unattached young men are apt to be taken for spies. Remember how Elizabethans felt about paupers—Poor Law, and all that—send them back to their home parish? There's slavery in some places. Thargvale, in particular."

"How barbaric!"

"Believe me, it is! And if not slavery, then military service. For the first year or so, I was caught up in a war."

Pause. "A war?" Mrs. Bodgley repeated the word with disapproval. The brandy was making her louder and more matriarchal than ever. Smedley wondered what Alice was making of her. Alice had not spoken in a long time. She was too close for him to see her expression. She was too close.

"'Fraid so," Exeter agreed.

"Like Afghanistan, you said? Bows and arrows? Some squalid tribal squabble?"

"Very much squalid."

"Edward, I'm afraid I feel a little disappointed in you! Could you not have left the natives to fight their own battles? I really can't see why it need have been any of your business. Your duty lay back here, surely?"

Smedley wondered what the good lady was going to say when she heard about the scars and the face paint. Perhaps Exeter could guess, because he did not mention them.

"I felt that way too, Mrs. Bodgley. But it wasn't so easy. First, no army tolerates deserters. Secondly, I—" Exeter shot another brief, cryptic glance at Smedley, as if checking his reactions. "Well, I had responsibilities there, too. I had made friends, you see, who had given me hospitality, so I could hardly just run away and leave them, could I?"

"You weren't fighting in the ranks, though, were you?" Alice said.

Exeter pulled a face. "Not in the end," he admitted.

"They elected you leader?"

He nodded unwillingly.

"Leader?" Mrs. Bodgley paused, as if rolling the idea around in her mind. "Leader of what?"

"The combined Joalian and Nagian armies. In our terms not much more than a brigade, five or six thousand."

"Indeed? Well, that does make a difference, I admit."

It certainly did, Smedley thought. Brigadier Exeter? Field-Marshal Exeter! Bloody good show!

"Of course, it would be just like a Fallow boy to take command," Mrs. Bodgley mused approvingly. "Leadership! Initiative! The traditions of the Old School. The school magazine will— No, I suppose not."

"Oh, it was nothing to do with me," Exeter protested. "It was just my stranger's charisma."

"You are modest, Edward. It is starting to get chilly, isn't it? But let's stay out here a little longer. I hate the smell of those paraffin lamps. Do tell us about this war of yours."

Exeter laughed unconvincingly. "It wasn't very noble. I worked my way up from the ranks. By the time they elected me supremo, we were locked up in a besieged city with the finest army in the Vales certain to come after us as soon as spring opened the passes. The seasons are running about three months behind ours just now, so that would have been roughly a year after I crossed over."

"Your cause was just, I trust?"

"My cause was just to save our necks. There was no hope of winning anything, nothing at all. All we wanted to do was get home safely."

"Xenophon and the Ten Thousand!"

"On a very, very small scale."

Better still! Smedley had always approved of wily old Xenophon, and he was intrigued by this charisma business—could use bags more of it on the Western Front! "How did you get them to elect you leader?" he asked.

Exeter shrugged. "I didn't. It just sort of happened. Joalians are great believers in *pour encourager les autres*. They'd already beheaded one general. They were ready to shorten his successor and put me up instead. I said I would help, but only if they'd just demote Kolgan back to being my deputy. . . . I told you, strangers have charisma."

"But you'd got them safely into the city in the first place," Alice remarked quietly.

"True. But that was a magic trick."

"So how did you get them out?"

Exeter scratched his chin. "By reading, mostly," he said vaguely. "We had a whole winter to kill, and there were books in Lemod—that was the city, Lemod. I did a lot of reading. And I had Ysian to help."

"Who's Ysian?" Alice asked.

"Er . . . a friend, ah, native, I mean. A Lemodian. Helpful."

"Describe this friend!"

Even in moonlight, his hesitation was obvious. "A girl. I—I found her under a bed, actually."

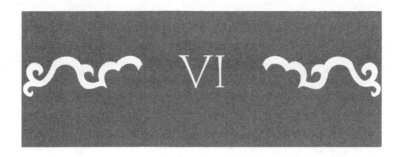

VI

Pawn Promoted

32

THE WEST END OF LEMODVALE WAS VERY HIGH AND THE CLIMATE WAS harsher there, but spring had come at last. Snow still lay on the hills, but in the last few days the temperature had risen dramatically, and now a drizzly rain had begun to fall. The world was about to turn green again.

Lungs strained and boots splashed in the slush as Dosh Envoy sprinted up the street. He could hear the heavy tread and labored breathing of Prat'han Troopleader at his heels. Prat'han was a bigger man by far, but he was weighted down by shield and club. Besides, while acting as D'ward's runner, Dosh had developed the best pair of legs in the army. Knowing that he could win and that winning would matter much more to the troopleader, he eased back slightly. Prat'han drew level. His face was bright red with effort and soaked with sweat. The idiot was wearing a fur suit he had looted somewhere and still persisted in wearing.

Their destination was in sight, and the two guards on the door were watching the race with interest. Prat'han put on a spurt; Dosh let him edge out in front. He was visibly in the lead as they stumbled up to the door and stopped, gasping. They leaned against the wall to catch their breaths. The guards cheered and clapped the winner on the back, but they had grins for Dosh also.

He was one of the boys, now. They spoke to him, joked with him, accepted him. If they were ever in doubt about what D'ward wanted, they would ask Dosh's opinion. He found the situation novel, amusing, and infuriatingly pleasant. He had never sought their approval—why should he enjoy it?

His sins had been forgiven the night he had helped the Liberator break into the city, almost half a year ago. They had been forgotten as soon as Anguan's pregnancy had become noticeable. Oh, once in a while one of the men would snidely inquire who had helped him with that, but the fact that it was cause for ribaldry showed that the former outcast was now accepted as a real man. Dosh's standard response was to explain that he was very versatile. That was absolutely true and always discomfited the inquirer.

"All here now?" Dosh asked as soon as he could speak. The guards nodded. "Come!" he told Prat'han, and led the way in. He was exceedingly curious to know what the Liberator was going to announce at this gathering. He hoped he had not missed anything important already.

The sign over the door said this was the house of Timbiz Wagonmaker, but now it was D'ward's. When Lemod had fallen, every man in the army had picked out a home and a woman to look after it—and him. The rest of the population had been slain or driven out, to conserve food. All the Joalian officers had moved into the palace, but the Liberator had chosen to reside with his troops. Although he had selected a home larger than most, he used it to hold meetings, and no one grudged him that symbol of rank. He was the hero who had taken the city.

He was the Liberator! Everyone knew it now, although he refused to accept the title.

The ground floor was one big workshop. There was no wagon under construction, but there was plenty of loose timber stacked around the walls. With the big double doors open the place was dim, and Dosh's eyes needed a moment to adjust. He realized how hard it had become to distinguish Nagians from Joalians. They had all survived the winter by dressing like Lemodians. In the last couple of days, some of the Nagians had begun to go around bare-chested. Not many, though. Dosh suspected that even full summer plumage would still leave the two armies looking much more alike than they had in the fall.

Everyone he had been told to summon had arrived—twenty-seven troopleaders, Kolgan, Golbfish. The new battlemaster preferred the Nagians' custom of informality, or else he refused to impose Joalian discipline on them. Everyone was sitting. Most of the Joalians were silent and ramrod stiff, while all the Nagians were chattering, and a few were lying stretched out on back or belly. Kolgan Coadjutant and Golbfish Hordeleader were seated on either side of a pile of planks, while D'ward himself sat cross-legged between them. He shot the newcomers a smile of welcome.

Dosh found himself a dark corner where he could watch the faces. He had not been specifically told to attend the meeting himself and could only hope he would be allowed to remain. He had nothing useful to contribute. Anyone he might conceivably be sent to summon was already present.

D'ward looked like a long-legged boy between the gangling, red-haired Joalian and the bulky prince. They were obviously in serious disagreement about something. His eyes went from one side to the other and back again as his deputies contended in angry whispers across him. He was saying nothing, and nothing in his expression revealed which side he favored, if either.

To see the flaccid, wide-hipped Golbfish resisting Kolgan was a phenomenon of note. Tarion would not recognize his half brother now; and when D'ward had been promoted to battlemaster, the Nagians had elected their prince hordeleader unanimously. If Golbfish ever returned to Nagland, Nag was going to be very surprised indeed.

D'ward threw up his hands to end the argument. Then he spoke to the assembly. His blue eyes twinkled. "To business! We have a slight disagreement here about the tactical situation. Let's have it out in public. Kolgan Coadjutant?"

The tall Joalian lumbered to his feet. He was scowling, but that was his customary expression. He wore armor over at least one layer of Lemodian woolens.

Dosh would love to know how Kolgan felt about the Liberator now—a juvenile savage from a minor colony running the Joalian army? The Clique would have his head when they heard of it. But Kolgan would have lost his head a fortnight ago if D'ward had not insisted that it remain attached.

"Honored Battlemaster," said the big redhead, "Hordeleader, and Troopleaders. The Thargians may be in Lemodvale already. If they are not, then they will come over Saltorpass the minute it's open. They will secure Siopass to close off our retreat, and they will march west to Lemod." He glared over D'ward's head as if daring Golbfish to disagree.

The room was humming with tension. Everyone was aware of the peril. This was why Kolgan had been deposed.

"There are lesser passes closer to us," D'ward remarked, "closer to Lemod."

Kolgan sighed patiently. "But the lesser passes open later. And even if the Thargians do manage to come that way, they cannot cut off our retreat, because they would be on the south side of the river—the wrong side."

"They could cross the river."

"No, they couldn't! The only place Lemodwater can be crossed is at Tholford."

Kolgan sounded very sure of that. Dosh grinned to himself. One of the first things the Liberator had done when Lemod was taken was to set Dosh to work scouring the city for books on the history and geography of Lemodvale.

"And our best strategy?"

"Our *only* strategy is to wait until Joal sends a relief force. Probably it will come over one of the lesser passes from Nagvale, but those will not open for several fortnights yet—that side of Lemodwall is higher, as you may know. Or they may come over Siopass, as we did, and then follow our route here. In either case, we must wait for relief. Lemod can resist a siege indefinitely."

"Thank you. Hordeleader?"

Kolgan sat down. Golbfish stood up, swathed in Lemodian woolens of ill-matched colors. He looked very bulky in them, but his bulk was still visibly pear-shaped.

"I agree with Kolgan Coadjutant on what the Thargians are likely to do. I disagree with him about staying shut up in Lemod. We do not know if Joal will ever send reinforcements. If it does, they will have to fight their way to us, every step. Lemod has never been taken by storm in the past, but the Thargians can starve us out. I say we march out to meet them in battle! If we are going to die, then let us die bravely in the open, not trapped like rats, eating our boots! We fought our way in here, we can fight our way out again."

His Nagians cheered him, of course, but without conspicuous enthusiasm. He sat down. Half a year ago, who would ever have expected to hear such defiance from the fat man?

D'ward glanced around the big chamber, as if inspecting reaction among the onlookers. Then he scrambled to his feet and stepped up onto the pile of planks. "My information is that the Thargian army is already in Lemodvale, and will be on our doorstep very shortly. Has anyone else heard similar rumors?"

There was a pause, a long pause. A few Nagian hands rose reluctantly. A moment later, some Joalian hands joined them. Angry whispers buzzed through the shop.

"Rumors!" Kolgan barked. "The city is sealed! Who can know?"

D'ward smiled down at the tall man's angry glare. "When we were the besiegers, the people inside the walls signaled back and forth to the Lemodians in the woods with flags. Did you not see them at the windows? And there are still many thousands of Lemodians here in Lemod. Those outside have been sending them messages. The rumors are well-founded."

Kolgan opened and closed his mouth a few times.

And so did Dosh.

The women!

The Joalian had worked it out also. "Can you trust a word they tell you?" he demanded angrily.

"Yes," D'ward said sadly. "Some of them. And I am not the only one who has been told, obviously. This is a problem, gentlemen. Some of you have won the love of your companions, and I am sure that hundreds of others have done so also. But most of those women are now with child. I am afraid that we must leave them all behind when we depart, and that—"

"Depart?" Kolgan shouted. "Go where? How?"

"Well, home, of course! You don't *want* to stay here do you?"

Even the Joalians guffawed at that, even Kolgan himself, but it was laughter with a brittle ring.

The Liberator folded his arms and looked around the room again. "A fortnight ago," he said loudly, "you honored me by electing me battlemaster. I asked you then to wait, and to trust me. You did both and I thank you for your faith. Now the time has come. This morning it started to rain."

He smiled faintly at the puzzled reaction.

"I am told, and I believe, that the Thargians outnumber us by three to one. The Lemodians must be even more numerous. While I respect Golbfish Hordeleader's courage, I refuse to send warriors against impossible odds. On the other hand, I also refuse to end my life as a slave in the Thargian silver mines."

The assembly growled agreement like a nest of fourfangs.

D'ward raised his voice. "When you have eliminated the unacceptable, you are left with the merely impossible."

He grinned and paused, as if waiting for suggestions. None came.

"No one's mentioned the rope bridges they maintain in peacetime. I looked into the possibility of building one, but it isn't practical. It would take days, and we'd need half the army on the other bank anyway, to defend the construction. If we could move half over, we might as well move all of it."

He waited a moment. Dosh wondered how many of the listeners had even known about the rope bridges. He had heard of them from Anguan and come to the same conclusion—they were not a practical solution.

Receiving no argument, D'ward continued. "It's true that the only permanent, all-weather ford on Lemodwater is Tholford. But at low water, there are other sites where active men can force a crossing. You may think that low water comes in late summer, as it does on most rivers. But Lemodwater is fed by glaciers. Its low point is right now! In a few days the rain and melting snow will start it rising again. Have none of you noticed?"

Dosh heard the mutter of surprise. Certainly he had not spared the river a glance lately, but he never stood guard on the walls. No one spoke up.

D'ward shrugged. "Well, you will see shortly. An army can go where traders and normal civilian traffic cannot. My information is that about three days ago, the Thargians arrived in Lemodvale over Moggpass, which is about twenty miles due south of us. That must have been quite a feat, but Thargians are a determined bunch when roused, so I'm told. They headed west, to Thimb'lford. Men can cross there at low water. They should be making their crossing today. Expect them at the gates by tomorrow night or the day after."

Dosh shivered.

D'ward waited until his audience fell silent. "Now do you see? They're going to be on our side of the river, the north side. So tonight we shall cross over to the south side! It must be tonight—the rain has begun. We jump the river, and then we make a forced march to Moggpass, which the Thargians have so kindly opened for us. Our only way out is to invade Thargvale itself!"

The room exploded in tumult.

D'ward yelled, "Quiet!"—and won silence. "I am your battlemaster! You will take my orders now, or you will depose me and cut off my head! Which is it to be?"

He was younger than anyone present, an untrained youth garbed in a motley collection of cast-off clothes, and yet he seemed to blaze. Deadly blue eyes raked the room. Not a whisper . . .

"Very well. Why does the wall go all around the city? I wondered about that when I first saw it. The only possible reason is that sometimes the river can be crossed! And right now the water is as low as it ever gets."

Men stirred in excitement. Dosh thought of the cliffs and that roaring white torrent. He shuddered. There would be Lemodians over there, and probably Thargians. Not very many, perhaps, but some.

"We need planks," D'ward said, "and all the rope we can find. We can bridge some of the gaps with pontoons. It won't be easy in the dark, but tonight we cross Lemodwater. If we can get one man over, we can get all of us over. Tomorrow we march on Thargvale. The Thargian army will be on the wrong bank—and the river is rising!"

Escape! He was offering them hope—a slim hope, but a chink of light in a sealed tomb. So what was a thousand feet of roaring foam, sharp rocks, ice floes, and Lemodian arrows? Nothing, compared to the Thargian host. The troopleaders sprang to their feet and cheered.

D'ward waved impatiently for silence. "This is what we shall do. Secrecy is essential! Some of the women here now support us, but many are still loyal Lemodians, understandably. They will try to signal. When darkness falls, they may set the place alight. We must round up every woman in the city, so there are no signals passed. Every man will need warm clothes, good boots, four days' rations. . . ."

The implications struck home to Dosh like a kick in the belly. He was going to be parted from Anguan! He would miss that wiry little Lemodian wildcat. He would never see that child she carried. He had always known that this must come to pass, of course, but the actuality was an unexpected blow. Why? Affection? Gratitude for some wonderful copulation? It was no more than affection, surely?

Perhaps he was more like other men than he had realized.

He wrenched his mind back to the Liberator, who was spouting a fountain of orders and directives. Obviously he had worked out all the details in advance. As soon as darkness fell, Golbfish and Kolgan were to lead separate columns across the river. Before then, they must obtain ropes and prepare floats, pontoons, and gangplanks. There were tree trunks and ice floes caught amid the rocks. Of course it would be dangerous. They could expect to lose men, drowned or frozen. The enemy on both banks would attack when they learned what was happening.

If a contested crossing of Lemodwater had been achieved in the past, the Liberator must have learned of it in his reading. He was not mentioning that, so it had never been done.

The withdrawal of the forces on the gates . . .

Oh!

D'ward asked for volunteers for that contingent and got them—but who could doubt that the rear guard was going to die?

Logic said it was impossible. The Liberator said it could be done, and his words carried conviction. It was madness, and it was going to happen. It was going to happen tonight. The troopleaders listened in stunned amazement. By morning they and their army would be on the far bank, or they would all be dead. A lot of them were going to be dead anyway.

Questions?

Most of the questions were about the women. The women were certainly a problem. The women had been taken as slaves and booty, but copulation was not called "making love" without reason. Many of the men were reluctant to leave their concubines now. D'ward was adamant: The women must stay behind. Never see Anguan again . . .

The council took a long time, but the basic plan had been accepted. Only the details needed to be hammered out, and D'ward had answers for every objection. Dosh sat back in his shadowed corner and marveled at this spectacular display of leadership. He could not recall any hint of it in the *Filoby Testament*. Success or disaster, the coming night had escaped the seeress's foresight.

Eventually the Liberator had the troopleaders convinced—he had them roused to quivering excitement. When he dismissed them, they stampeded to the door to begin their preparations. Evening was coming fast.

"Dosh Envoy!" he called, and then he sat down on the pile of planks.

Dosh stalked forward expectantly. Only Kolgan and Golbfish remained.

"Battlemaster?"

The Liberator was hunched over and silent. He raised his head with what seemed a great effort, and Dosh was shocked to see the change in him. The vibrant war leader of a moment ago had disappeared. D'ward was only a haggard, exhausted boy, as if he had been drained of strength.

Kolgan frowned, seeming as puzzled as Dosh was. "Something wrong, sir?"

"Just tired."

Was rhetoric such an effort? True, he had roused almost thirty men to wild enthusiasm, every one of them older than he. Some of them had been twice his age and far more experienced in warfare. He had inspired them to rush out and attempt the impossible, knowing that many of them were going to their deaths. It had been an amazing performance, but why had it left him looking like a corpse?

He smiled weakly at Kolgan, and then at Golbfish. "Thank you for keeping silent there. You have questions too, I know."

Kolgan laughed harshly. "I do. No women, no cavalry, no pack animals? Just a bunch of men on the run? What happens in Thargvale, if we ever get that far?"

A spark of blue fire returned to D'ward's eyes. "I don't know. Do you want to come with us to see, or would you rather stay behind?"

The big man recoiled. "I beg your pardon, sir. It is a bold inspiration! Of course I support you."

D'ward grunted. "Hordeleader?"

Golbfish said, "Did your reading tell you that the river can be forded here at Lemodvale?"

"No. It sort of implied that no one had ever been crazy enough to try it."

The prince's big, suety face split in a grin. "Then by the five gods, I should love to see those Thargian faces when they discover we've gone!"

D'ward chuckled. He rubbed his eyes with thumb and forefinger. "You two go and reconnoiter the best routes. I'll meet you on the battlements by the clock tower steps in an hour."

The two deputies saluted.

"Wait!" D'ward licked his lips. "One last thing before you leave. There's some rope over there." He pointed at Dosh. "Tie this man up."

33

Kolgan Coadjutant and Golbfish Hordeleader hurried over to the door and departed. Dosh sat in dread stillness, his wrists and ankles bound to a chair. Fear churned in his belly, making him nauseous.

D'ward was hunched over again, head in hands. After a long moment he looked up and forced a smile.

"Relax!" he whispered. "I'm not Tarion."

Of course he was not Tarion, but the memories were terrifying. "What are you going to do with me?" Dosh was ashamed to hear the quaver in his voice. "You won't leave me for the Thargians?"

"No! No, of course not!" The Liberator straightened up wearily. "I just don't want you rushing off to the shrine to report to Tion. That's what you would have done, isn't it?"

Dosh fumbled for words that would not come. "But . . . but, Battle-master! Surely you don't think you can keep a *god* from knowing what's happening?"

"Yes, I do. Yes, I can, for a while anyway." He smiled thinly. "I know more about gods than you do, my lad! Why does Tion need you to report to him if the gods already know everything, *mm?* I don't think he would tip off the enemy, but one never knows. You won't be hurt if you behave."

He heaved himself to his feet and walked over to the stairs. He disappeared up them, moving like an old man.

Dosh strained at his bonds, with no success. He could probably trust D'ward's promise not to leave him behind, but he was still determined to escape. His master's orders gnawed at him, compelling him to rush to the shrine and report this new development. And just being tied up was a torment in itself.

He glanced around the shop. There must be something. . . . Yes, there had been a pile of scrap iron lying in the corner where he had sat during the meeting. If he pushed with his feet, he could tip the chair over back-ward. Then he would break his arms or wrists. Try something else.

If he could somehow tip himself forward to put his weight on his feet, then he might manage to shuffle across the room like a snail carrying its shell. He had been left some movement in his shoulders, so if he tipped the chair back a little with his toes, then threw his weight forward, he might manage to rock it enough to—

A voice said, "Stop that."

He stopped.

A girl was standing over him with a balk of timber in her hands.

"Hit him on the head hard enough to dent a cooking pot—that's what D'ward told me to do."

"Would you?" he asked.

"Yes."

"Then I'd better behave myself, I suppose." He had not met Ysian more than two or three times, had not exchanged a dozen words with her. Anguan alone took a lot of satisfying and for variety there had been other playmates around much safer than Ysian Applepicker—D'ward's mistress had been off-limits.

There was something different about her . . . her hair. She had gorgeous dark auburn hair, which she had worn in a thick pile on top of her head. He had often wondered how she would look with it hanging loose and no clothes on, and how it would feel to play with. Now she had cut it short. Criminal! It made her look even younger. It made her look boyish, for she was short and thin. Her nose was small and peppered with freckles. She wore a long dress of some dark material, a shadow in the fading light of evening. He could make out a tightness to her jaw, and he decided she was capable of carrying out her threat. The glint in her eye suggested that she might even enjoy doing so. Definitely boyish.

"Pull up a chair," he said. "I won't run away."

Ysian thought for a moment solemnly, then sat down on the pile of planks D'ward had used, watching Dosh fixedly and still holding the club.

"We may be here some time," he said.

"I expect so."

"Tell me about yourself."

She kept her eyes on him like an agate idol. "What is there to say? This was my home. When D'ward took it over, I came with it."

"What happened to your family?"

For a long moment she did not answer, but when she spoke her voice was unchanged. "My aunt and uncle are out there in the woods somewhere. My cousin died in the battle."

D'ward had been right, as usual. The guerrillas had been keeping the women in town informed; the women who had fallen in love with their masters had passed them the news. It was inevitable that Ysian would be one of those traitors. The Liberator's charm could melt warriors twice his age. A juvenile mistress would not have a chance.

"I am sorry," Dosh said. "Truly, I am! I did not start this war. I am not even a warrior."

"I know. You were the other prince's plaything."

He withheld the obvious retort that she was D'ward's. "You are well-informed."

"We women gossip."

That might be humor or cynicism, he could not tell. How much of his life story had he told to Anguan, and how much had she babbled to the women of Lemod? Ysian's features had not changed expression since she arrived. She was only a kid, but he sensed he was matching wits with a very shrewd woman.

"What else do you know about me?"

"That you are a liar."

"All men are liars!"

She did not reply. Admittedly his position put him at a considerable disadvantage, but he was annoyed that she was besting him in the conversation.

"I have never lied to D'ward."

"Yes, you have!" She glared. "He asked you to find him a copy of the *Filoby Testament*, and you told him there were none in the town. I know there were. You threw them in the river."

"That is not true!"

"I saw you. I followed you."

He gritted his teeth. "Does he believe that?"

"I told him about the books, but it was too late. You had found them all. He said he was not surprised. He said you had been sent to spy on him and that was why you had taken service with the prince, back last summer. He said there is a prophecy about him and a prince and you never mentioned it to him, so he knows you are not to be trusted. He thinks you are one of those people who cannot help lying all the time."

That was probably true. Telling the truth always seemed sort of risky. Still, lying was probably just a habit. He was as loyal to D'ward as his other loyalty permitted—but he could not explain that.

"You told D'ward about Moggpass."

She did not deny it, just sat and watched him as if he were a cake on a griddle.

"If he cannot trust me, how can he ever trust you? You betrayed your people to the leader of the army that killed your cousin. Why? What sort of woman does that?"

"He knows he can trust me."

Dosh snorted. "But you cannot trust him!"

"I trust him absolutely." Her confidence was stupidly childlike and infuriatingly unshakable. He felt a sudden urge to crack it, to hurt.

"He took the city! He slew your family! And you think you can trust him? What madness is that? He is going to leave you tonight! What will your own people do to those who have aided the enemy?"

"I am coming with you tonight. I shall be your guide."

"He told the troopleaders that none of the women would come."

"Except me."

"He will not take his own woman and make his men leave theirs. He is not that sort of leader!" Why else had she cut her hair off, though?

Ysian shrugged—the first gesture he had seen from her. "I was raised on the south bank. I know Moggpass. I can help."

"He is lying to you, you know."

"No!"

Aha! Now the tinder was starting to smoke.

He sighed with great sadness. "Women in love are rarely reliable judges of character, Ysian Applepicker."

She bared her teeth at him. He chuckled, imagining her as wrestling partner. Usually he preferred boys tough and girls tender, but he would relish a sharp tussle with this firecub.

"What makes you think I am in love, Dosh Envoy?" she demanded.

"Ha! He is the Liberator. No one can refuse that man! I just watched him twist thirty warriors to the shape he wanted, all at the same time. Even I really do try to please him, as much as I can. No woman could resist him for a moment!"

Ysian tossed her head, perhaps forgetting that she had cut her hair. "You are jealous of me, Houseboy! Jealous because I live with D'ward!"

He flinched at the use of his former name, then sudden inspiration. . . .

"Why are you laughing?" she shouted.

"I don't need to be jealous of you, girl! Do I? Nothing to be jealous of!"

She blushed furiously, confirming his guess. She really did look ready to club him, and for some reason that made him laugh even harder.

"We have more in common than I thought!" he taunted. "There's another way to win a woman's loyalty, isn't there?"

Only D'ward would have thought of that, or been capable of it.

34

Golbfish stood at Kolgan's side on the battlements, staring down at the river. He felt ashamed of himself. The flow was half what it had been when he first came to Lemod, and he had never noticed the change. Beaches of shingle fringed both banks; ledges and boulders dispersed the channel; tree trunks and ice flows bridged some of the narrower gaps. An agile man could certainly work his way to the middle. Beyond that, the widest, fastest stretch . . . well, that was what friends were for.

The sides of the gorge were vertical in places, and not much less than vertical everywhere else. He wondered who stood in the woods on the far side, watching the city.

He spoke for the first time since leaving Wagonmaker's. "By the five gods, he's right again! It is a way out, and the only way! He saw it and we did not."

Kolgan growled. "I wish I knew how he does that."

Golbfish had asked the Liberator that question once, but the answer had been something about a temple of learning somewhere, and he had not understood. "Where will you try?"

"Down there looks good," the Joalian said, "but how could we get to it?"

They paced the parapet for an hour, until each had chosen a point of attack. The Nagians would try downstream, the Joalians upstream. The leaders would have to guide their men across by memory.

"Think we can do it?" Golbfish asked glumly.

"Cross? Some of us, yes." The tall man glared across at the far cliffs and tugged at his red beard. "But to invade Thargvale with no cavalry, with very little surprise, with a larger army already in the field and able to cut our line of retreat . . . You know this is madness?"

The alternative was worse.

"Have you ever been to Thargland?"

Kolgan shrugged. "Once. As a youth, I accompanied an uncle of mine on an embassy to Tharg. I was not impressed."

"You are a Joalian. You would not be impressed by a Thargian shitting gold bars."

"I would certainly have them appraised by a competent minter."

Golbfish chuckled, but it was a social chuckle, and false. "Tonight the river. Tomorrow the guerrillas, the forest, and the pass. We must take life one day at a time now and be grateful for it."

"Aye!" Kolgan said sourly. "And even if we fight our way home, Your Majesty, our troubles will not be over. Your brother will be well established on your throne now, with an army of his own, and my foes in the Clique will have drawn up detailed plans for my funeral."

This would not do. Leaders must maintain their own morale if they were to maintain their troops'. Golbfish squared his shoulders—as much as his shoulders would ever square.

"Look on the bright side. However it began, this is no longer a squalid territorial squabble. We are caught up in the affairs of gods. Many things are prophesied of the Liberator, some clear and some obscure. Many things are likewise prophesied for a man named D'ward, and now we know that D'ward and the Liberator are the same. The most famous of the prophesies is that the Liberator will bring death to Death. If you wanted to find Death, Kolgan Coadjutant, where would you go looking?"

Kolgan raised his eyes to the southern peaks, his red brows bunched in a fearsome scowl. "Are you suggesting he is going to lead us to the city itself?"

"What use is a prophecy that is never fulfilled? Tharg would not take us very far out of our road, as I recall."

"It would be a shorter road, because we should never return."

True! Golbfish admitted to himself that he held no great hopes now of ever seeing Nag again. "When you were in Tharg, did you visit the double temple?"

"I saw it, although it was not then complete. Not all the pillars were erected, K'simbr Sculptor was still working on the image of the Man as Creator. But I have looked upon the face of Death." He spat contemptuously. "No one but the Thargians would raise such an abomination!"

After a moment he added, "And their cooking takes the skin off your tongue."

Before Golbfish could comment, D'ward came stalking along the parapet. He seemed to have recovered his strength, although his face was still drawn.

"Possible?" he demanded.

"We'll take casualties," Kolgan growled. "But it won't be a massacre."

The Liberator nodded and leaned on the battlements. "Get as many men working on supplies as you can. Ropes, planks . . . food for the march, of course. Wineskins and barrels for floats. Have to lower the barrels down the cliffs in nets, but keep all preparations out of sight until dark, of course. A swimmer won't last two minutes in that cold. Oh . . . I didn't say so, but Ysian comes with us. She knows the terrain."

Golbfish caught Kolgan's eye. When the Lemodians returned, they would be hard on traitors.

Kolgan was disapproving. "Sir, this will not be an easy march, even for battle-hardened warriors. For a girl . . ." He let the suggestion die aborning.

D'ward was staring down at the river. "Do you know the narrowest escape I have had in this campaign so far, Coadjutant?"

"Your entry into the city, I assume, sir."

"No." He looked up with a grin. "The next morning, when I first met Ysian. She came at me like a whirlwind. She very nearly skewered me with a butcher knife."

The men laughed as men do when their leader makes a joke. "You tamed her, sir!"

"Or she tamed me. Now, anything else?"

"What of Dosh Envoy?" asked Golbfish. "I thought you trusted him?"

D'ward smiled thinly. "In some things. He has a higher loyalty that you'd be happier not knowing about. He'll come. Don't worry about him once we're across."

He looked up at the drizzling clouds. "Pray for rain," he said. "Pray for lots and lots of rain."

Just before the light failed completely, Golbfish buckled on a sword. He sent a squad down the cliff face to rope out a path and string ladders. He followed with the next contingent, descending into black madness. Men kept coming steadily after that, with ropes, with timber, with anything that might float.

An hour or so later, bruised, battered, and freezing, he stood on the south shore.

He had been one of the lucky ones. Everyone went roped, with two companions feeding out the line behind him, but anyone who slipped landed in ice-cold water and was usually smashed into the rocks before he could be hauled back. Planks worked loose from their moorings, barrels sank, ropes failed, ice floes rushed out of the night like monsters. Men vanished in mid-sentence and were gone forever. Darkness and the roar of the river made communication almost impossible. The current brought down Joalian bodies.

As soon as he had a score or so of men with him, Golbfish secured ropes to guide the rest. Then he told a squad to follow him and set off up the cliff. When the Lemodians learned what was happening, they would start rolling boulders down on the invaders.

The slope was steep—rock and mud, dribbling water. He knew he was at the top when he banged his head on a tree root. He hauled himself over the lip and rose shakily to his feet. The darkness was absolute, but *something* alerted him. He ducked. A blade whistled overhead. He dragged out his sword and slashed at the night. He felt a sickening, squishy impact, heard a cry, and knew that he had just drawn his first blood. He moved quickly to the other side of the tree and peered around helplessly, listening. His victim was sobbing and muttering prayers, somewhere on the ground.

Again an unnamed sense warned Golbfish of movement, and he flailed his sword at the empty air. He was a warrior now, a killer. Behind and below him, he could hear his own men coming.

"Watch out!" he shouted, parrying blindly. His blade struck another with a loud clang. He dropped to a crouch and swung again, knee high. A man screamed and fell into crackling undergrowth.

The only way to tell friend from foe was by speech—challenge, and if he did not reply in the right accent, try to kill him. If he just tried to kill you, don't wait for the reply. But the resistance was surprisingly light and soon faded away completely.

Having secured a beachhead in the woods, Golbfish detailed a squad to accompany him and set off to establish contact with Kolgan.

The Joalians were having a worse time of it. There was another blind skirmish in the undergrowth, and again the defenders withdrew. Soon Nagians were hauling Joalians over the cliff edge and securing ropes for those coming after. There was no sign of Kolgan himself.

Golbfish returned to his own column and was dismayed to discover less than a hundred men in position. He waited for a while to see if the Lemodians would launch a counterattack. Nothing happened; the woods were silent. He scrambled back down to the river. The army was crossing, but at this rate it seemed likely to take days. He fought his way back across the river—an even more hair-raising procedure than the first trip, for he frequently had to work his way around other men clinging to the same rope or boulder.

He harangued the crowd milling on the beach. He assured them that their comrades were crossing safely and had not just gone to a watery grave. He ordered more lines set up, more avenues mapped through the maze.

He climbed back up the north cliff in a shower of gravel, mud, and descending warriors, and somehow even forced his way up one of the rope ladders dangling on the walls. More haste! he commanded. Faster!

He reeled off in search of D'ward and found him overseeing the defense at the gates, for the Lemodians had guessed what was happening. Even there, though, the assault was strangely halfhearted.

Golbfish reported. D'ward listened, thanked him, and ordered him back to the south bank. He set off to cross the river a third time. He saw with relief that the exodus was gathering speed.

There were no moons. By midnight the rain had become a downpour, making the darkness absolute. Undoubtedly many men died at the hands of their friends as gangplank or rope failed and too many struggled to occupy the same perch. Hundreds drowned or froze or were smashed on the rocks.

At dawn Golbfish found himself in command of the army in the orchards of the south bank. Kolgan had fallen while climbing the cliff, breaking his shoulder. He was huddled in a daze of agony and shock on the shingle. The river was littered with bodies and the shore with wounded.

Rain still fell in torrents. The river was visibly rising. Lemod was back in the hands of its rightful owners, blazing in several places from fires set to slow down their return. There was no sign of pursuit. Praise the gods!

Dosh Envoy appeared in the first gray light, accompanied by a boy whom a second glance showed to be Ysian in male clothing. The sight of her blue lips persuaded Golbfish to let fires to be lit. The two camps had been amalgamated and he had posted a cordon around the perimeter, almost a solid fence of men. The Lemodians were still not attacking, not even re-verting to their old guerrilla tactics. Why not?

Everyone was coated in mud. Half the survivors seemed to be limping or staggering blindly in deep shock. One skinny youngster arrived hobbling, with his arms around two friends. He pulled loose from them and steadied himself on one leg, hanging on to a branch.

"How many?" he barked, and Golbfish realized that the kid's eyes were blue.

"Casualties? Four or five hundred, I think."

The muddy scarecrow winced. "No opposition?"

"Very little. How many did you leave behind?"

"Damned few," D'ward said. "How many can't walk?"

Golbfish shrugged. "There are at least fifty still down on the beach. Up here . . . I don't know. Another fifty?"

The Liberator groaned and wiped an arm across his face. It remained just as filthy as before. "You all right?"

"A trifle fatigued, perhaps. You, sir?"

Chuckle. Another groan. "Twisted an ankle, that's all." The Liberator laid his injured foot on the ground and showed his teeth in a grimace. "My first battle," he muttered.

Golbfish saw how his eyes were glistening, and felt a curious twinge of sympathy. Like him, D'ward was not a genuine soldier, was not hardened to being responsible for the lives of followers. Most leaders would have been cheering madly at this point, exulting in a brilliantly executed withdrawal. Twice now, D'ward had pulled off stunning reversals; twice he had made brilliant generalship look like child's play, and all he was concerned with was the cost.

"The river has taken its toll, but it was not the massacre the Thargians would have inflicted."

"We must see they don't get their chance yet." D'ward eased himself to the ground. "Summon the troopleaders." Ysian came and knelt beside him. She tried to wipe his face with a rag, and he waved her away irritably.

Soon the troopleaders gathered around, a bedraggled, shaken retinue, barely half the number who should have been there. D'ward appointed temporary substitutes and sent for them—there was no time for proper elections, he said. He seemed to know the names and abilities of every man, Joalians as well as Nagians.

Still sitting in the mud, leaning against a tree, he outlined what everyone already knew and did not want to think of. They had escaped from one trap, but only into a greater. The Thargians might recross the river and try to intercept their quarry before it could reach Moggpass. If not, they would head east to Tholford and block the road back to Nagvale. There would undoubtedly be many more armed men in Thargland itself. The reckoning had only been postponed.

"Now we must march," he said. "Anyone who can't must stay. Form up."

The men were exhausted, but the alternative was death or slavery. The troopleaders exchanged glances, but no one objected.

D'ward hauled himself to his feet. Half a dozen men rushed forward to help, but he refused them. In obvious pain, he began to hobble forward. In a moment someone offered him a staff, freshly cut, and he accepted that. He was setting an example, but that was all he was capable of.

Kolgan had arrived, but he was still too shocked by pain and exposure to be any use at all. Marveling at the strange fate the fickle gods had thrust upon him—and cynically amused by it also—Golbfish took effective command and issued the necessary orders.

One woman and less than five thousand men set off on a journey of conquest and deliverance. The steady, chilling rain was both a physical torment and a promise of hope.

Behind them, the abandoned wounded screamed and pleaded until their voices faded into the distance.

35

"THARGVALE IS BEAUTIFUL," EXETER SAID. "NATURALLY. IT'S VERY fertile, the climate is moderate, and it's ruled by an aristocracy."

"What has aristocracy got to do with beauty?" Smedley asked drowsily.

Mrs. Bodgley had shepherded her guests indoors to the drawing room and settled them in chairs. A single oil lamp cast a soft light on the four faces, while two moths held races around the glass chimney. Fortunately the chairs were excessively uncomfortable, or Smedley would not have been able to stay awake at all. Alice had reluctantly consented to play, insisting she was hopelessly out of practice. She had then executed a couple of Chopin études from memory. Very well, too, so far as he could tell. And now they were back on Nextdoor again.

"Oh, *really*, Captain!" His hostess's tone suggested that he was showing himself to be excessively ill informed. "It's a matter of tender loving care! The only people who can look after land properly are those who plan to hand it on to their children and grandchildren. Gilbert's father planted an avenue of oak trees, knowing he could never live to see their majesty. That was fifty years ago, and they need another hundred at least. Gilbert himself absolutely refused to countenance mining operations on our place in the Midlands. That sort of thing. Men who think only of their own lifetimes *exploit* land. Those who think of their families *nurture* it. Do help yourself to another cigar if you wish," she added, as though regretting her scolding.

Smedley thanked her and heaved himself out of the lumpy chair even more gratefully. He went to the humidor. No Bodgleys would admire the oak trees in their prime. The Bodgley line had died out when Timothy was murdered. There was no one left to smoke the cigars, even.

Alice's eyes were twinkling in the lamp's gentle glow. "You can carry it too far, of course, like anything else. William the Conqueror depopulated whole counties to make royal deer forests. People have rights, too."

Mrs. Bodgley considered the point and seemed to decide that it was a dangerous heresy. "Not necessarily. People come and go, but land is forever."

Exeter flickered a wink at Smedley as he returned to his chair. "Do you suppose that aristocrats' tendencies to make war all the time is a form of population control, weeding out the peasants?"

The lady saw the hook at once and bit it off. "Probably! Lancing a few of the men would be kinder than letting women and babies starve, wouldn't it?"

"Depends which end of the lance you're on, I expect. But land and war do seem to go together. The Thargian military caste is just as bad as Prussian Junkers."

Dogs of war howled in the night of the mind. "Dueling scars?" Smedley demanded.

"No, I don't think they go that far."

"Thargvale is like England?" asked Alice.

"It has the same organized, cared-for look. The vegetation is very different. Thargian trees are colorful. We have copper beeches and then dull old green. They have blue and gold and magenta and various other shades as well. But the great estates are beautiful. The farmland is one big garden. The wild parts are beautiful too—and yes, some of those are deer parks. There are no picturesque little villages, though, or not many. The slave barns are kept out of sight."

"Sparta?" Mrs. Bodgley murmured.

"Similar," Exeter agreed. "I didn't see much of it at first. Partly because it was raining cats and dogs, partly because I twisted an ankle leaving Lemod and it took everything I had just to keep walking. The river crossing was a tricky business all round. Old Golbfish was the hero of the hour, organized the whole thing and rallied the troops. We were lucky with the weather. The river began to rise, so the Thargian army daren't come after us. The Lemodian guerrillas left us alone. By the second day we were into Moggpass. The Thargians had opened a trail—bridging streams, cutting through the avalanches, and so on, and that helped a lot. By the fourth day or thereabouts we came panting down into Thargvale and could start the looting and pillaging. We were half a year late, but that's what the original intention had been. Everyone had a great time."

"Except you?" Alice asked.

"I healed up quite quickly, actually. The troops were feeding me mana, although they didn't know it. Not that I deserved it, but that made no difference."

Smedley fought down a yawn. The carriage clock on the mantel estimated the time at around eleven. As soon as he finished the cigar he would excuse himself and head off to bed. Exeter's little war was interesting, but he had no need to hear any more about war for the next hundred years.

Alice was wearing a dangerously sweet smile. "So Pocahontas led you to the pass, did she? Then she went back to her own people?"

In a very flat voice, Exeter said, "Yes, she led us to the pass. She couldn't go back to her family, although we went very near her home. They would have treated her as a traitor, even though she was only a child."

"I see. Sorry. I was being bitchy."

Mrs. Bodgley gulped audibly. "Er, what did these Thargian Junkers of yours have to say about the looting and pillaging?"

Looting and pillaging were not part of the Fallow curriculum.

"Almost nothing! That was very strange indeed! They shadowed us with cavalry, lancers on moas. We could see them in the distance, but they never closed. They picked off stragglers and patrols, but only Joalians. Nagian blood was never shed."

"Odd?"

"Very! Favoritism! It began to cause dissension, as you may imagine. Golbfish insisted that the enemy was trying to pry the allies apart, split the Nagians away from the Joalians, and he managed to keep the peace more or less—he was a wonder, that man! After a couple of days, when the pattern became obvious, he suggested that Nagians and Joalians exchange equipment, helmet for shield, spear for sword. We tried that, and even the army itself could hardly tell which was which. The Thargians stopped attacking at all.

"We kept up the pace. Forced marches, thirty miles a day. It was a race. Moggpass had held us up a little. After that we had a clear run across Thargvale to get to Saltorpass and home. Thargian roads are excellent, as you might guess. In order to cut us off, their main army had to run the gauntlet of Lemodflat, and I told you what that's like."

"Obviously you won the race, or you wouldn't be here."

Exeter rubbed his eyes. "No. We lost. Well, not exactly. The Great Game came into play again. I say, it feels deucedly late! We didn't get much sleep last night. . . . Do you think we could continue this breathtaking saga in the morning?"

"Well, of course!" Mrs. Bodgley said. "But you can't leave us hanging like that! Give us a clue. What do you mean by the Great Game?"

"The Pentatheon, the Five. I told you how Krobidirkin got me involved in the Joalian campaign, and possibly Tion was in on that also. I still don't know all the details. The Game is so complicated that even the players can't keep track of the rules, and everyone has his own way of scoring. But when Zath learned that the gates of Lemod had been opened under a quadruple conjunction, he knew exactly where the Liberator was. So he leaned on Karzon, who is the Man, who is also patron god of Thargland. That was why the Thargians weren't killing us—the priests in Tharg had received a revelation from Karzon."

"I'm lost," Alice said.

"Zath wanted me taken alive."

"Alive?"

"So he could make absolutely certain I died, of course. This time he was going to do it himself and see it was done right."

ᕙ 36 ᕘ

NOONTIME SUN BEAT DOWN ON THE DUSTY ROAD. THERE WERE NO mountains in sight to the south at all—a situation that seemed wrong to Dosh, as if a necessary part of the world were missing. Thargvale was very big, the army very small. With the scouts and foragers and skirmishers spread out amid copses, hollows, and hedges, five thousand men could vanish into the landscape. Trudging up the road with Ysian at his side, he could easily disbelieve in those five thousand men.

That was a delusion, a fancy. In fact Talba's squad was just ahead, out of sight over the rise. Beyond the hedgerows, patrols flanked the army's progress on either hand. Gos'lva and his cavalry troop were close behind—unfortunately.

Since Lemod the cavalry traveled on foot, like everyone else. They were close enough to call out ribald remarks, usually about the incongruity of the pervert squiring the battlemaster's concubine. Away from the city, out in the field again, Dosh was no longer one of the boys. Jittery men needed a butt for nervy humor, and he was an obvious target.

"Hey, Pogink Lancer?" bellowed a voice.

"Yes, Koldfad Lancer?" roared another.

"Tell me, Pogink Lancer, why Dosh hath no spear?"

"I don't know, Koldfad Lancer. Why hath Dosh no spear?"

The punch line was predictably obscene. The cavalry's humor had never been of the best; descent to ground level and the status of mere mortals had not improved it. Their current blisters, fatigue, hunger, danger, and other tribulations must be very good for their souls but were obviously failing to keep their primitive minds from carnal fantasies.

Dosh bore no weapons because D'ward still used him as a runner. He probably traveled twice as far as the rest of the Army did in a day. He didn't usually let the abuse worry him, and didn't know why he was feeling the bite now.

"Hey, Koldfad Lancer?"

"Yes, Pogink Lancer?"

"What do you think of the way those hips move?"

"Which hips are you admiring, Pogink Lancer?"

"You don't have to stay here and listen to them," Ysian said quietly.

Dosh glanced down and saw a puzzled look in her big, clear eyes—the eyes of a child. She had been limping along at his side in silence for some time, apparently paying as little attention to the humorists as he did . . . paying, it must be admitted, very little attention to him either. The pack she bore was as big as any man's, her boyish form bent almost double under it. Every man in the army was half again as big as she was, but she kept up. She never complained, so far as Dosh knew. He sought her out and escorted her when he wasn't running errands, but the two of them rarely spoke much. The only thing they had in common was that they were both misfits.

A runner could not carry a pack, either. Ysian had shared her rations with him.

"They're just getting randy," he muttered, and then wondered if she would even understand what he meant.

Apparently she did. "This rape and pillage expedition hasn't produced much of either so far, has it? And they are not as perceptive as you are."

"Don't let them vex you. D'ward had his own reasons for bringing you. It's none of their business. Want me to carry that pack for a while?"

Ysian shook her head, hefted the pack higher on her shoulders, and continued to limp along.

D'ward was bringing up the rear, as he usually did. He had given himself the task of inspiring the stragglers, the wounded and the weakest, although every day men would drop in their tracks and perforce be abandoned to the doubtful mercy of the Thargians. Golbfish was in the van, leading the rout.

The land was deserted. The Thargians had burned the houses and driven off all the livestock. There were no women to rape and precious few goods to pillage—which mattered little, as the invaders had no pack beasts to carry booty. Whenever the weary foot-sloggers did manage to catch a stray zebu or auroch, it went straight in the pot. The rations brought from Lemod were exhausted; the spring fields were bare. A few more days of this, and hunger would bring the army to its knees.

Thargwall to the north was a glittering parade of ice and fresh spring snow. Somewhere behind it the Thargians must be marching too. Mountains loomed to the east also, closer every day. Within those crags lay Sal-

torpass, the road home, but could the weary, starving invaders ever hope
to force it, and then Siopass after? This campaign seemed destined for fame
as one of the greatest military blunders in Valian history. Joalia had sacked
Lemod, thanks to D'ward, but otherwise all it had achieved was to force
the Thargians into wasting a strip of their own homeland. Dosh found that
a very small consolation indeed.

Like the peaks of Thargwall, massacre and surrender loomed ahead, ever
closer, and the survivors would go to the silver mines. The two misfits
could hope for nothing better. Dosh was serving his chosen god, and to die
for Tion would guarantee him an eternal place with the blessed among the
constellations, but the girl had no reason to be there. She had been useful
as a guide in Lemodvale—why had D'ward not left her there? Had he no
gratitude at all? Dosh would have expected better of the Liberator, somehow. The *Filoby Testament* never mentioned any Ysian, as far as he could
remember. That meant nothing; the prophecies were very patchy.

He was on top of the rise now, with Talba and his men in clear view
ahead. He stared around at the countryside—half expecting, as always, to
see a second Thargian army advancing in wrath. Specks in the far distance
were some of their scouts, lancers on moas. They rode circles around the
invaders, watching like buzzards, pestering like mosquitoes, and yet now
they had stopped attacking at all.

A temple!

A cluster of trees and ancient stone buildings standing all alone, halfway
up a hillside in the middle of a pasture, where there was no visible reason
for any sort of settlement at all—that could only be a sanctuary of some
sort. The trees' spring foliage was beaten gold, but so was the glint of the
central dome, and gold said *Tion*. Dosh could not resist that call. He did
want to; he was eager to serve his master.

"Better see if D'ward needs me," he muttered, and stepped to the verge.

Gos'vla and his men marched by; he gave them the finger and they
shouted obscenities at him. As soon as they had gone past, he dived through
the hedge. He sat down in the weeds and waited for the rear guard to pass.
The last troop went by him singing lustily, which was reasonable evidence
that D'ward was with them, encouraging and inspiring as only he could.

Dosh stayed where he was a little longer. Then he scrambled to his feet
and began to run across the fields.

37

Smears of dust in the distance told Dosh that the Thargians were still skulking. They might very well intercept him before he could ever catch up with his companions again. He was neither Nagian or Joalian, so he could not guess how they would treat him. It was better not to speculate. No matter, he had news he must pass to his master.

Half a fortnight ago D'ward had asked an unsettling question: Why should a god need spies to tell him things? Dosh had puzzled over that a lot until he worked out the answer. A god did not *need* anything. Gods were omniscient. It was the act of service that was important, and it was important only to Dosh himself. As a huntercat was trained to fetch prey, so he was being trained to serve, so that his soul might be worthy of a place in the heavens. Sacrifice was of value to the worshipper, not the god. The more it hurt the better it was, whether the sacrifice was a scrawny chicken or an act of service. Tion did not need Dosh, but Dosh desperately needed Tion.

The settlement was an abbey, he decided as he drew close. A nunnery was possible but a monastery more likely for an avatar of Tion.

Gasping for breath, he trotted through the gateway, slowing to a respectful walk within the sacred precincts. The buildings were very old, thickly coated with moss—five of them crouching among the trees and one larger edifice standing off by itself in the open. From the size of its windows, that one was probably a scriptorium. The order could not be very large, a dozen monks at most, and he wondered what they did with themselves, all alone out here in the hills. He caught a glimpse of a gowned figure bent over, weeding a herb garden, but saw no one else around. Prosaic washing waved on a line.

The minster was recognizable by its dome and central location. His wet shirt flapped against his skin as he strode up the steps. One side of the double door stood ajar, and he stepped through into clammy dimness.

The little chapel was entirely barren of furniture, not even an altar. It held only the image of the god, lit by beams shafting down from high slits in the dome. It certainly represented some aspect of the Youth, but a chunky, unappealing carving in veined marble, with his customary nudity partly concealed by a scroll he held vertically in both hands.

Dosh had been given a personal ritual to summon his master. Gods always designed such ceremonial so that they would not be duplicated by any trivial accidental gesture, and in his case he had to begin by taking off his clothes. That required privacy. He stood on one leg to remove a boot and almost fell over as a tall figure floated forward out of the shadows. Where had he . . . Oh, there was a door in the corner.

The monk was elderly, but his back was straight and his shaven face and head made his age hard to estimate. The bones were well shaped under the parchment skin; in his youth he would probably have been worthy to serve the lord of beauty. His yellow robe shone in the gloom; his sandals made a faint shuffling noise on the stone floor. A glittering necklace dangling to his waist suggested that he was the abbot himself. He was frowning.

"You come to pay reverence to Holy Prylis, my son?"

Fortunately, long winter nights of pillow talk with Anguan had given Dosh a grasp of Lemodian, and Lemodian was not unlike that dreadful Thargian croak. He understood, if only just. Prylis was god of learning—hence the scroll.

Clearly the holy father did not approve of sweat-soaked worshippers arriving out of breath, shirt unfastened, muddy boots. He probably expected Dosh to kneel and kiss that chain now, and then he would order the peasant off to some freezing pond to bathe before commencing his worship.

Dosh made the gesture of Tion, but he used his left hand and simultaneously extended two fingers of his right. It was probably a recognition signal of one of the Tion cults, although Dosh had never been sworn to a mystery. Just where he had learned that sign, he could not recall. Perhaps the god himself had instructed him. It always worked.

It did now. The old priest bowed low. He did not even raise his head fully, did not look directly at his visitor again. Murmuring, "I shall see that you are not disturbed, my son," he departed, sandals whispering hurriedly on the flags. The outer door closed behind him with a thump, making the chamber even darker. Much better.

Dosh stripped, shivery in the dank cold. The series of postures he was required to assume would normally be regarded as utter blasphemy in a temple, but one of the Youth's attributes was Kirb'l, the Joker. Dosh bowed to the idol, turned his back, bent over. . . .

"What in the world are you doing?"

He shrieked and jumped and twisted around. There was no one there. Furious enough to forget his nudity, he strode over to the little door in the corner and threw it open. Beyond it lay a small chamber containing a table heaped with books. There was no other furniture, no other door. The voice had not come from there.

Trembling now, he hurried back to the idol and abased himself on the cold stone floor.

"Well?" asked that same sepulchral voice. *"You have not answered my question."*

"Lord, I was merely performing the ritual that you taught me."

"Oh!" There was no doubt now that the voice was coming from the statue. *"Tion did, you mean?"*

Dosh gibbered for a minute. "But are you not Holy Tion also, Lord?"

The god uttered a peculiar *tee-hee* noise, almost a snigger. *"Well, not always. Not at the moment. What is he up to now? What in the world are those scars on your face? Start at the beginning and tell me the whole story."*

"But . . ." Dosh had performed his ritual several times, in shrines or temples, and always it had brought the Lord of Beauty himself. But of course this time he had not completed the ritual, had hardly begun it. Were not all Tion's avatars Tion? That was what the priests said. Why, then, did this one refer to the Lord of Beauty as "he"?

It was not his place to question. "Lord, I have been following the Liberator, as you . . ."

"Yes?"

"As you . . . I think you told me to. I don't remember!" He began to panic. "I have to report to you what the Liberator does, don't I? That's right, isn't it? You must have . . ."

"When did it begin?" asked the voice. It had lost some of its spooky, echoing quality. It sounded almost gentle. *"Did you by chance win the gold rose in the—our, I mean—festival?"*

"Yes! Yes!"

"What year?"

"Six hundred, ninety-seventh festival, Lord."

"And then what happened?"

"I . . ." Dosh moaned. He trembled. He felt faint. "I don't remember! I stood on the dais with the rose in my hair, giving out the prizes in the festival. Then . . . I don't remember!" The next day he had gone to the palace in Lemod and asked Prince Tarion for work and been hired on the spot. That was almost a year ago now. . . . But that did not add up! "Four years? That festival was four years ago, wasn't it?"

"Yes, it was. Put your clothes on, lad." The god's voice had lost its divine menace altogether and become almost chatty. *"I can see you're freezing. Don't worry about the missing years. You're much happier not remembering, I'm sure. Keep talking. You mean that the Liberator is actually here, in Thargvale?"*

Dosh confirmed that as he shivered into his wet garments. Three years! Three years stolen out of his life!

"That's very serious! Dangerous! Did the Service send him here, so soon?"

"The who, Lord?"

"The Service! The Church of the Undivided, if you prefer. Hmph! Obviously you don't know about them. My mast—my senior aspect has not been totally frank with you. Well, this is all very interesting, yes? Tee-hee! I must meet the Liberator. Go and fetch him."

Dosh gulped in dismay. D'ward and the army would be miles away by now. How could he, Dosh, ever persuade the Liberator to turn it around and come back? Even less likely was the possibility of his coming alone, with the Thargian cavalry prowling over the countryside.

But to disobey a direct order from the god was unthinkable. It might condemn him to more years of . . . of what?

Hatred! Three years of his life had been stolen!

Anger and sorrow burned up in his throat. He turned and stared hard at the inanimate image. This was another god altogether. He must not let his sudden fury at Tion spill over onto Prylis. He must not antagonize the god of learning, who had granted him this wisdom.

And the Liberator—D'ward had done far more for him than Tion ever had. Must he now lead D'ward to his death?

"Lord, how can I ever persuade the Liberator to come? There is danger!"

"Mmph! See what you mean. Well, your new insight will be a sign to him, and . . . yes . . . we shall find you some assistance. Go outside."

More bewildered than ever, Dosh genuflected to the god, then stumbled over to the door. He stepped out into blinding sunlight. A hand grabbed his hair and hurled him forward. He pitched down the steps and sprawled on the gravel. Through sudden tears of pain he saw shiny boots all around him.

". . . is no Nagian!" said a harsh voice.

"Not with hair that color," another agreed. "We can kill this one."

"Feed him to the worms."

"Sacrilege!" someone bleated. "You violate the holy sanctuary!"

"Take him outside the gate, then," said the first.

Dosh heard a strange moaning noise and realized it came from himself. Rough hands grabbed his arms and hauled him to his feet. He was surrounded by eight or nine Thargian lancers—hard, wiry men, in green and black leather riding gear, in bronze helmets, all clean shaven in Thargian fashion. He tried to speak and merely gibbered.

The abbot was flustering around in the background, wringing his hands and still protesting the sacrileges: violence on the steps of the minster, moas desecrating the gardens, general lack of respect. Followers of Karzon could not be expected to pay much heed to a priest of Prylis, and these troopers were not about to create precedents like that.

"Move, scum!" said the leader.

As Dosh was jerked forward, the minster doors behind him flew open with a boom.

"*Stop!*" roared a voice of thunder.

The hands released him. He staggered and almost fell.

"*Come in here, all of you!*" No mortal could be that loud.

The image still seemed to be marble, and yet it was also flesh. The scroll was almost vellum, and Prylis still held it before him. His eyes were more visibly alive than the rest of him, shining as blue as D'ward's. His hair had taken on a golden hue.

The abbot and the Thargians groveled before him. Behind them, Dosh knelt respectfully, then stared disbelievingly at the idol. That pose with the vertical scroll—it was deliberately obscene! Why had he not noticed sooner? *New insight* the god had said. . . . The Joker mocked his worshippers!

A voice of thunder rolled around the chapel: "*Barbarians! Say why we should not smite you for your sacrilege?*"

The lancers moaned and gabbled.

"Lord!" their leader croaked. "We followed orders. We were told that Holy Karzon—"

"*This place does not belong to Karzon! You, Ksargirk Captain, are sworn to his vile cult of the Blood and Hammer, we see. You also, Tsuggig Lancer, and Twairkirg Lancer . . . and Progyurg Lancer, too. Savages! Renounce your oaths!*"

The soldiers howled.

"*Abjure or die and be forever damned!*" the god screamed, louder than ever.

In quavering mumbles, the four men renounced their oaths to whatever the Blood and Hammer was—some warriors' cult of Karzon, presumably, probably nasty. Dosh decided he was enjoying this unexpected change of fortune. Prompted by the divine bellow, the bullyboys denounced the Man and swore never to seek his patronage again. They were practically wetting their breeches with terror now.

It was nice to have friends in positions of authority.

"*Now swear eternal obedience to us! All of you! Swear that forever more you will worship the Youth above all gods.*"

Could it be that the god was enjoying this also? There was an odd timbre to his thunder, which in a mortal might have hinted of bluster. How often would an obscure, unassuming deity like Prylis indulge in such assertive behavior?

The troopers swore allegiance to Tion with great reluctance, some of them almost weeping. Dosh suspected that the apostates would arrive in the heavens most speedily if Karzon ever heard of this breach of faith—or if any of their friends as much as suspected, either.

"Now," the god said in a slightly less deafening roar, *"there is a great evil abroad in the world, and you are called to strive against it."*

"Tell us its name, Lord," said the captain, sounding encouraged.

"Its name is Zath!"

The troopers exchanged horrified glances.

"You are charged to give all help to our trusted servant Dosh Envoy, whom you sought to slay. You will obey his orders without question or hesitation and if necessary to the death, until such time as he releases you. Rise, Dosh Envoy."

Dosh stood up. One by one the Thargian lancers knelt to him and swore unlimited obedience. Yes, he was definitely enjoying this! He was going to continue enjoying it, too. That young one . . . Progyurg? Yes, Progyurg Lancer was a really cute-looking kid. . . . Obey without question or hesitation, *mm?*

For some reason, Dosh suddenly thought of D'ward. Tarion certainly saw nothing wrong in using the authority of rank to satisfy personal whims. Progyurg himself would certainly not argue, because Thargians put obedience to superior officers before anything else in the world, but D'ward would disapprove. Dosh felt sure of that, although he did not know why or how he knew. Well, he would think over the morals of the situation before he detailed Progyurg for special duties.

"Holy Father Abbot?" boomed the god.

The old man was still groveling. "Lord?"

"Dosh Envoy may need your assistance also. Aid him. Um. That seems to be all, doesn't it? Tee-hee! Well, I suppose you are all our servants now and we give you our blessing."

The image was marble again.

Poor Progyurg Lancer toppled to the floor in a dead faint.

ꝏ 38 ꝏ

THE ARMY HAD CAMPED AMID THE RUINS OF A GREAT MANOR. THE big house was a smoking, stinking ruin, but some of the many outbuildings had survived. Together with stone walls around yards and paddocks, these gave shelter from the cool wind that had sprung up at dusk, and they concealed the little campfires. Eltiana's red eye stared down from the darkening sky; the stars were gathering.

The Sonalby troop was crammed into a tiny courtyard. Ysian spotted Prat'han right away, and began jostling her way quickly toward him, stumbling over legs. Nagians accepted her much more readily than the Joalians did. She was D'ward's woman, and if D'ward had chosen to bring his concubine along while forbidding anyone else to do so, that was his leader's privilege as far as they were concerned. They would be shocked speechless if they knew that D'ward had never as much as kissed her. Dosh Envoy had guessed, but Dosh was a creepily perceptive person.

The Sonalby troop especially regarded the Liberator as one of themselves; they seemed to approve of his choice of woman, and now they greeted Ysian with whoops and crude jokes in the gabbling Nagian accents. They were *definitely* not thinking of her as a baby sister, which was a nice change. When she said she was looking for D'ward, of course, the humorists shouted that she mustn't tire the poor man, should at least wait until bedtime, and so on. The others laughed and agreed. She was used to that now. In half a fortnight with the army, she had learned a great deal about men that she had never known before, and one of the things she had learned was they rarely thought of anything other than sex. Their single-mindedness was quite astonishing.

Big, gangling Prat'han was squatting by one of the fires, roasting something on a stick. He yelled at the jokers to be quiet. Then he shone big teeth at her. "The battlemaster has gone scouting with the Thoid'lbians, lady. They wanted to see if they can climb that ruined tower. Should be back soon. Stay and keep us company, for we are all lonely for the sound of a woman's voice." The audience shouted agreement.

Ysian was very conscious of so many men close around her, a very odd feeling, and not unpleasant. Their attention was flattering. But she had come to see if Prat'han would help her rescue Dosh, and now she realized she could not ask him in public like this. Relations between Nagians and Joalians were bad. She knew D'ward was worried; she must not do anything to make matters worse. Prat'han must know that too, so he might refuse to get involved. Or too many of the troop might get too much involved, and she would have started a riot. Bother!

"I really can't stay just now, Troopleader. I'd like to. Maybe later."

Prat'han said that was a pity. The men needed the company of beautiful women to keep their morale up. Then he held out his stick to her. Sonalby, he explained, had met with good fortune that afternoon—a marshy pond, full of fat lizards. The tails were a great delicacy, and she must eat this one while it was hot. He smiled proudly.

She took the stick and tried not to look at the smoking lump on the end of it. She would not eat lizard if she were dying of starvation, but it might be just the excuse she needed to intrude on the terrible things she had seen happening.

"This is very kind of you," she said. "It smells delicious! You won't mind if I take it with me, will you?"

"Alas! We are heartbroken. Where must you rush off to so urgently?"

"Oh . . ." Ysian was already edging away over the tangle of legs. "A friend needs me. Something I must do before D'ward gets back."

Of course they chose to misinterpret her words, but nothing she could have said would have been proof against their coarse humor. With the raucous suggestions scorching her ears, she hurried off into the shadows. Her father had never talked like that. D'ward never talked like that. D'ward was different. She rather wished he were not quite so different. She thought he would approve of what she was doing now, because she knew he disliked deliberate cruelty as much as she did. She was so mad she did not care overmuch whether he would approve or not.

She detoured around the charred and stinking remains of a stable to avoid a camp of Joalians. She reached the shed she wanted. The door was ajar, casting a thin wedge of lamplight over the cobbled yard outside. The horrible noises had stopped. Ignoring sudden quiverings in her insides, she kicked the door open and marched right in. The hut was larger than she had realized, bare except for a workbench along one wall; from the smell, it was probably where wool was baled at shearing time.

Two of the Joalians were sitting on the bench, feet dangling. Two more were leaning against their shadows on the wall. Dosh lay curled up in the middle of the floor, his arms bound behind him and more rope around his ankles. The old scars on his face were hidden by blood and fresh welts, his legs were bruised and scratched. Rips in his shirt showed more bruises on his ribs, repulsively bright on his fair skin.

"Well!" One of the Joalians on the bench paused in licking his knuckles. "Brought us some supper, did you?"

"Not for you!" Ysian did not look at him. She knelt down beside Dosh and pulled out her knife. D'ward had given it to her when they left Lemod, telling her to keep it handy always.

"Hey!" the Joalian shouted. "What do you think you're doing?"

"He can't eat with his hands tied, Troopleader." She sawed at the rope around the prisoner's wrists. It had bitten into the flesh, and his hands were hideously red.

He peered at her out of the corner of his eye, looking very astonished. He gasped as the rope parted.

The Joalian leader pushed himself off the bench, his boots thudding on the flagstones. He was big and swarthy and hook nosed. His shadow leaped up behind him, huge and menacing. "Who said you could do that? And why should a traitor eat before honest men?"

However disgusting the grisly lump on the stick seemed to her, all four guards were eying it hungrily.

"He's not a traitor until the battlemaster says so! Here!" She thrust her revolting offering at Dosh, who was struggling to sit up.

"Need a minute," he muttered, chaffing his hands.

"You give that to me!" The Joalian bent to grab it from her.

Ysian whipped it around behind her back. "Go and get your own food! This is for Dosh Envoy." She tried to glare up at him, but kneeling was not a good position for glaring.

"Dosh Traitor you mean! Just because you're the battlemaster's harlot doesn't give you the right to order me around, missy!" He tried again to take the stick from her. "You don't have his authority to do that!"

"Yes, she does," D'ward said, marching in. Golbfish Hordeleader's cumbersome bulk filled the doorway behind him.

Ysian relaxed with a rush of relief. She had been starting to think that things might shortly begin to get somewhat out of hand. Dosh grinned at her, showing blood on his teeth. She handed him the stick. He took it in his swollen fingers but did not try to eat.

The Joalians had come to attention. Tall and fearsomely blue-eyed, D'ward glanced them over, then spared a longer, harder look for Dosh. He was making no effort to hide his anger, and it filled the shed like a winter frost. He spoke first to Ysian.

"What are you doing here, *Viks'n*?"

"I brought Dosh Envoy some supper."

"Why?"

"I thought they might stop torturing him if I was here."

D'ward sighed and gave her his exasperated look, which always annoyed her tremendously. "Well, cut his feet loose too. Now, Dibber Troopleader, I want an explanation. Report!"

"Sir! Saw this man consorting with the enemy, sir!" The Joalian waited, as if nothing more need be said. When nothing more was said, he spoke again, but with much less confidence. "This afternoon you passed the word for him, sir. He wasn't found, sir, was he? About sunset, sir, we saw him in the distance with a band of Thargians. We watched him try to sneak into camp unobserved . . . arrested him . . . sir. . . ."

D'ward's eyes shone like blue steel. "You did not report to Kolgan Co-adjutant or Golbfish Hordeleader?"

"Er . . . waiting for you, sir . . ."

"So you questioned him yourself?"

"Er, yes, sir." The troopleader's face glistened wetly under the lantern— he was scared and serve him right!

"Did he tell you anything?"

"Some lies about acting on your orders, sir."

"And you know he wasn't, do you?"

An insect thudded into the lamp and bounced off. In the awful silence, it sounded like a drumbeat. When D'ward spoke, his voice was even softer but full of menace.

"Dosh Envoy, did any of them try to stop what was happening?"

"Not that I heard." Amazingly, Dosh was now nibbling at the lizard tail. He seemed remarkably cheerful, considering the beating he had suffered.

D'ward pronounced judgment. "Dibber, you exceeded your authority. Go back to your troop. Inform them that you have been demoted and they are to elect a successor. He is to report to Golbfish Hordeleader immediately with recommendations for your further punishment. That means all of you. Go!"

The prince moved his mass aside, and the four men stampeded out into the darkness. Golbfish pulled the door closed, with himself on the inside of it. He was smiling, yet somehow he did not look pleased. Ysian stood up, planning to leave the three men to their deliberations. She had done what she came for. She thought she deserved a little more appreciation for it, too.

"You'd better stay, *Viks'n*." D'ward heaved himself up on the bench, feet dangling. He stared down at Dosh with disgust. "Oh, you! What sort of mess are you in this time?"

"Got a message for you," Dosh said, still chewing. Apparently he was actually enjoying the revolting meal. He could not have been eating well lately.

Puzzled that she was wanted, but quite pleased, Ysian moved back against the wall. She caught the prince's eye. He nodded and smiled at her, and she did not understand that, either. She liked the big hordeleader. He always spoke to her as if she were a lady.

"From?" D'ward said.

Dosh glanced warily at Ysian and Golbfish. "A friend of a friend. A servant of a former master of mine. The one you guessed."

"Aha! You can talk about him now?"

Dosh nodded. "The servant removed the master's . . . directive." He choked. "That bastard! That mudpig! He stole three years of my life!"

He tried to rise. Golbfish went to help him, and he staggered to his feet. "This aspect's all right—I think. He wants to meet you."

D'ward raised his eyebrows.

Golbfish made a rumbling sound. "Now wait a minute! Let's hear where you went—and how you came back. And what about the Thargians?"

Dosh leaned both arms on the bench. He must be in a lot of pain, though he was trying not to show it. "Liberator—"

"Don't call me that! You'd better speak openly. I trust these two, and they deserve to know what secret they're keeping. Out with it!"

"Sure?" Dosh said impudently. He was never as respectful to the Liberator as everyone else was. "Well, I went to a temple, to report to Tion. I met his avatar Prylis—god of learning. I gave him my report, but . . . Well, he isn't Tion!"

"Of course he isn't. None of them are. What else?"

"He wants you to go to him. Very important, he said. Some Thargians had followed me. Prylis bound them to my service. They have to obey me!" Dosh tried to laugh, winced, and rubbed his ribs regretfully.

Ysian caught Golbfish's eye again. He was frowning, but he did not look as surprised as she would have expected. Perhaps D'ward had told him some of the strange things he had told her—things that would have shocked her parents to the core, things she would have believed to be dreadful heresies had she heard them from anyone but D'ward.

"I saw that temple," Golbfish said. "If you went there, then how did you catch up with us?"

Dosh twisted his bruised lips into a parody of a smile. "I rode a moa."

"That's impossible!"

"That's what I thought, but it isn't. Not if you ride double. The brute didn't like it, but it brought me."

After a moment, D'ward said, "I'll have to trust you. What does this Prylis person want with me?"

"Dunno. Don't question gods."

"Maybe you should." D'ward stared down at his knees for a while, swinging his feet. "How far away is this temple?"

Dosh shrugged, wiping his mouth. "Ten miles, maybe. My lancers will take us. You can be back before morning."

"Battlemaster!" Golbfish exclaimed. "You cannot seriously . . ."

But obviously D'ward was planning to go. How could he trust his life to Dosh Envoy? Ysian did not *like* Dosh. D'ward had told her why the other men disliked him, but that should not matter to her. There was just something *wrong* about him—not wrong enough to justify what had been done to him tonight, though.

"I have to risk it, Highness," D'ward said. "It could be very important. If I'm not back by dawn, lead the army into the pass—and keep going, understand! On no account wait for me or look for me!"

"Battlemaster—"

"Can't pass up a chance to have a god as an ally, can I? Consult Kolgan, but you make the decisions, apart from the orders I just gave you. I'll tell him." He turned to Dosh, who was trying not to show his pleasure at the Liberator's faith in him. "You coming too? Can you make it in your condition?"

"I'm the toughest bastard in the whole army."

"I know you are. Very well, I'll make my rounds now, and you get yourself cleaned up. Nobody else must know I've gone, or half the Nagians will come after me, no matter what I say! As soon as—"

"Me too!" Ysian said. She was *not* going to be left behind like a child!

The three men all turned to stare at her; she racked her brains for some convincing reason why she should not be left behind like a child.

"Now, ma'am!" Golbfish said. "This is no expedition for a—"

"Me too! D'ward, you told me where the safest place was!"

The safest place was next to him, he had said, because the *Filoby Testament* predicted many things he would do before he died. Besides, even if the army escaped back to Nagvale and Joalvale, what would become of her, a Lemodian traitor? Even if she could ever return to Lemod, no decent man would marry her now. Next to D'ward was the only place she wanted to be, ever. She could never tell him that, but if he ever asked . . .

He was grinning. "Quite sure, *Viks'n*? It'll mean a couple of hard rides and no sleep all night."

"Quite sure!"

"Thargian patrols may catch us and kill us."

"You don't believe that or you wouldn't be going!"

He chuckled and gave her one of his rare, wonderful smiles that always lit up the world. "Come, then." He gestured at Dosh. "Help this traveling disaster clean up, will you, *Viks'n*?" He jumped off the bench and disappeared out the door, leaving the two men staring after him in disbelief.

"What's this *Viks'n* he calls you?" Dosh demanded.

"Just a pet name."

Golbfish shrugged. "In classical Joalian, '*viksen*' means 'courage.' "

Dosh said, "Oh."

Ysian had not known that and felt pleased. D'ward had told her it was the name of a small animal with red hair, and her hair was *not* red. It was dark auburn.

༖ 39 ༒

As THEY CREPT OUT OF THE CAMP, D'WARD TOOK YSIAN'S HAND. She thought *progress!* Then she decided he was just being protective again, babying her. The only time he had ever touched her was when they had been crossing Lemodwater, escaping from the city. His strength on that occasion had impressed her a lot, but she would not agree that he was necessarily more surefooted in darkness and rough terrain just because he was a man. Not without a demonstration, anyway.

And this could never be a truly romantic stroll, since Trumb had risen, three-quarters full above the branches. His eerie green light made people look like corpses, definitely not romantic. Eltiana's rosy glow was the moonlight for lovers. Besides, Dosh was there too, leading the way. He was moving like a corpse, or at least a half-dead person, and ought to be in bed. So not romantic. More like goose-pimply and exciting. Nevertheless, she let D'ward continue to hold her hand, squeezing his fingers discriminatingly from time to time.

They avoided the sentries' notice—which annoyed D'ward a lot. Then Dosh said he had better go ahead in case of accidents, and in a minute she had D'ward to herself.

"Are you being romantic or just baby-sistering me again?"

He released her hand. "Sorry."

"Sorry for what? You really are the most maddening man!"

His eyes and teeth showed bright in the moonlight. "Now what have I done?"

"It's what you don't do that bothers me! It is very insulting for a woman to find herself ignored like this when she has made her inclinations perfectly clear!"

"With the knife, you mean? Oh, I certainly understood the message. I have never been so scared in my life!"

"That was before I got to know you. Why don't you even kiss me?"

He sighed. "I've told you, Ysian. I am promised to another. You're a sweet kid and—"

"I am not a kid!"

"And rarely sweet?"

"Exceedingly sweet. Try me."

"I ought to put you over my knee and spank you."

"Promise to take my pants off first?"

"Ysian! You should be ashamed of yourself."

"I am ashamed of myself. I've tried everything I know—" At that point she tripped and almost fell. D'ward did not even try to catch her.

It was humiliating.

After twenty minutes or so, they came to a bridge over a stream. A voice from the shadows up ahead demanded, "Password?"

"Flower of shame," Dosh replied. "Captain Ksargirk?"

"Yes, sir."

"There are three of us. You take this man. And the, er, boy can go behind Tsuggig. I'll ride with Progyurg."

"His mount is only a five-year-old, sir. Better to—"

"That's an order!"

"Whatever you say, sir."

Ysian grinned to herself, wondering if D'ward noticed how much Dosh enjoyed flaunting his authority; the Thargian certainly had.

A chance to ride a moa had seemed like a big adventure. Moas were big—she had never realized just how big. More Thargians led the steeds in from the darkness. The long necks seemed to stretch halfway up to Trumb, and the saddles were higher than the men's heads, even D'ward's! How was she ever going to get up there? More important, when and how would she come down?

The lancers began hauling on reins, some of them lifting themselves right off the ground and hanging there. The moas snickered complaint, then one by one reluctantly folded their huge legs and sat.

"Ready, boy?" the Captain asked Ysian. "Hold on for your life, now!"

"Er, me? Ready for what?"

The nearest lancer vaulted into his saddle and at the same moment Ksargirk Captain and another man lifted Ysian bodily and more or less *threw* her at his back. She flung her arms around him and the moa went mad. It leaped straight up into the sky, while the other men cleared rapidly out of the way. It came down and went up again. It shrilled and brayed, kicked and cavorted. She clung grimly to the rider, her face pressed hard against his tunic. She clung so hard she wondered he could breathe, and yet she was bounced madly for what felt like several hours. Sometimes she came down on the moa's hairy rump, sometimes on the edge of the saddle, which hurt. Her legs flapped up and down like wings. Tsuggig cursed a stream of guttural Thargian that she could not understand and the moa ignored. She heard a few cries of pain from Dosh—he really ought not to be doing this in his condition! D'ward made no noise, but soon the whole night seemed to be full of bucking, rampaging moas. Oh, poor Dosh!

All nine moas made a fuss at being mounted, but the three with passengers were by far the worst. The other six calmed down after a few token leaps. Her lancer was the last to bring his mount under control, perhaps because it was the biggest, perhaps because both Dosh and D'ward weighed so much more than she did. When it began to behave itself, tired by its antics, he was given his lance, which one of the other men had been holding for him. Then Ksargirk Captain shouted an order, and the troop set off along the road. *Streaked* off along the road! Never had Ysian traveled so fast in her life. The moa seemed to cover eight or ten feet in a stride, but its gait was amazingly smooth. Hedges and trees went hurtling past, a blur in the night. The wind blew cold on her face, and although the saddle was too small for two, she soon decided that she was enjoying herself after all.

Clouds had covered most of the green moon when the weary moas strode into the grounds of the monastery. Two elderly monks were waiting with lanterns at the door of the temple, and one of them wore a golden chain, so he must be the abbot. Ksargirk Captain reined in at the steps, and then sprang nimbly from his moa's back. He made a very graceful landing, and saluted the abbot. A lancer dismounted the same way and took the captain's reins. Ysian looked down at the ground thoughtfully.

Tsuggig Lancer twisted around to peer at her. He was older than she had realized, clean shaven in Thargian fashion, but not really ugly. "You're no boy!" He had not spoken a word to her until then.

"I wasn't the last time I looked."

He made a growly sound, and then chuckled. "If you were when you got on, then you might not be now. But you did good. My pleasure. Can you get down without help?"

"Of course." Ysian pushed herself off and slid spryly down . . . down . . .

Her legs buckled under her and she fell flat on her back, banging her head on the gravel. Bother! The moa shrilled mockingly and shifted its hooves as if readying a kick. She scrambled up and moved to a safe distance to dust herself off, feeling oddly shaky. The ground seemed too close, as though her legs had shrunk, and much of the rest of her felt as if she had been flogged by the public executioner. D'ward had already dismounted and gone to help Dosh. She took a hard look at the forbidding figure of the old abbot and decided he might not approve of women in his monastery. She had better remain a boy.

Four of them went into the temple, for Dosh was barely capable of standing on his own, let alone going anywhere. He gave the abbot some very snappy orders to look after "his" men, then called on Progyurg Lancer to dismount and help him walk. He hobbled inside with one arm draped over the Thargian's shoulders and the other on D'ward's. Ysian followed.

No one had said she shouldn't.

Her experience with temples was limited. This one was small and dark, no more than a barren stone box, chilly and dusty smelling. It was not nearly as impressive as the temple of Eth'l in Lemod. As the lancer brought the lantern closer, the image of the god emerged from the gloom. Being an aspect of the Youth, Prylis was depicted in the nude, but he held a scroll of learning in a strategic position. Progyurg and D'ward lowered Dosh to his knees.

"Good lad," Dosh whispered. "Leave the light here."

"Sir!" The lancer departed. He was a nice-looking boy, not much older than Ysian herself, she thought. Not as handsome as D'ward, of course. The door thumped closed behind him.

She knelt and was surprised to see D'ward still standing. He had his arms folded and seemed to be shivering. The temple was cool but not as cold as that.

"Holy Prylis!" Dosh proclaimed. "I have done as you commanded."

Silence.

The flame in the lantern danced. Highlights squirmed on the shiny surface of the statue, but nothing else happened.

"I am the Liberator," D'ward said. "You summoned me."

More silence.

"Perhaps he's asleep," D'ward said.

"Gods don't sleep!" Ysian protested.

"I'll bet they do!"

"This is annoying!" D'ward added, but she could tell that he was more angry than that. "I have an army to look after and a war to fight. We must get back before dawn. How do you waken a god, Dosh?"

"Nibble his ear?"

"I'd break my teeth. No better ideas? What's behind that door?"

"A little room with a table. Nothing else. It doesn't go anywhere."

"Prylis!" D'ward shouted. "We've come!"

Even more silence.

"What if you try your ritual? No, I suppose not."

"Definitely not!" Dosh groaned and eased himself down into a sitting position. "Looks like we'll have to wait for morning."

"Damned if I will . . . Ah!" D'ward walked over to the door in the corner. He opened it, went in, closed it behind him . . . and again there was silence.

After a minute or so, Dosh said, "Go and look for him, *Viks'n*."

"That's not my name! Only D'ward calls me that!"

"Then, my lady Ysian, will you go and look for him—please?"

She clambered to her feet and walked over to the mysterious door in the corner. Behind it there was only darkness. She went back to Dosh and fetched the lantern. Shadows leaped around the edges of her vision as she carried it. As Dosh had said, there was a little room there, with a table piled high with books. Apart from that, there was nothing at all—no other door, no window, and no D'ward.

Ysian and Dosh waited. After half an hour or so, she realized that she could hardly keep her eyes open and he was unconscious, or at least he could only groan when she tried to rouse him. So she went out and asked the abbot to send some monks in to get Dosh—he should be put to bed and cared for, she explained. She told Ksargirk Captain that he and his men could stand down; she asked the abbot, very politely, if she might have something to eat and a place to sleep. She thought nothing more was going to happen before morning.

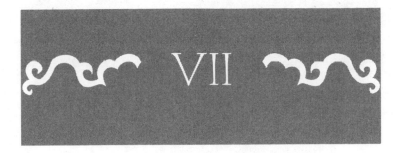

VII

Revealed Check

ᳱᵔ 40 ᵕᳩ

SMEDLEY CAME DOWN VERY LATE FOR BREAKFAST. HE HAD A SOUR, sandy feeling behind his eyes, and he had cut himself twice while shaving. Worst of all, the underwear he had rinsed out before going to sleep had not dried completely in the night. He would not be able to hire a valet until the war was over. Of more immediate importance were adequate clothing and some fags.

The great Victorian dining table would have seated at least a dozen. Exeter sat alone at it, poring over a thick book propped amid a field of dirty dishes. He looked up wryly.

"Morning," Smedley grunted.

"Good morning! *Beautiful* morning! Lovelier now for your presence, of course."

"Put it where the monkey put the nuts. Any tea in the pot?"

Smirking, Exeter removed the cozy and swished the teapot. He removed the lid and peered inside. He pulled a face. "Lots, but I think someone's been washing boots in it."

"Just what I need!" Smedley sat down.

Exeter poured. "The ladies have gone off to shop and call on the erudite Nathaniel Glossop. There's a couple of congealed eggs there and some petrified bacon. I'll warm it up for you—seems there's laws about not wasting food. . . ."

"Just the tea will do, thank you."

Mercifully Exeter said nothing more for a while. He closed his book and carried it out of the room. When he returned without it, though, he was still infernally cheerful. "Looking up Prylis. Not the one I met."

Smedley ended his contemplation of the heap of soggy toast. "Prylis?"

"Chappie who invented the wooden horse. Didn't take out a patent, though, and Odysseus swiped the idea. Probably spoke much better Greek than the one I met. Sure you don't want eggs and bacon?"

"Quite sure."

"We both need our shirts ironed. I'd try it, except I don't know how."

"Me neither," Smedley lied. To avert further small talk, he said, "Tell me about Olympus."

Exeter crossed his legs and hugged one knee with both hands. He stared for a moment at Smedley with his impossibly blue eyes.

"Told you, old man. It's very much like a station in the colonies some-where, an outpost of civilization in the bush. The *tyikank* and *entyikank* live in nice houses, the natives are the servants. Like Kenya, India, or all those other places. Main difference is the natives are as white as we are. Redheads, most of them. The *tyikank* are a mixed bunch, but a lot of them are English originally. Recruited here. Some aren't. A couple are from other worlds altogether. Some of them have been on Nextdoor a deuce of a long time, but the Service itself isn't all that old. The guv'nor was one of the founders."

"But what do they do?"

"Argue. Plan. Squabble. Go out on missionary work." Exeter continued to study Smedley as if watching his brain cells twitch. His own face was illegible as the Sphinx. "One committee's still working on the True Gospel. Another runs an intelligence branch, tracking what's going on—politically and theosophically both. Anything that may help overthrow the Pentath-eon."

That steady gaze was starting to get under Smedley's skin. "You make it sound as if you don't approve."

"Oh, it's a wonderful idea. A worthy cause. The strangers are definitely parasites. Some of them do a little bit of good in passing, like Tion and his festivals. A lot of them are . . . well, horrors."

Smedley poured another cup of tanning fluid. "I suppose if you're going to live forever you don't rush at the hedges?" He looked up, and the blue eyes were still boring into him. "If it's such a wonderful idea, why are you being so shifty about it?"

Exeter sighed, put his foot back on the floor, and turned to stare out the window. "It's just not that simple, old man. It's not like Dr. Livingstone and the witch doctors. It's not Saint Eggbeater burning down the druids' grove. These Johnnies have *power*! Real power. Start blaspheming in their temples and you're liable to drop dead. Nothing like a public thunderbolt to impress the masses—and then the mana just pours in to replace what's been spent."

"So start a new religion, a good one! You mentioned a Church of the Undivided. The Service is behind it?"

"It *is* the Service. The trouble is that the old gods have cornered the market. Say you find yourself a node—there's still good ones around—and you set up a new god, then you get asked what is he the god *of?* Anything worthwhile will have its own divinity already, and he or she will be an avatar of one of the Five. The Pentatheon have all bets covered. Even the Undivided tends to get identified with Visek, the Parent, so the mana benefits them . . . him? Her? Visek's sort of androgynous. . . . Visek hasn't taken sides yet. I think the Service does him more good than harm. More good than they want to, certainly."

It was definitely not the right time of day for riddles, but Smedley had started this. And he did want to know more about Olympus and the Service. If he didn't find out from Exeter now, he would probably never have another chance. Who could resist the chance to learn about an alternative world?

Or was he just looking for a cause?

"You said some of the gods—strangers—some of them are all-right types?"

"A few." Exeter began fiddling with a spoon, drawing lines on the tablecloth. "A few are secretly Service supporters. Lukewarm, mostly. Fence-sitters. One or two have converted, but not many have got away with it."

"Converted?"

"Mm. Like the Irish goddess Bríg, who became Saint Bridget. Or Cybele becoming the Black Madonna—back in the Dark Ages, scores of pagan deities became Christian saints. But in the Vales they're all vassals of the Five. If Tion, say, catches one of his minions consorting with the enemy, then he is seriously peeved."

"If Christianity did it in Europe, then why not try Christianity on Next-door?"

Exeter looked up with a smile. "And where exactly is Jerusalem? Who did you say these Romans were? Egypt? The Red Sea? I've been on the other side of this conversation a few times. What I got told then was that one big advantage Christianity had over the pagan gods was that it had a real historical basis, instead of just myth. But that's in this world. On Next-door it isn't."

"So what is the Church of the Undivided?"

"A hodgepodge. A Unitarian concoction of ethics and morals: Christian, Socratic, Buddhist, et cetera—the Golden Rule plus a universal god too holy to be named. That's an attempt to shut out Visek. As I said, that doesn't seem to work awfully well. It's a frightfully antiseptic sort of religion. No passion, you know?"

Smedley reached for toast and butter. "You're saying there's really nothing you can do, then?"

Exeter sighed. "There's nothing *I* can do, no. I'm branded as the Liberator and anything I tried to do would be warped by the prophecy and lead to killing Zath. That brings on catastrophe."

"Why?"

Exeter looked irritated. "You'll see if you just think about how it would have to be done. It would need an enormous amount of mana. How do I get that? What would I have to become?"

Yes, Julian should have seen that. If Exeter had invented all of this, he must have spent a lot of time working out the details. It was as logical as whist. "You'd have to start playing by their rules, you mean?"

"Playing their game. That's why I shan't ever go back there. As to whether there's anything *you* can do, old man . . . you want to try?"

Smedley was not ready to face that question yet, but his pulse rate had jumped a fraction. "I'm asking what the Service can do."

"Keep trying and hoping." Exeter's eyes were gleaming. Was he poking fun at the Service? Or at Smedley, for believing this fantasy? Or was he a supporter, coolly understating his enthusiasm? No way to tell, with him.

"But not praying? How do the faithful pray to a nameless god?"

"The whole point is that they don't. They pray to the apostles to intercede for them, because only the apostles can speak to the god. The apostles are not gods themselves, because he's Undivided; they're just the Chosen. Strangers from Olympus, of course." Exeter smiled wryly. "The Service doesn't have the manpower to put a missionary in every pot, but they do try to have someone drop by every couple of fortnights. You understand why they have to do it that way?"

"So everybody shares in the mana? Does that work?"

"It works after a fashion. A chicken sacrificed to the Undivided in Joal, say, will not provide the Service with anything like the mana it would give Astina if it died to her glory in her temple there. Mana will flow between nodes, but there's a lot of steam leaks out. No other reason?"

Then he raised a quizzical eyebrow and waited.

Smedley began to feel nettled. "You're three years ahead of me and it's too early in the morning."

Exeter laughed, taking pity on him. "Right-oh! The real problem, my boy, it that we're all human. The reason the apostles are set up as a sort of nameless divine committee is that power corrupts, as Alice said the other night. The Service has had agents go over to the other side. They discover what they can do with mana and they like it. Set a chap up in his own chapel and pretty soon he begins to feel like it's *his* chapel, and these are *his* people. Sooner or later one of the Five will send a henchman around. Some of our chaps sell out. There was an Italian named Giovani who became Jovanee Karzon, god of wagons. All the best attributes have been taken, but there's always room for more. Did you know the Romans had a patron goddess of the-light-in-rooms-where-women-are-giving-birth?"

"No," Smedley said grumpily, thinking that he did not want to. Having buttered the toast, he supposed he had better eat the horrid stuff. "You're saying it's hopeless?"

"No. Here's what I think, on the level: It may work! They may over-throw the Pentatheon. They're not fools, they're dedicated and well-meaning, all of them. But it's going to be a long, long struggle. Two or three hundred years at the least. Christianity took longer. Islam was faster, but more brutal. If you think of mana as being like money, then the Five are stinking rich and getting richer. The Undivided is scratching for crumbs. . . ."

The doorbell rang.

The two exchanged glances. Then Exeter pushed back his chair and stood up tall. He adjusted his tie and straightened his jacket. "That may just be the Women's Institute soliciting contributions for the church fete. Or it may not be." He strode out, closing the door.

Smedley continued to masticate long-dead toast. Why was he so fasci-nated by the idea of Olympus? Was he just trying to flee from reality—the war, his mutilation, lost friends, the changed face of England? If he nurtured secret fancies of magic giving him his hand back, then he was seriously bonkers. Cold logic said he should not make any decisions yet, not for a long time. On the other hand, his nerves were improving. He had not wept since leaving Staffles. Dreaming of Olympus and Exeter's fantasy world was probably a lot healthier for him at the moment than brooding over his own reality. He had always been too prone to introspection.

He heard voices as the door began to open.

"I'll put the kettle on, then. You go in."

In came portly Ginger Jones, attempting to polish his pince-nez with a silk handkerchief and keep hold of a pair of bicycle clips at the same time. He looked hot. "Morning, Captain!"

"Morning, sir. Any news?"

Ginger put his specs on his nose, his handkerchief in one pocket, and his bicycle clips in another. "No. Oh . . . thought you might need these." From yet another pocket, he produced two packets of Player's.

Smedley's heart melted. "May you be blessed with many sons and your herds prosper!" He fumbled for matches.

"Lord, how would I explain that to the Head?" Ginger sat down chuck-ling. "Thought I'd drop over and hear some more of the Exeter-Through-the-Looking-Glass saga." He glanced up as the man in question returned. "I posted your letter. Caught the evening collection, too."

"So it should arrive today," Smedley said, "if it is going to arrive?"

Exeter sat down. "If it's going to arrive, then it has already arrived. It wouldn't even hit the bottom of the pillar-box. It would go straight to somebody's desk.''

The others each waited for the other to comment. Eventually Ginger said, "Explain that, would you?"

"I can't. The magic may have been removed, since it does no good now, or it may be still there. But when I was a kid at Fallow and Head Office were keeping an eye on me, then the letters I put in that box went straight to them. I hope there was a spell invoked by that address written in my handwriting. I may be wrong—there may have been a guardian living in the neighborhood, in which case he or she will likely have gone now. I think Creighton would have told me if there had been, but I don't know. Told you it was a long shot.'' He shrugged.

"Indeed!" Ginger muttered. "I'm trying to remember if I heard the letter drop.''

Smedley did want to believe. "It's rather like the portal idea, two worlds touching at a point.''

"Mana can certainly be used to warp space," Exeter said, "especially on nodes. The inside of Krobidirkin's tent was bigger than the outside.''

"Wonderful idea for luggage.''

"Or blocks of flats.'' He grinned. "Imagine the rent you'd collect! You remember that business with the long strip of paper you give a twist to and then paste . . . ?''

"Möbius strip?''

"Probably. Sounds right. Old Flora-Dora spent half a term trying to get the idea into my skull. All I remember now is that you start at a point and go all the way round, and when you come back you're on the wrong side. It gave me nightmares. Now the chappie Prylis I mentioned last night had a library, a corridor lined with books. At the end you turned right, and there was another corridor lined with books. At the end of that you turned right again. You went around and around in a square—round and round and round, and you never came back to where you started. All the windows had a north view. This was all behind the church, and yet there was nothing there.''

"I hadn't thought of the Fallow postbox in quite that way," Ginger said. "No use taking it apart to look?''

"None. The question is," Exeter added, "if it works as I hope it does, then whose desk does it lead to? Head Office or the Blighters? I warn you— this may turn out to be a jolly interesting day.''

41

GOLBFISH MOVED THE ARMY OUT AT DAWN. HE DID NOT LIKE DOING so, but the Liberator's orders had been explicit. No one demanded to know why he and not D'ward was setting up the order of march; among five thousand men, the commander's absence would not be noticed for a while yet.

Golbfish himself stayed near the front with Kolgan at his side. The big man's sword arm was in a sling, his face haggard with pain. When the inevitable battle came, he would not be able to fight. If the gods were merciful and the army miraculously won its way home to Joal, he would certainly be put on trial before the People's Assembly. The verdict and sentence could never be in doubt. His beard showed more white than red now.

Food supply was becoming critical. Armies usually went marauding in the autumn, when harvests still filled the barns; no sane infantry ever went anywhere without cavalry to support it. Even Golbfish knew that. Plumes of dust in the distance showed where the Thargian scouts were tracking the invaders and watching their progress. The enemy had mobility—if the Joalians turned aside to pillage, the livestock was removed and the stores destroyed long before men on foot could reach them.

"Why don't they attack?" Kolgan demanded more than once. It was all he ever spoke of. "Why don't they harass us? Why not molest our patrols? Why are they letting us go?"

To that paradox there was no answer. At first the enemy had picked off Joalians whenever they could and left Nagians alone. Now they ignored Joalians also, not meddling even with small bands. All they did was ravage their own land, then stand aside to let the invaders pass. No people should behave like that, least of all the proud and warlike Thargians.

Around mid-morning, the road crested a height of land. Golbfish paused a moment or two to look back at the weary multitude trailing behind him. "It shows already," he muttered.

"What does?" growled Kolgan.

"Yesterday they sang as they marched. Today they're not singing. They're slouching and straggling more than marching."

"They're hungry." Kolgan turned away. Golbfish stayed to watch a little longer, but then he too resumed the journey. Yes, lack of food was a major problem, but lack of D'ward was a greater one. The army might not be aware yet that he was absent, but it was missing him.

The road curved down into a wide valley, but instead of crossing the river, it turned to the north and headed straight toward Thargwall. Consulting his maps as he marched, Golbfish concluded that the river must be Saltorwater; a conspicuous notch in the peaks probably marked Saltorpass itself. If the army could cross over that and reenter Lemodvale, then there was some hope of Joalian reinforcements coming to the rescue. Unless his slimy half brother had changed sides already, Joalia must still hold Nagvale and probably Siopass.

But Saltorpass was the first problem and a perfect site for an ambush. Thargia was in a much better position to bring up reinforcements than Joalia was. If Golbfish were running the Thargian campaign, he would let the invaders into the pass and then bottle them up from both ends. A few days' starvation would force complete surrender, which would yield the maximum harvest of slaves. Golbfish was certainly not running the Thargian campaign, and the men who were might prefer a more violent ending, with Saltorwater running red. That would be more Thargian, more traditional.

The valley was wide and relatively treeless, the fields divided by unmortared stone walls. Here and there, ruined farms still smoked, but the people and their livestock had gone. The only consolation Golbfish could find in the situation was that his right flank was now protected by a raging milky torrent. He withdrew the patrols from that side and spread others farther to the left, but he sensed the jaws of a trap closing around him. He was hungrier than he had ever been in his life.

Wherever D'ward was, he would not be able to rejoin the army until darkness shrouded this barren landscape. He had said he would return, and he had meant what he said, but Golbfish could not help but wonder if the Liberator had gone to meet his ordained destiny elsewhere.

About noon, patrols signaled enemy activity to the north. Shortly after that, forces could be seen gathering on the height of land to the west. There was a lot of dust to the south, too.

The herald came in the middle of the afternoon, and he came from the south. By then every man in the army knew it was surrounded. He was a welcome sight, so he was allowed to pass unmolested. Talking would at least put off the battle for a while. Riding a white moa and bearing a flag of truce, he raced along the columns, being waved forward with no worse abuse than jeering and insults. Undoubtedly he was counting and assessing as he came. He would not be much impressed by that footsore, bedraggled array. Joalians had lost their shiny smartness; Nagians were no longer painted savages. They had merged into a hungry, hopeless rabble.

Advised of the herald's coming, Golbfish hurriedly summoned a few of the closer troopleaders to form a retinue. The Liberator's absence was obvious now. They growled mutinously when he refused to explain. He had no time to explain and no explanation that he was willing to give them anyway. Kolgan sneered in the background, saying nothing to help. D'ward had left Golbfish in charge and Kolgan knew that, but Joalians found loyalty an elusive concept. The Thargians would insist on dealing with a Joalian, so Kolgan was going to be battlemaster again by the end of the negotiations.

What was there to negotiate, though?

Shogby?

Centuries ago—according to a legend that the Thargians insisted was vile slander—they had surrounded a Randorian army at Shogby and had offered mercy. If one quarter of the invaders would surrender and go voluntarily as slaves to the silver mines, they had said, the remainder would be allowed to depart unharmed. After long debate, the Randorians had accepted, drawing lots among themselves to select the sacrificial victims. The next day the Thargians had surrounded the departing three quarters and offered the same terms again.

The first ice of winter and the word of a Thargian, said the proverb.

The herald reined in before the leaders. His ceremonial whites were drab with dust, his mount was labored and steaming, but he stared down from its back with predictable arrogance and the traditional sneer of his craft.

"I come in the name of Holy D'ward!"

Not the Liberator—D'ward Tion, god of heralds. His ritual was brief and to the point. He leaned down, holding out a leather bag. Golbfish dropped a silver coin in it. The herald shook it to demonstrate that there were now two coins in there and that he was therefore bound equally to both sides. He straightened up and came right to business.

"I bring terms from the ephors to your commander."

Golbfish held a spear and shield, wore a loincloth. At his side, Kolgan was clad in Joalian armor and helmet. Around them stood the motley retinue of both peoples, most wearing a random assortment of garb and weapons so that their individual races were not immediately evident—but the herald's gaze was fixed on Golbfish alone.

That was odd. No, that was bad. It probably meant that the Liberator had been captured and interrogated. But apparently the envoy wanted to deal with Golbfish, and D'ward had left him in charge. His childhood ambition, he recalled, had been to write great poetry. "I am leader. Speak and be brief."

The herald's grim smile implied that there was very little to argue about. "The noble Ephors Grarknog and Psaamb send these words: They have twice your number at your rear. Your flank is held by an army little smaller. The noble Ephor Gizmok blocks the pass ahead with a force greater than any I have yet named. The ephors would—"

"That's good!" Golbfish barked. "Glad to hear it. We have been getting very bored lately." His companions laughed on cue. The sound was brittle.

"The ephors would meet with you at sunset. In—"

"The usual Shogby terms, I presume?"

The herald scowled. "Will you hear my message or not?"

"If you will stop insulting my intelligence I will give you a few more minutes." Being deliberately rude was a new experience and quite enjoyable.

"Then hear. In token of their good faith, the noble ephors have refrained from attacking your men these past several days, as you must know. Moreover, they have now halted all movement of their forces and will not advance farther until after the parley. They point out that you are totally at their mercy. Nevertheless they wish to offer you terms."

"Women chatter, men act. Tell them to write their terms on their swords and deliver them in person." Golbfish gestured dismissal and started to turn away.

"They will offer safe passage for all your men, back to Joaldom!"

Golbfish returned to his previous orientation. He was ignorant of military matters, but he did know history and he did know politics. He also knew how the haughty Thargians must feel about the presence of invaders within their home vale. Nothing in the world would persuade the ephors to let them escape scot-free.

"Oh, begone!" he shouted. "You foul the air with your lies and posturings."

"You will not even agree to a parley?"

"I have better things to do with my time than talk about Shogby!" Golbfish was amused how airily he threw that mortal insult at a Thargian warrior. Even a lifelong coward could be assertive when he had an army at his back. "Go tell the Milogians of mercy!"

That was worse. The herald's pallor showed even under the road dust. "You may yet suffer the fate of the Milogians!" His voice croaked with fury.

Golbfish had run out of insults. "Begone!" Again he started to turn away.

"Hear me out!" the herald yelled. "The ephors will come in person to your camp. They will bring with them the Most Holy K'tain High-priest, primate of all Thargia." He swallowed as if the next part was going to taste ever worse. "In support of the terms they will offer, the ephors will furnish whatever hostages you demand, including their own sons if necessary."

Golbfish realized his mouth was hanging open and closed it quickly. He glanced at his companions and wondered inanely why he had not heard the clatter of jaws dropping all around him. "Ah . . . That's all?"

The herald shuddered. "Could there be more? In all our great history, no such offer has ever been made to an enemy of Thargia. I agreed to deliver it only on condition that my tongue will be cut out when I have returned with your answer. This has been promised me."

Golbfish looked at Kolgan, but the Joalian seemed to be too shocked to speak. He felt little better himself. Even if this was all a trick, merely to make such an offer should be suicidal humiliation for the ephors.

"Why?" he demanded of the herald. "Your words are beyond belief. You claim to have us at your mercy and then throw yourselves at our feet? You will have to explain, or I must assume that Thargians have merely discovered humor."

The man wiped his forehead, where sweat had turned the dust to mud. "I have exceeded my mandate. Pray ignore what I said about tongues. Grant me your answer."

"At sunset . . . within our camp . . . How many?"

"I am to ask for twelve, but accept fewer if necessary."

Either the herald was insane, or Golbfish himself was. He made the stiffest demand he could imagine. "You will deliver fifty fat bullocks to our lines within the hour. Your forces will hold their present positions. At sunset you may send just five suppliants—two ephors with one son apiece, plus the priest. Unarmed, on foot, in civilian clothes."

An army crushed by defeat would have howled at such humiliation, but the herald barely hesitated. "You are leader of the Nagians and you grant them safe conduct upon your personal honor?"

Odder yet! Why had the man been told to make that strange stipulation? Why *Nagians,* when the Joalians were the real enemy?

Then Golbfish realized what was different this time, what was warping warfare, history, religion, and politics into this nightmare tangle. He licked his lips to hide a sudden smile. "I am leader of the Nagians and the Joalians both, and I grant safe conduct upon my honor."

"Then it is agreed! The curse of Holy D'ward to Eternity upon him who says otherwise."

The herald wheeled his moa and flashed away like a leaf in a whirlwind. He was only a speck on the horizon by the time Golbfish emerged from a screaming, cheering riot of Joalians and Nagians. They were clapping him on the back and pumping his hand; they were hugging him and kissing him.

Nobody, they exulted, had ever humbled a Thargian emissary like that. Never. Fat bullocks within the hour? Ephors unarmed and on foot! Ephors surrendering their sons? In the end he was hoisted shoulder-high and paraded through the army as his feat was shouted from troop to troop. They seemed to believe that he had suddenly become a military genius. He found it amusing. He knew D'ward would, if he were there.

He did not try to explain to them. The herald had spoken with the leader of the Nagians. *The Thargians thought they were dealing with the Liberator.* What was going to happen when they discovered their error?

42

"THAT'S IT!" EDWARD SAID. "HARROW HILL! WHAT ELSE?" HE jabbed a finger at the map and looked up, beaming triumphantly.

Alice doubted things could be so easy. "They show standing stones there," she agreed, peering. "Why Harrow?"

"Anglo-Saxon. *Hearh* meant a hilltop sanctuary."

"Is there any language you can't speak?" Julian demanded.

"Chinese. And I'm not much good in Thargian. You need a sandpaper throat to pronounce it. But this looks right, and here's the village where we met the Gypsies—Vicarsdown. See the meadow by the river? It all fits."

The five of them were gathered around Mrs. Bodgley's dining room table, examining the maps Mr. Glossop had provided. He had also sent a list of half a dozen megalithic sites around Greyfriars, but obviously Edward was already convinced he had found the one he wanted.

Alice distrusted enthusiasm. "Second choice, just in case?" she asked. Harrow Hill was only nine or ten miles from the Dower House, so she could guess what was going to happen this afternoon.

She had had a busy morning, visiting old Glossop with Mrs. Bodgley and then shopping in Greyfriars. The town itself had not changed in three years, but the effects of the war had been depressingly obvious. That a wealthy lady would have to fetch her own groceries instead of having them delivered—that had been one big difference. The eerie scarcity of young men had been another. Not that their absence had been all bad. Buying men's underwear in Wickenden Bros. Gentlemen's Outfitters might have been a lot more embarrassing had the clerk not been a woman.

Edward completed his survey of the list and shook his head. "Looks like Harrow Hill or nothing. We can run over there after lunch. It's a lovely day."

"Is old Elspeth up to another outing?" Smedley asked.

Mrs. Bodgley shook her head. "Better not. Her wind isn't what it used to be. Mr. Glossop allowed us to borrow his bicycle, though. It's a lady's model of unimpeachable antiquity, but if you don't mind being seen on it, Edward, it should take you there and back."

"I don't mind being *seen*. Being *noticed* might be sticky. Running into old Inspector Leatherdale, for example."

"Why don't you take my bike?" Ginger suggested. "Miss Prescott will doubtless be pleased to accompany you." His expression was unreadable, light reflecting off his pince-nez.

About to suggest that Julian go in her place, Alice caught herself in the nick of time. She had not brought any clothes suitable for cycling, but Edward was beaming at the prospect. "I'd love to," she agreed. "Very kind of you."

"Then that's settled!" Mrs. Bodgley said heartily.

"Ripping!" Then Edward frowned. "One thing, though . . . we shall have to take an offering."

The lady blinked. "What sort of offering? Kill a white lamb, you mean? Or a five-bob note?"

"Something significant." He looked apologetically at Alice. He was flat broke, of course.

"I think I may have something." Mrs. Bodgley swept from the room.

An awkward silence remained. This was the twentieth century. Pagan gods were a permissible subject for conversation, but actually making sacrifice to one would be behavior beyond the bizarre.

"Blood, of course," Edward muttered, "but it would be more fitting to have brought something tangible in this case, I think. . . ."

Alice decided that blood sacrifice was out of the question. She could not possibly summon up enough faith . . . which was the whole point, presumably. Half a crown in the plate was as far as she would go for a pre-Christian woodland numen.

Mrs. Bodgley sailed back in majestically. "I presume you can deliver an offering from me, on your behalf?" She might have been referring to the church jumble sale.

"Certainly."

"Then take this to your, ah, associate." She handed Edward a small silver tankard. "Timothy's christening mug. As a token of my gratitude for his helping my son's friend. And this . . . I gave you this once, so it is yours, but it still has Timothy's name on the flyleaf and Inspector Leatherdale returned it to me. It has no real value, yet I expect it could be termed significant under the circumstances."

Edward took the book and glanced at the title. Then he blinked several times and swallowed, at a loss for words. Eventually he mumbled, "Thank you very much. It's a wonderful choice."

Alice looked away. Probably they all did, for nobody said any more. The English were never very good at dealing with emotion.

It was indeed a lovely day. Mr. Glossop's bicycle was Jacobean, or even Elizabethan, with a pedal brake and a flint saddle; but it worked. Despite a niggling worry that her skirts would catch in the chain, Alice realized that she was going to enjoy this outing. Three days ago she had believed her cousin dead, and here she was cycling along a country lane with him, under beeches and elms just starting to blush with autumn. Wild roses and chestnut trees were laden with fruit.

In the Grange park, the sheep had been herded aside, and the convales-cents were indulging in a strange sort of cricket match. With half the players in bandages or even casts, the rules must have been specially devised. She turned her mind from them; she wanted to forget the war today.

"England!" Edward sighed.

"Are the Vales comparable?"

He pulled a face, as if that was the problem he wanted to forget, but he answered. "Not many. Thargland comes close. The colors! I suppose a blue and purple forest sounds grotesque, but it has its own beauty."

A hill intervened then, and they concentrated on pedaling. As they started downhill, Alice put her doubts into words.

"Edward? This is fun. I am enjoying it, but are you seriously promising to introduce me to a genuine woodland spirit? Human originally but from another world and endowed with magical powers? Centuries old? I must admit—"

"No. Probably not. If we went at night, perhaps, but he's very shy. I don't think he'll appear in daylight."

That was a relief. "So what are you hoping to achieve? What will you do, actually?"

"Pray," he said solemnly. "Thank him again for what he did for me three years ago. Leave the offerings, explain that I need to send a message to Head Office. Tell him the message, probably, and just ask him to pass it on. That's all."

Even that sounded weird. With almost anyone else, she would have wondered about sanity; she would have suspected obsessions or just tomfoolery, but Edward had never been a leg-puller. Even as a boy, he had been trustworthy.

"So how will you know if you've been heard?"

"I think I'll know."

And then he would set off to wangle his way into the Army! She did not want to think about that. Why fight for a homeland that wanted to hang you? A hay wagon loomed in the road ahead, rumbling along behind a solitary horse. They pulled out to pass it and started up another slope. On either hand the fields were golden.

"You can't predict strangers," Edward said. "They don't face early death as we do. Their viewpoint is so different. . . ."

"How many have you met?" she asked. "Just Puck in this world, but how many on Nextdoor?"

"Four or five. That's if you don't count the Service people, of course. Most of them haven't been strangers long enough to lose their humanity. They're communal, too. That helps. The god types are solitary."

"Skulking on their nodes like spiders in a web?"

"Exactly! Well put. Mad as March hares, a lot of 'em. But charming! They all have charisma, you see, so you can't ever dislike them."

He frowned at some memory or other and fell silent.

She prompted. "Tion and the herder one?"

"Tion and Krobidirkin. Then Prylis—delightful, entertaining, and a thoroughgoing rotter!"

Intrigued, Alice said, "In what way?"

Edward pedaled in sulky silence for a while. "I suppose I shouldn't judge him," he said—but so reluctantly that he obviously did. "He was just playing the Great Game as he thought it should be played, and he did save my life because of it. A real Zath hater."

More silence.

"Tell me about him."

"Prylis? He's one of Tion's minions, god of learning. Originally he was from somewhere in Macedonia, I think. Don't know exactly when. His ideas of history and geography never seemed to match mine. He was delighted to have a visitor from his old world, more or less. The last one had brought him up to date with current affairs at the time of Charlemagne. We talked in a wild mixture of Greek and Thargian and Joalian, but his Joalian was centuries old, and whenever he got excited his Macedonian and Thargian accents combined to make him completely incomprehensible. He had more books than the British Museum."

It was not like Edward to hold a grudge, and he was not explaining this one.

"He sounds no worse than eccentric."

"Oh, he was personable enough—and knowledgeable, as you'd expect in a god of learning. He showed me maps of the Vales, he talked of the lands outside—deserts to the southeast and Fashranpil, the Great Ice, to the north. There are jungles west and south, with travelers bringing back tantalizing hints of salt water beyond, but even Prylis can't tell if it's an ocean or a closed sea. There's a trickle of trade goods coming across the desert: sapphires and spices, carved onyx and amber, but nobody knows who or where they come from.

"He spilled out centuries of history for me, biographies of gods, legends and beliefs, great poets and great art, politics and customs. I learned more about the Vales in those two days than I had in the previous year. Just about anything I wanted to know he could tell me . . . except where Olympus was, oddly enough. The Service wasn't in his books and didn't interest him. Reforms had been tried before, he said, and he quoted some examples, but whenever they became a serious nuisance the Five just took them over or stamped them out. But the quirks of the Vales and the vagaries of its peoples . . . anything I wanted to ask he would answer. Thargvale wasn't such a crazy place to put a temple of learning as it seemed. Thargians are Philistines who care about little except war, but they're usually strong enough to keep the war in other people's vales. Prylis had been left undisturbed for centuries. By arriving with an army, I'd earned a spot in the history books already, just out of ignorance. Lovers of learning shouldn't mind the pilgrimage to his digs anyway, he said, which was true enough. He did have humor! We sat up all the first night, talked all day, two days. He charmed me, beguiled me."

Edward scowled darkly. "He kept me from my duty."

Ah! That was the crime he could not forgive.

43

BEING TOUGH HAD ITS LIMITS AND DOSH HAD REACHED THEM. HE HAD reached them once or twice before in his life, but never so convincingly. Dibber Troopleader and his sadists had enjoyed themselves very expertly under the guise of questioning him, and then the ride on the moa had completed the job. He remembered bringing D'ward to the temple, but that fulfillment had released the compulsion the god had put on him. After that, not much registered for a while.

He could recall being carried somewhere and laid on a bed. A wizened old man who must have been the house leech had tended him, strapping up his broken ribs, poulticing his well-kicked knees, salving his abrasions, dosing him with sour-tasting potions to ease the agony in his belly. Mercifully, he had slept after that.

He had awakened in confusion and a great deal of pain. Sunlight trickling through a high grating had revealed rough stone walls, bare floor, and a few dry sticks of furniture. For a long time Dosh had just lain on the boardlike bed, not daring to move a single tortured muscle and unable to hazard a guess as to where he was. Then the old man had come back and insisted on fussing with bandages; but after that he had spooned warm broth into the patient, which had been welcome. The man's yellow robe had reminded Dosh of where he was, but he had asked no questions. He was too weak to do anything about the answers.

He had slept again, wakened in darkness, slept more.

The next time he was conscious, a boy was standing over him, frowning. Good-looking lad, er, lass. It was Ysian in a skimpy tunic, standard male attire in Thargland. Women wore long skirts, which in Ysian's case would be a shame.

"Good morning," he muttered. His lips hurt. Everything hurt. He was afraid if he moved a finger he would start having cramps, and that would be disaster.

"It's afternoon."

"How long have we been here?"

"All yesterday."

"What's Ksargirk Captain doing?" A good commander always thinks of his men, especially Progyurg Lancer.

"They've all gone. The abbot sent them away."

"What right does he have?"

"He said the god told him to."

"Oh. Where's D'ward?"

"I don't know! He went through that door and disappeared. The abbot says he is with the god and not to worry."

Obviously she was worrying, though. The army would be a long way off by now, and the moas gone. Didn't matter about the army, Dosh thought. Much safer away from the army. His job was to keep watch on the Liberator, not the army.

In a startling flash, he remembered that his job was over. He was no longer bound to report to Tion, that unspeakable . . . Words failed him, thoughts failed him, hatred choked him when he tried to think of Tion. Prylis had removed Tion's binding. So Dosh was a free man again, for as long as he could stay out of the god's clutches. He had never been a free man before. Was he free now, for the first time in his life? The Liberator . . .

"What's wrong?" Ysian demanded.

"Not much, except I'm one big bruise. I have to get up. Don't be alarmed if I scream."

"I'll help you."

"I'd rather do it at my own speed." He flexed an arm. Ouch! "So are you having fun?"

"What does that mean?" she snapped.

"You're the only woman in the place, aren't you?"

"Sh! I told them my name was Tysian. They think I'm a boy."

He tried the other arm. Worse. "Do they? Do they really?" Could even monks be in doubt about those legs?

"Well, I think one or two suspect, but they're very kind."

"Mm? Found any good-looking young novices?"

Ysian said, "Oh, you're horrible! Don't you ever think of anything else?"

"Not unless I have to. Have you even looked?"

Without a word, she spun around and left. She slammed the door behind her.

Pity. He had been going to ask her to send them his way.

Ironically, the young novice who came to feed the invalid shortly thereafter was a very good-looking youth indeed, which was not unexpected in a devotee of Tion's. He showed no personal interest in Dosh, and while teasing Ysian was possible, Dosh in his present condition dared not venture advances that might be taken seriously. He felt quite disappointed in himself. He dozed off the moment he finished the meal.

The ensuing night was long, broken by sleepy thinking-times into several nights, end to end. He thought a lot about this strange notion of freedom and what it might be good for. He had had many masters before Tion—mortals all, but masters—plus a very few mistresses. He must have been about ten or so when his father sold him to Kramthin Clockmaker. He could still recall his joy when he learned that he would be able to stay in Kramthin's warm, comfortable house, eating fine food, never being hungry. What Kramthin had required of him in return had been much less unpleasant than his father's drunken beatings. Kramthin had been the first. Dosh had been traded a few times and then decided to handle his own affairs thereafter. Whenever he had tired of one master, he had just run away and found another. They had not owned him in law, for only Thargia of all the lands in the Vales permitted slavery, and he had stayed away from Thargland until now. They had not bound him as Tion had. He had bound himself to them voluntarily, for food and shelter and affection.

The last of his masters, Prithose Connoisseur, had gone visiting Suss to enjoy the artistic offerings at Tion's Festival. He had entered Dosh in the contest for the gold rose, much as a breeder might enter livestock in a show. Dosh had been seventeen. He had won the prize easily and apparently that prize had made him Tion's own prize. Three years missing . . . What had he been during those three years? Servant? Plaything? Wallpaper?

Prylis had broken Tion's spell. Would he impose one of his own, and turn Dosh into a monk, copying manuscripts to the end of his days? Would he return him to Tion? Or was Dosh now a free man for the first time in his life? Could he survive without a master?

At some later point in the night, his mind returned to the problem. All men but kings served other men, for that was the way of the world. The talent that had supported him until had become a doubtful commodity when Tarion ripped up his face. Copy manuscripts? Dig and reap?

Chastity or monogamy? Fun though lechery undoubtedly was, it had brought him more than his share of grief. D'ward seemed to get by without it at all. That was going too far in the opposite direction, much too far, but perhaps Dosh ought to introduce a little moderation into his life.

Who—him? Honest labor? Nothing like a few aches to bring on repentance, he decided. In a day or two he would be his old self. He went back to sleep.

44

T̲HE NEXT TIME HE AWOKE THERE WAS LIGHT BEHIND THE GRATING and birds were creating a damnable racket outside. Dawn. What morning? It had been Heelday when he first came to the monastery. Had it been Ankleday when Ysian came? This must be Shinday at the least. The army was either well out of Thargland by now or all dead. If the gods dispensed justice, though, ex-troopleader Dibber and his bullyboys were just settling in to a long, hard lifetime in the silver mines.

Dosh stretched. He sat up with a jerk. He fingered his ribs and detected only a trace of soreness under the bandages. He pulled down the blanket and looked at his knees. Not a mark. Not one bruise on him. His fingertips went to his face. It was smooth.

He leaned his chin on his arms and pondered. In among the litter of forgotten dreams, he found vague memories of voices in the night. Two men? He was able to raise no details, but he knew who one of them must have been, and could guess at the other. Well! So what about breakfast?

He swung his feet to the floor and saw that someone had been leaving him presents: on the solitary chair lay a brown Thargian tunic, a sword, sandals, a belt pouch with an intriguing jingle. The sword annoyed him, but he knew that Thargian law required freemen to go armed. He had no skill or experience with a sword. His weapon of choice was the concealed knife. He was quite good with that.

He had just finished counting the money—sixteen silver marks—when the door creaked open and a Thargian stalked in. No, it was D'ward, with his face clean shaven and his hair cut short, wearing a tunic and a sword. He even had the mean Thargian scowl—or at least an icy glitter in his eyes. When he saw that Dosh was awake, it thawed a little.

"Sleep well? Feeling better?"

"Did you come calling in the night?"

"Yes."

"With a friend?"

The angry glint returned. "*You* could call him that. I . . . He paid you for services rendered."

"I'd better go and thank him, I suppose."

"I suppose so too, but don't make an epic of it. Some merchant's just donated a very rare book to the temple, so the god is undoubtedly too engrossed to hear you. We're not wanted in the refectory for the same reason—the abbot's entertaining the wealthy gent, trying to squeeze an endowment out of him to enlarge the scriptorium. There's grub in the kitchens, cold water in the washhouse. You'd better shave off your beard if you want to pass as a local. Prylis removed your scars. I expect you'll want to thank him for that, too." He turned to the door.

Too much too soon! "Wait a minute!" Dosh caught his breath. It sounded as if D'ward was extremely knowledgeable about the workings of the monastery and the habits of the resident deity. What had been happening? "Where are we going?"

D'ward drummed fingers on the door before he looked around. "I know where I'm going. You can please your own sweet self, as far as I care. Pick a direction and start walking. If you want to come with me, we can chat on the way, but I won't loiter. I plan to eat on the hoof."

Dosh bit back a snappy retort and asked, "Any news of the army?"

"Yes."

"Well?" What was gnawing at the Liberator? Dosh had never known him to be crabby before.

"They're safe."

"*Safe!?*"

"I'll tell you later. Jump to it!" D'ward pulled the door open.

"Wait!"

He looked back with a glare. "Now what?"

Dosh smiled cherubically. "Has anyone ever told you that you have beautiful legs?"

D'ward could slam a door even louder than Ysian.

Chewing on hard bread and hunks of cheese, three wayfarers strode along the track in the dewy dawn. D'ward was in the middle, setting a murderous pace with his (beautiful) long legs. Despite his considerable handicap in height, Dosh was prepared to take him on at distance sprinting any day, but Ysian was struggling to keep up. To look at, they were a trio of young men, with no packs, one long dagger, two swords, three money pouches. Dosh still had his favorite knife, which didn't show. All in all, Holy Prylis had done them proud.

Apparently the war was over, at least so far as they were concerned. The future shone much brighter without a massacre in it. There seemed no obvious explanation for D'ward's vile mood, unless he was concerned about getting safely out of Thargvale, which certainly might pose problems. By law, strangers were spies unless they could prove otherwise.

"Where are we going?"

"Down to the river," D'ward said. "Thargwater. There I'm going to catch a boat. It's downhill all the way—I should be in Tharg in a couple of hours."

Tharg itself? "And what are we going to do in that city of celebrated boredom and illustrious ugliness?"

D'ward wrinkled his nose. "You please yourself. Ysian and I are going to the Convent of Ursula."

"*We are going where?*" Ysian screeched.

"Goddess of justice. I have been assured that her convent is a worthy sanctuary, and the sisters will take you in and care for you. I have a letter from the abbot."

Dosh strode along in silence as the ensuing altercation waxed loud and long.

Seemingly D'ward regarded Ysian as a child and felt responsible for her. Some child!—Dosh had known women who had borne two children by her age, but apparently the Liberator had other standards. He had sacked Lemod. One result of that act had been to brand all women remaining within the walls as ruined, harlots beyond all hope of marriage. For that reason, he had allowed Ysian to accompany the flight and guide the fugitives to Moggpass. He had then accepted her word that her family would put her to death for treason if she went home. Dosh suspected that she had been exaggerating there. But D'ward felt responsible, and now he had decided to hand his burden over to the stern nuns of Ursula. In a few years she would be old enough to make up her own mind what to do with her life, he said.

Ysian's rebuttal began quietly, but his stubborn responses soon had her yelling, interrupting the last of the birds' dawn chorus in the branches overhead and scaring the leafeater lizards in the ditches. She was a mature woman, she screamed. She would make her own decisions right now. He would have died in Lemod without her help. He was utterly heartless and she hated him. She loved him more than life itself. The nuns of Ursula were notorious sadists. She would follow him to the corners of the world. She would sleep on his doorsteps forever, anywhere he went, and haunt him for the rest of his life, and she was going to kill herself before nightfall and him soon after.

There was more, but suddenly both she and D'ward collapsed in helpless, hysterical mirth. Dosh was shocked to realize that she had been putting on an act and it had fooled him completely. Admittedly she was on the far side of D'ward, so he had not been watching her, nor listening very closely either. Yet he felt peeved at being fooled. He felt like an outsider in the presence of lovers—which was exactly what he must be. *Jealous, my lad?* He had never really seen these two together except in very public settings. Observing them now—leaning on each other for support, gasping for breath, tears of laughter streaming over their cheeks—no one could ever doubt that they were hopelessly in love. Ysian knew. D'ward was apparently not ready to admit the obvious.

The nervous release did not last long. Soon he returned to his angry urgency, and the three of them resumed their progress. Abandoning the argument, D'ward turned to Dosh. "Where are you headed?"

"I want to stay with you."

"Why?"

Interesting question! Dosh debated several answers, and then decided to tell the truth, just for once. What was the truth, though? The silence dragged out for half a mile before he found it.

"I want to learn from you. You're different."

D'ward said, "Hmm?" The river was in sight in the distance, a line of trees twisting along the valley floor. "How does it feel?"

"How does what feel?"

"Telling the truth."

"Dangerous. Like being naked in a crowd."

Ysian laughed.

"Have you a trade you can take up?" D'ward said. "Or a skill of some kind?"

"I'm good at massage."

He winced, misunderstanding. "Where are you from? Where was your home?"

Dosh decided to push the experiment in veracity a little farther. "Never had one. My people were Tinkerfolk."

"What are Tinkerfolk?" Apparently the query was serious and he really did not know.

"They're nomads. Wanderers. They mostly live in tents or wagons, although every city has a tinkers' hole somewhere. They do odd jobs, poach, steal. Most people think they're all liars, whores, thieves, and spies."

"What are they really?"

"Spies, thieves, whores, and liars."

The others both laughed at that, which felt good. The road led to a hamlet with a jetty. There were boats there, waiting for hire.

"Listen," the Liberator said, serious again. "You can't come where I'm going. You've got the same problem Ysian has. I'm sorry, but I can't help either of you. I have a potent sort of charm that I can't control and I really can't explain to you, either. You saw how it worked on the army—I began with a spear and ended up as battlemaster. I had five thousand men all wanting me to scratch them behind the ears. Ysian thinks she's in love with me, and so do you. I like both of you, but I can't return the sort of love you want and I am promised to another woman, so I can't help her, either. I'm truly sorry, but that's the way things are. *Viks'n*, you're better at this local snarl than we are. See if you can hire a boat to take us to Tharg."

"How many?"

"Two."

"Three," said Dosh.

Marg'rk Ferryman was not much more than a boy, built of sticks and string as if he had not eaten in several fortnights. His skiff was a smelly, leaky little hulk, and its sail bore innumerable patches. He toadied and groveled for passengers rich enough to pay him a whole silver mark for a half-day's work. He addressed each of them as "Warrior," which was the correct honorific for Thargian freemen. Had he known Ysian was a woman, he would properly have called her "Mother." That said a lot about Thargian values.

Propelled much more by the current than the forlorn breeze, his boat drifted out into Thargwater and headed southward. Marg'rk clutched the tiller with a bony hand, smiling obsequiously whenever anyone looked in his direction. Wide, swift, and smooth, the river oiled through a rich countryside. The banks were ornamented with fish traps and jetties, water mills and multicolored trees. High-horned kudus plodded along towpaths, hauling barges. Cargo boats crawled upstream under the muscle power of slaves. The hills beyond were figured with vineyards and orchards, or fields being plowed and sown. Here and there, grand aristocratic mansions graced the landscape.

Ysian sat amidships, being unusually quiet. Even cropped short so barbarically, her hair shone with red-gold highlights. She was brooding ominously. Dosh suspected the convent would have to survive without a new postulant, whatever D'ward might think.

The Liberator sat beside her, the mast between them, crouching to see under the edge of the sail. He scowled, fidgeted, and squirmed. He had not yet explained why he so urgently wanted to reach Tharg. Impatience was out of character for him.

Dosh sprawled in the bow with his feet in a stinking litter of nets and baskets, pots and bilge. After a while he removed his tunic and leaned back in his breechclout to soak up some spring sunshine. His two companions carefully avoided looking at him. Prudes! He had all the essentials covered. They wouldn't care about anyone else; they just knew he would accept any reasonable offer and were frightened to look in case they were caught window-shopping.

"Warrior D'ward?"

"Yes, Warrior Dosh?" D'ward had developed an intense interest in the reflections of windmills.

Dosh peered past Ysian at the boatman, who leered back nervously and mawkishly. That lout would not understand Joalian. "Are you going to Tharg to bring death to Death, as has been prophesied? And when you have that one stuffed and mounted, will you do Tion too, as a favor for me?"

"That's not why I'm going to Tharg." D'ward straightened his long back, and the sail hid his face.

"You told me our former comrades-in-arms are now safe. You promised to say how."

D'ward sank back into a slouch, and his scowl became visible again. Why was he so edgy? "Prylis told me. The Thargians gave them safe conduct back to Nagvale."

"More miracles? The *Thargians* did? You're serious?"

"They sent emissaries, a couple of the ephors in person. That alone is unprecedented. Golbfish did the negotiating. He demanded the whole world and they gave it to him: food, hostages, formal oaths sealed with sacrifice. The Thargians will hold back the Lemodians to let the Nagians go by. They groveled, they implored. Anything he wanted."

That ought to be unbelievable or else hilariously funny, and yet D'ward was disconsolate. Obvious question: "Why?"

"Plague," D'ward said, staring blankly at the left bank. "People are dying by the hundreds all over Thargland. They take ill in the night, and they rot for three days and then die. Funeral pyres bejewel the night and sully the sun by day—Prylis's words, not mine."

"Padlopan's the god of sickness, but—"

"This is Zath. The people think it's an epidemic, but Prylis says Zath's called in his reapers from all over the Vales, brought them here into Thargvale, and he's taught them a new form of sacrifice. A reaper death used to be quick. Now it's slow and even more horrible. And they're working overtime."

Zath was an aspect of Karzon, the patron deity. Why would a god destroy his own people? Dosh caught Ysian's eye; she looked away quickly. She was frightened about something.

"Human sacrifice?" he said with disgust. "You're saying that what reapers do is human sacrifice?"

"What else would you call it?"

"I don't know. I just never thought of it that way. Human sacrifice is something done by the savages in the southern jungles or read about in old, old history. Uncivilized. We don't do that anymore!"

"Reapers do," D'ward said grimly. "Zath does."

"I suppose you're right. What has this plague of reapers got to do with—Oh, my god!''

"Not your god, I hope. But you've got the idea. Karzon—or Zath—the distinction seems to be getting blurry . . . One of them has sent a revelation, telling the priests how to turn aside the divine wrath and end the epidemic.''

"Deliver the Liberator's head?" Dosh said.

Ysian's face was sickly pale.

D'ward's mouth twisted in a mirthless grin. "That's not what he said. Gods have pride. Everyone knows what the *Filoby Testament* prophesies about the Liberator and Death, although most people believe that the Liberator is still a year-old baby somewhere in Sussland. For Zath to name the Liberator would be a confession of weakness. He might have named D'ward, but even that would draw attention to the prophecies. He didn't have to name names. He knew I was responsible for the fall of Lemod. He knew I would be acclaimed leader—that was inevitable, although you won't understand why. So the revelation just demanded the leader of the Nagians, no name mentioned.''

"That's why the Thargians stopped killing us?"

"That's why. They didn't want to kill me by mistake. The leader of the Nagians must be brought to the temple and sacrificed there. Death in battle will not suffice. The ephors were willing to let the whole Joalian army go—willing to feed them and escort them home, do anything they asked. They demanded only one thing in return.''

Dosh rubbed his oddly smooth cheek—no stubble, no scars. "So Golbfish gave himself up?"

D'ward nodded miserably. "He's on his way to Tharg right now. We should arrive about the same time he does.''

"He's going to die by mistake?"

"No. Well, a Thargian mistake, but the prince is quite smart enough to have worked this out for himself by now. He must know that he's the wrong man, but his captors don't. He was in command and he has Nagian merit scars on his ribs—that would be enough for them. Zath may guess when he gets a look at him, but a god can hardly back down at that stage. So Golbfish will die, and the plague will end, and meanwhile his men are on their way home already, escorting enough hostages to make sure they get there.''

D'ward licked his lips. "It's a good deal from Golbfish's point of view. He dies, but he would likely have died anyway. This way his entire force gets home safely. No honorable leader would refuse such an offer. I'm sure he didn't even argue.''

"You don't seem very satisfied by the arrangement.''

"Prylis pulled me out of the trap and put in Golbfish instead." D'ward bared his teeth.

"You enjoy being bait?"

D'ward did not deign to answer. For a while nobody spoke. Dosh registered vaguely that the boat was tacking and the river had turned to the west already. The city might be coming into view. He did not look around—he was too busy trying to work out why D'ward should be so upset.

Baffled, he finally asked.

The Liberator looked at him oddly. "What don't you understand?"

"He's going to the temple," Ysian said bitterly, "to give himself up, tell them they got the wrong man!"

"But that would be utterly insane! D'ward . . . ? Really?"

"Aren't you?" she demanded.

"I must, *Viks'n*." He was looking at Dosh, not at her, and there was a curious appeal in his cerulean eyes, as if he wanted approval or reassurance. "A man's got to have honor. Right, Warrior?"

"No!" Dosh said. "No! No! Not right! What you're planning won't work, and even if it would, I'd still think you're bloody crazy."

ᐁᘯ 45 ᘺᐃ

"I THINK YOU'RE CRAZY!" ALICE SAID ANGRILY. "IT WON'T JUST BE Boche bullets you'll have to avoid. All those hundreds of boys who knew you at Fallow are all out there now, subalterns, mostly. It will only take one: 'By Jove! That fellow looks just like that cricketer chappie, Exeter. I say! Wasn't he the one who murdered old Bagpipe Bodgley?' And then, my lad, you'll be in the—"

"You're nagging," Edward said.

They were in Ye Olde English Tea Shoppe in Vicarsdown. The village was bigger than he remembered, he said, and she had retorted that it would still fit inside Piccadilly Circus, which was not true. But the tea shoppe was an authentic Elizabethan building and delightful, although it must have had some other purpose originally, because authentic Elizabethans had drunk

ale, not tea. It was tiny, cramped, and rather dark—pleasantly cool. They
were drinking tea. They were eating homemade scones spread with straw-
berry jam and cream thick as butter. It was too precious a moment to waste
quarreling.

Edward's eyes were cold as a winter sea. "Furthermore, those hundreds
of boys are not all out there now. Half of them are dead. And you persist
in treating me as your baby brother, which I'm not, anymore."

She lifted her cup. "Yes, you are. You always were my baby brother to
me, and you always will be. When we're both a hundred years old, with
long white beards, you will still be my baby brother." She took a sip of tea,
watching to see if he would accept the olive branch.

"I don't think I'll like you in a long white beard," he said reflectively.
"Promise me you'll dye it?"

She laid down the cup and reached across for his hand. "I promise I shall
stop thinking of you as a baby brother if you'll tell me about Ysian."

"What about her? I didn't take advantage of her. I hope that doesn't
surprise you."

"Not in the slightest." She knew it would surprise most people, though.
"Did you love her?"

He pulled his hand away and began heaping cream on a scone like a
navvy loading a wheelbarrow. "I've told you everything. She's a very determined young woman—I have rather a weakness for those, you know.
She was sixteen and I was a stranger. She fell for me like a ton of bricks,
naturally. It wasn't me, just the charisma."

"You haven't answered the question."

"No, I didn't love her."

"What happened to her? When did you last see her?"

"About a year ago. Mrs. Murgatroyd took her on as cook, at Olympus.
She's a good cook, although of course she knew only Lemodian recipes."

Romance cracked and shattered into fragments. "But not educated? Just
a native wench? Not good enough?"

He stared at her in disbelief, face flaming cruelly red. His knife clattered
down on the china plate.

"Oh, Edward, I'm sorry!" she said quickly. "That was abominable of
me! I'm sure you behaved like a perfect gentleman. Oh, I mean—"

"I was a stranger," he said in a very quiet, tight voice. "Strangers never
die, except from boredom or violence. I know I don't look any older than
I did when I left here. Ysian is eighteen or nineteen now, I suppose. Ten
years from now she will be twenty-nine, and ten years after that, thirty-
nine. Had I stayed on Nextdoor, I would still be much the same as I am
now. Why do you think the Service sends people Home on leave—especially bachelors? One reason is that they have to marry other strangers! Love

between stranger and native is unthinkable. It leads to unbearable heartache. It leads to . . . to abominations. The Chamber— Never mind."

"I hadn't thought of that. I'm sorry. You didn't let yourself fall in love with her, you mean?"

He went back to destroying scones. "I did not tell her I loved her. I never gave her any encouragement whatsoever. I used you as an excuse, actually. Hope you don't mind. Had I been free to react to Ysian like a normal man, I'd have thrown my heart at her feet and rent my garments and piled ashes on my head and writhed in the dirt until she promised to marry me. That wasn't possible, so nothing was possible. Just friends."

How wonderful the world would be if emotion could be dosed with logic so easily! *I am sorry, Sir D'Arcy, but your married status inevitably precludes any further communication between us. . . .*

"Look!" Edward pointed out at the sunlit village beyond the little dia-mond-pained windows. A Gypsy wagon was being hauled along the street by an ancient nag. Dogs barked, small boys ran after it.

He watched as it disappeared around the corner. "Last time I was here, a Gypsy told my fortune. That's a different wagon, though."

"You believe in that stuff?"

He twisted his face. "I didn't used to, but that one hit the mark pretty well. She said I'd have to choose between honor and friendship. Sure enough, I was forced to abandon Eleal when I might have been able to help her."

"Come off it, Edward! That might just as well have applied to Ysian."

His eyes glinted like razors. "I don't rat on my friends very often. Aban-doning Ysian, if that's what I did, was the honorable thing to do. You might like to know the rest of the prophecy, though—Mrs. Boswell the Gypsy also said I'd have to choose between honor and duty, that I could only find honor through dishonor. Explain that one, because I can't!"

Was there a chink here to work on? "Well, if your duty is to enlist, but the honorable thing is to avenge your parents' murder—"

"Never give up, do you?" Even Edward could lose his temper. If that happened she would have lost any hope of making him see reason.

"You haven't seen Ysian in a year?" The girl was the only bait she had to coax him back to Nextdoor and away from the Western Front.

He flashed a look of exasperation at her. "Told you," he mumbled. "She's at Olympus, working for Polly Murgatroyd. She's very nice—Polly, I mean. I wrote to her before I crossed over—to Ysian, I mean. . . ." He frowned, dabbing at his mouth with the napkin. "As the man who promised to deliver the note then tried to kill me, she probably never got it."

"You weren't at Olympus?"

He shook his head, chewing. "I took two years to get there and when I did, I didn't stay long. The Committee decided it was too dangerous, both for me and for everybody else—didn't want Zath sacking the place in the hope of catching me. I was packed off to Thovale, which is very small and rural, but not too far away. I helped set up some chapels there. I became a missionary!" He laughed gleefully. "Holy Roly must have turned in his grave! But we all do . . . they all do it."

"You'd make a good preacher." She could just imagine him running his parish like a school dormitory.

"I didn't! I can't ever believe that I know better than everyone else. I don't like telling people what they must think. It's immoral!"

"Doesn't a stranger make a good preacher?"

"Yes," he admitted glumly. "I could pack in the crowds. I converted heathens to the Church's new and improved heathenism. My heart wasn't in it, though. Jumbo Watson can convert a whole village with a single sermon. I've seen him do it."

Alice abandoned the Ysian campaign. If he could stay away from the girl for a whole year to do something he did not believe in, then thoughts of Ysian were not going to discourage him from enlisting.

"The Liberator?" she said. "It's a noble title—calls up memories of Bolívar, William Tell, Robert the Bruce. Doesn't it tempt you at all?"

He rolled his eyes in exasperation at her persistence. "Not too terribly frightfully, no. There were a couple of times—and the *Filoby Testament* predicted them both. I almost gave in to Tion, because he said he would cure Eleal's limp. That was a very close-run thing! And then in Tharg, the prince—" He popped a jammy, creamy morsel in his mouth and chewed blissfully.

"What about the prince?"

"That didn't work either, but it came close, too. That particular prophecy ends, *but the dead shall rouse him*. That's me, rouse me. And that part did work, Alice, because I saw the dead—in Flanders. How many lives has this war cost?"

"No way of knowing. What you read in the papers is all censored."

"Well, the dead speak. They say it's my turn. I have to do my bit, and that's that." He glanced at his wrist and then at the grandfather clock in the corner.

She sighed. Two more miles to Harrow. Her legs ached already. "Time to go, isn't it?"

Edward nodded. "Wish I hadn't eaten so much." He surreptitiously slid the last scone into his pocket. He grinned sheepishly when he saw that she had noticed. "Another offering."

Alice shook her head in disbelief. It was Friday afternoon in England and they were on their way to meet a god.

46

SHAME! SHAME! TO THE MAN GOETH D'WARD, SAYING, SLAY ME! THE hammer falls and blood profanes the holy altar. Warriors, where is thine honor? Perceive thy shame. —Verse 266.

The divinely inspired gibberish echoed and reechoed in Dosh's head as he was swept along a milling street in Tharg. Insects droned, people shoved and jostled; heat and noise and stink. That passage made no sense at all at this point in history. How could the prophecy of D'ward's death be fulfilled before all the others about him? The trouble with the *Filoby Testament* was that too much of it made sense only after it had happened.

What about Verse 1098, then? That was the one that intrigued Tion so much. Something about the Liberator being slow to anger, and then, *Eleal shall be the first temptation and the prince shall be the second, but the dead shall rouse him.* It certainly referred to the Liberator. It might well apply to this very afternoon. Something was about to happen, something so momentous that it had caught the eye of the seeress all those many years ago.

Tharg was the largest city Dosh had ever seen, bigger even than Joal. It well deserved its reputation as the ugliest. The buildings were of somber stone, with high plain walls and tiny windows, every house a fortress. There was no color, no decoration, not a carving in sight. The men wore tunics of drab brown or khaki, boys yellow or beige, although all had a touch of the sacred colors at the neck. Women were not in evidence. Doors and shutters were tarred, not painted. The streets were narrow trenches, hot and airless, straight as spears.

They were also thronged with huge crowds of impatient, hustling, urgent freemen, all hurrying in the same direction he was heading, and most of them much taller than he. He was having trouble keeping D'ward in sight. Fortunately the Liberator was taller than most, his distinctive black hair bobbing above the tide like a cork. He was gaining. He seemed not to care that every man in the crowd bore a sword and aggressive jostling might be fatal. Very likely he was deliberately trying to lose his unwanted follower.

Gods did not make mistakes. That thought, too, Dosh kept repeating like a mantra. Prylis had extracted the Liberator from the army so that the ephors would abduct the wrong leader. When Prylis had released him this morning, had he not known what D'ward would try to do? Because he had let him go, then he must have been certain that it was now too late—mustn't he? Golbfish must be dead already, mustn't he? *Could gods make mistakes?*

Maybe a minor god like Prylis could. Everyone was heading for the temple, because there was to be an announcement—Dosh had gathered that much from remarks overheard. He dared not ask questions, lest he be denounced as a foreigner. Thargians were never nice to foreigners, especially Thargians in mobs, and the air stank of dangerous passions already. Angry, armed male mob . . . no women, no slaves? The women would all be at home in those narrow-windowed prisons of houses, being mothers.

Now where was D'ward?

Dosh rose on tiptoe as he walked, peering through the jungle of heads. Gone! No! There he was.

He had stepped into an arched doorway, and Dosh was almost past him. He pushed his way across the stream of the crowd, bumping and apologizing, being shoved and cursed and threatened. Thargians never apologized. He reached the wall and was flattened against it by the crush, then began edging his way back to the arch.

A flash of color above it caught his eye, a festoon of faded blue ropes. Blue was the color of the Maiden, and a net was the symbol of justice. He had always thought that was inappropriate. In his experience, the little ones got caught and the big ones got away. That wasn't what it meant, of course.

D'ward was speaking through a grille in the door. Ysian stood at his side, her face pale and rigid. She looked up at Dosh and bared her teeth. D'ward passed the abbot's letter through the grating. Dosh eased nearer in the hope of hearing what was being said. As he squeezed by Ysian, a sharp pain stopped him. He glanced down and confirmed his gut feeling that the problem was her dagger.

"Go!" she whispered.

He stammered and then decided that he had seen that expression in her eyes once before, when she had threatened to club him senseless. D'ward was still talking, pleading for haste. The pain came again. She could puncture Dosh's bowels with one swift jab. He stepped back. She followed, urging him on at knifepoint.

"Go!" she insisted. "Move!"

He turned into the crowd and was swept away. He felt her hand grab hold of his belt, but at least the dagger was making no more holes in his hide. In moments they were being rushed along the street by the sweaty tide.

"What do you think you are doing?" he demanded, twisting around to see her.

She was smirking triumphantly. "I am not entering any flea-infested convent! D'ward will go on to the temple. We are going to catch him before he gets there and stop him making a fool of himself!"

It wasn't a fool he was going to make of himself, it was a corpse. "By the five gods, girl, how do you ever expect—"

"Don't you call me a girl!"

"I call you an idiot! We'll never find him in this—"

The crowd had slowed to a crawl. Dosh stumbled into the man in front of him, and a vicious elbow rammed into his solar plexus, knocking all the breath out of him. He staggered.

"Watch where you're going," Ysian said, pushing him forward again.

In all cities, the holy places tended to huddle together. Temple Square was just around the corner from the convent. It was now full. Refusing to be balked, the mob in the street continued to press onward.

It occurred to Dosh that women might well be prohibited by law from entering the Man's holy place. If Ysian's deception was discovered, then he would be held responsible. On the other hand, he was more likely to die in the crush. It was already hard to breathe, and the crowd continued to squeeze tighter and tighter. It oozed ahead like a human glacier, a paste of compressed bodies. He wished he were taller.

"This will kill us!" he groaned, feeling the start of panic. Two hands gripped his arms and pulled them behind him. "What in eternity are you doing?"

"Cup your hands!"

"What?"

Ysian pushed his hands together. Somehow she squirmed and struggled and got one foot in them. Then she wriggled up his back and seated herself on his shoulders, her fingers locked in his hair and her weight threatening to buckle his knees.

"There!" she said. "Now I can see. Keep moving!"

The ancient temple of Karzon in Tharg, dating from the days of the kings, had been built of wood. During the Fifth Joalian War, it had been struck by lightning and burned to the ground. This evil omen had caused great despair among the Man's Men on the eve of the final campaign, but the famous Goztikon, thirteen times ephor, had declared the sign to be one of hope. He had publicly pledged his life and the lives of his seven sons that the god was promising renewal for Thargia; the Man's Men would prevail, he swore, and would return to build a new and mightier temple to the glory of their god.

So it had transpired. The armies of the Joalian Coalition had been crushed

in the bloody battle of Suddopass. The survivors had worked out their lives
in the quarries to further the building of the temple. Artisans and craftsmen
from all over the Vales had spent twenty years on it. The indemnities levied
on Joalia by the peace treaty had included the greatest artist of the age,
K'simbr Sculptor, who had been specifically requisitioned so he might raise
fitting images of the god.

Gods. Whereas the Man in his primary aspect had always been god of
both creation and destruction, he had hitherto been represented by a single
likeness. In the new great temple, he was shown twice. One giant image
was plated with copper, which would weather to the green of his color.
The other was of silver, to turn black. Officially both were Karzon, but the
ignorant multitude soon spoke of the second image as being that of Zath,
his aspect of Death. The avatar had been promoted to equality.

Eased forward irresistibly by the bodies pressed in all around him, Dosh
shuffled into the southwest corner of the square. Over the shifting oceans
of heads he saw the temple towering into the sky, two walls of stupendous
pillars running off to east and north. They were so thick and the gaps
between them so narrow that from his angle they completely blocked the
interior from view. They were oppressive, domineering, overwhelming.
The temple of Karzon was a giant gray granite cage, the ugliest structure
he had ever set eyes on.

The crowd pushed relentlessly at his back, urging him closer.

"Not yet!" Ysian proclaimed, having to shout over the din. She twisted
Dosh's head around. "Wait over there!"

"I can't get out."

She took hold of his ears and pulled. He yelled, causing his nearest neighbors to look at him in surprise. He blinked away tears.

"I shall pull them off!" Ysian said, kicking him with her heels.

She probably meant it. He began to fight his way out of the crowd.

He broke free of the main current after a considerable struggle and reached
the shallows at the edge of the square. There were many people there too,
but they were mostly not moving, just staring at the temple, fearing to risk
their lives in the compacted mob. He leaned back against the wall, gasping
and sweating. His shoulders were breaking.

"Get down!" he groaned. "You're crushing me."

"Stop whining! You said you were the toughest man in the army, didn't
you?"

"I'm not a fornicating moa!"

Other children in yellow tunics floated above the crowd, riding their
fathers' shoulders. None was anywhere near Ysian's size. He would wager
that none was a girl, either. Many older youths had clambered upon the

plinths of the columns, and some had scrambled even higher, apparently finding toe- and fingerholds within the carvings, clinging there like human lichen. Every few minutes one would lose his grip and fall, dragging others with him, down into the melee. Whatever screams or oaths resulted were lost in the steady, torrential roar.

Dosh was farther from the corner now. He could see through the closest pair of pillars, and what he saw was the back of the statue of Zath. Silvery black, it stood ten times the height of a man, muffled in a reaper's cloak and ominously stooped, as if to study the multitude huddled around its feet. He was happy not to be there, looking up at the face of Death. Beyond it he could see an edge of the statue of Karzon, mostly just the great hammer he held, his symbol.

Ysian kicked her heels into Dosh's ribs. "Here he comes!"

If he had room to move, he could grab her arms and flip her off him, but in this mob she would fall on top of at least one man, probably two, and then there would be reprisals. As it was, his arms were so tightly crushed against his sides that he could not raise them even to defend himself from her attacks.

"D'ward's coming!" she insisted. "Move. This way." She took him by the ears again and twisted his head to the left.

He yielded to the inevitable, starting to shoulder himself forward. He would probably have made no progress at all had Ysian not begun using her feet with deliberate savagery on the innocent bystanders. The inevitable retaliation was all directed at him, of course—he was jostled, jabbed, punched, cursed at. Any minute someone would manage to draw a sword and gut him.

"Faster!" she demanded. "We'll lose him."

Of course they would. There was no chance of catching him. D'ward was bigger and taller, and he was the Liberator. He had admitted that he had a special sort of charm. He would charm his way through the crowd. He was not carrying Ysian.

Yet Ysian did add some weight to Dosh's efforts. He discovered he could lean on the men in front of him and they would pull away to avoid being pushed over and trampled. If he lost his footing, that would happen to him.

Ysian yanked at his left ear. "That man in green coming! Catch him!"

In a moment, Dosh saw the man she meant. His green tunic marked him in the drab brown crowd and probably meant that he was some sort of temple flunky—priest or guard. He was very large, very beefy, and obviously very determined to move closer to the temple. That meant closer to D'ward.

Somehow Dosh managed to slip in at his back, and after that they made better progress. The big fellow did not seem to register that he had acquired two hangers-on as he wrestled his way toward the pillars. Dosh leaned on him, urging him forward.

The noise was fading, and now there was another sound, a steady drumbeat. Dosh had no idea what was happening inside the temple, but the ominous *boom-boom-boom* made his scalp prickle. Was Golbfish being brought in now? Human sacrifice? No god of the Vales had demanded human sacrifice in thousands of years. What would they do to him? Cut off his head? Tear out his heart? Burn him alive?

Poor old Golbfish! He had turned himself from an effete slob into a warrior and a leader. He had made himself worthy to rule the kingdom that was his by right, and now he was dying to save his men. What must he be thinking?

"Almost there!" Ysian bounced a few times with excitement. Dosh shrieked at her. He thought she meant the great pillars now looming over them, but then he saw the familiar black hair just ahead. Perhaps this madness was going to pay off after all. Then what? D'ward had refused to listen to reason on the boat; he was not likely to be amenable to logic now.

But Dosh had not been joking when he told D'ward he knew massage. He also knew a few sneaky tricks of self-defense that had come in handy more than once when the romping had become too rough. *If* he could actually get within reach of D'ward and *if* he could then work his arms free and *if* he could put his hands around D'ward's neck—then he could put D'ward to sleep very easily.

Then . . . then D'ward would slump to the ground and be trampled to paste? That part of the plan needed more work. The drums were beating faster. All that was needed was to delay D'ward a few more minutes and it would be too late for him to stop the sacrifice. Now the man in green had caught up with D'ward and was right behind him. He had become a barrier instead of a trailblazer, for Dosh could not get by him.

They were within a few feet of the pillars when the man in green abruptly caught hold of D'ward's arm and jerked him around. He himself twisted to the right. Dosh stumbled to catch his balance, recovering to the left. The crowd surged back in tightly around them again, packing all three men in together, face-to-face, with Ysian's legs between them.

The whole congregation had fallen silent under the surging *boom-boom-boom* of the drumbeat.

"What?" D'ward demanded angrily, struggling to break free of the grip. He had not even glanced at Dosh or Ysian. "Oh—it's you!"

"Who did you expect?" the man in green demanded, in a voice as thunderous as the drums. "What in creation do you think you're doing here, you young idiot?" He was the taller by two or three inches and considerably huskier. He had a dense black beard and a jutting hooked nose. He seemed young, yet he was the sort of man one instinctively addressed as "sir" . . . or "master," in Dosh's case.

Ysian's fingers were knotting painfully in Dosh's hair. He could hardly breathe in the crush, glancing from the Liberator to the other man and back again. Their faces were directly above his, yet neither of them seemed to know he was there. He did not want to guess who this other man might be.

D'ward smiled, but the effect was grotesque—all eyes and teeth, as if the skin of his face had shrunk. "You've got the wrong man in there!" His voice was hoarse.

"I know that, fool! And tomorrow he dies. You think that's an accident? Have you any idea of the trouble that cost us? What do you think you can achieve, coming here?"

"I can take his place. My place!"

"You won't save his life if you do! Even if Zath chose to spare him, which he wouldn't, the ephors could not forgive the humiliation. He's dead now, dead as surely as he will be when they dash out his brains tomorrow."

D'ward grimaced. "I won't let them!"

"And how are you going to stop them now?"

The drumming was a continuous menacing roll, rising louder, echoing among the pillars.

"I can go there and say who I am! I can tell them they have the wrong man. If I say I'm the Liberator—"

"You would drop dead."

D'ward's face was white with misery or terror or fury—Dosh could not tell which, and perhaps it was all of them. "Then if you helped me, stood beside me—"

"Fool!" The big man roared the word, yet none of the surrounding crowd paid him any heed at all. How could anyone resist his authority? "Zath has more power than all the Five together. *You can do nothing here except die as well!*"

"There must be something I can do!"

"No, there isn't! Maybe one day, but not today, nor tomorrow." The massive fingers squeezed harder into D'ward's arm. The man seemed ready to bite him. "Now—will you live or die? Must I force you?"

D'ward's eyes glinted feverishly. "Use mana here and you'll attract his notice, won't you? We're on the node."

"Why are you so anxious to die?" They were bellowing at each other now, yet the mob packed around them seemed oblivious.

"Why should it matter to you if I die?"

"Because we want you to fulfill the prophecy! Your time is not yet, that's all."

D'ward closed his eyes and shuddered. He slumped in despair, as if only the press of the crowd held him upright. "All right! If that's your price, I'll do it. I'll be the bloody Liberator, I'll take your orders, I'll do whatever you want, but you've got to pull the prince out of there. I *won't* let another man die in my place."

"Sorry. I can't do that."

"Then damn you!" D'ward screamed. "Let me go!"

Before the man in green could answer, the drum roll stopped. A brief silence . . . a faint voice making an announcement . . . the crowd within the temple screaming in joyful unison . . . the crowd outside howling for the news . . .

The man in green heaved his great shoulders back to free his other arm and cracked his fist upward against the point of D'ward's jaw. D'ward's head jerked back. He went limp, held upright only by the man's hold on his arm and the squash of bodies.

Nobody could move, or the crowd would have been dancing. As it was, they all kept bellowing their lungs out. The news spread: The sacrifice would be made. The plague would end.

The man's eyes came down to Dosh with no surprise or sudden recognition. It was as if he had known all along who Dosh was and that he was right there.

"Bring her and follow me," he growled.

Then he hoisted D'ward effortlessly onto his shoulder and plowed off through the crowd, parting it like tall grass.

Still unconscious, D'ward dangled head down in a sandwich between the man in green and Dosh, who clung tightly to the man's heavy leather sword belt and let himself be dragged. He was barely supporting himself, sagging under Ysian's weight. As the crush began to slacken, he crumpled to his knees. Ysian broke free and tumbled. The big man turned and hoisted each of them in turn upright. His strength was . . . superhuman?

Who was he? Better not to wonder . . . but he probably was . . . Who else could he be? Why?

"Hang on!" the man commanded, leading the way again.

Dosh was certainly not about to disobey, lest hard experience prove his suspicions correct, and of course Ysian would not let D'ward out of her sight. The crowd was dispersing in jubilation, flowing out along the streets from the temple, cheering and singing. Dosh clung to the man's belt, towing Ysian by the hand. Gradually the mob thinned. South, east, two more blocks south . . . the man (the Man?) knew exactly where he was heading.

He turned into a dark opening. "Stairs!" he growled, and headed down them into blackness. Dosh and Ysian descended warily, fumbling at the rough stone wall for guidance. They descended three sides of a square well, into a littered and putrid-smelling hall. A door creaked open, and they followed their guide into a dim crypt, full of people.

The air was heavy with a multitude of scents: the dank rot of the chamber itself and its sweating walls overlain by odors of candles; bodies and unwashed bedding, herbs, and strongly spiced cooking—especially cooking. They brought back a rush of memories that stunned Dosh. He recoiled, cannoning into Ysian.

Men were scrambling to their feet, women hastily covering their heads, small children scampering to the comfort of mothers. There were easily thirty people in that dingy cellar, barely visible in the faint light of a few high ventilation slits. The men crowded forward—stocky men wearing tatters that seemed ready to fall apart, men with golden hair and beards. Their eyes were pale in the gloom, shining like their knives.

As soon as they had formed a cordon between their families and the visitors, they halted, deferring to an elderly man in the background. He stood amid a litter of bedding, bundles, and broken furniture. He was spare, silver haired, and dignified. He alone wore a rich robe, amid this ragged rabble. He bowed stiffly.

"You do us honor, noble Warrior."

It was a tongue Dosh had not heard in a score of years. The lump in his throat was already agony, and it seemed to swell at the sound of those words.

"Call off your panthers, Birfair Spokesman!" the man in green answered in the same speech.

The old man barked a single word. The other men reluctantly sheathed their knives. Their pale eyes moved to inspect Dosh. He knew he was in grave, grave danger now. He edged closer to the big man. The Tinkerfolk were granting him respect, although they obviously did not think he was who Dosh thought he was, or they would all be flat on their faces.

Whoever he was, he slid D'ward loosely to the floor. "This is the one I told you of. He is resting. I suggest the women bleach his hair before he awakens. It will save argument."

The old man smiled and bowed again.

"The others—" The big man gestured to indicate Dosh and Ysian. "That one is a woman. The other is one of your own. Take them also, if you will."

Birfair rubbed his hands. "At the same price, noble Warrior?"

A snort. "Very well. For the woman." The big man tossed a pouch to him. It struck the floor with a loud clank. "See she is not molested—she may be important. The man can pay his own way."

"Certainly, if he is one of ours, as you said." The old man's poxy, palsied face was more apparent now, as Dosh's eyes adjusted to the dark. "He is a diseased whelp of a degenerate sow, spawned in a cesspool."

"I shall rip out your stinking guts and thrust them down your throat with your feet," Dosh retorted. It was only a language test. His accent was rusty.

Karzon shrugged. "How touching to restore a lost son to the loving bosom of his people! I want all three of them out of the city as fast as possible. I don't care how you arrange it. After that, your brother can work for his gruel. He may have some skills you can use, if you're not too fussy. The other two will need your charity."

"The noble warrior has already provided most generously."

"And I expect value! When my muddle-headed young friend awakens, explain to him that he must stay away from Lympus."

"Lympus," the old man repeated.

"Yes. A place. It is being watched and will not be safe for him to approach for a long time."

"We shall obey."

"You'd better!" The man in green turned to the door.

It closed in Dosh's face as Dosh dived after him. Mysteriously, the door was now locked. It had probably been locked earlier, which would explain why the Tinkerfolk had been taken by surprise.

He spun around to get his back against it, knife in hand. Three young men were moving in on him already, coming cautiously but steadily, eyes and teeth shining. Birfair had made no promises about him. He had gold, a tunic of fine cut, and a valuable sword he did not know how to use. He also had his life. Whether he would be allowed to keep that would depend on how much he charged for the others.

Endgame

47

LUNCH HAD BEEN BAD ENOUGH, BECAUSE EVERYONE HAD WANTED TO talk about the war news—rumors were floating around Greyfriars that Passchendaele had fallen—but whenever anyone had mentioned it, someone else had changed the subject. *Mustn't upset our hero in case he starts weeping!*

That had been bad enough, but after Alice and Exeter departed on the bikes, Smedley found himself alone with Ginger Jones and Mrs. Bodgley, the three of them fighting their way through conversational swamps—nothing safe to take a stand on, nothing safe to talk about.

He went outside to try gardening, not that he could do much good. Black Dog really hounded him then. His hand hurt. His leg throbbed. He thought of challenging Ginger to a game of one-handed croquet, and that brought on visions of one-handed golf, one-handed grouse shooting, one-handed cricket, and one-handed loving . . . as if he would ever find a gal interested in a cripple. One-handed car driving?

He went for a walk, but it did no good.

He came back to the Dower House, flopped down on one of the garden benches, and wondered why he had ever been crazy enough to let himself become involved in Exeter's affairs and how he was going to extricate himself. There was no decent alternative in sight, either, just the family mausoleum in Chichester. The last meeting with the guv'nor had ended in both of them yelling and Julian sobbing at the same time. Thousands of aunts. Sunday was his birthday. . . .

"Cut it out!" said a voice.

He whipped his head around and saw that Ginger Jones was sitting in a deck chair under a tree. He had a newspaper spread over his chest, as if he had been napping under it and just pulled it down.

"Beg pardon?"

The old man's glasses flashed in the sun. "You were never a moper, Julian Smedley. Don't be one now!"

"I'm not moping." Smedley turned away.

"It's just another stage," Ginger said. "I've seen dozens like you these last couple of years." There was a rustle of paper and a grunt as he heaved himself out of the deck chair. "At first you're so relieved to be out of it that you don't care what it cost." His voice came closer. "Then you begin to realize that you have the rest of your life to live and you are not as other men. You think it isn't fair. Of course it isn't fair." He was right behind Smedley now.

"I'll try to do better next term, sir."

He might as well have saved his breath.

"I've seen dozens, I say! Lots of them would be delighted to give you a hand in exchange for what they've lost. Lungs, eyes, both legs . . . There's one chap who was a fairly close chum of yours—I won't tell you his name— and he looks absolutely splendid. It's just that he isn't a real man anymore, at least not as he sees it. Care to swop with him?"

"Why don't you go and help Mrs. Bodgley knit some warm woolly undies for Our Brave Fighting Men?"

"Because I'd rather stay here and carp at you. I'm telling you that you were never a whiner and you won't be in future. It's just a stage. It will pass. Soon the real Julian Smedley will surface again."

"I really can't tell you how much I look forward to that."

"And then you will start to do what we all have to do, which is play the cards we are dealt. I should have had Exeter give you this lecture. He's better at it than I am. He says he will get you to Nextdoor if you want to go."

"What!?"

Ginger shuffled to the other bench and sat down, moving as if his back hurt. "I asked him before lunch. He'll do anything for you, Captain, because of what you did at Staffles. If Nextdoor's what you want, he says, then he'll help. He thinks you would do well there. The Service will take you at his word, he thinks. But is that really what you want?"

Smedley was, for a moment, speechless. Then, "Do you believe him?"

"Yes, I do. Don't you?"

"I don't know. It all fits . . . but it's fantasy, Ginger! Ravings! Opium dreams."

"I believe him."

"You're not just saying that to cheer me up?"

Jones shook his head. "You knew him when he was a caterpillar. You were chrysalises together and now you're both butterflies. You know him as well as anyone will ever know him. You shared adolescence. You will never know any man better than you know him. Is there anyone, anyone at all, whose word you would take over the word of Edward Exeter?"

Smedley considered the question seriously. He had to. After a while he said, "Probably not."

"Me too. Now come indoors with me, because I want to take a look at that leg of yours. Have you changed the bandages today?"

The gashes were swollen and inflamed. Ginger wanted to phone for a doctor and only agreed not to when Smedley promised to do so the next day if things got any worse.

Then they went downstairs for tea.

It was cooler in the sitting room than in the garden, Mrs. Bodgley said, because it faced east. Smedley thought it gloomy, unlived-in, lonesome. The crumpets were from Thorndyke's, Mrs. Bodgley said, and Wilfred was an even better baker than his grandfather had been, although of course nobody would ever tell the old man so. The jam, Mrs. Bodgley said, had come from the county craft fair and she thought it must be Mrs. Haddock's recipe. The gentlemen agreed it was excellent jam.

Mrs. Bodgley then narrated several tales of events that had happened when she was in India. The viceroy's court in New Delhi, some jolly times up in the hills in Simla. Something about her visit to Borneo . . . the Raffles Hotel in Singapore . . .

The Empire on which the sun never sets.

Smedley laughed at the jokes, taking his cue from Ginger.

But his mind was on Nextdoor, a whole new world. Civilizing the natives, a worthy cause. His missing hand wouldn't matter there, because he would be *Tyika* Smedley and have house servants. The war would never be mentioned. He would dress for dinner and the *entyikank* would wear long gowns. He would do good for the people. He would live forever. He would gain mana and get his hand back.

Dream.

Gravel scrunched.

A car?

Mrs. Bodgley frowned. "That sounds like a car."

Inexplicably, the muscles in Smedley's abdomen all tightened up like wire cables. He remembered the bombardment at Verdun.

The doorbell jangled.

Mrs. Bodgley rose. "I am not expecting visitors. Do you wish me to introduce you by an assumed name, Captain Smedley?"

"No," he said. "If that is necessary, then it will do no good."

Which made no sense, but his hostess nodded her chins and sailed from the room. He glanced at Ginger, who was scratching his beard, light reflecting inscrutably on his pince-nez. Neither of them spoke.

Voices in the hall . . .

". . . the year Gilbert was elected chairman," Mrs. Bodgley was booming. "I was probably more nervous than you were!"

They both rose to their feet as she cruised in again, followed by a man. A man with fishy, protuberant eyes—eyes with a jubilant gleam in them.

"Of course the captain and I have met." He extended his left hand. "And Mr. Jones! Or may I call you Ginger now, as we always did before, behind your back?"

"If I may call you Short Stringer, as we always did behind your back. Oh, blast!" Ginger's pince-nez fell to the floor.

Stringer reached it before he did, wiped it on his sleeve, and returned it. "Yes, thank you, tea would be wonderful. Driving is dusty work."

Smedley felt ill.

Ginger had lost the ruddy glow that the sunny afternoon had given him. He pawed at his beard.

Mrs. Bodgley seemed quite unconcerned, happy to welcome an old acquaintance, one of her uncountable honorary godchildren. Perhaps she really was unconcerned—had anyone ever given her the Staffles part of the story? Did she realize how impossible this situation was, how deadly? She went to the china cabinet with a hesitant glance at the open door. "Do be seated, please, all of you. Your friend . . . ?"

"I'm sure she will find us," Stringer said blandly, selecting a chair. The gleam was back in his eyes again. His flannels and blazer were immaculate, but he seemed weary—as he should if he had driven across the width of England.

"Just freshening up," Mrs. Bodgley murmured quietly. "One lump or two, Mr. Stringer? Or would you rather I also called you Short?"

"Not unless you wish to be challenged to pistols at dawn. My friends all call me Nat. Only a few old Fallovians call me Shorty. Captain Smedley, I fancy, calls me an impossible coincidence."

"I might call you other things were Mrs. Bodgley not present," Smedley said, crossing his legs. His fist was clenched. Both fists were clenched. He consciously relaxed the visible one. The other he could do nothing about.

A teacup rattled on its saucer. He had shocked Mrs. Bodgley. Alerted to the conflict, she glanced from face to face in bewilderment.

"Nothing to what we were calling you two nights ago," Stringer said with asperity. "That was hardly pukka, what you did, Captain Smedley."

"You were long past due for a fire drill. Your presence here demonstrates that my suspicions were well-founded." Julian toyed with the idea of blacking one of those piscine eyes, and it tasted good. He was shaking, but that was only anger and all right.

"Well-founded but misdirected. Ah!"

A woman marched into the room and stopped, raking it with a glower like a burst of fire from a Hun machine-gun nest. She was tall, angular, unattractive. She wore a cheap-looking brown dress and carried a cumbersome handbag. Her hair was bound high in a bun. Smedley had last seen her behind a desk outside Stringer's office at Staffles.

The men started to rise again. Mrs. Bodgley said, "Ah, there you are. May I intro—"

"Where is she?" Miss Pimm demanded harshly. "Where is Alice Prescott? Is she with him?" She glared at Smedley.

He had nodded before he realized.

"Who?" Ginger said loudly.

She did not look at him, as if his effort to deceive was beneath contempt. "The Opposition has a mark on Alice Prescott, has had for the last three years. She went to Harrow Hill with him?"

Mrs. Bodgley made a choking noise and sank back in her chair.

"Where?" Ginger said.

"Oh, don't be childish!" Miss Pimm snapped. "I can tell that Exeter is a few miles southwest of us. *We* have a mark on *him*! I assume he went to Harrow Hill to consult the presence again. If his cousin is with him, then he is in deadly danger."

"How do we know," Smedley's voice said from where he was sitting, "that you are not the Opposition?"

"You don't. But it makes no difference. You will cooperate anyway."

"Mana!" Ginger said, and sat down hurriedly. "You have this mana he talks about!"

She looked at him seriously for the first time. She was the only one standing; the others sat and stared like children in a classroom.

"Yes, I am with Head Office, although you will have to take my word for that."

"I don't think I understand," Mrs. Bodgley muttered faintly. Had her self-possession ever failed her before? "Will you sit down and have a cup of tea, Miss Pimm?"

"No. There is no time. Mr. Stringer, we must hurry."

The famous surgeon sighed and drained his cup. He muttered, "You're sacked!" half under his breath.

Smedley and Ginger exchanged glances of panic.

"Perhaps you could explain?" Mrs. Bodgley said with an effort.

Miss Pimm slung the strap of her bag over her shoulder. "I repeat, there is no time. Nine years ago, I promised Cameron Exeter that I would guard his son. I almost failed. The boy is back again, and I still have some residual obligations to fulfil. I don't believe the rest of you are in any danger now. I shall intercept Exeter before he returns here. Even if the agent the Opposition has sent is a vindictive type, he will have no reason to vent his spite on you. Come, Stringer!"

"Wait!" Smedley barked. "What exactly are you planning to do?"

She stopped in the doorway and turned as if to give battle. "I am going to do what I was planning to do at Staffles before you stuck your oar in and disrupted everything, Captain Smedley. It was your blundering intervention that alerted the Opposition."

"The Blighters, you mean?"

"We sometimes call them that. Stringer?"

"Exeter says he will never go back!" Smedley shouted.

"I fail to see that it is any business of yours."

"I do. I want to go."

He had said it. He was shocked to hear it.

But he had said it, so he must mean it.

With the reluctance of a frozen pond melting, the formidable Miss Pimm's pale lips thinned into a faint hint of a smile. "After all the trouble you have caused me, you demand favors? Talk about brass! I know you are a man of initiative and fast decisions, Captain Smedley, but do you know what is involved? Do you understand that it means considerable danger and to all intents and purposes is irrevocable? It means loss of family and home and friends. It is a leap beyond the bounds of imagination."

He nodded. His heart was beating a mad tattoo. Damn Chichester and the old man! Damn the aunts! Sunday was his birthday—twenty-one, key of the door. He smiled, to see if he still could. "Just show me."

"You are ready to come now? Immediately?"

"Yes."

"Then you impress. Very well. Come along and we'll see if it is possible. I make no promises." Miss Pimm summoned Stringer with a flick of her head and stalked from the room.

Everyone stood up again.

"*La Belle Dame Sans Merci!*" the surgeon growled, following her. "Thanks awfully for the tea, dear lady. I have so much enjoyed our long chat this afternoon. Don't bother to see us out. We really must do this more often. Get the lead out, Captain! She won't wait for you." He disappeared into the hallway.

Smedley was shivering like a dog in the starting gate. He looked to the others. "Anyone else feeling suicidal this afternoon?"

Neither had any close family. They were both aging. Ginger at least believed the tales of Elfenland—Smedley wasn't sure if Mrs. Bodgley did. Get away from the war! Live forever! Be restored to youth and health! How could anyone refuse the chance, no matter how long the odds?

Ginger removed his pince-nez and rubbed it vigorously on his sleeve. Then he replaced it and sighed. "No. I think not. Not me."

Outside, the car engine rumbled into life.

"Mrs. Bodgley?"

The lady was pale. She bit her lip. Her hesitation was longer, but then she shook her head. "No. At my age . . . no. My memories are here."

"Then I must run. Thank you, Mrs. B. Thank you both for . . . everything." Oh, God! His eyes were flooding. He grabbed her and kissed her cheek. He clutched Ginger's outstretched hand awkwardly and pumped it, thumping the man's shoulder with his stump.

"Bye!" he shouted, and ran out of the room. He blundered into the umbrella stand, ricocheted off it, raced along the hall and out the front door. The great silver Rolls was just starting to move along the driveway. He sprinted after it, and a door swung open for him.

～ 48 ～

THE ROAD WAS NARROW BETWEEN TALL HEDGES. IT WAS CANOPIED by branches of great trees and full of fragrant green coolness. But it was steep. Alice gasped a final, "Whoof!" and gave up. She put her foot down and wiped her forehead.

"From here I walk!" she said. "How much farther?"

Edward halted at her side. "Just around this corner, I think."

She dismounted, pulled her skirts clear, and began to push the bike.

He took it from her, pushing both. "Look on the bright side. We can freewheel on the way back!" He was grinning, quite unwinded. He was in much better shape than she was.

"Mmph! Well, you can do the talking on the way up. You have never told me how you found Olympus."

"There isn't much to tell. You've heard all the exciting bits. How far had I got? Karzon? Well, he dumped us on a band of Tinkerfolk—"

"Why? I mean, I thought he was the Man, and Zath was one of his."

"Ah! Zath's supposed to be, but he hasn't been for quite a while. There had never been an actual god of death before him. Who would want to be? There are several fictitious deities like that, just a temple or shrine with no stranger behind them. People worship there just the same. In every case, a member of the Pentatheon will claim suzerainty, so not all the mana is lost. I think Death was merely an abstract notion until some minion of Karzon's asked for the title and Karzon let him take it. What his real name was, I don't know and it doesn't matter.

"Anyway, Karzon had made a bad mistake. Zath founded his own cult, bestowed the Black Scriptures on it, sent out the reapers. Human sacrifice is an enormously potent source of mana. Even though the murders were not committed on his node, he gained power from every death. By the time the Pentatheon realized what he was up to—and that probably took half a century or so—none of them dared challenge him."

"They couldn't combine against him?"

Edward guffawed. "Combine? After thousands of years of playing the Great Game? No, they can't think like that. They let Zath continue on his jolly way, all trying to get on his team. About fifty years ago, he arranged for a new temple in Tharg, with himself as co-deity. The Five, in effect, have become six."

"I think I get the gist. So Karzon supports the Liberator and the *Filoby Testament*!"

"Enthusiastically! He daren't let Zath know that, of course. He was hoping that little old me would achieve what all the gods of the world were scared to try. Well, I won't!"

Alice groaned. They had rounded the corner. The road ahead was straight—and straight up.

"Oh, I remember this bit," Edward said. "The gate's at the top."

"I hope my heart will stand it. Do you think we ought to be roped?"

They began to climb. Edward continued to push both bikes, yet he still had enough wind to talk.

"Karzon shipped us out of the city, disguised as Tinkerfolk. They're very much like our Gypsies, only more primitive, because the whole culture is more primitive. They wander all over the Vales, trading, stealing, spying. They're all blond as Scandinavians. It's said they abandon any baby who isn't, in the belief that it must be a half-breed. I wouldn't put it past them. Dosh was borderline, only just blond enough. He probably had a rough childhood because of that.

"By the time I woke up, he'd already been in a fight. He'd killed one, wounded three others, and was just about a goner from lack of blood himself. I still had some of the mana the army had given me, and I used it to revive him instead of curing my own headache, which at the time felt very altruistic, believe me! They were a rough-and-ready bunch of scoundrels."

Obviously! Alice had no breath to comment.

Edward chuckled. "But I had an interesting summer, that year! We crossed a pass into Sitalvale, then another into Thovale, and eventually wandered over into Randorvale. I passed very close to Olympus, although of course I didn't know that, and in any case Karzon's warning to stay away from it made good sense. Dosh disappeared in Thovale. By killing a man of the tribe, he'd acquired a wife, and she was a genuine, steam-powered firecat. Or perhaps it was just the primitive living conditions he didn't like. I don't know where he went, but I'm sure Dosh will survive. He's incredible."

"How?" She panted. Running with Gypsies! She wondered what Julian Smedley would think of this confession if he knew. Or the masters at Fallow.

"Just tough! All the Tinkerfolk are, but he could out-tough most of them any day. As for morals . . ." Edward fell silent for a dozen paces, and apparently decided not to discuss morals. "At first they treated me as a baby, but they had accepted gold and sworn oaths to cherish me, and they kept their word. They didn't know the man who had hired them was Karzon, but they knew he was somebody to fear. I wanted to earn my keep, so I became an expert in livestock trading. Every vale seems to have a different collection of herdbeasts, none of which look anything like our horses and cattle, but they're all traded in much the same way. Charisma came in very useful there, and I cheated outrageously—a stranger can be so plausible! I could extract more money for a worn-out useless runt than even old Birfair himself could, or buy a champion for less. Eventually they came to accept me as useful, a real man."

Alice decided that her cousin had depths she had not suspected and would prefer not to know about. Julian's hair would turn white if he heard this, an English gentleman going to the dogs, becoming a vagrant huckster.

"By autumn, though, I'd had enough of rags and dirt and hunger. Ysian was pining. We were in Lappinvale by then, which at the moment is a Thargian colony. And one day I saw a man I knew."

Alice stopped to catch her breath. He looked at her with concern.

"I'm all right," she said. "What man?"

"You can wait here while I go and see Mr. Goodfellow."

She shook her head. She wouldn't mind being winded were Edward not so confoundedly cool looking and relaxed. He turned to stare up at the hill ahead, and then peered around at the distance they had come, but his mind was away on another world. He smiled in secret amusement.

"I had never met him, but I had been told of him. In the higher, cooler vales, they have a riding beast they call . . . Well, there are a lot of different names for it. It's the Rolls-Royce of Nextdoor. It's enormous, big as a rhino. It's pretty much a mammal, but it looks like a cross between a stegosaurus—that's one of the dinosaurs in *The Lost World* with a row of bony plates down the middle of its back. . . . It's a bit like that and also like a Chinese dragon. It has scales, yet it's warm-blooded. It eats grass, and it's a wonderful steed—gentle, intelligent, willing, the only thing better than a terrestrial horse. I thought of them as dragons, so that name will do.

"One day I saw a herd of them just outside a village we had been cadging off. There were tents there, and I guessed soon enough that this was the encampment of a man who traded in them. I sauntered over to take a closer look.

"I got shouted at, of course. I was a tinker. I had bleached hair and blue eyes and my clothes were mostly holes held together by hope. I would have made a scarecrow look like a lord. The wranglers tried to chase me away, because I must be a thief and a ne'er-do-well. Most of them had a little gold circle in their left earlobe, and they all wore black turbans. That told me this was the outfit Eleal had described. Ready?"

"Think so." She began plodding again. He sauntered along at her side, still pushing a bike with each hand.

"So I withdrew to a safe distance and squatted down by some bushes and waited. After an hour or two, the man I wanted came marching back from the village. He was very big, and he had an enormous copper-colored beard. You know the legend of the sailor who has a girl in every port? Well, this fellow has one in every village. . . . I assume that's where he'd been, but perhaps I'm doing him an injustice. He may have been there on business. I doubt it. Anyway, I cut him off before he reached his tents.

"He barked an obscenity and tried to go round me.

"I said, 'T'lin Dragontrader? We almost met, once.' That stopped him!

"He scowled at me and said something I won't repeat.

"I said, 'How are things with the Service these days?'

"He went back two steps with his eyes almost popping out of his head. I knew that he was an agent of the Service, you see, because Eleal had told me. He's a native, not a stranger, and he spies for the political branch. He threw some sort of password at me then—'The grass grows softer when the rain is cool,' or some such gibberish.

"I said, 'Frightfully sorry, but I don't know the answer.' I gave him another code that I'd been told once. He recognized it, although he didn't know the answer, because it was for the religious branch and he's political. In the end I just said, 'I am D'ward Liberator.'

"I thought he was going to faint. We sat down beside the bushes, and we had a long chat. He admitted that the Service was hunting for me—they'd heard of the fall of Lemod, too, of course, and realized I was still alive. He knew they were not the only ones after me. I asked him to pass the word. Then I remembered Ysian and decided that being a dragon trader would be nicer than being a tinker. So I informed T'lin that he had just acquired two more hands.

"He didn't argue, actually. He's a very loyal follower of the Undivided— a likable rogue, very shrewd. I went and got Ysian. Old Birfair and the gang were genuinely sorry to lose us, and I had to write a note to Karzon, testifying that they had fulfilled their side of the bargain. I doubt if any of them could read, but they were grateful for the insurance. Then we went to T'lin's camp and put on some respectable clothes and became dragon traders. Look out."

They moved to the side of the road as a car came growling up the hill to pass them. It was a bright red roadster, puffing stinking clouds of exhaust. The driver wore goggles and a sporty cap.

"May his radiator boil and his tires all burst!" Edward said cheerfully as he strode out again. "Only a real bounder would drive a motor that color. We wandered around the Vales a bit, and settled down in little Mapvale for the winter. By then I'd been almost two years on Nextdoor and was getting pretty desperate, but we got no word back from Olympus before the passes closed. I loved the dragons, though."

They walked for a while in silence. They were past the worst. The gate must be just around the corner, set back in the hedge, probably.

"Did you meet Eleal again?"

"No, never. T'lin had changed his schedule, and he had not run into the troupe since the reaper almost got him in Sussvale. He thought they were still in business."

"And Olympus?"

"Ah! One morning, early in the spring, I was exercising a couple of bulls—boars—stallions? What the deuce do you call a male dragon in English? Anyway, I ran into a chappie riding a beautiful young female, of the color they call Osby slate. Of course we stopped to admire each other's stock, and of course I asked him if he would like to sell or trade.

"He was a lanky, rangy youngster with sandy hair and a notably big nose. Well fitted out. He admitted he would consider an offer. . . ."

Something funny was coming, judging by the grin.

"We must have stood there and haggled for two solid hours. I tried every trick I knew. I really wanted that filly! I blew my charisma to white heat. I argued and wheedled. I kept going up and up, and he wouldn't come down one copper mark. I was completely flummoxed. And finally he held out a hand and drawled in perfect English, 'I don't believe I want to part with her after all, old man. I'm Jumbo Watson. I was a chum of your father's.' "

Alice chuckled at Edward's infectious glee. "Nicely done?"

"Oh, beautifully! I wanted to melt and soak into the sand." He laughed aloud. "You should hear Jumbo tell the story! He puts on this incredible Tinkerfolk accent, although we'd been speaking Joalian. I have died a thousand deaths at dinner tables over that episode. But that's Jumbo."

"What's wrong?"

"Nothing. I took to him right away. We got along like a house on fire. We rode dragons over the ranges to Olympus, which was a corker of a trip at that time of year, and he was absolutely solid. He was gracious to Ysian, which is more than can be said of some. . . . He has the most marvelous dry humor, a regular brick."

"There you are—that's how I got to Olympus. It's a charming spot, very scenic, a little glen tucked away between Thovale, Narshvale, and Randorvale. Didn't dare stay more than four or five fort . . . about a couple of months." He fell silent for a moment, and then seemed to discard what he had been about to say. His smile had gone.

"I'd been two years on Nextdoor, and that was the first time I'd had any news of Home. I was horrified to hear that the war was still on and at the same time glad that I hadn't missed it all and would still be able to do my bit. I sat around for a few days, bringing them up to date on what I'd been doing and learning about the Service and so on. Then I politely asked for the first boat Home. That's when the wicket got sticky.

"The Service is badly split over the Liberator prophecies, you see, and always has been. The guv'nor had never gone for them. Once I got to Olympus and learned all the ins and outs of the business, then I was thoroughly against it, too. Break the chain and be done with it! Jumbo was pretty much leader of the anti faction, and I agreed with him wholeheartedly. Killing Zath would only lead to worse trouble. I wanted to come Home and enlist.

"Creighton, incidentally, had been one of the pro-Liberator group. In spite of what he told me, he came Home in 1914 specifically to make sure I crossed over on schedule. Much good it did him personally! But the pro-Liberator forces were in a majority, and they kept me dangling, on one pretext after another."

They were almost at the summit, and Alice decided she could cycle again. Before she could say so, she saw that Edward's mind was very far off.

"And what happened?"

"Mm? Oh, well, I did come back, didn't I? Eventually. And here I am. It's a beautiful day and I'm Home and I want to enjoy every minute of it."

She sensed evasion there and went after it—instinct, she thought, like a dog chasing anything that runs. "How, Edward? How did you come back?"

Long pause . . . Then he shrugged. "That was Jumbo's doing, too. One day he turned up at the chapel where I was massaging the heathens' souls for the Undivided and more or less said, 'If you wait for a flag from those blokes on the Committee, you'll wait a thousand years. I can fix it up for you.' He took me to another node and taught me a key to get me Home, and he swore that there would be people waiting at this end to help."

"What! You mean he deliberately dropped you on that battlefield in Flanders? He's the traitor you've been talking about! *Jumbo* tried to kill you?"

Edward nodded. He stared at the road ahead with eyes as hard and cold as sapphires. With a shock, she remembered that her young cousin could be dangerous. He was a sacker of cities.

"You see why I need to send word back?" he said. "And it may be worse than that, even. Five years ago, when the coming of the Liberator was almost due, the Service sent a couple of men Home to talk to the guv'nor, to see if he still felt the same way about matters. They wanted to meet me, too. I was sixteen by then, and they thought they should be allowed to inspect me. The guv'nor forbade that, although the only one who ever learned his reaction was Soapy Maclean. Jumbo came straight to England. Soapy went to Africa."

She took her bike from him. "And died at Nyagatha!"

Again Edward nodded. "The Blighters roused the Meru outlaws. But who tipped off the Blighters? Who told them where Cameron Exeter was? I think that must have been Jumbo, too. I think he was working for the Chamber even then. He killed our—"

She looked where he was looking. They had come to the gate. It was no farmer's gate. It was a steel gate, with a padlock. It bore a sign that said, WAR DEPARTMENT and POSITIVELY NO ADMITTANCE EXCEPT ON HIS MAJESTY'S SERVICE and other stern things. Beyond it, a freshly paved road climbed across the field to the crest of the hill—once, she assumed, crowned with a copse of oaks and a few immemorially ancient standing stones. Now it was surrounded by yet another fence and a gate with a sentry box. The woods had gone. In their place was an antiaircraft battery, a twentieth-century obscenity of iron sheds and repulsive ordnance.

"Puck!" Edward said with cold fury. "They've despoiled his grove! It's all gone. They drove him away."

First Stonehenge, now this. Another of the roads back to Nextdoor had just closed. But obviously that was not what was distressing him. He had just stumbled on a friend's grave.

Alice fumbled for words of comfort. "He had lived beyond his time, Edward. All things pass."

"But he was such a likable old ruin! Harmless! He helped me—a kid who meant nothing to him at all but was in serious trouble. He wouldn't have hurt a fly!"

"On the contrary, Mr. Exeter," said a voice from the other side of the road, "he was a meddler, and for that he had to pay."

✎ 49 ✎

I T WAS THE MOTORIST WHOM EDWARD HAD CALLED A BOUNDER. HE
was short and thick, standing in the weedy grass of the verge, half hidden
in the hedge. He wore his floppy cap at a cocky angle above a haircut short
enough to be called a shave; his brown tweed suit looked absurdly hot for
the weather. He had removed his goggles. Despite his breadth, his features
were not flabby. They were hard, and his eyes were a peculiar shade of
violet.

He was smiling and he had his hands in his pockets, yet Alice had an
inexplicable feeling that he was pointing a gun at her.

"Should I know you?" Edward drawled.

"If you believe in knowing your enemy. I have been waiting for this
meeting for a long time, Exeter. The prophecy has run out of mana at last."

Fighting to quench panic, Alice wondered why she did not turn around
to face this threat. She had not moved her feet, and neither had Edward.
They were both standing in an awkward, twisted position, holding their
bikes; they had not moved their feet.

"You needn't worry about the prophecy," Edward said calmly. "I will
never go back. I will never become the Liberator. You have my word on
it."

"Ah! The word of an English gentleman!" The bounder sighed dramatically. He ought to be an artesian well of perspiration in those tweeds on a
day like this, but his face was pale and dry. "So you say now. Forgive my
doubts. I had rather make sure." She could not place his accent.

"Then let Miss Prescott leave. She is not involved in this."

"I think it will be neater to include both of you. Turn your bicycles
around, please, and prepare to mount."

Alice did as she was bid, and so did Edward. Why had she not refused?
Why did she not simply climb on the saddle and pedal away? Why didn't
Edward? Of course the nasty red roadster was parked just over there, so the
bounder could run them down, but why should they not at least try to
make a break for it?

Rabbits hypnotized by snakes?

Oh, that was absurd!

Then why not just go? Why not just scarper?

"What are you going to do?" she demanded, and was disgusted by the shrillness in her voice.

"Very little." The bounder shrugged his broad shoulders. "I've already done it, actually. I just have to say the word. An Army lorry is starting up the hill. You and Mr. Exeter are going to pedal down. You will pedal as hard as you can, both of you. When you reach that bend down there, you will cut the corner, over to the wrong side of the road."

"Humor him, darling," Edward said. "He's funnier as Lady Hamilton, but that's on Tuesdays. His keeper gets Fridays off."

"Ah, the impeccably stiff upper lip!" the man agreed in the same dry tone. "*Toujours le sang-froid!* I estimate you will be doing between forty-four and forty-seven miles an hour when you stop. That is quite adequate to remove most of the rigidity from your ossiferous framework, if you will pardon the euphemism."

"Never," Edward said. "I had better warn you, I suppose. You have overlooked something. The *Testament* is a self-fulfilling prophecy. Every time someone tries to break the chain, he just strengthens it!"

"A few more minutes," the bounder said casually.

"You don't believe me? Then consider: If Zath had simply ignored the whole damned rigmarole, then nothing would have happened. But he tried to kill my father to prevent my being born. The attempt failed, and it alerted the guv'nor to the prophecy. The guv'nor left Nextdoor in case Zath tried again, but that meant he met the mater in New Zealand and got married and I transpired. If he'd stayed on Nextdoor, then any son he might have had would be a native, and harmless. Don't you see?"

"Ingenious. But not convincing."

Leave! Alice thought. Just perch on the saddle and pedal away. Freewheel sedately down the hill, staying safely on the left side of the road, and this whole insane conversation will fade away like moonbeams. Why did she not do that?

"It goes on and on." Edward was still speaking quietly, but faster. "The massacre at Nyagatha was supposed to kill me, but it killed my parents instead. If my father had lived he would have told me the whole story and I would never have crossed over! I would have taken his advice. I worshipped him and would never have gone against his wishes. So you outsmarted yourselves again. Then you tried to kill me in Greyfriars, and the result of that was that I did cross over and the prophecy was fulfilled. If you'd left me alone, I'd have enlisted and probably died last year on the Somme!"

The bounder had barely moved since Alice first set eyes on him, but now he raised a hand to smother a yawn. "Sorry to drag it out like this. Another minute or so and you can be on your way."

"I'm warning you!" Edward said, louder. "The same thing happened in Thargvale. Zath tried so hard to snare me that he let the whole army escape, and me too. By trying to break the chain, you will only strengthen it. Don't, please! I'm on your side! I want out. I want my own life. I don't want this damned prophecy coiling around me like a serpent all the time. Just ignore it and it will go away. It will wither. I want to stay here on Earth and serve my King. *I do not want to be the Liberator!*"

"You won't. We are about to make quite sure of that."

"Then leave Miss Prescott out of it!"

The bounder chuckled, but his ugly purple eyes did not smile. "If you believed your theories, you would not ask that."

"Bystanders get hurt! That's why you should listen to me. You may get caught in the backlash yourself. Dozens died at Nyagatha, thousands at Lemod. I sail through unscathed, and the innocents get mowed down!"

"You won't sail through this time," said the bounder. "Pedal as hard as you can and cut the corner at the bottom. No braking! It won't hurt."

"Let Alice go!" Edward shouted.

"You both go. Ready? Now!"

Alice swung up on the saddle and began to pedal as if her life depended on it. She was just trying to deceive the man. She would stop pedaling in a couple of minutes, as soon as she was safely away. They could freewheel almost all the way to Vicarsdown from here, and perhaps even have another cup of tea in the Tea Shoppe.

Edward went by her, head down, legs going like aeroplane propeller blades.

How dare he! Show-off brat! She forced her legs to move even faster. The wind was whistling by her. Never had she known such a sensation of speed. The hill unrolled below her like a death warrant. The hedges on either hand streaked past in green blurs. Wind caught her hat and snatched it away. Faster, faster! Harder, harder! Steeper, steeper! Edward was still gaining, his long legs giving him an unfair advantage, his jacket flailing behind him like Dracula's cloak.

She could no longer move her feet fast enough to do any good. Her hair was unravelling. Her eyes were full of icy tears, and she could hardly see. The bike hammered so hard she could barely hang on to the handlebars. The corner was rushing up at her.

Edward was there already. He leaned into the curve, cutting across to the inside—and vanished behind the hedge. She struggled to stay on her own side of the road, but at that speed she dare not. Despite all her efforts, she was turning to follow exactly where he had gone. The lorry leaped into view, growling up the hill, dead in her path, filling the road. Alongside it, cutting out to overtake it blind, came a huge silver-gray Rolls-Royce. There was no sign of Edward at all and she closed her eyes.

ɞↄ 50 ↄɞ

In ONE CORNER OF THE BACK SEAT, MISS PIMM SNAPPED COMMANDS: "Faster! Cut this corner! Go faster!" Her voice was soft and yet it carried the authority of a sergeant major's. In the driver's seat, Stringer was howling in terror, but apparently doing exactly what she wanted, like a puppet on strings. The big car swung around the bends, trees and hedgerows streaming past in an impossible blur. Thank the gods there was no other traffic . . . so far.

In the other corner of the back seat, Smedley had clenched his real fist until the nails dug into his palm, and he could not feel his imaginary one at all, just when he needed it. This was downright maniacal! A country lane like this was only safe at about twenty miles an hour, and they must be doing seventy at least. And uphill at that! The engine would boil. Even a Rolls made a din at this speed.

"Prepare to overtake!" Miss Pimm said. She seemed quite relaxed, holding her oversized handbag on her lap. "There is a lorry ahead."

God in heaven! What had got into the crazy old bat? She had been perfectly sane until about fifteen minutes ago. And then . . . well, they had gone through Vicarsdown like a Sopwith Camel. A miracle they hadn't killed someone. When he had expostulated, she had told him to stuff a sock in it.

"Pull over—*now!*"

The Rolls seemed to tilt almost onto two wheels as it hurtled around the corner on the outside. The back of an Army lorry swelled instantly from nowhere to fill the gap from hedge to hedge. Stringer shrieked and somehow shot the Rolls into the slit on the right. Branches snapped and whipped along the coachwork.

"Stay on this side!"

Straight ahead! A cyclist! Smedley yelled, "Look out!" Stringer screamed at the top of his lungs. There was a momentary image of an impending disaster, a loud impact of metal against metal, and Edward Exeter was sitting alongside Mr. Stringer in the front. *Then another!* More noise . . . something like a wheel whistled past the window . . . and Alice Prescott was on the back seat between Smedley and Miss Pimm. "Stay on this side!" Miss Pimm repeated. A bright red roadster rushed straight at the windscreen, veered at the last second, missed the lorry by inches, and plunged headlong into the woods with a noise like an artillery barrage at close range. Smedley caught a glimpse of its wheels and chassis as it reared vertically, plastering itself against a tree. Then the Rolls was around the bend and humming up a long, straight hill on a peaceful, sunny afternoon.

"I think that went well, don't you?" Miss Pimm said, in the tones of one who had just pulled off a daring finesse in a game of auction bridge. "You may pull over to the left now, Mr. Stringer, and reduce speed."

Alice opened her eyes. Exeter said something in a harsh foreign tongue and twisted around to look at her. They were both brightly flushed and apparently out of breath. He studied Alice, then Smedley, and finally Miss Pimm.

"Is it legal to enter a car at that speed?" Smedley inquired weakly. His heart was doing a thousand revs. If he had been skeptical of magic before, he must certainly believe now. Those two had been *outside,* on *bicycles,* and boring straight into the lorry like *howitzers* and here they were quietly sitting . . .

"Mr. Stringer, why are you stopping?" Miss Pimm demanded sharply.

"I'm a doctor! There has been an accident. And, by heaven, the police are going to ask some—"

"Drive on! We need not worry about the law. Unfortunately, nobody was injured. The soldiers will discover that the other car had no driver, whatever they may have thought they saw before the crash. They will not be able to explain the bicycle debris either, but that is not our concern. Pray continue." The class will now hand in its dictation.

"I'm alive?" Alice whispered.

"Only just!" Miss Pimm said. "I apologize for my tardy arrival and the unruly procedure."

Exeter squirmed around to kneel on the seat, leaning over the back. "I saw you at Staffles!"

"Being a guardian dragon? And now I am the *deus ex machina.*"

His eyes gleamed with delight. "*Dea,* surely? And *in machina,* not *ex?*"

How could he possibly be capable of making jokes already? Alice was still paralyzed. Smedley had just discovered that he had bitten his tongue.

Miss Pimm smiled her barely visible, thin-lipped smile in appreciation.

"At the moment I am going by the name of Miss Pimm."

"But when I was at Fallow, I used to address you as Jonathan Oldcastle, Esq?"

"You did indeed! Well done." *Move to the top of the class.* "I don't suppose your handwriting has improved at all, has it?"

Exeter was grinning as if all this insanity were just enormous fun. "Unlikely. Colonel Creighton said you were a committee."

A faint spasm of annoyance crossed her face. "I was chairwoman."

"Was it the pillar-box? You had a spell on it?"

"No, Edward. It was your fountain pen. Turn left at the intersection, Mr. Stringer."

"*You read my diary?*"

"No. It was excessively uninteresting."

Exeter scowled and looked at Alice. "You all right?" He reached out a hand, but the car was too big for him to reach her.

She let out a long sigh. "Yes, I think so. I need an explanation!"

"We have time for that!" Miss Pimm adjusted her handbag on her lap. "The real credit goes to Mr. Stringer's brother, the brigadier. He recognized Edward. He guessed that whatever had happened was beyond the scope of normal military procedures and very gallantly took the risk of shipping him home, notifying—"

"Dumping the whole mess on me!" Stringer snarled, turning left at the intersection. "I will kill him! Where are we going?"

Nextdoor! Smedley thought. *Olympus!*

"Straight on until I say otherwise. I became aware of your cousin's return when he reached England, Miss Prescott. I placed a mark on him many years ago. It is not operative outside this world, and even here its range is limited. I investigated. I decided he was in no immediate danger. It took me a few days to make arrangements—"

"My secretary eloped with a sailor!" Stringer growled.

"Quite so. Love at first sight. The very morning I took up my new duties—"

"Excuse the interruption," Exeter said softly. "But what do you do when you are not being my nursemaid?"

"Many things. I am with the organization you refer to as Head Office, of course. My portfolio is the British Imperial Government, excluding the Government of India. Mostly I burrow around Whitehall like an invisible mole, arranging this and that. For example, it was I who was responsible for your father being appointed D.O. at Nyagatha. That was an interesting challenge, as he was twenty-five years old, with thirty years' experience."

She smiled her schoolmistress smile again—Smedley wondered what age she was. He realized that he could not tell. At times she seemed quite young, and at other times quite old. Dowdy and unattractive, she was yet lording it over all of them. Charismatic?

"We wanted to see if we could demonstrate the advantages of nondisruptive techniques in elevating the social systems of subject races. But I digress. As I said, that very first morning Captain Smedley came blundering in."

Exeter looked at Smedley and smiled fondly. "Bless him!"

"He turned out to be a confounded nuisance," Miss Pimm said sharply. "But he has named his reward, and we shall see what he does with it."

Exeter's smile widened. "What did he do wrong?"

"He involved Miss Prescott. The Blighters have a mark on her. When she suddenly left London on a weekday, they were alerted. The rest, I think, you can work out. Right at the junction, Mr. Stringer."

The surgeon snorted. "You haven't asked me what reward I want!"

"I catch images of myself being burned at the stake," Miss Pimm retorted, "so I shall not inquire about the details. Try to concentrate on the interesting weekend you are having."

"We must need petrol."

"No, we don't. We have a fair distance to go, and the Opposition will be after us. Did you get a good look at their agent?"

Exeter scowled. "If you mean that joker driving the fire engine, then I think so, yes. He had mauve eyes."

"Ah! Then it was Schneider himself. I thought as much."

"He's dead now?"

"Not at all. And as soon as a suitable vehicle comes within his reach, he will be on our heels. He has probably summoned reinforcements. You have bruised his vanity too often, Edward."

"I did warn him!" Exeter glanced at Alice. "And that is not all I should like to bruise."

"But you are a native here, so you have no chance whatsoever of doing so. You must leave him to us. Now I have to teach you all the key to the portal—"

"Not so fast! You want to cross over, Smedley?"

"All three of you will cross over!" Miss Pimm said sharply. "It is the only way to put you out of the Blighters' reach. I have better things to do than guard you twenty-four hours a day, Edward."

"Not me! My duty is to enlist. I will not return to Nextdoor."

Miss Pimm's eyes narrowed dangerously, as if she considered ordering him to wash out his mouth with soap. "Then why did you go to Harrow Hill?"

Exeter was looking dangerous himself, or at least implacably stubborn.

"I have a message to send, that is all. There is a traitor in Olympus, but if Julian is going, then he can tell them for me."

"Who?" she demanded.

"Jumbo Watson!"

"Absolute rubbish! I have known Mr. Watson for—for more years than you would believe."

Exeter sighed and shook his head. "I would very much like to agree with you, ma'am. I like Jumbo personally, like him a lot. But remember he was Home in 1912? Somebody tipped off the Blighters where the guv'nor was hiding."

"No, they didn't. Soapy Maclean came over by way of the Valley of the Kings. That portal had been compromised. We did not confirm that until much later. The only person to use it since was Colonel Creighton, in 1914, and there was so much confusion that summer that he managed to shake off the followers he had acquired."

"Really?" There was an oddly pleading expression on Exeter's face.

"Certainly. Jumbo was confident that your father would still oppose the Liberator prophecies and would try to prevent your fulfilling them—he had no motive to kill Cameron and Rona Exeter. Furthermore, the Blighters obviously believed that they had caught you in the massacre. They ignored you for two years after that. Jumbo knew you were at school in England, although I would not tell him where. You cannot blame Nyagatha on Jumbo, Edward."

Exeter sighed. "I'm glad! But he was the one who dumped me on the battlefield. It was a deliberate attempt to kill me, and it was certainly Jumbo who did that. Even if he wasn't the rat at Nyagatha, he's a rat now."

Miss Pimm frowned and bit her lip. After a moment she said, "I cannot recall anyone from Nextdoor ever crossing over by way of Belgium. That is not a portal known to the Service. So who told Jumbo about it?"

"Zath, I expect. The Chamber."

"Of course. Cannot we go a little faster, Mr. Stringer? We have a long way to go."

"I am a nervous wreck!"

"You will be a physical one also, if you try to resist me now."

Exeter caught Smedley's eye and grinned. Miss Pimm was a most formidable lady.

"Faster!" she said. "Undoubtedly the Chamber informed Jumbo, Edward. But how? They must have an agent within the Service, but who? If Jumbo were here, we could ask him who told him about that portal. We could ask him who taught him the key, and who assured him that there was a tended node at this end—which I assume he told you was the case?

You were deceived by someone you trusted, but perhaps that person had been deceived also?"

Exeter was nodding.

"You are making charges of the most serious nature," she continued. "Undoubtedly, the Service will bring whoever is responsible to trial and impose the death penalty if he is convicted."

"I will drink to that."

"But is Jumbo the culprit, or was he duped? Captain Smedley is an unknown on Nextdoor. He is also—forgive me, Captain—a man who has recently undergone a grave ordeal. If he turns up unannounced in Olympus mouthing accusations of treason against one of the Service's oldest and most senior officers, then he is not likely to receive a serious hearing. At the very least, the individual responsible will have enough warning to make his escape. If you want revenge, Edward, if you want justice, then you must deliver the message yourself. An accused person has the right to face his accusers."

Now that was telling him, Smedley decided joyfully. Exeter obviously agreed, for his frown was thunderous.

Alice was smiling. She was pretty when she smiled, not at all horsey.

Exeter said quietly. "My duty is to enlist."

A shadow of exasperation passed over Miss Pimm's crabby face. "Spoken like a true Englishman," she said cryptically. "But to do so here would be rank stupidity. I cannot guarantee that I shall always be available to pull you out of the wreckage. I will make you a much better proposition. Do you know the sacred grove of Olipain?"

"In Randorvale? I know where it is."

"And you can get there from Olympus?"

"It's not far. Three or four days' walk."

"Very well. I shall teach you the key to it. It leads to a tended portal in New Zealand. In fact, that was how your father came Home in ninety. Your mother was born not far from there."

She paused, but Exeter just waited for her to finish, eyes steady and unreadable.

"You will return to Olympus this evening, taking Miss Prescott and Captain Smedley. When you have laid your charges and given your evidence—when honor is satisfied, and I know I can trust your judgment on that—then you can make your own way to the grove of Olipain. You will not need to ask the Committee's permission, fair enough? That key requires no additional drummer. You will enlist in New Zealand. The Dominion forces are playing a noble part in this war. The chances of your ever being recognized in their theaters of operation are remote. That is a reasonable compromise, is it not?"

"I have no intention," Exeter said icily, "of sitting out this war guarding some bloody sheep farm on the wrong side of the—"

Smedley exploded. After he had outlined the Gallipoli Campaign and the reputation Anzac forces had earned on the Western Front, he subsided as suddenly as he began. He apologized to the ladies for his language. He had rather surprised himself, and he had certainly astonished Exeter.

"I didn't know!" He swallowed. "I'll have to swot up on all this! But I apologize. I accept your generous offer, ma'am."

"That is settled then!"

"Not me!" Alice roused herself for the first time, sitting up straight and seeming to pull herself together. "I stay here."

"Alice!" Exeter said.

Smedley wanted to tell him that he was being a fool. She kept a man's dressing gown in her flat. A woman had greater loyalties than cousins. For a moment nobody spoke.

At last Alice said, "No, Edward. I warned you. I have my reasons, Miss Pimm."

Miss Pimm nodded.

Exeter moaned. "Alice? Please? The Blighters may come after you!"

"No, Edward. If they are using me as a Judas goat, then I think I will be more valuable to them alive than dead. Correct, Miss Pimm?"

"I hope so. One cannot tell, but it may be so. You must go faster, Mr. Stringer. I shall warn you if there is any traffic coming."

"There is a car behind us. It has been there for some time, a Bentley, I think. Is it a threat?"

She closed her eyes for a moment. "Nobody I recognize. I shall watch them, though. Carry on. Now, do not be tiresome, Edward. Your cousin is quite old enough to make her own decisions."

"But—"

"No buts. Attend carefully, please, Captain Smedley. All portal keys are very ancient and very complicated. They involve rhythm, words, and a dance pattern. They arouse primitive emotions to attune the mind to the virtuality. Think of that as sanctity."

"Exeter described them." Smedley had begun to feel excited again. "He mentioned beating drums, though, and I'm short a few fingers now."

"I don't think that will matter, as long as someone is drumming for you. Have you ever felt a sense of *uplift* in church, when the anthem soars?"

"Um. Yes, I suppose so."

"You are not tone-deaf, I hope? You can dance?"

"No and yes, respectively." His leg was throbbing like the dickens, but he could move it.

"Then I foresee no difficulty. Your wrist has healed sufficiently that it will not open if the sutures are lost. We shall begin with the words."

O MBAY FALA, INKUTHIN,
Indu maka, sasa du.
Aiba aiba nopa du,
Aiba reeba mona kin.
Hosagil!

The gibberish ran round and round in Smedley's head. Fortunately there were only three verses to that key, each ending in the same shout of *Hosagil!* He thought he had the words, but the beat was nastily complex and contrapuntal, and of course the steps and gestures would have to wait until they arrived at St. Gall's. Even a Rolls was not spacious enough for dancing.

Ombay fala . . . Screw *Hosagil*, whoever he was.

Exeter ought to be in worse shape, because he was having to memorize two keys. Smedley could not imagine how he would manage that without mixing them up, but he had not changed a bit from their schooldays— cool, calm, and accomplished. He caught on to the rhythms right away, claiming a knack acquired during his Africa childhood, and he had always been a whiz at languages, which must help with the words. He would probably come first in the exam. Just like old times! In fact, Edward Exeter would be a downright pill if he wasn't always so straight and square, such a brick. No one could ever dislike him.

The sky was trying on pastel colors as evening approached. Stringer clung grimly to the wheel, rarely speaking. If Miss Pimm was not supporting her driver with spikes of magic, he must be well beyond the end of his tether. There had been no break for tea.

Now Exeter was prying information out of her, a process much like opening oysters with bare hands.

"And what is St. Gall's?"

"A church."

"Very old, of course?"

"Of course. There are," she continued in an obvious diversion, "two standing stones remaining in the churchyard. It may well be that some of the keys we know date from megalithic—"

"Do you use this portal often?"

"Quite often," she admitted with the reluctance of a biology mistress being asked to explain the function of reproductive organs.

"It leads directly to Olympus?"

"Yes."

"And back?"

She sighed. "Yes. We know keys for translation in both directions. That is rare."

"Then why are the Blighters not aware of it?"

"They are."

"They have sentries?"

"No resident stranger, no. No traps I cannot handle. Normally they don't care a fig about Nextdoor, remember! It was only the Chamber's appeal for help in destroying you that roused the Blighters' interest. They care more who comes in than who goes out, in any case. Anyone departing who has not entered will be marked in some fashion."

"Will that Schneider man have guessed it is where we are going?"

"Oh, yes. He may have alerted others to intercept us there."

Cheerful thought!

The car wound down a steep hill. Now Stringer was being allowed to proceed at his own pace, for there were cyclists, horse traffic, and a few cars. With all the *Ombay fala* guff, Smedley had lost track of what county he was in, but the building stone was the right buff color for the Cotswolds, and the landscape was picturesque enough. A large plate of hash and a tankard of bitter would go down very well about now. Would there be such a thing as beer on Nextdoor?

Waves of unreality . . .

At times he believed. Then it felt like the night before a big push, with the barrage to begin before dawn. Then a man looked at his watch every half minute and wondered if he'd ever see another sunset. Not quite that bad, but his gut was tight and his palm damp. *Aiba aiba nopa du* . . . Tonight he might meet the suspect Jumbo Watson face-to-face. Tomorrow go for a nice ride around on a dragon.

Other times he just couldn't. Then it all felt like an enormous leg-pull. *Aiba, aiba,* up your nose. Shamans and fakirs. Witch doctor dances moving people to other dimensions? What utter gullage that was! If such things were possible, then hundreds of people would have disappeared over the centuries.

But if they had, what evidence could there be? You couldn't prove it wasn't true!

Not in that direction, whispered his doubts, but when was the last time you read about a naked, shocked, bewildered foreigner stumbling out of the woods somewhere, unable to speak a word of the language? That ought to be easier to disprove, because at least you could demand to have a body produced. *Habeas* the bloody *corpus*!

"Sharp left at the end of this wall, Mr. Stringer," Miss Pimm said. "There is room to park."

Smedley snapped out of his reverie, realizing that the spire he had seen over the trees a moment ago must be St. Gall's.

"The vicar is expecting us." She did not deign to relate how she knew that. "But I ask both of you to be discreet in what you say to him. 'Them as asks no questions isn't told no lies,' or, 'No names, no pack drill,' as Captain Smedley is fond of remarking. This is a small parish, not well endowed. The Service supports his church with generous donations. He knows we use the building for unorthodox purposes, but it is easier for him if he can pretend to turn a blind eye. The current bishop is notoriously conservative in his views."

Exeter had twisted around to stare at her again. "You mean we are actually going to go through with this inside the church itself? Dancing around with no clothes on?"

Miss Pimm sniffed. "Would you prefer an audience? On a fine evening like this, the grounds are a favored locale for courting couples."

"Too many bodies in the graveyard," Stringer remarked loudly. It was comforting to know that he was still conscious.

She ignored the comment completely. "The node overlaps the building itself, especially to the east, so we could perform our ceremonies outside. However the center of the virtuality is just in front of the altar. That is where in-comers materialize, and you will translate more easily from there."

There was a stunned pause, and it was Alice who sniggered first. "Do they ever drop in on Sunday mornings?"

The old bag did not crack even a hint of a smile. "Olympus keeps careful track of the clock, naturally, and times its deliveries for the small hours of the morning. The vicar is accustomed to receiving unexpected visitors."

Stringer was braking. Smedley caught a brief glimpse of some houses about a half mile away, then the car turned into a narrow lane, lurching to a stop beside an iron gate set in a high stone wall. With a long sigh like a deflating tire, Stringer sprawled limply over the steering wheel. Miss Pimm uttered a snort of disbelief. About to say something cheerful to Exeter, Smedley took a second look at his expression, then at Alice's, and didn't. Instead he opened the door and clambered down. There would have to be an awkward farewell here. He had no taste for public sentiment. . . . She kept a man's dressing gown in her flat, dammit! He hurried around to open the door for Miss Pimm.

Someone had beaten him to it. As that someone was wearing a cassock, it would not be unreasonable to assume he was the vicar. He was short and plump, elderly and fatherly, white-haired and rubicund, obviously not a stranger but a *native*. Smedley's heart did a little jump at that thought. It meant that he really did believe.

Ombay fala, inkuthin . . .

He fumbled shakily for cigarettes and matches.

All five of the occupants had emerged from the car. Edward hovered very close to Alice, Stringer was stretching and rubbing his eyes. Miss Pimm and the vicar had obviously met before. They exchanged congratulations on the weather. She did not introduce her companions and he ignored them—extremely odd behavior for a cleric—then they all converged on the gate, with Miss Pimm and the vicar in the lead. Smedley found himself being squired by the surgeon, crunching along a gravel path. He could not hear Alice and Exeter following.

The churchyard was dark and rather spooky, overhung with gigantic yews and studded with headstones, half of them weathered to shapeless boulders. Rhododendrons had taken over much of it, while the straggly grass in the remainder badly needed cutting. Someone had made a start on that, and then abandoned the lawn mower in its tracks. There seemed to be no lovers dallying amid the shrubbery or skulking in the shadows, but the vicar's sudden conversion to gardening would have blighted the romantic atmosphere of the evening.

The church itself was small and extremely old, or at least the west front was, because the door was set in a rounded arch. "Norman, I see!" That was about the limit of Smedley's architectural expertise.

But not Stringer's. "More likely Saxon. That transept is younger, Early Gothic. Middle thirteenth century, probably. The spire can't be older than fourteenth."

"And the railway station beyond the far wall? Late Victorian?"

"That's probably the vicarage."

Garn! "Or the county jail."

"Ah, yes. By the way, Captain, I congratulate you on the way you spirited your friend out of Staffles. Adroitly done!" The surgeon's hearty tone was belied by his fishy eyes, which were friendly as barracudas'. "You did not limp on Wednesday."

"I scratched my leg going over the wall."

"We wondered which of you that was. Have you had it seen to?"

"I plan to have it cured by magic in another world."

Stringer snorted. He walked on in silence for a long minute, then sighed. "I think I need a holiday."

Yes, the war was tough, wasn't it?

Four of them had reached the steps. Alice and Exeter still loitered by the gate, staring into each other's eyes and whispering earnestly. He must still be trying to talk her into coming. Why could he not understand that the lady hankered after what came wrapped in that dressing gown?

"Hurry, please!" Miss Pimm called. "Reverend, we have had no chance for a meal and some of us have a long drive ahead of us yet. Would there be any shops still open in the village to buy something we could eat on the road?"

The little man looked alarmed at being required to make such a decision. "Not shops. I have some ham . . . or you could inquire at the Bull. Mrs. Daventry might run up some sandwiches for you."

Smedley suppressed images of a buxom lady climbing a mountain of sandwiches. He must be windier than he had realized. He took a long draw on his fag.

"You could pick me up back here in half an hour or so," Miss Pimm informed Stringer with a meaningful look.

He frowned at this cavalier dismissal, but obviously he had learned not to argue with his new secretary. He offered his left hand to Smedley. "Thank you for a most interesting few days, Captain. Do drop in if you're ever in my neighborhood, won't you?"

"And you likewise," Smedley said.

Alice and Edward arrived hand in hand, very tense about the eyes.

"I will send you a postcard as soon as I, ah, return," he told her.

"No, you won't!" Miss Pimm snapped. "That would be insanely unwise. I shall see she is informed of your whereabouts. For goodness sake, kiss her and go inside! Thank you for your help, Reverend."

"Oh, very welcome, I'm sure, Mrs.—er . . . If you need me, I shall be cutting the grass out here."

Better than trying to cut the grass in there, Smedley thought. Lord, he was getting hysterical! He pecked a kiss on Alice's cheek, nodded politely at the vicar, who jumped and returned a nervous smile.

He stamped out his cigarette. Then he followed Miss Pimm up the steps and into the cold gloom of the church. Edward came trotting after them and closed the heavy door with a slam. It echoed like a knell of doom.

52

Smedley tossed his shirt into the chest. There was a strange assortment of clothes in there already, male and female both, plus a couple of small drums. He sat on a chair to remove his shoes and socks. The floor was icy.

Damn it all! No matter what she had said, he would not remove his pants! Not yet.

He limped out into the nave. He could hear the rattle of the vicar's lawn mower outside, very faint and distant. With a drum slung around her neck, Miss Pimm was poised on one foot, left arm raised and head thrown back. "*Ogtha!*" she proclaimed, and brought her hand down to the drum, and raising the other. "*Ispal!*" She was teaching Exeter the gestures for the key that would take him to New Zealand. He was watching intently, showing no sign of discomfort at being stark naked.

Writhing with embarrassment, Smedley slipped by them. He wandered along the aisle, studying the pictures in the stained glass windows and the nosegays of color they shed. The arches at the east end were rounded, then they became pointed, Gothic. Either the original church had been extended, or a new generation of builders had taken over at that point. The oaken pews displayed prayer books and hymnals, laid out at even spacing, ready for the next day's service. The pulpit was modern and grandiose, perhaps a result of the Service's generous contributions, and too big for the church.

This was a very little church.

But it was a church, a recognizable C. of E. place of worship, and its like could be found all over the world. The sun never set on the Anglican Communion. It was all the things he had been brought up to revere, had taken for granted and respected all his life. His family went to church every Sunday. They almost never discussed religion. It was just there, part of a man, like breathing. Dancing around in the nude was not in the cards. It was uncivilized. Gentlemen did not do such things anywhere, least of all in a church.

"*Umbathon!*" said Miss Pimm in the background.

This was not going to work. This was a gigantic confidence trick. This was insanity.

Ombay fala, inkuthin . . .

He had not wept in days. Was he past that, now? Had he sunk to a whole new level of madness, with delusions of flying to other worlds and people leaping from bicycles into cars without actually moving through space? Was he, despite all the evidence of his senses, bound up in a straitjacket inside some padded cell?

He could feel his right hand again. It didn't exactly hurt, but he could feel it. He looked down at the bandage disbelievingly and tried to flex invisible fingers. He was in front of the altar rail already. This was the center of virtuality, she had said. Bunkum!

He shivered.

He turned away from the altar. Fresh yellow roses and chrysanthemums in brass vases. A fellow should not go mucking around in a church in a state of undress. Not proper! What in heaven would the guv'nor say? Or the mater, if she were alive—she would be truly shocked. Or the aunts, the monstrous regiment of aunts?

The other two were coming up the aisle. "Captain Smedley!" Miss Pimm's harsh voice took on a notable resonance in this old stone cave. "I asked you to remove your clothes."

"After the dress rehearsal."

"No, Captain—now! You will not achieve the correct state of mind if you are distracted by trivia. It will take you time to adjust. Off with them!"

He glared at her, then turned his back on her, pulling off his braces. But when he had everything off, he did not know what to do next. He could hardly leave bags and underwear for the congregation to find in the morning. He glanced over his shoulder. Miss Pimm was watching him with her arms folded. He could imagine her toe tapping.

"Give them to me," she said impatiently. "I'll put them in the chest as I leave. Oh, Captain! I saw my first naked man several hundred years ago, and none of the equipment has changed since then."

He gave her the bundle.

"Thank you. And your bandages. Then we can begin."

The governess instructed her pupils in the proper ritual movements for *Ombay fala.* They took it in slow motion, gesture by gesture, and Smedley felt worse and worse as the farce progressed. His nerves were not going to take much more of this. Exeter, he was glad to notice, was starting to shiver. At least when they began to dance in earnest, they both should feel warmer. He was shivering too, and he did not think that temperature had very much to do with it in his case. It was funk.

Oddly, Miss Pimm seemed colder than either of them, and she was fully dressed. She was snappier than a vixen in heat, shouting at them when they got it wrong. She kept glancing at her watch.

For once, Smedley realized, he was picking up something faster than Edward Exeter. Exeter was distracted, thoroughly miserable. Pining for Cousin Alice? Had he just realized that he could never see her again? He could not even send her a postcard. The Blighters would never stop hunting him until he fulfilled the prophecy or died. Or was he just unwilling to cross over?

Miss Pimm made herself comfortable in the front pew and adjusted the drum on her lap.

"Now we'll try it with music. First verse. Ready? One, two—"

"*Ombay fala*," Smedley chanted, lifting his left foot and raising his stump overhead, "*inkuthin.*" Exeter followed him around the circle. Surprisingly, they went right through the first verse without an error—at least it felt as if they got it right, and Sergeant Major Pimm did not interrupt.

"Not bad!" she admitted as they bellowed out the closing, *Hosagil!* "Edward, you forgot the words a time or two, didn't you? Captain, your timing is erratic. Is that leg going to be a problem?"

The scar on his wrist was blood red, but a neat piece of sewing. The trivial scratches on his leg looked much worse, ugly and swollen. He compared his two arms, wondering if the right one was already wasting away.

"Let's try again." Miss Pimm stole another glance at her watch. "Smartly! I certainly don't want to have to fight my way out of here. Take it right through, now. Keep on going until something happens. Ready? Oh, I almost forgot . . . *bon voyage!*"

It was the first real smile Smedley had seen on her face. It made her seem almost pretty, in a way he would never have guessed, but he was not in a mood to return smiles. He was expecting her to break into howls of laughter any minute, and start shouting *April fool!* "Thank you in anticipation," he said coldly.

Exeter said, "Thank you for everything." But he did not smile either, and Miss Pimm responded with a rolling tattoo of fingers on the drum.

Smedley shivered and waited for the rhythm to begin. This was all wrong! He had taken religion seriously as a child, because his parents had. Here it came. . . . *Dum-de dum-de dum-dum-dum* . . . At Fallow he had done what all the others had done. "*Ombay fala, inkuthin*," he chanted. In the senior forms he had joined the conventional rebellion into Buddhism, atheism, agnosticism, Unitarianism, or any esoteric -ism that had turned up. *Right leg, left arm.* Smedley himself had never been quite sure which of the -isms he favored. When he enlisted he had given his religion as C. of E. without thinking about it. "*Indu maka, sasa du.*" He had attended church parade on Sundays. In Flanders he had prayed his heart out a few times, screaming and sobbing to a merciful god, any god, any god at all. No atheists in foxholes . . . *Hop, bow, hop, bow.* When the danger had passed, he had always felt ashamed of his cowardice, and less of a believer in consequence. What sort of merciful god would have allowed the war to start in the first place—and why? Just so some terrified sods would repent of their sins? "*Aiba aiba nopa du.*" What sins had he ever had a chance to commit?

But even so, a chap ought not to profane a holy place. Even a heathen temple deserved respect. Even if it was a mud hut, even if only one single curly-haired darkie thought it was sacred, then a fellow ought to have the grace not to mock it. *Head back, elbows out.* St. Gall's was a Christian church, the sort of place his ancestors had worshipped in for hundreds of years. It deserved better than this obscene posturing, these primitive antics. *Echoes rolling back from the ancient stones.* It was holy. He could almost smell the sanctity. Normans had worshipped here, maybe Angles and Saxons. "*Aiba reeba mona kin.*" That meant *nine centuries* of humble people bowing down and glorifying their God. Their worship alone made it sacred. The thought was suddenly terrifying. Light blazed. He screamed and stumbled and fell facedown in the grass. *Hosagil!*

Bewildered, not understanding, he raised his head and blinked at the painful brightness. He lay in the exact center of a circular lawn, about the size of his parents' dining room, and the surrounding hedge was the color of a blue spruce, with the sheen of holly. He heard sounds of chirping, whistling, and hooting. He blinked harder to clear away tears. Beyond the hedge soared the most incredible snow-capped peak he had ever seen, blushing orange against a pale blue-gold sky. The air was tangy with a scent of wood smoke. It was evening or early morning.

He had done it! He had done it! He had done it! Yes! It was true. He had crossed over to another world. Grass. Odd, mint-scented grass. Day-light. The war, England, the guv'nor, the aunts, medals, the dead, the maimed—all gone. He had really done it. He wouldn't have to go to the Palace for his bloody gong after all. He had done it, really done it.

He laid his face on the back of his hand and started to sob.

53

It was the cold that stopped him, the unpleasantness of lying on dewy grass at dawn. He sat up and rubbed his eyes with the back of his hand and almost laughed. He hadn't had a weep like that since Wednesday's lunch in the Black Dragon. Done him a world of good, it had! *Two* worlds of good. Now he needed to find some clothes before he caught pneumonia.

He had done it. He had done it.

Behind him stood a small kiosk of unpainted wood, like a summerhouse. Alongside it was the only break in the hedge, through which he could see only a gravel path and more hedge on the far side of that. Assuming this place was not somebody's idea of a joke, it must be a secluded, private aerodrome for travelers arriving in a state of undress—which was a reminder that Exeter would be dropping in any minute, and the exact center of the circle might become crowded.

Miss Pimm had issued somber warnings of the aftereffects of passing over, and especially a first trip. Cramps and nausea and despair, she had said, and Exeter had nodded grimly. Usually it would last only a few minutes, but it was as unpredictable as seasickness. Smedley felt none of those, unless his weeping fit qualified. He felt fine.

So he scrambled up and limped over to the gazebo. The orange fire had already faded from the mountain and the sky was brightening. There were several other peaks to admire as well, painted in blinding white and ice blue. The hedge was high enough to hide everything closer, except a trailing, lazy cloud of white smoke, which accounted for the tangy smell in the air. Someone was having a bonfire.

What could be keeping Exeter? It was jolly good to have pipped him like this, and him on his third trip, too.

The gazebo contained a comfortable chair with a book lying on it, and a wooden chest. Like the one in the vestry of St. Gall's, that chest probably held all sorts of Apparel Suitable for the Discerning Traveler. The book was heavy, leather-bound, and apparently written in Greek, but yet no Greek Smedley had ever seen. Odd! When he looked inside the chest, he found one shoe and three socks. He took two socks and put them on, but that hardly seemed adequate wear, no matter how temperate the climate.

Undoubtedly the little kiosk was a sentry box. Someone was supposed
to be sitting here, reading that book, keeping watch in case visitors dropped
in. The rotter had deserted his post. Having breakfast, likely.

What on Earth, real Earth, could be delaying Exeter? Had the effort of
learning two keys at the same time confused him, mixing them up in his
mind? Or was he so reluctant to leave Alice and return to Nextdoor that
he could not summon up the correct mental attitude? Bother the man!

So what did Julian Smedley do now, poor thing?

He went to the gap in the hedge and—being extremely cautious not to
expose too much of himself—peered around the edge. He looked straight
into the face of a young man doing the same thing from the other side.

The other man yelled. They both jumped back in alarm.

Smedley broke into roars of laughter.

Slowly the newcomer edged into view around the hedge, one big, wide,
green eye at a time. He was barefoot, wearing only a loincloth. His beard
was close-cropped, while his hair hung down his back like a woman's. Both
were a startling shade of copper, and his very fair skin's efforts to tan had
coated him in several million freckles. He was one all-over freckle. He was
also jumpy as a field full of grasshoppers, ready to flee at the slightest prov-
ocation.

He said something, but the only word Smedley caught was *tyika?*

"Sorry, old man! Don't speak the lingo. Got any English?"

The man nodded vigorously, still jittery, but apparently reassured. "I am
speak English well, *tyika!*" He had a singsong accent. "My name is Dommi
Basketmaker, but once Dommi Houseboy, and having hopes again to be
so." He was no older than Smedley himself, short and broad shouldered.

"I'm Captain Smedley. Dommi, you said? Weren't you bearer for, er,
Tyika Exeter?"

A huge grin split Dommi's face into unequal halves, revealing a set of
perfect white teeth. "Indeed I had that highly pleasurable honor a year ago,
for a transitory time only. *Tyika* Kisster a most felicitous *tyika* to serve, a
very benignly inclined *tyika!* I had been informed that his honor will be
returning shortly and have had apprehension of perhaps being permitted
again to serve him, which I would be most earnestly appreciative." His joy
wavered into sudden despondency. "But, alas—"

"Well, he's due any moment now." Smedley wondered how that information could have reached Olympus ahead of him, though. "And he
will be arriving in the same state of undress I am. And I am deucedly cold,
to boot. Why don't you run off and dig up a couple of sets of clothes for
us, soonest?"

"But . . ." Dommi's gaze wandered over Smedley, noting the missing hand and the gashes on his calf. "Of course, *Tyika Kaptaan*! At once, most imminent!" He spun around and vanished. Sounds of feet running on gravel faded into the distance. *Bare* feet? Ouch!

Well, that took care of clothes.

Exeter was taking a damnably long time! He had two translations to his credit already, so he ought to be able to manage another, surely. Had he changed his mind? Having seen Smedley cross first, was he going to rely on him to unmask the traitor, whether Jumbo or another? No, he would not go back on his word to Miss Pimm. Or had Schneider arrived at St. Gall's and queered the show? She had said: *I don't want to have to fight my way out of here.*

Smedley decided that there was nothing he could do about that. He had no idea of the return key, and he could have contributed nothing to the fight, if fight there was. He might never know what had happened after he left.

He might have to introduce himself to the Service, instead of being recommended by Edward Exeter, Liberator. Should have brought his *curriculum vita*. Damn! That could be unpleasant. He'd have to talk about the war. Well, one day at a time . . .

He should have asked Dommi to bring some breakfast. His mouth was watering. He sniffed. Mm. Yes, there were definite hints of meat in the all-pervading smoke. Perhaps someone was roasting an ox on that bonfire? Or frying bacon.

Curiosity took him back to the gap in the hedge. He peered again, and this time there was no other face advancing to meet his. As he had suspected, the other hedge was just a screen across the entrance, providing privacy. The gravel path curved out of sight and his view was blocked by shrubbery and tall trees. They were not English trees, but a tree was a tree anywhere. Some of the colors were a bit off.

He looked the other way.

A body sprawled on the path about twenty feet away, but there was no doubt that it was dead. It had been hacked to pieces. Hair and clothes were unrecognizable, black with dried blood, and he could not tell whether it had been a man or a woman. He could hear insectile buzzings even at that distance. A couple of things like feathered squirrels were chewing at it.

He looked beyond. Smoke drifted up from the remains of a house, a black field of ruin. He retched at the memory of the odors that had made his mouth water. In the background, amid the trees, other houses smoked, many other houses, all razed. Black specks on the ground might well be other bodies. Olympus had been sacked.

A few men were moving around, and although they were far off, he could see that they were not dressed like Englishmen. They were dressed like Dommi, meaning virtually undressed. The natives had risen against the *tyikank*. It was Nyagatha all over again.

Now one of the savages had learned that there was a *tyika* who had been missed. Dommi had not gone to fetch clothes, he had gone to fetch his friends, with assegais or machetes or whatever they used to kill white men . . . *tyikank* . . . Dommi was as white as Smedley, but he was a native, and there could be no doubt what had happened here yesterday, or perhaps the day before.

Smedley was alone, naked, penniless, and friendless on a strange world where he could not speak the language and the native population was out to kill him.

He really ought to have settled for Chichester.

He ought to disappear into the woods as fast as he could move.

But what if Exeter arrived as soon as he left?

How long until Dommi and his pals arrived?

Somebody screamed, but Smedley did not think it was him.

ᖇᖊᖋ 54 ᖌᖍᖎ

EDWARD EXETER WAS THRASHING LIKE A LANDED FISH IN THE MIDDLE of the grassy enclosure. He kept on screaming.

Smedley ran over to him and knelt down, having to ward off flailing arms and legs. He shouted a few times, but it did no good. In a few moments, though, the paroxysms grew quieter. Exeter subsided into a twitching heap. His muscles kept knotting and unknotting horribly, and he cried out every time.

"Exeter? It's me, Smedley. Anything I can do to help?"

Anything I can do to shut you up?

Exeter's eyes were closed. He was obviously trying not to move. "Julian?" he whispered. "Hold me."

Hold him? He was a *man*, dammit! And neither of them had any clothes on. With distaste, Smedley lay down behind him and tried to put an arm around him. All he did was set off another riot of cramps and spasms, and more shrieks of pain.

"Keep it down!" he hissed. "They'll hear you!"

"Hold me, damn you!"

Right. Smedley rose to his knees, took hold of Exeter's hair, and hauled him up into a sitting position. Exeter screamed. Smedley wrapped both arms around him and hung on as tightly as he could.

The fit passed. Exeter gasped and leaned his head back on Smedley's shoulder. After a moment he whispered, "Thanks! Just keep holding me."

That was all very well, but there was a band of headhunters on the way. This did not seem like the moment to explain that, though.

"What delayed you?"

"Dunno," Exeter whispered. His eyes were closed, and he was barely breathing. "Just couldn't get it to work."

"I thought the Blighters had got you."

Exeter shook his head, and that small movement set him off again, thrashing and moaning. Damn! but he was loud. He was going to be sore for days after these cramps. He was knotted like a fishnet.

"I do believe we have run into a spot of trouble here," Smedley said.

Footsteps on gravel! He looked around in alarm, bracing himself to face a murdering mob, but it was only Dommi, alone. He came hobbling in, clutching a bundle. He was covered with soot, streaked pink with sweat, and he had developed a severe limp.

"*Tyika* Kaptaan!" he cried. "I was as quickly as I could. And *Tyika* Kisster! It is most fortuitous to set eyes on your honor again, but at such a sad timing. I have brought the clothes, *tyika*, but I fear they are only the best I could find in the house of *Tyika* Dunlop, and many of them have singe marks upon them, and are soiled. It was the only house I was able to make entrance to."

Exeter's eyes opened wide.

"That's great, Dommi!" Smedley said hoarsely. "Could you hold *Tyika* Exeter for a moment for me?"

Muttering solicitously, Dommi knelt down and relieved Smedley of his burden. The exchange set off another round of cramps in Exeter, but he bit back his screams. Grateful, Smedley crawled away and rummaged through the bundle the bearer had dropped. He found typical tropical kit: shorts and shirts and sandals and long white socks. No underwear. As Dommi had said, the white cloth was scorched and soot stained. He began to dress.

Dommi was spilling out the horrible story between sobs. "It was a great madness, *tyika*! On Necknight, a great madness came upon us in the village. We gathered torches and all weapons which were at hand for us, and we marched in whole company upon the compound of the *tyikank*, singing hymns in the praise of Holy Karzon, whom our ancestors were ignorant to worship, but we know well to be the Demon Karzon and yet did not hail as such that night." He was weeping like a fire hose. "There was terrible slaughter, *tyika*, and raping of the *entyikank*, and, oh, awful things were done. The houses were all been burned. I cannot explain this madness, *tyika*! There were others there, not belonging to us, not Carrots like us but strangers. They wore black, *tyika*, all black! I fear they were the dread reapers of whom our mother would frighten us when children we only were. It is most likely that they were the cause of our madness, *Tyika* Kisster, is it not? All of us Carrots are most humbly disposed toward the great *tyikank* who have done so much to educate us and civilize us, and we are very truly grateful for what you have done for us. It must have been the robed ones who provoked us."

The reason he had been limping was that he had a bloody great burn on his foot. He must have gone into one of those smoldering ruins to find the togs.

"There's a body just outside," Smedley said. "The houses have been burned."

Exeter licked his lips. "Zath again," he whispered. "It's all over now?"

"Indeed yes, *tyika*! We Carrots are remorseful in the most extreme about what we have done, but we could not help ourselves. I myself was one of them who did these terrible things. Now we are chagrined most deeply and wish to make amends. It is to be hoped that many of the *tyikank* and *entyikank* and domestic Carrots managed to escape out into the woods, *tyika*. We have been trying to count the bodies, but we also slew all the Carrots we found wearing the noble liveries you *tyikank* had so generously provided for us, and it is hard to tell who is among the dead and who is not there. Many escaped, I am hopeful . . ."

He choked down more sobs. "We even burned the library, *tyika*!"

Very gingerly, Exeter eased himself into a sitting position. Blood dribbled from his mouth, shockingly red against his pallor. "I am sure it was the reapers who were to blame."

"It had been reported that you would have imminent return." Dommi whimpered. "I am most glad that your honor did not return sooner and so share in this unfortunate killing."

Exeter hugged his knees, staring blindly across at the hedge, not moving. "The house of the *Tyika* Murgatroyd? Was this attacked?"

"Indeed yes, *tyika*. No house escaped."

"The servants of *Entyika* Murgatroyd? Ysian, the cook?"

Dommi covered his face with his hands.

"Well?" Exeter demanded, not looking at him.

Ysian? Wasn't that the name of the girl Exeter had found hiding under a bed somewhere? How had she ever got to Olympus?

"No, *tyika*. She did not escape. I saw."

"How did she die?"

"Not to ask, *tyika*!"

Exeter's eyes were burning cold, but he was still gazing at the hedge, or through it. "Tell me, Dommi. Please tell me. I know it wasn't your fault."

"*Tyika*—there were awful things done. Please not to say them."

Exeter mumbled something that made no sense, but sounded vaguely like, "Oh, Vixen!"

"What? Smedley demanded.

"Nothing. Pass me those bags, will you, old chap?" Moving very deliberately, he began to dress. "Dommi, go and collect the Carrots."

The valley was narrow, less than a mile wide. From a flat floor, the sides rose precipitously, soaring almost unbroken to the incredible peaks all around. It held a river, open meadows, and many-colored woods. It would have been spectacularly beautiful two days ago.

They walked past burned ruins and trampled flower gardens, many strewn with dismembered bodies. By the time they emerged from the trees, Exeter was able to walk on his own, just steadying himself with a hand on Smedley's shoulder. They had come to tennis courts, where a band of terrified natives awaited their arrival, two score or more. Men, women, and youngsters, they all had red hair. Many carried shovels, but seemed unsure what to do with them or where to begin. They all looked ill with guilt and horror. Even Smedley, hardened campaigner from the Western Front, was utterly nauseated by what he had already seen, and that was only a small part of Olympus. Plumes of smoke were still fouling the valley.

Exeter was greeted with apprehension and relieved murmurs of, "*Tyika* Kisster!" Others were running in through the trees. He waited as the crowd grew, leaning on Smedley. He was still trembling and very weak. It had been a bad crossing.

"Self-fulfilling!" he murmured.

"What?"

"The *Filoby Testament*. It seems to be self-fulfilling. Dommi said he was expecting me back from Thovale, so the Committee must have summoned me—but I'd gone to Flanders! If Zath hadn't sent me there, I would have arrived here in time to die, you see. And if he hadn't done this, I would still be going on to New Zealand."

Smedley looked at him in surprise. "Now you won't?"

"If Zath can't break the chain, then how can I?" Exeter released his grip on Julian's shoulder and straightened up to address the nervous mob of Carrots.

"It was not your fault!" he shouted. "It was Demon Karzon who drove you to this, Demon Zath. The saints will not abandon you, for it was not your fault. The Undivided knows the truth and where the guilt lies."

They reacted with screams of joy, like children.

"But you must demonstrate your grief. You must bury the dead with honor. Women go and start digging graves in the cricket ground, big graves. Men collect the bodies. We shall bury each household together, *tyikank* and servants together. The saints and the Carrots who lived together shall lie together. It must be done by sundown!"

It was done by sundown, when the snowy peaks of Kilimanjaro and Nanga Parbat turned to blood. The dead could not be numbered, for many bodies had been piled in the burning houses and others had been butchered into anonymous lumps of meat. Nevertheless, it was clear that many more Carrots than *tyikank* had died—most of the strangers would have been able to use their mana to escape, Exeter said. The remains were tipped into pits and covered over. Olympus was a ghost settlement.

Almost out on his feet with exhaustion, Smedley watched and marveled as Edward Exeter conducted a funeral service over the mass burial. He faced a congregation of several hundreds, probably the entire population of the native village, and he spoke in the local tongue, so that Smedley did not understand any of it, only the tears of the assembled Carrots. Whatever Exeter said, he began softly and ended with great vehemence, and his audience was impressed. When he had done, they cheered wildly, which seemed like a very peculiar closing for a funeral.

The next day some of the surviving *tyikank* came creeping out of the forest, hungry, frightened, and exhausted. Missionaries began returning from duty in the field. They were all surprised to find work gangs already clearing away the ruins, cleaning up, erecting temporary dwellings. They were even more surprised that the leadership was being provided by a young man none of them had ever met, an officer in the Royal Artillery, known to the Carrots as *Tyika* Kaptaan. The lad was doing a fine job, too.

Exeter had gone. He had departed in the night, alone, and nobody knew where. According to reliable Carrots, he had revealed to them in the eulogy he had delivered over the graves that he was the prophesied Liberator. They were not supposed to know that, of course, but it had always been impossible to keep the English-speaking domestic Carrots from eavesdropping and passing rumors, so many of them had already known. Now, apparently, Exeter had sworn that he was destined to bring death to Death, and thus fulfil the prophecies.

It was, he had said, an affair of honor.

He had not said where he was going.

As the fortnights passed with no news of him, a consensus arose that either Zath's watchers had caught the fellow on his way out, or else he had just gone native again. He could safely be forgotten.

Some of the pessimists would not believe that, especially Jumbo Watson. He predicted that Olympus had not seen the last of Edward Exeter. He pointed to the *Filoby Testament* and in particular to the cryptic Verse 1098:

Terrible is the justice of the Liberator; his might lays low the unworthy. He is gentle and hard to anger. Gifts he sets aside and honor he spurns. Eleal shall be the first temptation and the prince shall be the second, but the dead shall rouse him.

ᶜᵔ 55 ᵔᵛᶟ

47 Bamlett Road,
London, W1
16th September, 1917

Dear Miss Prescott,

With very deep regret, I must inform you that word has been received that my brother, D'Arcy, has made the Supreme Sacrifice. A telegram from the War Office reported today that he has been killed in action. We have no further details at this time.

I was at the house when the telegram arrived. My sister-in-law was, as you will understand, quite distraught, as were we all. I have only just got home, and have written to you as soon as I could. You may have seen the news in the evening papers already.

A memorial service will be arranged and announced in the usual way.

I am sure that you share our grief, even if you will not be able to acknowledge it in public.

I am,
Yours sincerely,
Anabel Finchley (Mrs.)

Appendix:
The Moons

NEXTDOOR IS A PROBABILITY VARIANT OF EARTH. THE STARS VISIBLE from its surface are the same as those visible from Earth; the sun is apparently the same.

However, Nextdoor has four moons. Prof Rawlinson's theory that they might have been gouged out by the impact of one or more meteors is not without merit. The Pacific was commonly believed in his day to be the scar left when the Moon was torn from the Earth. Modern theory supports an impact origin for the Moon, although the Pacific is now known to be billions of years younger. The impacting body would have had to be the size of a small planet, considerably more than a meteor, but in some respects Rawlinson was ahead of his time. He was particularly perceptive in anticipating recent insight on chaotic systems; even a minute difference in the size, velocity, or angle of such an impact could generate enormous variations in the final results. This would account for not only the varying number of satellites but also the slight discrepancies in the length of the day and year on Earth and Nextdoor.

Only Trumb displays a sufficiently large disk to hide the sun and create a solar eclipse. This occurs on every orbit, but is visible only in the daylight hemisphere. The following refers mainly to eclipses of the respective moons by the shadow of the planet, lunar eclipses as we know them.

The outermost moon, Eltiana, has a period of twenty-eight days, very similar to Earth's Moon, but it is much less conspicuous, little more than a bright red star. Its equatorial orbit causes it to be eclipsed every month, although on average only each alternate eclipse will be visible from a given location.

Ysh displays a small blue disk. It has a useful and dependable period of almost exactly fourteen days, the origin of the fortnight used as a basic division of time. Like Earth's Moon, Ysh has an inclined orbit and therefore is likely to be involved in eclipses only two or three times a year. Many eclipses will be obscured by weather or their occurrence during daylight hours. An observed eclipse of Ysh is a rare and ill-omened occurrence.

Trumb, the green moon, displays a large disk. Its synodic period is 4.44 days and its orbital inclination too slight to matter. It is eclipsed on every orbit, although half the eclipses occur below the horizon.

The tiny yellow moon, Kirb'l, may be a captured asteroid. Its orbit is elliptical and inclined at 15°, which is close to the latitude of the Vales. To complicate matters, its orbit precesses rapidly under the influence of the other moons, and the body itself is asymmetric, rotating every two hours with marked changes in albedo. It has a synodic period of 1.5 days.

At perigee, it appears to move from west to east. This may occur almost overhead, at times of minimum declination, or may be invisible below the horizon. Eclipse is very common at perigee, but Kirb'l is never eclipsed at apogee. At intermediate positions it moves north or south and may or may not be eclipsed.

The astronomer priests of the Vales find Kirb'l completely unpredictable.

In Round Three of "The Great Game"
Edward Exeter takes on the god of Death
in a fight to the finish.